# BLACK
# DOVE
# WHITE
# RAVEN

*Also by*

## Elizabeth Wein

CODE NAME VERITY

ROSE UNDER FIRE

# BLACK
# DOVE
# WHITE
# RAVEN

Elizabeth Wein

**HYPERION**
Los Angeles New York

*Special thanks to Dr. Fikre Tolossa for sharing his expertise on Ethiopian history and culture*

Copyright © 2015 by Elizabeth Gatland

All rights reserved. Published by Hyperion, an imprint of Disney
Book Group. No part of this book may be reproduced or transmitted
in any form or by any means, electronic or mechanical, including
photocopying, recording, or by any information storage and retrieval
system, without written permission from the publisher. For information
address Hyperion, 125 West End Avenue, New York, New York 10023.

Printed in the United States of America

First Hardcover Edition, March 2015
First Paperback Edition, May 2016
10 9 8 7 6 5 4 3 2 1
FAC-025438-16046

SUSTAINABLE
FORESTRY
INITIATIVE

Certified Chain of Custody
Promoting Sustainable Forestry

www.sfiprogram.org
SFI-01054

The SFI label applies to the text stock

Library of Congress Control Number for Hardcover: 2014044446
ISBN 978-1-4231-8523-9

Visit www.hyperionteens.com

*For Susan*

# BLACK
# DOVE
# WHITE
# RAVEN

SINIDU TOLD ME I SHOULD AIM FOR THE SUN.

I still have a plane. There must be *some* way I can get Teo out safely. I think Momma's hoard of Maria Theresa dollars is enough to pay for the travel. I am hoping my new passport is waiting for me in Addis Ababa. But Teo . . . Teo is trapped. I have thought about trying to get him a British passport—Colonel Sinclair has friends who have not left Ethiopia. I could throw myself at them in disguise as Helpless Young American Girl All Alone.

I wonder if I could sweet-talk someone at the British Legation. But Momma couldn't even sweet-talk the Americans in our own legation, and of course the British probably can't do a doggone thing for Teo even if they want to. Legations have not got all the powers of embassies, and I don't know if they are even running anymore, since the invasion and the shooting started. I don't know anything that's happened in the past four months, except what I've seen from the air.

What about the French? Momma was still friendly with Pierre Ferrand and those Imperial Ethiopian Air Force pilots last time we were in Addis Ababa. But we're not French, either, and I don't even know if they're still here.

It is a waste of time trying to pass Teo off as Italian. I think I pretty much burned that bridge when I stole a plane from the Italian air force.

Sinidu is right. I am here at Lake Ashenge, north of Korem, and the emperor is in the hills above the town. There isn't anyone else who can help me.

I have nothing to lose. I am going to dare it. I will aim for the sun.

~~March 4, 1936~~
Yekatit 25, 1928

3

Humble greetings to Your Most Imperial Majesty, Haile Selassie I, Emperor of Ethiopia!

I am writing to you (politely, I hope) to beg you to forgive my brother, Teodros Gedeyon, for the bond he owes your servant Ras Amde Worku and to grant him an Ethiopian passport.

We have not met you, but we saw you just before your coronation and again when you landed for a few minutes at Tazma Meda. You know our mother, the photographer and flier Rhoda Drummond Menotti, who works in your progressive clinic there. You used to let her land on your airfield in Akaki near the capital. Her aircraft has also been flown honorably in your service by my brother, Teodros. He was given his pilot's license by the same man who trained your own Imperial Ethiopian Air Force pilots.

Your Majesty, I am a white American myself, and I don't believe you will expect any national loyalty from me. But my foster brother is an Ethiopian citizen because of his Ethiopian father. I count on your mercy and wisdom as I beg you to shower your blessing and generosity on Teodros. I have lived in Ethiopia since I was a little girl and am brokenhearted to have to run away as it is falling.

I am on my own. I am desperate. I don't know where else to turn for help. But I know that you can grant Teo a passport. You have children, too, I know, and some of them are not grown up yet—Princess Tsehai is our own age, and Prince Makonnen is very young. You must understand what it is to fear for your family.

I thought I would send you some things my mother kept, our baby stories and our older stories, some writing exercises, and our flight records. I hope they help you understand what has happened to us.

I am embarrassed that everything is written in English. Teo

4

and I both speak Amharic, but we don't write it very well, and I know that your translators are busy. My apologies! Also, I'm embarrassed about the writing, which is silly here and there, especially in the beginning. But we both like to write, and sometimes I feel as if the only thing I *can* do is write. It helps me think. Maybe you know what I mean.

I beg to tell you all that we have done for Ethiopia—and for you—this year.

I anxiously await your response and remain

Your obedient servant,

Emilia Drummond Menotti

P.S. The captured Italian aircraft is also for you. I hope it is payment enough for the big favor I am asking.

## THE ADVENTURS OF BLACK DOVE
## AND WHITE RAVEN

*This story is by Em M and it is writen down by Teodros Dupré*

Once upon a time there was a very beaoutiful lady that was able to wear every costume and she coud make things and save peple and her name was White Raven. She travled in her flying machene with her partner named Black Dove. Sometimes he coud be invisable. They flew everywere together and that means they were always in the soup together. One day in there plane they saw a big gray cloud and when they got close they saw that it was made all out of birds flying very close together. They flew arond the cloud and they landed safelly. The End

*(May 1928)*

Theme for Miss Shore by Emilia Menotti
Subject: "My Earliest Memory"
Beehive Hill Cooperative Coffee Farm
Tazma Meda, Wollo Province

19 October 1934 (Teqemt 9, 1927)

YOU DON'T HAVE MUCH CHOICE ABOUT WHAT YOUR
parents make you do until you're big enough that they can't tie
you down. I am not sure this is my earliest memory, but it is the
oldest one with details in it. It is of being tied into the open cockpit of a Curtiss Jenny flying machine by Cordelia Dupré. When I
was little, Delia took up more space in my head and heart than my
own father did. In fact, she still takes up more space there. Delia
is the most important thing that ever happened to our momma.

I know that this memory takes place when I was five years
old because I was five years old when Momma and Delia bought
the Jenny, their own airplane. It was a biplane that looked a
lot like the one we have now, one wing above the other, with
open cockpits. Well, there were four of us to fit into the Jenny's
two cockpits, counting me and Teo. Teo and I weren't very big
when we were five, but Momma and Delia figured out ways of
taking us along.

This memory is not of my first flight. My first *flight* was in
France in 1919, when I was five *weeks* old, not five years. My father,
Papà Menotti, did the flying. Momma carried me against her belly
in a scarf tied around her waist and under her big leather flying
coat—they didn't want anyone at the airfield to know they were
taking me along. It was the day of my baptism. Momma's parents

are Quakers, and they don't hold any kind of religious ceremony, but Papà is Roman Catholic and Momma wanted to make him happy. So she agreed to have me baptized if they did my "baptism in air" on the same day. Momma thinks I might have been the youngest person ever taken for a flight in an aircraft then.

But I don't remember that. What I remember is, when I was five years old, Delia lifting me out of Momma's arms and putting me into the Jenny. Delia was crouching between the wings, and Momma was standing on the ground, holding me up to her. I remember reaching to Delia, how pretty she looked in her leather flying helmet, which was exactly the same dark brown color as her skin, with her hair peeping out around the helmet like a soft, crimped frame for her face. She had on pink lipstick because she and Momma had just finished performing in an air show, and Delia always prettied herself up for the crowd. She lifted me into the plane and plunked me on the seat in the cockpit, squeezing me in next to Teo.

"There they are, in the soup together!" She laughed. "Rhoda, get up here and look at our kids—they are a double act, just like us."

It was the first time they'd ever taken us flying in the US of A because they'd never owned their own plane before. None of the owners of the borrowed planes they flew wanted to get a bad name if their plane being flown by a woman (Momma)—or, even worse, by a Negro woman (Delia)—crashed with a couple of little kids inside. If anything like that had happened, it would have shut down an aircraft owner for good. But now that Delia and Momma owned their own plane fair and square, they could do whatever they wanted.

Momma must have stood on her toes to peep up over the edge of the cockpit, and she and Delia both laughed.

"Tie 'em down," Momma said, and Delia laughed again.

I craned my neck to see Momma hop up onto the fragile body of the aircraft behind us, straddling the fuselage like it was a horse. (Once, when she'd first started wing-walking, she put her foot through the fabric of the lower wing and broke her ankle and couldn't get it out. Delia had to land the plane with Momma all balled up in the wing struts. Delia was the best pilot alive.) Momma watched while Delia tied us down, and I remember Delia doing it—how I felt like I was going to be the safest person in the whole world when she was finished.

I remember Delia's slender, dark fingers and her rose-red varnished nails. On her left hand, there was a shiny pink scar in the shape of a heart, which she had got when she was learning to fly and spilled hot engine oil on her hand. She strapped us up with white silk aviator scarves because the aircraft harnesses were too big for us; then she tied us together.

"Now, you hold on to each other," Delia said. "Like this."

She crossed Teo's left hand over to mine and crossed my right hand over to his, so our arms were woven together.

"You are going to be the new Black Dove and White Raven, so your two mommas can retire!" Delia told us. Momma laughed. I clung to Teo's hand because—I remember this *so well*—I thought she'd meant we were supposed to make the plane go, and I was worried that I didn't know how to. (Now I know she tied us down so that we couldn't grab hold of the control wheel in front of us. There was one in each cockpit.)

Delia told us, "Now, if you feel scared, just hang on tight to each other and squeeze. Three squeezes means, 'Are you scared?' and four squeezes means, 'I am not scared.' If you tell each other you're not scared, you'll feel brave. Then lean back so you can watch your momma, 'cause she's going to do the showing off. You know you'll be safe because I'm going to do the flying!"

I remember feeling *so relieved* it wasn't going to be up to me.

"Oh, put a cork in it, Del," Momma said crossly. Delia was always teasing Momma about not being as good a pilot as she was.

Teo repeated in my ear, "Put a cork in it," because it sounded goofy. We both snickered.

When she'd finished tying us up, Delia pulled on her leather gloves, covering her tiny hands and hiding her pretty nails and her shiny scar. She leaned down and kissed us one at a time, leaving pink lipstick on Teo's forehead and probably on mine, too, and she said again, "Now you are a double act like me and Rhoda."

Their double act was not onstage but in the air. They were called the Black Dove (Delia) and the White Raven (Momma), and they did an aerial show together, barnstorming in flying circuses all over the US of A. They did aerobatics (mostly Delia, because she was the better pilot) and wing-walking (mostly Momma, who was not scared of getting out of a flying machine and riding it like a horse while it was in the air). Wing-walking doesn't mean "walking" so much as it means "daredevil fooling around outside the airplane while it is flying." Even just standing up between the cockpits counts. But also doing a handstand over the pilot or eating a picnic lunch on top of the wing. Sometimes Momma did parachute jumps, too. People are always impressed by *anybody* doing stunts like these, but especially a pair of pretty girls.

*Black and white, night and day*—that was what people used to say. On the ground, when people were watching, Momma and Delia milked that contrast all they could. But on their own and in the sky, they never paid any mind to black and white—they were just two crazy people who loved flying.

"All set, Rhoda?" Delia asked.

Momma answered smartly, "Aye, aye, Cap'n!" because whichever of them was piloting was the captain; and then Delia climbed into the pilot's seat. Momma was straddling the plane, her wrists twisted into the straps she'd rigged in the wires over our heads as a kind of safety net. Someone on the ground in front of us must have swung the propeller to get the engine going. I remember feeling very excited but not nervous—if I leaned back, I could see Momma perched right behind me. Teo and I hung on with our arms crossed and nudged each other in the ribs.

"We are in the soup together!" I echoed Delia.

"Put a cork in it!" he echoed Momma.

We laughed like cackling chickens. It doesn't take much when you are five.

And then the plane started to move, and soon it was bumping over the grass, and then, without me or Teo even realizing what was going on, we were flying. We were so little we couldn't see out of the cockpit. All we could see were Momma's arms in the straps over our heads and the upper wing like a big sail and the blue sky all around us, and all we could hear were the engine and the wind singing in the wires. And Delia was flying.

That is my earliest memory.

NOW I AM DONE WRITING FOR MISS SHORE, BUT IT is making me think about Delia, and I want to write about her some more, so I am putting it in another of Miss Shore's blue theme books, which I pilfered from the "school cupboard" in the Sinclairs' dining room. It has been more than seven years since Delia died, which is nearly half my lifetime ago, and I worry that I am starting to forget her. It would be a terrible thing to forget Delia, or how she and Momma made that promise to each other.

It was a little bit later. I don't know where we were. I *know* it must have been somewhere in the South, because we were in some stranger's kitchen—we always stayed in people's houses south of the Mason-Dixon, instead of in hotels or boarding houses, because it was too hard for Momma and Delia to get rooms together.

It was a big kitchen in the airfield owner's house. There was an old-fashioned icebox *and* an electric refrigerator on white metal legs, and a brand-new gas range that matched the refrigerator, all shiny white enamel with nickel trim. Delia had flown the plane from wherever we'd just left, and Momma had brought me and Teo with her on the train. Momma was making us scrambled eggs when Delia came in.

Delia was still wearing her leather coat and trousers, but she'd taken off her flying helmet and replaced it with a modish gray cloche hat that fitted tight over her sleek, marcelled hair—she was always so much more stylish than Momma. Delia carried her helmet and goggles in a pink-and-gold-striped cardboard hatbox over one arm and she had her pigskin flight bag over her shoulder. She was also holding the big paisley carpetbag she packed her things in when we were traveling. She dumped everything down on the kitchen floor and swooped over me and Teo for a hug and a kiss. Then she looked up at Momma and said sadly, "McKinley won't let us do the show for a mixed audience. Whites only."

Momma banged the cooking fork so hard against the iron fry pan that me and Teo jumped. We must have been seven by then. Old enough to understand what was going on.

Momma's wispy gold bangs were matted to her forehead. She stuck out her lower lip and blew at them. Then she frowned so that her gray eyes went narrow and you could see that little dent between her eyebrows. But she wasn't mad at us, or at Delia.

"We're staying in his house," Momma said. "He'll let us all sleep under the same roof, in the same bed, and help ourselves to the food in his icebox to feed our kids. But he won't let colored folks and white folks watch our air show together?" She rammed the fork back into the eggs and stirred them messily. A big piece of egg flew out and sizzled on the black charcoal beneath the range's brand-new gas burners. "Well, I'll talk to him."

"Just 'cause you're the White Raven is not going to make him change his mind."

Delia wasn't being sarcastic or mean. She'd talked to the airfield owner already, and she knew he wasn't going to budge.

Momma stabbed at our eggs like she was going to kill them.

"Now, Rhoda!" Delia gently took the fork and fry pan out of Momma's hands. Delia was still wearing her pretty hat and her flying coat, and she squeezed Momma around the waist. Then she started to stir the eggs herself.

Momma stomped over to the kitchen window and looked out with her arms folded over her chest. If a human being could look like a covered pot about to boil over, she was doing it.

"It's *not fair*, Delia," Momma said. "It's not fair and it's not right. Bessie Coleman wouldn't ever fly if she couldn't have a mixed crowd watching. She'd have refused, and we should, too."

"We don't have Bessie's draw," Delia said, "or her backing. Maybe someday we'll get a newspaperman to sponsor us like she did, but that has not happened yet, and her falling out of a plane and killing herself didn't do us any favors. We just don't pull the crowds like she could, and that means we don't make the money. And we have more mouths to feed."

Momma stood, simmering.

"We have got to do it, Rhoda. We have got to go ahead and play to whatever crowd we get."

"I won't."

"Well then, I will do the show myself," Delia said.

Momma turned around to glare at her. "You dirty double-crosser."

Delia took the iron fry pan off the stove and started to pile forkfuls of egg into two saucers that Momma had put out for us.

"I never double-crossed anybody," Delia said calmly. "I'm just feeding the kids."

Momma let out one enormous, choking sob and swiped the back of one hand angrily across her eyes.

"*It's not right*, Delia. They don't do this in Pennsylvania or New York, and when they tried it in New Jersey, we didn't cave in like this. We never caved in like this before."

" 'Cause we haven't had to yet." Delia took hold of Momma's shoulders and made her sit down with us at the table. "Listen, honey—I want to tell you my wild idea."

Then she knelt between me and Teo with one hand on each of our shoulders now. "I want to tell you *all* my wild idea."

Delia got up and sat down across from Momma and held out her hands over the table. Momma took them. Teo and I sat watching with our scrambled eggs getting cold in front of us. We knew that wall they were up against. Crossing that invisible border between Pennsylvania and Maryland took you into another world, where you had to play by a different set of rules. Delia probably hated them more than Momma did, but she was better at playing along.

"You want to go back to France?" Momma asked. Her voice was low and husky. "I'd go back there in a heartbeat. Remember how no one cared when we sat together at the café in La Chênaie, drinking Chartreuse and rocking our babies in the same baby carriage? A colored girl and a white girl wing-walking and flying aerobatics would pull *sensational* crowds in France." Momma paused. "How do you say *Black Dove and White Raven* in French? *La Colombe Noire—Le Corbeau Blanc*."

"*Blanche*," Delia corrected. "You are a girl."

"No. *Raven* is masculine," Momma said.

"But you're not," Delia laughed.

She realized she was still wearing her hat and let go of Momma's hands for a moment to take it off and lay it on the table. Teo shot me a warning look, and I carefully moved my plate closer to me so I wouldn't risk getting grease on the hat's soft charcoal-gray surface. But Delia wouldn't have noticed. She had something more important on her mind. She pulled Momma's hands back across the table and said quietly, "I don't want us to go back to France. I want to go to Ethiopia."

This is the moment I remember—not my earliest memory, but the *best*. Delia and Momma gripping each other's hands across some stranger's enamel kitchen table, staring hard into each other's eyes. Their hands were clasped in front of us, Momma's strong and pale, Delia's slender and brown. Momma's gold wedding ring and Delia's rose-red painted nails. *I want to go to Ethiopia.*

The Europeans still use its old name, Abyssinia. But the Americans who are enchanted by it call it by its own name, in its own language: Ethiopia.

"That's crazy," Momma said, giving Delia's hands a shake and a squeeze like she was trying to wake her up.

"*It is not crazy.*" Delia was forceful, but she still didn't sound like she was being stubborn or mad—her voice was just warm and determined. She really meant it. "I told you it was a wild idea, but it is not a crazy one.

"I have been thinking and thinking," Delia went on. "Maybe I wouldn't have ever heard of Ethiopia if I hadn't gone to France and met Gedeyon and had Teo, but I bet I would still have the notion to go to Africa. You and me both used to listen to that Marcus Garvey talking about Liberia being the new black African homeland. I don't have reason to go to Liberia, but my son is half Ethiopian. I want him to feel at home there."

"But that's like running away," Momma objected. "And Ethiopia isn't *my* homeland."

"No, your homeland is that Alice-in-Wonderland horse farm in Pennsylvania, where nobody fights wars and nobody gets lynched, and you go every Sunday to those starchy Friends meetings, where nobody ever sings or says anything, and you left when you were eighteen because it was so boring! You know that isn't the real world!"

"What about the NAACP trying to change things lawfully for Negroes in the USA?"

Delia hesitated. And finally she said, "They are changing too darn slow. They help people in court; they don't do a thing on the street. Being a mother is making me selfish. I don't want my boy to have to wait. Ethiopia is a country of African people run by Africans, and it always has been. It's not like Liberia, set up by the USA as a colony for freed slaves. Ethiopia is the only country in Africa never to be colonized!"

Delia knew what she was talking about. She went on. "They have got their own culture and their own language—Rhoda, you still look at those wonderful books of photographs Gedeyon gave me in France. You were looking at them before we left Pennsylvania. You know you want to see it. Imagine if you could take pictures like that yourself!"

"You temptress," Momma teased.

Teo and I loved those pictures, too. Even before we could read the books, we made up stories around the pictures. Churches a thousand years old carved in rock. Crazy-looking hornbills so top-heavy it looked like their beaks ought to make their heads fall over. Black-and-white monkeys with beautiful, long tails, and men playing strange stringed instruments, and women in embroidered robes weaving patterned baskets. Crowned priests carrying fringed umbrellas and horsehair fly swatters.

"And now Ethiopia is respected enough to be a member of the League of Nations," Delia said. "They just sent a diplomat to the American president! It's turning into a modern nation—let's be the first to go!"

Momma sighed again, shaking her head. "It's a dream, Delia! Ethiopia is *poor*. People there don't have money to pay to watch a pair of girls wing-walking."

Delia was ready for this.

"We could make a business for ourselves finding game for white hunters. Or taking exotic aerial pictures for magazines. You nursed people before—I bet they need nurses. We could fly to out-of-the-way places and help out. I don't know, but *something*! So our kids will grow up in a place where no one will ever say to them, 'You can't ride with each other, because one of you is colored. You have to eat in different rooms because of the color of your skin.'"

That was something Teo and I hated. We all hated it.

"I don't want my boy to have to *fight* for his right to get a drink of water or eat in a restaurant," Delia said. "I want to live in a place where people can do what they like, and it is ordinary."

Staring her straight in the eye, Momma gave Delia the single, curt nod that she used to tell her she was ready for aerobatics. It meant she was ready. Ready to go. She just hadn't said it out loud yet.

"Teo's dad is dead," Delia said. "But even before Teo was born, I had to work things out for my own self, and I am not counting on any man to help me now. You and me need to do this ourselves. And we can. Cut back on little things—nail varnish, new clothes—"

"That's *you*," Momma said. "I don't spend on myself."

"All those dang magazines," Delia reminded her. "Film for your camera."

Momma laughed. She tightened her hold on Delia's hands.

"So this is what we do," Delia said decisively. "We do these dumb whites-only shows. You practice keeping up that poker face you are so terrible at holding, and we play to whatever crowd they give us and we don't complain and we don't kick up a fuss about who they let in. It's selfish; I know it. But it won't take too long. Two years, maybe? We'll make the money and then we'll go!"

"You *are* a little crazy, Delia," Momma said fondly.

"You were with me from the start and you are with me now!" Delia gave Momma's hands a shake. "Think of the sky, Rhoda! Think of the sky in Ethiopia! What'll it be like to fly in the African sky?"

They clung to each other across the table.

"Rhoda? Say you'll do it with me." She squeezed Momma's hands three times: I saw her do it. *Are you scared?*

Momma squeezed Delia's hands back. I counted to four. *I am not scared.*

Momma vowed to Delia, "We'll do it. In two years' time. We'll do it."

IN THAT HOUSE, WE HAD ONE BIG IRON BED WITH creaking springs for all of us to sleep in, and that was our favorite kind of place to stay. When we all had to be in one big bed, me and Teo got squeezed in between Momma and Delia, and there is no place I ever felt safer or warmer or happier. That night, I remember how Momma and Delia kept whispering and planning back and forth over the top of us:

"If we do a show in Washington, we can see if there is an Ethiopian embassy or at least a legation if they have no embassy yet—"

"That crazy Horatio Augustus knows all kinds of people. *And* he owes us money."

"My folks can take the kids for a spell. For the whole summer, so we can fly shows back-to-back—"

"Aw, the kids can come along with us while we do that. They are big enough to behave. They are nearly big enough to learn to fly!"

"Now, *that* would be an act," said Momma, and they both laughed.

THEY MADE A PLAN. THEY KEPT TRACK OF THEIR funds in a special notebook, and they did everything they could to save for our new life in Ethiopia. Delia stopped painting her nails and Momma stopped buying magazines. Teo and I sat paging through the old ones while we waited on people's porches or in the shady corner of some aircraft hangar. The pictures we looked at in magazines were always the same after that night to remember—except every now and then, when Momma sold a picture she'd taken herself, and *Harper's* or *Popular Science* would send her a copy of the issue that had her photograph printed in it. She didn't stop buying film.

They still hadn't saved what they needed when the Delia-shaped hole got blasted in our world.

Here's what we know about the crash:

It was a bird strike. That's when a bird hits the plane in midair. Delia was flying in the front cockpit, and Momma wasn't tied in—she had just climbed down into the backseat after a wing-walking show. They were only twenty feet above the ground when it happened. The propeller shattered, and a piece of it hit Delia in the head. The Jenny stalled itself hard into the ground and flipped over. Momma, in the rear cockpit, was thrown clear; they think Delia was killed instantly, when the propeller hit her. But if it wasn't the propeller, she didn't survive the crash.

It happened in Illinois in the summer of 1927. I was eight and Teo was seven. The bird was a prairie falcon.

Momma was in the hospital for a week, stone-cold unconscious for the first two days. The cook from the diner next to the airfield took care of me and Teo until Grandma and Grandfather came out to get us. Then we waited for Momma to wake up.

I know this is hard to believe, but we didn't know anything was wrong until the night they let Momma out of the hospital. We were just so used to having other people keep an eye on us—so used to getting left with a pile of Lincoln Logs on some stranger's kitchen linoleum or playing with a cardboard box full of kittens on an unfamiliar front porch for an afternoon. We hadn't been at the airfield when the Bird Strike happened, so we didn't see it, and nobody told us about it. When Grandma and Grandfather got there, they thought we already knew, so they didn't tell us anything, either.

Even Momma herself didn't know what had happened when she came to stay in the hotel where we were with Grandma and Grandfather. She was nearly as much in the dark as we were because she'd been out cold for so long. But Momma figured it out. And so did we, the first night we had her back. I think we figured it out because for the first time ever—*ever*—it was just Momma and me and Teo all together in a strange bed. We weren't sandwiched safely between anybody. We were all by ourselves on each side of Momma, a strange, pale ghost of herself, wearing a bruise like a purple raccoon's mask, lying on her stomach and shrieking into the pillow as if we weren't even there.

"What am I going to do?" she choked wildly. "*What am I going to do?*"

That was how we knew Delia wasn't coming back.

When I woke up in the middle of the night, Teo and I both had our arms tight around Momma. She was sound asleep, but every now and then, she'd make a little gasping sob like she was still crying in her dreams. We knew we had to take care of her because Delia couldn't do it anymore.

After the Bird Strike, we all went back to Grandma and Grandfather's farm in Bucks County, Pennsylvania, and Momma stayed in her bedroom for six whole months.

Teo and I are a double act, like Delia said. We have each other. So the Delia-sized hole in our lives is bigger for Momma than it is for us. The only thing that has ever come close to filling that hole is the African sky, and that is why we live here now.

Theme for Miss Shore by Emilia Menotti
Subject: "Home Is Where the Heart Is"
Beehive Hill Cooperative Coffee Farm
Tazma Meda, Wollo Province

Oct. 26, 1934 (Teqemt 16, 1927)

MOMMA HAS FOUR SISTERS (SHE'S THE OLDEST ONE), and her parents run a riding school called Blue Rock Farm in Bucks County, Pennsylvania. Teo and I lived there for three years after Delia died, and that is where we learned to take care of ourselves. Momma was too busy crying to pay much attention to us the first year we lived on Blue Rock Farm, and then she went away to Africa without us for the next two years. When Teo and I came to Ethiopia for the first time, it really felt like we were coming home. Because that was when, finally, after three years, we were back with the Momma who we knew and loved.

But when we first came to Blue Rock Farm in the summer of '27, Momma mostly stayed in her room till Christmas. We'd only see her if we went in there looking for her, or met her in the hall on her way to the bathroom.

"It's like living with a ghost," Aunt Connie complained to Grandma. She was still in high school at Fox Friends in Lambstown, the only one of Momma's sisters not already grown up and married. "I don't believe Rhoda could be more miserable if her own husband died!"

"She couldn't be more miserable," Grandma agreed. "Don't judge her, Connie. She has lost her soul mate."

I loved that phrase: soul mate. We asked Grandma what it

meant, and she said, "Two people who understand each other without talking about it. Two halves of a whole."

"Like being married?" I asked.

"No," Grandma said. "It could be anybody. Father or mother or sister or friend. A teacher or someone you work with. Anybody. Any two people who understand each other so well that one of them can fly blindfolded and the other will stand unafraid on the wing of the plane."

We have never been sure if she was exaggerating or if Momma and Delia really did that once. But *soul mate*. You would trust your soul mate with anything, so they might have.

Now Momma was alone.

Teo and I learned to take care of ourselves during that first year, but we learned to take care of Momma, too. Together. We'd figure out what we were going to pester her with, and then we'd let Teo do the pestering. He can be very persistent and very patient, and she'd wake up a little for Teo. She couldn't ignore Delia's baby.

Here's the kind of thing Teo would do. He'd shove an open book under her nose and say something like "Momma, you *have got* to tell us why this tree has fallen on the boy and if he'll be okay—Momma, how come he's only got one hand? He only has one hand in all the pictures, not just this one here, where the tree is squashing him."

The fallen-tree picture is the most terrifying and intriguing picture in *Freckles* by Gene Stratton Porter, and neither of us could read yet.

"I'm sleeping now. Come back later and I'll tell you."

"I'm going to leave the book here by your head, okay, Momma? Don't lose the page," Teo would warn. "And it's one of Aunt Connie's books from her special shelf, so don't throw it. She's already mad at us for getting the cover wet."

"Please go away, kids." Momma would turn her back on us and pull a pillow over her head.

"Come on, Em, let's make her coffee."

In an hour, we'd trail back up there with coffee, and Teo would start on her, patiently, all over again.

"We made you a story this time. Em made it up and I drew it. Look, Black Dove and White Raven have got a moving bed—it is under a tent that the wild ponies are carrying on their backs. Look at this bed the ponies are carrying!"

Momma liked to look at our stories. She liked *The Adventures of Black Dove and White Raven*. But then she'd get mad at me because I kept using Delia's gorgeous clothes for dress-up. It was okay for Momma to float around the house in Delia's silver kimono, for some reason, but not for me.

"Look, Em, can you just keep your nose out of Delia's things for a little while?" Teo scolded me. "'Cause every time I think Momma's going to start talking to us again, you turn up wearing Delia's earrings and then Momma does nothing but cry for two days. You are not helping."

And I stopped. It was hard, but I really did. Grandma used to give us scraps of rickrack and buttons to make up for it. Teo made me a pair of White Raven wings. They are not actually raven wings, but American goldfinch wings, the flashiest bird we could think of. I brought them with me to Ethiopia, and I still wear them sometimes, unless we are going out on a feast day, when it makes more sense to blend in.

"You just have to be careful with Momma for a while," Teo told me. "She's broken. Like a jug with a broken handle that you try to glue back together. It looks all right, and it'll still hold water. It's still a good jug. But you better not ever pick it up by the handle. You have to wait for the glue to dry, and even then it might not hold."

I squinted at him. "Come again?"

"You know what I mean. Just keep out of Delia's things."

"How come she likes our stories when we draw them but she doesn't like to see us act them out?"

"She can pretend it's her and Delia when we draw them," Teo said. "She can put herself in the story when she's listening to it. But when she's watching someone else all dressed up, it isn't her."

One day Momma followed us down to the kitchen when we went to make her coffee. It was about a month after the Bird Strike, and her face was still bruised—she was all yellow around the eyes. She sat at the kitchen table in Delia's cream silk pajamas with the pink shell pattern and read *Freckles* out loud to us all morning.

When Grandma came in from the stables at lunch time, and we were all sitting there with the coffeepot still on the burner and all the coffee boiled away, Momma looked up at her and complained, "Mother, can we send these kids to school so they can figure out how to read to themselves?"

Grandma swept the coffee off the stove and then swooped down on Momma to kiss her on top of her frazzled gold hair.

"First thing in September. Oh, Rhoda, I've just been waiting for thee to ask." Grandma always says *thee* to her daughters and to us, old-fashioned and familiar, because she is a Quaker. "Does that mean thee's going to stay home for a while?"

"No place else I'm planning to go."

THAT WAS WHEN WE REALLY BECAME THE NEW Black Dove and White Raven, when we began making up their Adventures.

When we first started, we just drew everything, like comic strips, because we didn't know how to write. Some of those pictures were pretty weird. We decided that Black Dove (Teo) could make himself go invisible, and White Raven (me) was a glamorous master of disguise. So sometimes we'd just draw Black Dove's equipment, like a plane that looked like it was flying without a pilot, or a runaway train he was stopping. (Teo got carried away making up interesting-looking planes and trains.) And there are no pictures of White Raven that actually show *her*, because she is always in disguise.

We drew a lot of these stories, but we also acted them out. We specialized in reunions and rescues. Every episode ended in celebrations with real cake and bunting in the kitchen or the barn, with Grandma and Connie and Sallie the housekeeper usually dragged in as party guests. Everything *always* came out all right in *The Adventures*. We cranked out happy endings like we were starving for them. Well, I guess we *were* starving for happy endings.

School was an endurance exercise that brought us back to reality five days a week. The only good thing about it was learning to write, which was what made *The Adventures of Black Dove and White Raven* really take off. Teo was the only black person in our grade in New Marlow, Bucks County, Pennsylvania, but there were also a couple of black kids who were sisters, one in the grade ahead of us and one in the grade behind. There were two teachers for the whole school, the Misses Larson, who had first started teaching at prairie schools in the Dakota Territory just after the railroads were built. They weren't as old as you'd think, because they'd started teaching when they were not quite sixteen. (Now that I am not quite sixteen myself, thinking about the Misses Larson makes me feel uneducated, unemployed, and old.)

The Misses Larson were good teachers, but not so good at figuring out what was going on in the playground. There were always a couple of mean kids who called us names. They picked on Teo not only because he was black, but also because he always managed to end up covered with dust whenever he went to the chalkboard or paint if we were painting, or he'd come in from recess with twigs or spiderwebs in his hair from climbing in the mulberry tree at the edge of the schoolyard. They picked on me because everybody thought Momma was a crazy woman. *They locked up your ma yet? She grow wings yet? Bet you have to tie her up at night so she won't fly away. Ha ha ha ha ha ha ha.*

And mind you, this is in the place Delia complained was too nice to be real.

So Teo struggled not to be noticed and I pretended to be somebody else, and here's the kind of thing we'd end up doing.

"Those rats with the spitballs are waiting behind the steps again," Teo pointed out as Miss Ida Larson rang the bell to announce that recess was over. We had to lurk between the fence and the mulberry tree for the whole lunch hour so no one noticed us. We'd been at the New Marlow School for two whole months. "They do it every Friday. Do they think we're nitwits?"

"They do it on Friday because they know Miss Larson will forget about it over the weekend," I answered. "Let's just not go back in. No one will notice."

"What'll we do instead?"

"Whatever Black Dove and White Raven would do. Fly someplace interesting."

"We can't fly," Teo said practically. "How about we take a train? We can pretend we're rescuing people on the Underground Railroad!"

"You mean *go somewhere*? Not just stay here in the schoolyard but actually *leave*?"

"Sure! What's the difference to Miss Larson if we're here or home or anywhere else? Can you find the river? 'Cause those big trains go by with open doors all the time. We could get off at Lambstown and meet Connie after school, and she could bring us home on the trolley."

We knew about the Underground Railroad because Grandma's Quaker mother had actually run an Underground Railroad station in Philadelphia, a safe house for runaway slaves going to Canada. We didn't know it wasn't a real railroad. We imagined secret trains running without lights in the middle of the night.

"That might be your *best idea*," I exclaimed.

"Grandma won't think so, but Connie won't tell," Teo said with confidence.

So I led us through the woods to the railroad bed by the Delaware River, and after about twenty minutes of climbing around on the rocks below the embankment, meeting up with our imaginary runaways, we heard a train coming and scrambled back up to the tracks. Three engines creaked past at low speed in a cloud of steam, followed by at least a hundred wooden freight cars. They were going so painfully slow that anyone would be tempted to climb in. When one of them came along with an open door and an iron running board, it just looked too easy.

Teo hesitated—I did not. It *was* easy. (We were lucky that day; we did it about half a dozen times in three years, and it was mostly hair-raising. But we never got caught.)

"Come on, Black Dove! No one can see you!"

He laughed with delight. I am always pretending to be White Raven right out in the open, but he is sort of shy about pretending to be his made-up hero, and it tickles him when you treat him like that is what he really is. I held out my hands, but he took a running jump and hopped up next to me without any trouble. The car was full of empty bushel baskets and feed sacks. We sat side by side in the open door with our feet dangling, rattling through the wet-smelling fall woods at about five miles an hour.

"No one can see me, but you need a disguise," he said. "Grab one of those sacks when we get off."

After we hopped off at the other end, we spent an hour under the steel girder bridge at Lambstown weaving orange and yellow maple leaves into the feed sack for a Swamp Angel disguise (we got that name from *Freckles* but improved on its meaning). We discussed the perils of ending up chained in a jail cell, which we didn't really think would happen to *us*, but which was no doubt going to happen to Black Dove. Teo managed to lose his cap *and* tear his sweater. Connie was not too thrilled to see us at her trolley stop, but she softened up when we told her she was rescuing us from slavery. I guess she felt the same way we did about the New Marlow School, even without people slinging names and spitballs at her.

AW, WRITING THAT ESSAY FOR MISS SHORE IS JUST making me want to work on *The Adventures.* This pilfered theme book is a great disguise for when I get fed up with doing schoolwork. Remember the story where White Raven became a bareback rider in the circus so she could distract the owners while Black Dove freed all the bears? That episode was a direct result of the Drummond sisters' riding show on our first Thanksgiving at Blue Rock Farm. I don't want to forget that, either, just like I don't want to forget Delia.

All of Momma's sisters and their husbands and their babies (two very new, two just walking) came to stay for Thanksgiving the year of the Bird Strike, and they decided to do a circus in the riding school for me and Teo and the babies. They'd always done this on Thanksgiving when they were little, and they hadn't all been home together for five years. They were excited about having an audience. Even Momma came out to watch. She didn't bother to get dressed, but she put on her old leather flying coat and her tall boots because it was cold, and covered her head with a blue silk scarf of Delia's. She looked a little strange, but at least she was *there*.

Except for Connie's act, the aunts' show was pretty tame because they were so out of practice; but Aunt Lorna and Aunt Jean did a really funny clown act—pushing each other and falling off horses and jumping on backward. Aunt Connie was fabulous and scary—she made all the other aunts crouch down in a row on the ground and got her horse to jump *over* them.

Grandfather had a fit. "You girls all get off the ground—make it snappy!"

The aunts didn't pay any attention. They weren't at all scared. Afterward, when Connie trotted back to where we were all watching, all her big sisters defended her.

"She's the best part of the show!"

"Connie's the starlet!"

Momma was quiet until she said, "Connie, take those stirrups off."

Connie shot her big sister a startled glance, and Momma gave that one quick, steady nod.

Connie seemed to know what it meant. She slid like melted butter from Jasper's back, handed the reins to Aunt Alice, and started to unbuckle one of the stirrup leathers. Aunt Jean sauntered over to help with the other stirrup while Alice lengthened the reins.

Momma took her coat off and stood in the chilly November air wearing nothing but Delia's pretty silk pajamas and her riding boots—and then she took off her boots, too. She wasn't even wearing socks.

"Rhoda!" Grandma scolded. "Thy feet!"

Momma rolled her eyes.

"Thee knows I have to do it barefoot, Mother. Jeannie, come on. Make me a step."

Aunt Jean laced her fingers together, and Momma put one naked white foot into the cup of Jean's hands, and then she vaulted up into Jasper's saddle.

Momma had the lengthened reins bunched up in one hand, and she leaned forward and wound the fingers of her other hand through Jasper's mane. Jasper started trotting, neat and brisk. Momma got up on her knees, still crouched forward. It was exactly the way she crouched on the fuselage of an airplane, bent forward and hugging the plane with her knees. It was exactly the way she'd crouched behind me on that day Delia had tied me and Teo together in the cockpit of their new Curtiss Jenny.

Jasper trotted around the school with Momma kneeling barefoot on his back, the pink-and-cream silk pajamas fluttering in the breeze. Momma urged him into a canter.

The aunts must have known what she was going to do. Grandma and Grandfather, too. But me and Teo didn't have an inkling. Even though we'd seen Momma wing-walking a thousand times—even though we *knew* that was what she did best, that she got paid for it, and even though we'd sat in a plane and watched her while she did it—neither one of us ever in a million years guessed you could ride a horse the same way you could ride an airplane.

Jasper cantered smoothly around the ring.

My jaw dropped as I watched Momma pull one knee up and then the other, planting her feet squarely across the saddle, gripping with her toes. She straightened her knees, still holding on to Jasper's mane, so that she was nearly standing, bent over double, like a ballerina touching her toes. Then she let go of Jasper's mane, let out the reins, and stood up.

Jasper just kept on cantering. And there was Momma, standing barefoot on his back, her arms spread for balance, straight as an arrow, with the blue silk scarf pulling free of her hair and the silk pajamas billowing around her lanky body like a circus costume.

It was the most amazing thing our momma had ever done, and that was saying something.

She let Jasper go around the ring twice while she stood careless and proud on his back. Then she knelt back down and sat. She let him trot around back to me and Teo.

"Oh, Momma, I want to do that!" Teo cried.

He scrambled through the rails, and she bent over with her arms held out to scoop him up.

All the grown-ups let out yowls of protest.

"Don't you do it, Rhoda—"

"He only just started riding—"

"You're too thin! You won't be strong enough to hold him!"

She hoisted Teo up in front of her.

"Jiminy Christmas. What a bunch of nervous Nellies."

Then she trotted away from us around the school.

Everybody shut up after that because they didn't want to scare her—or Jasper—or Teo.

Momma pulled Teo's shoes off and tossed them against the fence. She didn't stand up again herself, but she helped Teo stand. Momma wasn't touching him—just making a protective circle around him with her arms. And I know he was the safest person in the whole world with Momma's arms around him like that.

Teo didn't smile, because he was concentrating. His eyes were fixed somewhere far in the distance, and he hardly wobbled at all. He'd never done *anything* like that before, something that made everybody look at him. Nobody would call him a daredevil. But when he fixes on something he likes to do, he sure can be full of surprises. I haven't ever been so proud, or so jealous, of anybody in my whole life as I was of Teo right then. Black Dove is supposed to be *invisible*.

They went around the ring twice, just like Momma had done, with Teo standing and Momma behind him with her arms in a ring. Then she made Jasper walk again, and she swept Teo tight in a hug. Then she started to cry against the back of his neck.

She didn't ever do it again. We went a little bit crazy trying to get someone else to help Teo do it, but no one else would. The one thing we were absolutely not allowed to fool with on our own was the horses, so we never tried it ourselves.

We both sort of wish we had.

I am not going to show *any* of this to Miss Shore. I will have to start again.

"Home Is Where the Heart Is"
*by Em M.*
(Or "How We Ended Up in Ethiopia")

MOMMA MET PAPÀ MENOTTI BECAUSE SHE WENT TO Italy to be in the Army Nurse Corps during the Great War. Grandma and Grandfather were not happy about it. They didn't want her to be involved in a war at *all*, even helping to fix people. They are Friends—Quakers. They don't believe in going to war. So Grandfather was mad at Momma, but it is a known fact that she is his favorite girl and he will let her do anything she gets her mind stuck on—standing on a cantering horse, marrying a soldier, flying a plane, taking her children to live in Africa.

So Momma was a nurse and Papà was a pilot for Italy, and his plane crashed and he was picked up by the Americans. Momma ended up taking care of him and then falling in love with him. After the war, she brought him back to Pennsylvania just long enough for them to get married, and then he took her to France because he had a job as an instructor at a flying school there. He hired Delia to go with them to France as Momma's maid because Momma was going to have a baby (me).

Of course, Momma had never had a *maid*. Grandma and Grandfather are always working in the stables and the riding school, and they hire men to help them. They also hire an old Pennsylvania Dutch woman to cook for them and do the housework, but Sallie never waited on Momma and her sisters when they were little, and she used to yell at me and Teo if we didn't make our own beds. For darn sure Momma never had anyone around who was just *there* with nothing else to do but fill the tub for her and comb her hair and carry her shopping bags. And if you knew Momma, you would know that (1) she hates water, (2) she bobbed her hair *herself* when she was thirteen so she wouldn't have to take care of it, and (3) if she ever went shopping, *nobody* was going to carry her bags but Momma herself.

But there wasn't really anything for Momma to do in France except take baths, comb her hair, and go shopping. So she and Delia did it together. After not very long, they were buying things for both of them—they'd get matching hats and fur collars for their coats. They'd sit drinking coffee together in parks and cafés, and practice their French—Momma had learned some in high school, but Delia didn't know any till they got to France. They'd go see moving pictures together. And they could, because nobody in France cares if black and white people go around together, especially if they are both pretty, young women.

Papà was the only one who could have cared, because he was paying Delia's wages. But Momma was happy and Delia was happy, so Papà Menotti was happy, too. Gedeyon Wendimu, Teo's Ethiopian father, was one of Papà Menotti's student pilots. That was how Delia met him. France and Britain and Italy all have interests in Ethiopia—the French paid for Ethiopia's first railway, and Ethiopians who want to study in Europe go to France. The emperor himself speaks French. Gedeyon was in France because he was the secretary for an official who came to Paris to set up a brand-new Ethiopian Legation. Gedeyon didn't realize Delia was hired help when he met her. She got introduced to people as Momma's *bonne amie*, her good friend.

Teo and I were born so close to each other, eight months apart, that Momma and Delia used to wheel us around in the same big wicker baby carriage as if we were twins. The story is that people got confused when they peeked in at us.

While they were hanging around the French airfield where

Papà was working, Momma and Delia met Bessie Coleman. Bessie was the first Negro woman in the world to get a pilot's license, and the first American—black or white, man or woman—to get an international pilot's license. She had to go to France to do it because no one would teach her in the USA. She took French classes so she could go.

If it weren't for Bessie Coleman turning up on their French airfield, it might not have occurred to Momma and Delia that they could learn to fly, too. But Bessie did. Papà Menotti was not her chief instructor, but he gave her a couple of lessons. When Bessie flew solo for the first time, Momma and Delia were watching. Bessie took off and flew the plane and landed it again safely, all by herself.

Momma and Delia were waving and cheering as Bessie climbed out of the cockpit of the Nieuport, a little biplane that looks a lot like a Jenny, and she stopped to shake their hands. She was a little bit older than they were, and Momma said they felt like they were meeting a queen.

"You are an inspiration!" Delia told Bessie.

"Prove that to me by getting yourself into the air!" she answered. She grinned at Momma, too. "And you. I see you sitting here all morning just watching! Why don't you both learn to fly? You're lucky to be here, and there is no time like the present. You can take turns sitting with your kids."

There is a photograph—one of three dozen in Momma's little French airfield album—of me and Teo sitting up straight in our carriage, both of us wearing matching crocheted hoods with rabbit fur edging, parked on the grass lawn outside the flight school. Momma is kneeling next to Teo, and Delia is kneeling next to me. They are both dressed in long leather flying coats and white scarves, and everyone is smiling. Bessie Coleman took the picture for them.

Everything changed again because Papà had to go back to the Italian air force—in Tripoli, in Italian North Africa, the Italians were fighting to control their colonies.

Falling in love with a nurse in wartime had been one thing, but Papà didn't want to take his wife and toddler, not to mention everybody else, to go along with him to strong-arm rebellious desert nomads. Momma said she'd go back to Pennsylvania and stay with her parents while he was away. But Papà stopped paying Delia's wages—Momma obviously didn't need a maid and Delia obviously wasn't one—and when Momma and Delia went back to Pennsylvania, they started doing flying circuses. They did it to make their own living and to pay for their flying. Bessie Coleman was doing flying circuses, too, by then, and they thought they could be like her. That was when they became Black Dove and White Raven. Until the Bird Strike.

Papà Menotti knew about what had happened to Delia. Until Momma shut herself in her bedroom after Delia died, Papà and Momma always wrote to each other. He sent her money sometimes, and he sent us presents—silver charms and bags with leather fringes and beautiful geometric rugs and blankets that Grandma used for bedspreads. After Delia died, Grandma wrote to him in Italian North Africa every month or so and she'd always get me and Teo to send him stories and pictures. He usually got a friend of his to write back to us in English. And when he did, we'd read his letters to Momma.

We'd been at Blue Rock Farm about a year when Papà Menotti left Tripoli.

"This letter is from a boat!" Teo crowed. "He is at sea!"

"Where's he going?" Momma asked. The mail came before breakfast, and we read it to her before we went to school, while she was still in bed. Momma got up and got dressed most days by then, but not till after we were out of the house. First she had to scan three different papers for news of Ethiopia, like it was a lifeline, the only thing she could still do for Delia. (She even used to get a subscription to a Negro newspaper published in Chicago.) When she'd given up, usually in disgust that nothing she cared about got reported, she'd go work in the stables. She didn't feel like talking to anyone, so she didn't help in the riding school, but she worked hard enough behind the scenes that Grandfather paid her.

"Italy Somewhere," I said with authority. We'd only been in school a year.

Teo had picked up reading a lot faster than I had. He read *everything*, all the time, even then. It made me lazy because he could read to me when no one else would. "Em, you nitwit. He isn't in Italy. He is going to another place in Africa—Italian Something—Italian Somaliland."

Momma sat up straight in bed. It was like she'd lit up suddenly, like a light had turned on in her head.

"Italian Somaliland!" Then she sagged again. "You must be reading it wrong."

"Here, Momma, you can read it yourself." Teo twitched the letter out of my hand and gave it to her. It was a letter from her husband, but it wasn't even addressed to her. It didn't cover most of a page; it was just a chatty, cheerful note in broken English that someone else had written, with Papà telling me about the ship he was traveling on. It had gone through the Suez Canal, and they'd taken apart five airplanes to pack in the ship to take with them.

Momma's face grew brighter as she scanned the page. When she finished, she looked up, and she was smiling the first real smile we'd seen on her face for a long time.

"Orsino really is going to Somaliland!" she told us.

"What is Somaliland?" we clamored. "Why is that good? What does it mean?"

"It's in the Horn of Africa," Momma said. She beamed at us. "It's another Italian colony in Africa. Africa is huge—*huge*—it's like he's making a trip from New York to Los Angeles through the Panama Canal. But now Orsino's going to be *right next door* to Ethiopia! Italian Somaliland and Ethiopia share a border. He's going to be so close! We could . . . we could finally go!"

"To Somaliland?" Teo asked, alarmed.

"No, honey, to Ethiopia! Italian Somaliland is the perfect place to start—the perfect way for us to get in. It's just over the border—and the Italians are bringing airplanes there, and that will turn the distances into *nothing*."

Teo and I both knew Ethiopia was Delia's dream to start with. But we knew it had become our momma's dream, too, because we paged through her French books of travel photographs with her, and we knew she scoured the papers for Ethiopian news, and we knew she never did anything with the money Grandfather paid her, like she was still saving it for something big. But our connection to the Underground Railroad seemed realer than our connection to Ethiopia. Ethiopia didn't seem like a real place at all.

We got excited and bounced on her bed. "Can we go before school starts?" I begged. "Can we take all of my White Raven outfits?"

"Do you have to buy another plane?" Teo asked. "Can we fly there ourselves?"

Momma gave a bitter, choking laugh. "It's a little bit farther than you think." She hesitated. "I'd have to go by myself, at first, and stay with Orsino in Somaliland. I don't think he'd let me bring you two to stay with him, not all of a sudden. I don't even know if we could raise children there. I'd have to go and see what it's like. He'd be happy with me there—and maybe later on—I could take a trip to Ethiopia."

"By yourself?" Teo and I chorused.

"I'd have to, to start out. But you could stay here and live with Mother and Daddy and Connie—not for too long. Stay in school and learn to read! And I could find some work to do, and a place for us to live. . . . Papà Menotti would help me—"

Teo started to cry. Momma swooped him into a hug.

"It will be the best adventure we've ever had," she told us, "living in that beautiful country, where there won't be anyone calling you names just because you and Emmy don't have skin that matches! You are half Ethiopian yourself, and we are going to see the place where your father was born!" She opened her arms to include both of us. "Come here, Emmy." We snuggled against her, excited and startled and bewildered. "We are going to make Delia's dream come true!"

Then she laughed a little, a real laugh, not a bitter, sarcastic one. "What'll Mother and Daddy think!" She hugged us close. "You ready for a fight?"

We looked at her and gave her the Nod—her own single, certain nod. Both of us at once, like we'd practiced. It was the only thing to do. We knew the Ethiopian sky was the only thing big enough to fill the Delia-sized hole in Momma's heart. The only thing to make us into a family again.

That is the best I can do to explain how home can be where the heart is. Delia's dream was to come here to Ethiopia, and Momma's heart is with Delia's dream, so this is home.

## EPISODE FROM "THE SLEEPING QUEEN"

*(Summer 1930?)*

The two explorers thought their job would be easy. White Raven had a good idea to look in the magical briar forest for the castle where the queen of Antemeridia was hidden. They knew that a princess had fallen asleep in a castle there before, under a spell for a hundred years. Maybe Queen Morning Glory was hidden there, too.

Black Dove and White Raven were smart about getting through the forest. They took a boat along the river that used to lead to the castle. But when they got there, they were surprised to find that the castle was gone. There was nothing left but one broken tower. All the rest had fallen down an enormous waterfall.

Black Dove tied the boat up to the tower. He and White Raven got out and looked down over the edge of the waterfall.

They could see the other towers that fell down standing upright in the water far below.

*Queen Morning Glory could be sleeping safely in one of those towers,* the explorers thought. But the waterfall was too dangerous for them to sail their boat down.

Suddenly, the Prairie Falcon swooped overhead.

"The longer you wait, the longer the queen will be under the spell!" the Prairie Falcon teased. "For every day it takes you to get to her, she will have to sleep for another year!"

The bottom of the waterfall was too far away and too deep for them to climb down or swim to.

Black Dove said, "The queen has already been asleep for three years. Her subjects want her back. We don't need to waste another day hunting for her. Let's kill that stupid bird instead. Then the spell will be broken, and it will be easy to find her."

Theme for Miss Shore ~~by Teo~~
By Teodros Gedeyon Dupré
Subject: "My Father"
Beehive Hill Cooperative Coffee Farm, Tazma Meda

~~Teqemt 23~~
2 November 1934

MY FATHER DIED BEFORE I WAS BORN. SO FAR, I HAVE been raised by girls: Delia, Momma, Grandma, and you could even count Aunt Connie in there, I think. And Sinidu, Momma's best friend here.

My real father was called Gedeyon Wendimu, and he was an Ethiopian working in France right after the Great War ended. But he died of influenza in 1919, three months before I was born. There is Grandfather, of course. But I don't think of him as my father. When we lived with Grandfather, Emmy and I mostly read and drew and acted out our made-up stories in the hayloft, and then Grandfather would stomp around, muttering to himself, because we'd made a mess of the hay when we'd slid down the chute making a pretend getaway for the forty-sixth time.

It was uncomfortable going to baseball games with him. People pointed and whispered, and we'd think at first it was because I'd put my sweater on inside out again without noticing. Then, suddenly, some ticket seller would call Grandfather a "nigger lover." He never got mad. He'd just bow or tip his hat and say something absolutely irrelevant like, "Yes, my morning glories are out in full force right now."

One time when someone made a sneering remark at us, Em

43

snarled back, "Least he doesn't look like a dogfish like you," and Grandfather stunned us by grabbing the backs of our collars and marching us right out to the streetcar without going to the game.

"Name-calling is a pointless way to fight a battle" is the only thing he said to us for the whole hour and a half it took to get home. But he helped me figure out my sweater.

I love Grandfather, but I don't think of him as my father. Maybe I'll start off writing about him anyway, and a few other fatherly fellows, and hope I get somewhere.

GRANDFATHER BROUGHT US HERE TO ETHIOPIA IN 1930, two years after Momma left Pennsylvania and three years after the Bird Strike. It meant that he and Grandma were away from home for two months—Aunt Lorna, the one who doesn't have a baby, went to take care of the riding school while they were gone. We took so many different boats and trains to get here that it didn't really sink in that we were *in* Ethiopia until Momma met us at the train station in Addis Ababa. Of course, I also remember how we couldn't get off right away at Dire Dawa, because there was a pack of hyenas prowling on the platform, and that one time the train had to stop because there were camels on the line.

I remember those things, but what I really *noticed* was how people stared at Grandfather, and then quickly dropped their eyes when he tried to shake hands and talk to everybody who got near him.

Em and I didn't realize then that there is a separate passenger car for white Europeans and Americans to travel in if they want to. I guess we traveled with the Ethiopians because of *me*. But no one ever stared at *me*. I was invisible at last.

When we got off the train in Addis Ababa, Momma was waiting for us, but Em and I felt as awkward as if we were meeting her for the first time. We hadn't seen her for two whole years. She threw herself at Grandma while me and Em lurked behind Grandfather, hanging on to each other's hands so tightly it made my own hand ache after a while.

"Mother—*Mother!*" Momma cried out. "I got your wire from Djibouti, so I knew you'd be on this train, but before that, I came to meet every train for the past *three days*! I can't believe you're here at last—we're *all here!*"

Then Momma dove at me and Em, and swept us into her arms like an enthusiastic puppy dog. "Oh, sweetie pies, you *kids*! You know what they sometimes say for a greeting here? *'Selam'*—'peace.' Isn't that wonderful? *Peace* for a greeting! And *'Tafash!'*—'You've been lost.' *You've been lost!* But *we made it.* We're all here!"

She let go of us. Em and I grabbed each other's hands again and ducked behind Grandma this time, while Momma hugged Grandfather. She seemed like the Momma I remembered from when we were little, but that person had disappeared three years ago after the Bird Strike, and this one was a stranger.

She chattered on. "I've got rooms for us at the Hotel de France. It's not the fancy hotel, but it's European—there are a lot of reporters staying there for the emperor's coronation. It's *beautiful* we're all going to be here for the coronation!"

*The emperor's coronation*—this sounded like something Em and I would make up, not something that would really happen in a place where we were living. We were instantly hooked. Em peeked around Grandma's shoulder.

"Why is the emperor being crowned now?" she asked.

I came out of hiding, too. We still hung on to each other's hands. "We thought he was already emperor," I said.

Momma gazed at us, grinning hopefully, trying to reel us in. "He was the regent for his cousin, who was the old empress. *Regent* means he was running the show for her," she explained. "Now the empress is dead, and he's going to take a new name and a new title and take the throne! We won't be able to see the coronation ceremony, but we'll be able to see some of the procession from the hotel porch. The soldiers wear lion-skin capes and carry spears. The priests wear crowns and carry silver crosses, and the new emperor's wife rides in a red car with guards standing on the running boards—you will *love* it. And we'll get to watch the dress rehearsal for the flying show at the race course!"

Then Momma turned and talked fast in Amharic to the kids who were unloading our bags from the train into the cart she had brought.

Em and I glanced at each other. She mouthed at me: *A flying show?*

We hadn't seen a flying show since the Bird Strike. Grandfather wouldn't take us even when there was one as close as Lambstown. He took us to the new art museum in Philadelphia that day so we wouldn't have a chance of sneaking away to the air show on our own.

I grinned. I *wanted* to see a flying show. I wanted to see a flying show in Ethiopia. I wanted to see it with Momma, after all these years. I was ready. I was itching to learn how to fly someday, and Em knew it.

"Sounds good," Emmy said quietly.

Momma's hair was longer, tied back in a ponytail, and her skin was darker, and she was wearing a white cotton shawl like a thin blanket wrapped around her shoulders—a *shamma*, like everybody wears, only we'd never seen Momma in one, and it made her look mysterious and foreign. Em and I crowded up against each other's shoulders. Momma said, "Mateos and Orsino are going to meet us at the hotel tonight—"

"Who is Mateos?" Grandma interrupted.

"Mateos Wendimu—Gedeyon's brother. Teo's uncle! He's an advisor to one of the *rases*—the royal lords. And Orsino is coming—remember Papà Menotti, sweeties?"

We didn't actually remember Em's father—we hadn't seen him since we left France when we were babies. But he still wrote to us, and of course we knew who he was, so we nodded.

"He'll be stopping in at the hotel tonight," Momma said. "He and I don't—" She swept her beautiful smile over us all like a lighthouse beam without finishing that sentence.

She said, "It's a pretty long walk to the hotel—but I bet you all need to stretch your legs after that terrible wooden train! I borrowed the mule. It belongs to Mateos. There's so much to tell you!"

From Momma's letters, we already knew we were going to live with her on a tiny airfield operated by an English socialist and his American wife—the Sinclairs. Momma hadn't told us much about them except how handy it was that they had their own generator and fuel tank for their coffee farm. She talked much more about Ezra, the Ethiopian doctor she worked for in the village of Tazma Meda, and about his wife, Sinidu, who helped them in the clinic.

"Ezra is also the local governor," Momma told us now. "He got his medical degree in Britain, which is where he met Sinclair, and they formed a partnership to organize the local farmers. Sinclair rents his land from Ezra and runs the Beehive Hill Cooperative Coffee Farm. It's a model progressive community! The clinic is better-equipped than we were with the Army

Nurse Corps in Italy—we are so *lucky* in Tazma Meda. Ezra is the only local doctor in the whole country with a European medical degree. It isn't fair that there aren't a thousand other Ezras for the rest of Ethiopia! And his wife, Sinidu, is my favorite person in the whole of Africa. Sinidu is like—she is my best friend."

Grandfather shook his head, listening and fiddling with his pipe. Momma was his darling, and he was used to her wild enthusiasm about people working together for a better life. But her torrent of excitement and information made you feel like you were being swept up in a hurricane.

"And this summer, Ezra and Sinidu and I have been running a flying clinic, too, so now we can reach the most remote villages in Ezra's district! I do the flying, and Ezra does the doctoring. Orsino has let me keep the plane that he bought when I was with him in Italian Somaliland. It's a three-seater Romeo, built to a Dutch design—perfect for us! At least until Sinidu has her own babies it will be perfect, because that will certainly happen sooner or later. I have never seen a man as crazy about his wife as Ezra."

Grandfather said with a wink, "Oh, I'll bet I have, Rhoda. One who gives his wife an airplane."

"Now, Daddy! The plane will also be perfect for me and the kids. And you will love Sinidu, too—everybody loves Sinidu. She is the one who taught me to speak Amharic!"

"Is she going to teach us Amharic?" Em asked, wide-eyed.

"The second you meet her she will start," Momma promised. Then she hesitated.

"But we can't go back to Tazma Meda right away," she admitted after a moment or two. "My plane is parked by the aircraft sheds at the race course, and I can't move it till after the coronation. Security is very tight there until the ceremonies are over. But that means we're going to be in Addis Ababa for the whole thing! And Orsino's really excited about seeing the kids again, and Mateos is pretty excited about meeting Teo. There's an American pilot here, too—Horatio Augustus. You remember Horatio Augustus, don't you, Daddy? He's that stuntman who did all the parachute jumps over New York City."

"Black man?" Grandfather asked. "In a red suit?"

"The Ebony Eagle," Momma corrected. "Don't you make fun of him. He did a lot of stupid tricks to get publicity, but now he's a high-ranking officer in the new emperor's air force. He's teaching young Ethiopians to fly."

Grandfather fished in his jacket for his pouch of pipe tobacco and looked around as if he were expecting Colonel Augustus to pop out from behind the wooden building. "Well, he *did* wear a red suit!" Grandfather said. "He jumped out of a plane wearing a red suit like a ringmaster *and* playing the saxophone."

"Yes, and I used to hang upside down by my knees from the landing gear wearing a bathing suit and a silver garter," Momma reminded him.

"Thought that stunt was pretty dumb, too," Grandfather commented, and all the grown-ups laughed.

"Horatio Augustus *still* owes me and Delia twenty-five dollars for a parachute ride and his name on our poster. And *then*, when we were going to do that show on Long Island, he turned up and took our spot at the last minute, and the airfield let him because he was the famous Ebony Eagle and we were just a couple of girls with babies and who shouldn't be jumping out of planes for a living. But Augustus is a big man now. The new emperor himself asked him to come from the US to pilot for him! And you have to get along with *everybody* here. The flying community's *tiny.*"

"Augustus get along with Orsino all right?" Grandfather asked.

"*Honestly*, Daddy. No one argues over *me*. I'm married!"

Grandfather put the tobacco pouch back in his jacket, shaking his head, and bent away from the breeze to try to light his pipe. He and Grandma have always wished that Momma would just go live with Papà Menotti forever.

There was a mule pulling the luggage cart, and Momma lifted Emmy and me onto the mule's back, one at a time, me first. Em rode in front. It was getting dark by the time we left the station and set out through Addis Ababa for the Hotel de France. You could smell eucalyptus trees fluttering their leaves in the chilly breeze, but there was also dust and stink everywhere. There weren't any sewers. There wasn't any electricity. There was only the one paved road, and we were on it. It wasn't like a modern city at all, and it was hard to make sense of it in the dark.

"Scared?" Emmy whispered.

*"Love it,"* I whispered back, and she laughed.

*"Yes."*

Grandma and Grandfather were trying to be brave.

"Hope you know where you're going, Rhoda," Grandfather joked hollowly.

Grandma hung on to his arm with determination. "Guns everywhere," she grumbled. I knew she was feeling grim about having to leave us here forever. "Everyone is a soldier. And there was that big battle last spring . . ."

"That was a civil rebellion by traditional lords who resent the modern changes the new emperor made while he was regent," said Momma. "And he absolutely put an end to that conflict."

"And *slavery*! How could Delia have thought to raise her child—or thy own—in a country that hasn't yet abolished *slavery*? When thy own grandmother ran a station on the Underground Railroad!"

"Why do you think the new emperor has to defeat the reactionaries trying to stick to their medieval rules?" Momma protested. "It's not like the antebellum South here! There is a boatload of new emancipation laws, and no one's been born into slavery for a decade. People are jumping straight from the Middle Ages to the twentieth century, and they're doing it as fast as they can!"

I was absolutely looking forward to seeing evidence of the Middle Ages—lion skins and spears and treasure. And if there was slavery, maybe me and Em could work for an Ethiopian Underground Railroad in real life.

"No ruler can afford to let his most powerful landowners go on squabbling," Momma continued. "Don't *fuss*, Mother! A lot of the guns you're seeing were picked up at the Battle of Adwa in 1896 or even Magdala in '68! In which case nobody has ammunition that fits any of them. It's a badge of honor to carry a rifle from Magdala, like wearing a medal."

She took a breath and went on.

"Think of the founding fathers! We did all this a hundred and fifty years ago. These people are building a new country *now*. And you will *love* Beehive Hill Farm. Tazma Meda is the perfect model—there's a school, the clinic, the cooperative, and they're even going to build a radio tower there."

The big city of Addis Ababa (the name means "new flower") seemed alien and mysterious and a little deliciously sinister as we made our way across it for the first time. Stars poked through like holes in the cloth of the sky and shed no light on anything. Darkness flooded down winding paths of close-packed stick houses showing an occasional flicker of flame here and there through the gaps in the walls. The thump of the mule's hooves beneath us, and the murmur of Grandma and Grandfather muttering to each other behind us, began to put me and Em to sleep.

But the hotel was a blaze of light and a buzz of noise in

the soft highland blackness. In spite of the weird, new city, it reminded me of our long-gone life of barnstorming with Momma and Delia, snuggled into a different bed every couple of days. Walking up to the Hotel de France was like coming home some summer night in the mid twenties after an air show, everybody a little nervous about the new place but excited that the show went so well. It felt like that again. I didn't realize until that moment what I'd been missing.

Neither me nor Em can remember going inside or sitting down. The one thing we agree on is that, when we looked around in the bright acetylene light, we'd never seen such a mix of black and white faces in one dining room.

"Teodros! *Emilia! Mia bella cara!*"

Papà Menotti was waiting for us. He swept us both into an enormous bear hug. We hadn't seen him since we left France when we were babies. He cried *real tears* over Em even though he couldn't think of anything to say in English to either of us besides, "Well, well, *well!*" He had presents for us—a lace veil for Em, which is still one of her prized possessions (she wraps herself in it sometimes and wears it instead of a *shamma*), and a die-cast toy *Spirit of St. Louis* monoplane for me.

He didn't speak English at all—he talked to Momma in French. He spoke to me and Em by patting us on the head and clapping us on the back and stroking our hair. He ordered big plates of pasta for everybody. It was like being in a restaurant in South Philadelphia. Every now and then, he'd take Momma's hand and hold it quietly, longingly, until she twitched it away from him again.

They are both tall and thin. They are about the same age. They look like a couple. But Momma doesn't pretend to be his wife or to be in love with him or act any differently around him than she does with anybody else—she just puts on being married like a flying suit when he is there. Like her wedding ring, which she never takes off. It's not because she cares about it. It's just part of her wardrobe.

Momma had to talk a lot of French that night. The hotel is run by a French couple, and we met the Imperial Ethiopian Air Force chief, Pierre Ferrand, and two other French pilots—all of them here because of France's support for Ethiopia. We met Mateos, my uncle. He came in late and joined our table, and for a few minutes, he sat so quietly we didn't even notice he was there. (He really has got the trick of invisibility—I wish he could give me lessons. He moves as silently as a hunting cat.) Then, after he'd watched us for a while, he leaned across the table to shake hands first with Grandfather and, at last, with me. After a moment of hesitation, he sized me up, grinned, and grabbed me in a full-arm Ethiopian handshake.

I saw, in a flash, that I knew him. His smile was exactly like my father's in one of those French airfield album photos, and it was exactly like my own smile, too. I was so startled I stood up and jumped backward into Grandfather's seersucker and made him accidentally drop his pipe.

Momma leaned forward eagerly, gesturing at all of us around her.

"My family."

She repeated it in Amharic so Mateos would understand. She added in English, "Teo, this is Ato Mateos, your father's brother—your uncle. It's thanks to him I have the clinic job in Tazma Meda. His boss is a railroad official, an Ethiopian who was educated in Europe, just like Ezra, the Tazma Meda doctor. They both studied at the University of Edinburgh. And Ras Assefa, the railroad official, is the brother of the man your father worked for in France. Everybody is connected. I owe so much to so many people!" Momma beamed.

Then, suddenly, she started up, half rising from her chair. She'd seen another person come in. We all looked in the direction she'd turned. The man she was looking at threw his cloak to a barefoot bellhop and advanced on our table.

*"Rhoda Menotti! Rhoda Menotti and her family!"*

It was like being announced by a ringmaster. Heads turned. The speaker was a tall, broad-shouldered black man wearing a sky-blue uniform with gold epaulettes. American and European reporters glanced up at him and watched with interest. The Ethiopians ducked their heads, looking sideways or in the other direction.

I glanced at Mateos to see what he was doing, and he was sitting still and straight in his white *shamma* cloak, gazing at an empty spot in the corner of the room as if he were sitting by himself. And no one was looking at him.

I sat still and straight across from him with my head tilted down, gazing between Em and Papà Menotti, thinking: *Mateos and I are both invisible. None of the rest of us is, but we are.*

It was a fantastic trick.

It was easy because the man who had shouted Momma's name was so incredibly flamboyant.

Grandfather stood up and held out his hand with Drummond determination. He and Colonel Horatio Augustus could not have been more extreme opposites if they were negative film images of each other. Grandfather was all bristling white hair and mustache, in his gray-and-white-striped seersucker suit still dust-lined from the train journey. He looked old and frail and pale. He was up to the challenge, though.

"Colonel Augustus, it is a *delight* to meet you. The Ebony Eagle himself, the man in the flesh! You won't believe me, but I was in the crowd to see you off in the *Abyssinia I* in '24 when you tried to fly to Africa!" Grandfather gave a bark of laughter. "By jiminy, that show was what I call exciting—"

"Ah—" said Colonel Augustus, trying to interrupt, while Momma glared at Grandfather to get him to shut up. Augustus might be loud, impressive, and a show-off, but he was just like Momma: leaving behind his old life and starting a new one.

"Too bad it had to end in the Hudson River," Grandfather went on, still pumping Colonel Augustus's hand enthusiastically. "But, Colonel, I am one of those supporters who gave you an *A* for effort. *A* for effort! I contributed thirty-five dollars to your fund. Twenty-five by mail and ten when they passed the hat. I did it for Rhoda and her air circus partner. You remember Delia Dupré—remember their flying act, Black Dove, White Raven?"

The other people in the dining room were all sitting on the edge of their seats. Grandfather nodded and blew into his mustache. He announced to nobody in particular, "Yes, sir, this man is a real daredevil. I knew then he was going to make it big." He turned back to Colonel Augustus. "And now look at you—an officer of the Imperial Ethiopian Air Force! It is a thrill to meet you, sir, a real thrill."

Maybe Colonel Augustus was offended about being reminded of his crash, but he wasn't going to make a fuss when Grandfather said he'd backed him with thirty-five dollars.

"Sit down, Daddy," Momma repeated, and added with cool and simple welcome, "Colonel Augustus, come on and join us."

Colonel Augustus sat down between me and Em. He clapped me on the shoulder and offered me his hand to shake, grasping my arm like Mateos had done. But Mateos had made it feel like a secret handshake. Augustus made it feel like he was performing a circus act for hundreds of people to applaud.

"You must be Teodros. Teodros Gedeyon, the Black Dove's Ethiopian son—welcome to your homeland!"

"I'm Teo," I said cautiously. I hadn't considered Ethiopia as my homeland yet.

"Teo's American," said Em.

"Ethiopian by birth!" Augustus insisted.

"I was born in France. I come from Pennsylvania," I told him. This made Colonel Augustus laugh.

"You are, dare I say it again, Ethiopian by birth. The law is that the child of an Ethiopian father is an Ethiopian citizen. The law that applied to your father applies to you."

Em turned to Grandfather, who'd taken care of our tickets and passports and telegrams and official stuff like that. "Is that true?" Em asked.

I shot him a desperate look, too, silently begging him for adult help.

"Teo's American on my passport," Grandfather said gruffly. "He's one of us." Then he said to Momma, "You're going to have to put Teo and Emmy on your own passport now. You can do it at the legation here."

"And has the Black Dove's talented partner taught you to fly yet?" Colonel Augustus asked me directly.

"Jumping cats!" Em exclaimed. She knew how much I wanted to fly, and also that it was a dangerous topic to bring up around Grandma and Grandfather, so dangerous that we hadn't even risked telling Connie. "Teo isn't but eleven years old, and Momma hasn't seen us for two years—of course he doesn't know how to fly!"

*"Emilia!"*

Several grown-ups scolded her at the same time for being rude.

But Momma swooped in to rescue us all. She pulled her chair around next to mine. "Of course my kids are far too young to learn to fly."

There was more to it than that. Neither me nor Em had been in an airplane since before Delia died. We were going to have to travel to Beehive Hill Farm in Momma's new plane; we knew, sure as shooting, that Momma must be worried about that trip, and that Grandma and Grandfather were worried about it, too. Even if it was her own plane that she'd been flying around Ethiopia for a year now.

"I hope that teaching Delia Dupré's son to fly will be my pleasure someday soon, Mrs. Menotti," Colonel Augustus said heartily.

"Teo's not here to learn to fly," Momma said flatly.

There was an awkward silence.

But Colonel Augustus didn't give up easily. "Teodros Gedeyon was born to be a pilot! Wasn't his mother one of the earliest licensed fliers of her sex and race in the world? Wasn't his father one of the earliest African men to take to the skies before his untimely death far from home—?"

(He really did talk like that.)

"—And does the new emperor not dream of an Imperial Air Force of young Ethiopian men born to the skies? The Black Dove's son is destined to follow his mother into the air and fly for Ethiopia!"

As it happens, we have been here for four years, and we still don't know how to fly and we are fifteen years old now.

It is an itch that I have learned to ignore. I know I will not be in Tazma Meda forever. Em will tell you I can be very persistent and very patient.

"Colonel Augustus," Em said with a winsome smile, "don't you owe Momma and Delia a favor? Don't you owe them twenty-five dollars for putting your name on their poster?"

I couldn't believe she remembered that. She was being White Raven, distracting the enemy so Black Dove could go invisible again. I did Mateos's trick of looking off into an empty corner of the ceiling, while Em looked Colonel Augustus straight in the eye.

"You should take care not to look a person in the eye here in Ethiopia," Colonel Augustus warned her gamely. "You must never look your elders or your superiors in the face. And when you meet the new emperor—"

Neither of us had ever met such an expert at changing the subject. Em's mouth dropped open.

"*Meet the new emperor?* Really?"

"*If* you meet him, remember what I'm telling you now: you must bow three times."

"Like this?" Em slowly closed her eyes. "I am not looking in your face." She gave three big nods. "I'm bowing three times."

Colonel Augustus laughed. "Just like that!"

"Let me try again."

I nodded along with her. If she was being White Raven, working on *The Adventures* in her head, my job was to back her up invisibly so I didn't give away her game.

Behind me, Momma suddenly pulled me against her and held me tight.

"*Oh, my beautiful kids.*"

"WHAT DO YOU THINK?" EM WHISPERED TO ME IN PRIVATE after Grandma and Momma had tucked us in under the mosquito netting in a dark, strange hotel room. "I don't know about Momma."

"Me neither," I agreed. "It will be nice to have her to ourselves. Right now she belongs to too many people and she isn't really *ours*."

"Yes." Em paused. "We will miss Grandma and Grandfather."

"And Aunt Connie."

"Yeah, but we're okay without them mostly. We won't miss those awful Sunday Quaker meetings," Em pointed out softly. "Or the kids at the New Marlow School."

"I'll say so!" I agreed.

Em reached up to poke at the mosquito net on her side of the bed. On my side it was already all untucked where I'd kicked it by accident. "Teo, you're such a slob. Be *careful* with it."

"We could use something like this in the game. A rain-cloud disguise," I said.

"I thought that, too!"

Momma and Grandma and Grandfather were sitting in the next room with a kerosene lamp, and the door was open a crack so there was just enough light for us to see the gauzy shadow of the mosquito net making a tent around us.

"We can still go home with them if we want to," Em whispered disloyally.

I nodded. After a few seconds, Emmy grabbed my hand and squeezed three times: *Are you scared?*

*I am not scared,* I squeezed back.

For a while, we lay in the dark listening to the rise and fall of Momma's low, excited voice and Grandfather's occasional chuckles peppering her plans. I thought of Momma pulling me against her.

*Oh, my beautiful kids.*

"Momma is okay," I said. "It will be okay with her. I think she is better." It felt risky to even say it out loud.

Em laughed softly. "The glue is dry," she whispered. "They were holding the jug by the handle, too, talking about Delia like that in the restaurant tonight. I guess we ought to stay. Ethiopia is what Delia wanted."

"It's what *Momma* wants now," I said.

———

WE WERE IN THE HOTEL DE FRANCE FOR ABOUT A WEEK, just as Ethiopia finished preparing for the man who had been known as Negus Tafari Mekonnen to be crowned as the emperor Haile Selassie in 1930. We went on a mule ride up into the hills to see the dead Empress Taitu's old palace (not the empress who'd just died, but the wife of the emperor before that). We had a tour of the new part of the city, which looks like buildings from Washington, D.C., in the middle of a farm that has been taken over as a camping field for soldiers. We did not see any electric lights the whole time we were there. We went to a glorious but baffling church service that lasted three hours (Em and I both fell asleep—just like in Sunday meetings), and we toured a school and the Menelik Hospital. We went to the American Legation to get our names put on Momma's passport. Then we saw a show at the British Legation, which was all done by men in kilts, and we got to shake hands with one of the king of England's sons, the Duke of Gloucester, and a cousin of the king of Italy. We saw Ethiopian dancing and got served the best *injera* and *wat* I have ever eaten, even now. Momma swapped some empty film canisters for pretty carved eucalyptus twigs to brush your teeth with. Em and I were so impressed with all the cloth merchants working in the middle of the markets, with their portable Singer sewing machines, that we wrote a story later called "The City of Tailors."

Ethiopia was magical. It was worth waiting for. It was kind of exhausting, too, but mostly it was magical. Who needed electricity and baseball games when you had a city full of flames and stars and camels hauling salt blocks out of the desert?

Then we went to see the flying show.

It was supposed to be a private rehearsal for the coronation, but it seemed as if the whole city knew about it. Everything about Negus Tafari Mekonnen's regency had been focused on change, and on making things better for people, and one of the modern things he'd been working on was putting together an air force. Now he wanted to show it off.

Getting through the crowd to the place where we were supposed to meet Mateos, you'd never have guessed we were in the twentieth century. It could have been five hundred years ago, for all we knew. The strange crowd of yodeling women in white cloaks and men in lion's-fur collars carrying medieval-looking spears was like a riptide carrying you along. I hung on to the back of Grandfather's seersucker jacket with both hands—Em was attached to Grandma. Momma pushed ahead of us because people let her past when they noticed her—of course she was the only white woman wearing a *shamma* and a sun helmet in the whole crowd.

Then Grandma disappeared.

*"Rhoda!"* Grandfather yelled at Momma.

Momma swung around. "Just over there—they've got a barrier up, and we need to be on the inside. Mateos will meet us there. It's only a piece of rope—"

*"I've lost thy mother,"* Grandfather cried.

"And Emmy!" I said.

"Oh—" Momma's first gasp was one of irritation. She glanced around over our heads. I don't know what she saw, but I was just eleven and I couldn't see anything but people's chests and arms, white cloth and animal-skin belts and the occasional rifle hanging over someone's back. Momma yelled, "Come to the meeting place. Wait there and I'll find them. I don't want to lose you, too."

She led us, fighting her way to the lines of rope barriers around the racetrack that was used as an airfield. There were imperial soldiers guarding the barriers. They were barefoot— khaki uniforms and sun helmets, but barefoot like everybody else except us. People were crowding around us as though they were trying to get on the last trolley home from the ballpark. Momma took hold of one of the ropes, lifted it up, and held the gap open for us to step through. There was a crowd on the other side of the rope barrier, too, but at least we were on the inside now.

"Now, wait. Don't move. I'll come back." She turned to go, and there was Emmy, leading Grandma by the hand, making her way toward us along the string of ropes. Momma's and Grandfather's mouths dropped open.

*"Oh!"* Momma gasped.

I linked my thumbs together to make my hands into a flying bird, the secret greeting of Black Dove and White Raven. Em grinned at me.

"Emilia is amazing!" Grandma exclaimed. "She knew exactly where we were going the whole time. Every time I'd start to fret, she'd squeeze my hand four times and tell me that means *I— am—not—scared.* So confident! And this crowd—"

Em shook her head in disgust at the commotion Grandma and Grandfather were kicking up. "Honestly. Momma *said* we were supposed to meet Mateos here. It isn't hard."

*"Oh, thank heaven,"* Momma breathed, and as the little dent of worry smoothed out between her eyebrows, I suddenly realized how scared *Momma* had been.

I had seen her angry before, and I had seen her miserable. But I had never seen her scared.

We were supposed to be safe here, right? So what was she worried about?

At first I thought there must be some danger she hadn't told us about—bank robbers or ravenous wild animals or poisonous snakes. But now I think it was simpler than that. She was just worried about losing us again.

––––––––

MATEOS SEEMED TO APPEAR OUT OF NOWHERE. SUD-
denly, he had his arm around my shoulder and was leading us
to the front of the crowd as effortlessly as a starling cutting
through the sky. He called out lightly, "Woyzaro Rhoda—Mrs.
Rhoda!"

Under Mateos's guidance, everything suddenly became
easy. He moved quietly and quickly and somehow managed not
to bump into anyone, clearing a little pathway with the butt of
his spear. Within seconds, we were at the edge of the field.

Here there was another flimsy fence of ropes hung between
stakes in the ground. Ramrod-straight soldiers with expres-
sionless faces kept pushing people back from the ropes with
their spear shafts. Grandma hissed through her teeth as though
she'd got a paper cut every time she saw someone shaking a
spear. Mateos flashed that smile that was so much like mine,
and made a quick gesture to the soldiers with one hand—he
didn't even say anything. They let us pass along the barriers
until we were standing unbelievably close to the new emperor's
private box. Then Mateos gave us another grin, a quick wave,
and disappeared in the crowd, on some other official business.

Now all that lay between us and the imperial grandstand
were mats of woven straw overlaid with a long, dark red silk
carpet that nobody dared to touch. It was like the Yellow Brick
Road leading to the Emerald City, only bloodred. The soldiers
let me and Em stand at the front, right up against the carpet,
because we were so little.

Guess who poked her foot out when she thought no one
was looking, so she could touch the glorious red silk with a
bare toe that was sticking out of her sandal. That's right—Em
touched the private carpet of the man who was about to become
Emperor Haile Selassie. She is such a sucker for pretty things.

"Oh, Teo, try it!" she gasped.

I slipped one foot out of my tennis shoe and edged my toes onto the red silk.

This rug was absolutely the most beautiful, out-of-place thing we had ever seen, laid across the dirt of a temporary airfield. Our toes were side by side on the bright silk for about two seconds. When Em pulled her toe back, I looked up, following the carpet with my eyes to the point where it met the imperial grandstand. I didn't have a choice about where to look. That was where my eyes had to go.

And the new emperor was looking at us. That was the first time I saw him, and the only time I have seen him, but I knew right away that I was looking at the *negusa nagast*, the king of kings of Ethiopia, the man who was going to catapult this glorious medieval festival into the modern world. And he was looking right at us.

I snatched my foot back.

He sat alone, on a sort of raised platform decorated with the Ethiopian flag and bunting in the flag's colors, red and gold and green. There was a space of a few feet between him and his closest guards and ministers. He was *short*—he really wasn't a lot taller than me, and I was only eleven years old. Momma would tower over him. Most of the men standing near him would have towered over him, too, if he hadn't been sitting above them.

He wore a white European suit under a black silk cape and a white sunhat, and just behind him stood a servant holding a red silk parasol with gold fringes. A man with a white *shamma* over his uniform held a pair of binoculars ready for use. Another man stood carefully watching a pair of young lions that he was holding on leashes. Everyone else in the box was watching the other end of the racetrack, where half a dozen French fighter-bomber aircraft of the Imperial Ethiopian Air Force were moving out of their big shed. The emperor-to-be, though, was looking straight at me and Emmy.

*"Don't look him in the face!"* I gasped, remembering. "Bow three times!"

And I did. A moment later, copying me, Em did, too.

And he *laughed.* We both saw it. Then just one second of a smile as he turned his head away again, dismissing the outrageous foreign children who were watching his coronation rehearsal. He took the binoculars from the other man, and focused on the field, where the planes were taxiing in their plumed trail of dust.

"THIS IS THE FIRST TIME THESE PLANES HAVE BEEN flown by Ethiopian pilots," Momma said proudly. "They're all young men who got trained by the French fliers here, and by Colonel Augustus. It's the first time they're giving a display. There we go!" The first plane lifted into the air, and the little crowd around us began to cheer.

"She still likes flying," Em pointed out to me quietly.

"She just needed to be able to get in the air again without worrying about us at the same time," I said, as if I knew all about what was going on in Momma's brain. "She'll be fine now. All these pilots admiring her!"

"Hey, talking about them, where's Colonel Augustus?" Em asked suddenly.

Of course Colonel Augustus was such a big man, and his uniform was so gaudy, that we would have noticed if he were in the grandstand.

A look of concern and confusion clouded Momma's face.

"Where's the royal plane?" she murmured. "It should be on display outside the aircraft shed—the new emperor's planning to take a ride in it for the first time at the coronation."

There were three planes circling overhead now, and another three were raising a storm of dust as they taxied out to join them. I didn't see any other planes.

"They taxi it out of the shed whenever there's a parade. It's a white Gypsy Moth," Momma said, frowning. "It should be out here now. You'll know it in a minute—brand-new. Prettiest thing on the airfield! It came all the way from England by boat and train, and it's never been flown!"

"There," Em said, and pointed.

The new emperor's private Gypsy Moth was purring out of the new corrugated zinc shed at the far end of the field, and it was, for sure, the prettiest plane I had ever seen. It was a biplane like the French planes already in the air, but smaller and all over creamy white. While we watched, the little plane jumped into the air and skimmed across the field twenty feet above the ground. The white sunlight glowed on its white wings, and the plane passed *right* in front of us, so close we could see the pilot.

It was Colonel Augustus.

He waved as he passed. I don't know if he was really waving to *us* or to the crowd in general, but me and Em waved back like crazy. Momma grabbed our hands, one on each side of her, and forced them down. It was like having a lead weight hanging on your arm—you couldn't fight. She was *much* stronger than she had been when she left us. She was as strong as a man.

She hissed in a whisper, leaning between us so we could both hear, "Colonel Augustus isn't allowed to fly that plane. *No one* is allowed to fly that plane. So don't you go looking like you think it's okay."

Then she let go of Em's hand, and very quickly, so only the two of us saw her do it, she pointed at the emperor-to-be.

He'd jumped up from his royal seat. He was standing rigid,

watching, entirely focused on the little aircraft sailing right in front of his court, still no higher than twenty feet above the ground. The plane passed the royal box, but for a moment, I completely forgot to watch it—I could only watch the new emperor.

I couldn't see the expression on his face. But I never saw anyone's body look so *shocked*. He was like a statue—except his head moved. He turned his head to watch the plane pass by and continue across the racetrack toward the far side. He didn't wave at the waving pilot.

There was a row of tall, thin eucalyptus trees at the other side of the field. Colonel Augustus, in the Ethiopian royal plane that he wasn't supposed to be flying, was heading straight into them.

"Climb!" I heard Grandfather gasp, not very helpfully.

That was when I closed my eyes.

Em says she watched. I don't know if I believe her, because I *couldn't*. I couldn't watch a plane crash, knowing it was going to happen. Not a pretty little white biplane that looked a lot like a Curtiss Jenny.

Anyway, Em says she watched. The landing gear got caught in the treetops, the plane flipped, and Colonel Horatio Augustus, with two broken ribs and a broken arm, had to be extracted from the wreckage. They took him to the new hospital in Addis Ababa and patched him up. And then they took away his honorary Ethiopian passport and sent him back to the USA.

Momma didn't watch, either. She knelt down beside me and hung on to me in a stranglehold, burying her face. When she heard the crash, she gave a little grunt of a sob against the back of my neck. Grandfather knelt on the other side of her.

*"He thought he'd teach Teo to fly!"* Momma gasped. *"Never."* She sobbed into the back of my neck. *"No one* is going to teach

my children to fly. Not for the emperor of Ethiopia, not for Delia, not for *anybody. Never.*"

Grandfather looked up to see what was going on, and now I couldn't help squirming around a little in Momma's grip so I could look up, too. There were people racing out to the aircraft and pulling the pilot from the cockpit, and even I could see he wasn't killed. "He's *alive*, Momma," Em said, hanging on to Momma now herself. "And it wasn't a bird strike. It was just his own being dumb."

*"Never."*

We all sat down on the dust of the track at the edge of the red carpet. Momma cried into my back until my shirt was damp, and I started to wish she'd let go of me, but I was too worried about her—and she was still too much of a stranger—for me to dare try to wriggle away. So I just waited until she let go herself.

I MAY NOT HAVE A FATHER, BUT I HAVE GOT THE world's most beautiful mother. That's our momma—the White Raven. There is not a safer pilot in the whole world than our momma.

When the coronation was over and we were allowed back on the airfield at the Addis Ababa race course, she flew us all to Tazma Meda, and Beehive Hill Farm, two at a time. She didn't seem nervous at all—I guess she just likes to be flying the plane herself. I went with Grandfather, and Em went with Grandma, and then Momma flew Grandma and Grandfather back to Addis Ababa together a week later to get the train to Djibouti. They were badgering her right up to the moment they left about her going to live with Papà Menotti. As they were packing up to go (this is my earliest memory of Fiona Sinclair's bedroom, which is where they stayed), they were still pestering her about Papà Menotti.

Momma stared out the window at Beehive Hill and answered patiently, "Orsino is still stationed in Italian Somaliland. It's not possible for us to be together now that the children are here! They can't live on an Italian air force base. He bought me the plane, of course, but I don't owe him anything. We have an *agreement.*"

"It's called a *marriage*, Rhoda." Grandma sighed a little. "I wish we could stay longer. But I'm so glad we got here—thy real home. I feel better about leaving the children here in Tazma Meda. Addis Ababa wasn't real. Not the city, not the coronation, not the cloud of men around you like ants at a picnic. I can see thee and the children will be all right here, Rhoda. Even without thy husband."

If Momma can get along all right without a husband, I guess I can get along all right without a father. I have Momma and I have Emmy. They are enough to make a family.

# EPISODE FROM "THE SLEEPING QUEEN"

*(December 1930)*

Queen Morning Glory of Antemeridia was safely back on her throne, but her kingdom was still in trouble. She was hungrier than normal people. She had been asleep for three years, and she needed a thousand breakfasts to make up for it. She asked if someone would take a trip to the kingdom of Eclipsia to bring back honey and coffee.

This was a dangerous job because of Eclipsia's being so strange. Their honey came from beehives made of skulls. The skull hives hung in the coffee trees, and the honey was harvested by the princes and princesses of Eclipsia. Every one of them knew how to throw a spear, and they would kill you if you tried to steal anything. They would only sell honey and coffee to other people from Eclipsia.

"I am good at throwing spears," White Raven said. "I can disguise myself as a princess of Eclipsia and sneak some things to Black Dove when he is invisible."

"That is not a good idea," said Queen Morning Glory. "I don't want to pilfer anything from Eclipsia."

Theme for Miss Shore
By Teodros Gedeyon Dupré
Subject: "The Ethiopian Christian Church"
Beehive Hill Cooperative Coffee Farm, Tazma Meda

26 Teqemt (5 Nov.)

YOU WOULD BE AMAZED, BUT I HAVE PLENTY TO SAY about this subject because we spend a lot of time visiting Habte Sadek, the priest in charge of the monastery of St. Kristos Samra on top of Beehive Hill.

We met him on our first day alone in Tazma Meda. In those days, loads of people used to turn up to watch whenever Momma took off or landed from the airstrip at Beehive Hill Farm, partly because it was so exotic to see a plane there, and partly because she might be bringing in some tourist who would have a lot of Maria Theresa silver dollars to give away in exchange for a place to stay and meals cooked for him and a guide and maybe also a mule. Half the village and everyone on the farm had met Grandfather and Grandma, so there was a great big party of people who came to wave good-bye to them when they left. Em and I stood there waving with Ezra, the doctor, and his wife, Sinidu, Momma's new best friend.

Grandma burst into tears when she kissed us good-bye, which made Emmy cry, too. For a moment of panic, we were both scared about being left alone in this strange, new place with no one we knew—without even *Momma* all of a sudden.

"Oh, *Em*," said Momma. "I will be back soon! You and Teo are good at taking care of each other, and Sinidu will help you."

"And I have heard that you are both brave adventurers, and there is someone I want you to meet," Sinidu tempted us warmly. "Also, you do not want me to join in crying with you."

"It is very hard to make Sinidu stop crying once she starts," Ezra joked.

Sinidu was supposed to stay in our house and keep an eye on us till Momma came back. She had learned pretty good English from Ezra, and also from the Sinclairs and from Momma, so she could talk to us and translate.

Em and I stood with our elbows linked to watch and wave as Momma and Grandma and Grandfather left us alone in Tazma Meda for the first time. Linking elbows did not feel as babyish as holding hands. It was more like something a striker or a suffragette would do—facing a challenge together.

Sinidu didn't give us time to worry too much about being alone in our new life. Two minutes after the plane took off—the second it was out of sight—she grabbed hold of our hands, one of us on each side of her, and said in English, "Coffee!" She switched back and forth between Amharic and English. "*Buna!* Coffee! Say *'buna'*!"

"*Buna,*" Em said.

"Beautiful! *Konjo no*, that's 'beautiful'! Say *'konjo.'* "

"*Konjo,*" Em said.

Ezra laughed at Em's game cooperation. "Beautiful!" he repeated appreciatively. "Now Sinidu is going to take beautiful coffee to her uncle Habte Sadek up on Beehive Hill. And if you go with her, she will teach you how to speak Amharic even better than your *ferenji* mother—your foreigner mother."

Sinidu pulled us briskly away from the landing field. Ezra, on his way back to work in the village, called after her fondly, "Slow down or they will not be able to keep up with you."

"You are worrying about me, not about the *ferenji* children,"

Sinidu scolded. "They will keep up with me. I will see you back at the clinic in the afternoon."

Five minutes after Momma's plane took off with Grandma and Grandfather in it, Em and I were trailing up Beehive Hill after Sinidu, on our own in Tazma Meda for the first time. Ezra had been right about his wife's energy: Sinidu bounced up the stony slope ahead of us like a goat, barefoot. She carried a brazier and charcoal to boil the water and roast the beans for coffee, a black clay coffeepot, and a set of cups to go along with it. Popcorn to eat with the coffee. And a pound of green coffee beans. And a goatskin water bag on her head. She was so much faster than we were that she had to keep stopping to wait whenever she came to the sun-spotted shade of an acacia tree. Then she'd shout back to us:

"Say 'I'm going to walk as fast as Sinidu!'"

"How do you say, 'I'm going to walk five times as fast as Sinidu'?" Em challenged, bounding up to meet her.

"Say 'In my mother's flying machine, I can soar higher than a bearded vulture!'"

"What's the first thing Momma ever said to you in Amharic?" I asked her.

"'The sky over Beehive Hill is the most beautiful sky in the world!'"

Em and I both laughed. That is *exactly* what Momma would say.

Sinidu looked up, and we followed her gaze above us through the lattice of sparse leaves and branches into the blue. Two catbirds were calling unbelievably sweet songs to each other not too far off, and the high air was dry and cool, and we were five thousand miles away from the sadness and strangeness and meanness of New Marlow, Pennsylvania.

Sinidu repeated what she'd said in Amharic, still looking up.

Then she turned to us and said in English, "Your mother said it in the air, the first time she took me up in her flying machine. She is teaching me to fly in exchange for the Amharic lessons."

"Wow, teaching you to *fly*," Em echoed, impressed and envious.

"She won't teach us," I explained.

"I will help you change her mind!" Sinidu laughed.

Beehive Hill is not called that because of its shape. The shape is a coincidence, and a mistake if you think it looks like the kind of beehive you see in nursery-rhyme books. It is called Beehive Hill because long before there were coffee farmers in Tazma Meda, there were beekeepers. The holy men at the hermitage of St. Kristos Samra keep the bees and use the honey to make *tej*, Ethiopian honey wine. ("Say 'beekeepers'!" Sinidu told us. "Say *'tej'*! Say 'good business for Tazma Meda'!") All the acacia trees on Beehive Hill are full of beehives. They are long baskets that look like logs, and every tree has about a dozen beehives hanging in it.

It was like we'd been whisked into a landscape we'd made up.

"They look like giant cocoons," Em whispered to me.

I was already planning our next story. Black Dove could be captured by giant bees and tied up in a cocoon. And White Raven could rescue him. . . .

"Take care," Sinidu warned us, balancing all the stuff she was carrying as she rounded the last narrow ledge at the top of the trail. Em followed her first, me behind, and Em gave a little squeak of shivery delight as we came around the corner.

Where Beehive Hill looks out over the Beshlo River gorge, there is a little open cave full of skulls. It isn't covered up or anything—just dry bones sitting there in the wall of the cliff.

"Be polite," Sinidu said, "and do not look them in the eye. They might be important people."

It took us a minute to figure out that she didn't mean the skulls. She meant the holy men who were sitting in other shallow caves carved in the hillside, a honeycomb of rock bunk beds. There were two men in white robes reading there who didn't look up as we passed.

Suddenly Sinidu pulled up short and turned to us. "Say *'Habte Sadek'*!"

*"Habte Sadek,"* we repeated obediently.

"Again! Take care!"

We said it again, taking care.

"What is *Habte Sadek*?" Em asked.

"Habte Sadek is my great-uncle," Sinidu said. "He is the priest here. You should bow."

He was sitting on a rug on the sunny slab of rock in front of the elaborate sculpted entrance to the cave that is the St. Kristos Samra chapel. We all bowed. Em gaped for a moment, then looked away when she remembered to be polite. Habte Sadek is the only person I know who is flashier than Em.

He wore a silver priest's crown in tiers, like a tower. A boy a little older than us was holding a silk umbrella with gold tassels over the priest's head to shade him from the sun. (The boy turned out to be Sinidu's nephew, Yosef.) Habte Sadek's hair and beard were already completely white the first time we met him. Sinidu told him who we were, introducing us in Amharic. We heard our mother's name and the words for *flying machine.*

Em was twitching, trying to steal glances at the old priest without being obvious. I'd figured out from studying Mateos that the best way to steal a glance at someone is to look at the bottom of them, feet first instead of face first. So I knelt and bowed my head.

Habte Sadek's feet were like Grandfather's, lean and strong and steady, but his skin was as wrinkled and brittle and dry as the antique reins hanging in Grandfather's office. (Habte Sadek doesn't know how old he is.)

He spoke to us in Amharic, and his voice was low and musical. It didn't sound anywhere near as old as he looked.

"My uncle says you are the most respectful *ferenji* tourist who has ever come up here, and asks me to thank you," Sinidu told me.

Emmy and I are still Habte Sadek's favorite foreigners, and it is all because I wanted to look at his feet when I was eleven years old!

But it never hurts to be polite to people.

"So, I have told you that my uncle Habte Sadek is a priest in the Ethiopian church," Sinidu said. "That means he can enter the inner sanctuary and celebrate the sacraments. The others you see here are deacons, and they may only teach and preach."

Habte Sadek stood up. He was taller than Grandfather, terrifying and glittering. Sinidu chatted with him matter-of-factly. Finally she put down her water skin and the coffee things and turned to us. "Ethiopia is mostly Christian—we have had a bishop in Egypt since the time of the Aksumite Empire, since before Europeans became Christian."

"We went to an Ethiopian church service in Addis Ababa," I said.

"What did you think? Tell me what you thought, and I will repeat it for my uncle!"

"It was long," Em said diplomatically, and Sinidu could not help laughing.

"Long! Yes! I think so, too, because all the prayers are in Ge'ez, a language as old as the church itself, which nobody understands except the priests. But beautiful!"

"It is all beautiful," I said. Because it really is. *"Konjo no."*

Habte Sadek held up one strong, thin, dark hand and spoke to Sinidu.

"He wants to show you Beehive Hill's beautiful chapel," she interpreted. "*Ferenji* tourists like to see the little chapel. Not the honeycomb, though. Come on!"

"What's the honeycomb?"

"Tourists can't see the honeycomb," Sinidu repeated. So we understood we couldn't watch the beekeepers at work. "But you can see the chapel."

Yosef folded the sunshade umbrella. Sinidu told us, "Leave your shoes outside," and we took off our tennis shoes and left them on the wide stone step outside the cave. We never put them back on. We were home.

Yosef doesn't talk much. Without speaking, he gave us each a long, skinny mustard-colored beeswax candle to carry. When Yosef had lit all our candles, Habte Sadek led us into the dark.

Stepping into the chapel at the St. Kristos Samra hermitage, this little self-sufficient community for holy men who never left Beehive Hill, I suddenly figured out the point of all those boring Sunday meetings we sat through with Grandma and Grandfather for three years. *God is in you,* they kept telling us, *waiting for you to feel him there.* Stepping into the chapel at the St. Kristos Samra hermitage, I suddenly knew what they had meant. This was where I could find God, if I really wanted to.

I know Habte Sadek would not agree with me. He thinks we are all a bunch of *ferenji* heathens—we do not believe what he believes, because we do not know or understand his God or his religion, even if we all call ourselves Christian. *Emmy* does not agree with me. Emmy thinks the Ethiopian church is all show—all costumes and glitter. She likes the ceremony but only because it is so pretty. She goes along with it. It doesn't mean anything to her.

But it means something to me. I'm not sure what. I don't think their faith is my faith. But seeing the chapel at St. Kristos Samra made me realize, for the first time, that *I have faith.*

When Habte Sadek led us in there on our first day alone in Tazma Meda, the dirt floor was cool and worn smooth under our bare feet and the air smelled of frankincense and dust. We held up our candles, and the cave glowed gold and red, with little bright pockets of light around each of our candles. The walls are painted. Not just gold and red, but there is a lot of that, so it is what makes an impression on you when you first step in there. On the back wall of St. Kristos Samra's cave chapel is an enormous story in pictures, frame by frame like a comic strip. It tells the legend of Menelik, the son of King Solomon and the Queen of Sheba, stealing the Ark of the Covenant from his father and bringing it to Aksum in Ethiopia.

It is *so different* from the high white walls of the New Marlow Friends meetinghouse. Emmy thinks there is no connection between New Marlow Friends Meeting and the St. Kristos Samra hermitage. But I think it is the same God.

Habte Sadek turned to us so that he was standing in front of the painting. He didn't look like a priest or a teacher. He looked like a guard, ancient and fierce. Then he spoke, so suddenly that I jumped.

"'I was a soldier,'" Sinidu translated.

I stared at Habte Sadek's thin, dusty feet, longing to look at his face. Emmy was squeezing my hand so hard I thought it would fall off when she let go.

"Say it," Sinidu ordered. "'I was a soldier.'"

She translated what he told us, but also she made us repeat everything he said in Amharic so we'd learn it.

"He was a little bit older than you," Sinidu told us. "A silent boy like Yosef. The British brought cannons against him."

"Against a *boy*?" Em asked, wide-eyed.

"Against the emperor, Teodros! But also against anyone who defended him! So, yes, against my uncle, the young deacon, and his brothers and his friends dedicated to the church, fighting for the emperor and his ancient church treasures. My uncle was the oldest of the boys."

"Why was the emperor fighting the *British*?" I asked. Even then I knew that the British had *encouraged* Haile Selassie to fix up the country when he was regent, as did the French and the Italians. These foreigners had helped build Addis Ababa and get modern things, such as a radio station and a railroad and membership in the League of Nations.

"This was more than sixty years ago," Sinidu explained. "Emperor Teodros was angry at the queen of England because she kept ignoring him—for years! So then he asked her to help his army, and when she still ignored him, he took her diplomats as hostages. It turned into the Battle of Magdala."

Em and I glanced at each other, thrilled. I was named after the emperor Teodros.

Habte Sadek and a dozen of his friends, all of them church deacons and none of them any older than he was, made stretchers and loaded them so it looked like they were carrying the bodies of dead priests. Some of the boys carried the stretchers and some of them carried spears that they'd disguised as tall prayer sticks. But the stretchers weren't loaded with bodies. They were loaded with the *only* church artifacts at Magdala that *didn't* get looted by the English soldiers and carried off to the British Museum.

After Sinidu had told us all this, Habte Sadek turned around so that his robes and crown flashed in the feeble light of the yellow beeswax candles. He stood in front of the glittering caskets and candlesticks on the altar and spoke in his low, lilting, fierce voice. When he'd finished, Sinidu said, "Every treasure you see, the crowns and the gold and silver crosses, the jeweled censers and candlesticks, the gilded books—all of it except the paintings on the walls—my uncle and his friends and brothers carried over the mountains from Magdala. A church is nothing without its *tabot*, its copy of the holy commandments. So when they saved their *tabot*, they saved their church. They worked like spiders and mice, creeping beneath the noses of the English while they loaded their own wagons. *Spiderwebs joined together can catch a lion.*"

Habte Sadek made a little movement of his hand. Yosef lifted his candle and swept it around the chapel, splashing reflections of flame across the walls. And I knew something else, then, too—this place was holy because people had *made it holy*. They'd brought God there themselves.

"Teodros was defeated at Magdala," said Sinidu. "But my uncle remembers with pride how he fought for him. My uncle is the only one left of those soldier-priests. My grandfather, his brother, died before I was born. And his other brother went north to Aksum and never came back. But he took Habte Sadek's story to Aksum, to the priests at the cathedral of Maryam Seyon. They are the ones who guard the true Ark of Zion, the Tabota Seyon, the tablet bearing the commandments God gave to Moses. All *tabot*s are copies of the true Ark."

"What did they do when they heard what your uncle did?" Em asked. "Were they pleased?"

"They gave him the honor of choosing a new name for this chapel," Sinidu said proudly. "So now it is dedicated to the saintly woman Kristos Samra. Habte Sadek was born near Gondar, in the place where Kristos Samra lived hundreds of years ago."

Habte Sadek said something else, and he said my name.

"He is telling you that the emperor Teodros was Ethiopia's first great reformer," Sinidu explained. "Teodros modernized his army and unified the nation—he reached out to Europe and—" She paused, listening hard to get everything her uncle was saying. "And Teodros was the first to try to put an end to slavery in Ethiopia. And that you should be proud to bear his name. And since you are so interested in my uncle's boyhood as a soldier, he wants to show you how to throw a spear," Sinidu finished.

Now Emmy and I both fell completely, hopelessly in love with Habte Sadek.

He took us up a narrow stairway cut in the rock above the chapel, so narrow you had to climb it sideways or your shoulders wouldn't fit. Sinidu followed, and Yosef came after a bit more slowly, carrying spears. The stairs were steep.

The stairs came out on top of Beehive Hill and it was the most wonderful view in the whole world, looking all across the Beshlo River valley and the Simien Mountains to the north, with farmers' green terraces and coffee trees growing in the sparse forest below. Bearded vultures soared above us, and even though it was November, it was summer in the Ethiopian highlands.

We had seen it from the air, but now we were standing in it. Now it felt real.

So then we spent an hour judging a spear-throwing competition between Yosef and Habte Sadek. They made me try it, too. Yosef was very patient with my complete lack of accuracy. Habte Sadek could throw twice as far and as fast as Yosef. He had an arm like a Major League pitcher.

Em got restless because they would not let her try.

She was working hard at being White Raven in disguise as a polite girl tourist, she told me later. It is the only way she can make herself be polite sometimes. Equality comes in different forms, and it is a lot harder being a girl in Ethiopia than it was in Pennsylvania.

After a while, Em said to Sinidu, "Habte Sadek is still a soldier!"

Sinidu told him, and Yosef grinned and handed Habte Sadek another spear. He took it thoughtfully. You could tell he was pleased. But he had a serious answer for Em, which Sinidu repeated in English.

"This is only a game," Sinidu explained. "My uncle says he is a man of peace, so he uses the weapons of war to test his skill. To keep his eyes keen and his arm strong."

"Our mother does the same with her flying machine," said Em. "People can use them in a war, or they can use them for flying doctors around to fix people. Momma uses her flying machine for peace."

Sinidu told her uncle, and he laughed and said something that made Sinidu laugh, too.

"He says you argue like a churchman," Sinidu said. "Also that your flying mother is like St. Kristos Samra herself! Kristos Samra is the namesake of this hermitage and chapel. When her twelve children were grown, she devoted herself to God, and she flew to hell to make peace between God and Satan. Say it— Kristos Samra, the Mother of Peace!"

"Kristos Samra," we said. "The Mother of Peace!"

The Ethiopian Orthodox Church is not anything like our own, but I can say that I feel at home in the Kristos Samra chapel. Our mother has flown to hell and back, too. It is nice to live in a place that is dedicated to peace, whatever God they believe in, and even if war brought them here a long time ago.

Essay by Teo

Theme for Miss Shore by Teodros Gedeyon Dupré

Subject: "The Language I Dream In"

Beehive Hill Cooperative Coffee Farm, Tazma Meda

Teqemt 30, 1927

9 November 1934

HERE IS A CONVERSATION I KNOW I HAD IN ENGLISH.

Before I start, I need to explain that Momma never gets paid. She works as a nurse at the clinic in Tazma Meda, and every couple of months, she takes Ezra in the plane to hop around the province and help out sick people in other villages. Her salary, and Ezra's, are supposed to come from a new government public health program that also sends them medical supplies. And every so often, about twice a year, a couple of mules come up here with a supply of aspirin and morphine and hypodermic needles. But there is never any money, not even for Ezra. He can afford to live without a salary because he is the district governor and the landowner, and the Sinclairs pay him rent. Momma can just about afford to do it because she sells pictures to American and German magazines. She has been taking pictures since before we came to Ethiopia, since before she learned to fly, and she takes them on the ground as well as in the air. She has got a closet in the Sinclairs' house that they let her use as a darkroom.

I am one of her best-selling subjects.

Ethiopia is the first place I ever lived where as long as I keep my mouth shut, I can blend in like a native. This was my biggest

83

and most beautiful discovery when I set foot here for the first time. As long as I keep my mouth shut, even the Tazma Meda kids seem to forget that I am the crazy *ferenji* flying woman's boy, even though I go home with Emmy at the end of the day. During our first year here, we spent almost as much time chasing goats with the Tazma Meda kids, or throwing spears with Yosef, as we did reading.

We have been here four years now. Emmy will be sixteen in three months. She blends in less and less all the time, but I am getting better and better at it.

Even though I'd rather not be noticed at *all* in everyday life, I get noticed all the time in glossy magazines around the world. I wear a *shamma* and carry a stick over my shoulder just like the Tazma Meda goatherds. So I guess in a way I am a circus performer like the rest of the family whether I like it or not.

Here is the English conversation that I had with Em not long ago:

Me: "But I'm *not* Ethiopian. I'm American. If I stand wearing a *shamma* under a bee tree in front of the St. Kristos Samra hermitage, I'm still not Ethiopian."

Em, shrugging: "Your father is Ethiopian, which makes you officially Ethiopian, and you live in Ethiopia, and you wear a *shamma* all the time."

"But—so do you! But—"

"I don't see what difference it makes whether Momma takes a picture of you or of Yosef! This way at least the person she takes a picture of gets a cut."

"Momma says the caption in *Vu* magazine means 'Abyssinian shepherd boy.'"

Em gave a snort of scorn. "Well, you *look* like whatever the French people think an Abyssinian shepherd boy looks like. If they don't even call a country by its right name they won't care if they're looking at an actual shepherd boy or not. Why do *you* care, Teo? They're the ones getting buffaloed."

"Imagine if I grow up and design a train that runs on balloon power, or figure out how to make radios work without batteries or something, and instead of taking me seriously everybody just points to those pictures and says, *Well, you are a fake.* I would care. I bet Delia would care."

That made Em clam up for a moment. Then she said, "If you think it's wrong, tell Momma."

"Are you crazy? She got two hundred dollars for that picture."

That one picture was worth more than her nonexistent clinic wages are supposed to be for the whole year. You can't really argue with facts like that. It should make us just about the richest people in the whole district, except that all the money is spent on fuel and film and developing fluid.

"The thing is, Teo, you work so hard trying not to look like a *ferenji* that you're already a humbug."

I am the only one of us who can actually get away with not looking like a *ferenji*—a foreigner. And it is embarrassing to admit it, but Emmy is right. I spend my whole life trying to think of ways to make myself fit in. I watch Ezra. I watch Habte Sadek. I watch Yosef. I watch the Tazma Meda kids more than I talk to them. As long as I keep my mouth shut, I can make it work. Em is the most fluent Amharic speaker of any of us—mine is accented just like Momma's. But I am the only one of us who looks the part.

When we're in Addis Ababa, I can fool people into thinking I'm a farm boy. Or Em's servant. Neither one of us likes that, but it's a side effect of being together all the time.

Unlike me, Em wears whatever the heck she wants to wear in Tazma Meda. She is the crazy *ferenji* flying woman's crazy *ferenji* daughter, trailing around in lace shawls and green glass beads and flying goggles and sunsuits that she makes herself out of Mrs. Sinclair's patch bag. I think that in a corner of her head she is always pretending to be White Raven. She wants to be like White Raven, not afraid of anything, always able to fool people into doing what she wants and always able to figure a way to make everything come out all right in the end.

THIS THEME IS SUPPOSED TO BE ABOUT THE LANGUAGE I dream in. I've described a conversation I know I had in English, so here is a conversation I know I had in Amharic. This happened two days ago:

The clinic where Momma works is the newest building in Tazma Meda. It is stone with a corrugated iron roof that sounds like thunder when it is raining. There is a wooden ladder bolted to the wall at the back so you can get to the radio mast and the water tanks on the roof, so me and Em spend a lot of time climbing up there while we wait for Momma. You can spy on the whole village from the roof—the clinic is right on the edge of town because it's so new, and higher up than the rest of the houses.

I say you can spy on things, but you aren't really hidden up there, because anyone who looks up can see you. And people do look up at the roof of the Tazma Meda clinic because of the radio mast. The wooden tower got put up about two years ago, but Akaki Station only started transmitting last month. The mast takes up the entire clinic roof and is five times as high as the building itself. It is like having our own copy of the Eiffel Tower in Tazma Meda. Momma says it is very useful to use as a landmark for lining up to land on the airfield at Beehive Hill.

Em and I were sitting on the roof yesterday when the soldier from Gondar came riding up the valley and along the track into the village.

I saw him come to a halt, and I climbed down because I figured he would want someone to take his horse. Em stayed sitting on the roof with her legs dangling over the edge.

I jumped the last four feet to the ground and came to meet the stranger. I nodded politely and held out my hand. The soldier and I were both wearing khaki shorts and shirts and white *shammas*, both of us barefoot. We were not too different, two modern countrymen meeting in front of one of Haile Selassie's best new twentieth-century clinics. The rider frowned at Em, then spoke to me.

"There's a radio inside?" he asked in Amharic. "Does it transmit?"

That was not a question I was expecting.

I hadn't really looked at him before, I guess. I'd seen a tired man on a horse, carrying a rifle. Everybody carries rifles, so that wasn't too remarkable. But now I saw that beneath his *shamma*, his uniform was the greenish-khaki of an Imperial Guard, like we'd seen at the coronation. His rifle looked brand-new, not something his grandfather had picked up at the Battle of Magdala in 1868. He didn't look like someone who ought to be traveling alone in the middle of nowhere. He looked like he was part of an elite regiment.

"The clinic radio can only receive," I said. "But if you need to send a message . . ."

Momma has sometimes flown messages to Addis Ababa. But it isn't an offer I'd dare to make without telling Momma about it first.

"I need to ask my mother," I said. "She works in the clinic."

The stranger glanced up again at Em sitting on the roof with her bare legs dangling over the edge. We'd been working on a story where White Raven is disguised as the kidnapped queen of Constellatia, the Kingdom of the Stars, while Black Dove tries to rescue the real queen. So Em was dressed up as the queen of Constellatia. She had her hair frizzed out as far as she could get it and had stuck two beautiful, big bunches of highland roses in it. She wore a marshmallowlike fairy dress that we'd made out of two *shammas* sewn together with Sinidu's sewing machine, and she also wore a cardboard crown cut from a film packing box someone had sent to Momma. I'd painted it with ground-up pieces of glass from a broken jam jar of Mrs. Sinclair's. So Em was actually *sparkling*, sitting up there with the sun in her tiara.

The soldier looked at her for a long time. Then he must have decided that despite her womanly body under the weird outfit she wasn't old enough to be my mother, and was also the wrong color. (Of course, so is Momma, but he didn't know that yet.) He looked back at me expectantly, dismissing the sparkling queen on the roof.

I was dying to ask him what message he wanted to transmit, but I knew I had to be polite. "You should come inside and sit down while you wait. I can get you some water."

"Who is the head of your village?"

"Ato Ezra, Mr. Ezra. He's also the doctor here. My mother helps him. She's called Woyzaro Rhoda, Mrs. Rhoda."

"It is a matter of *urgent importance*," the man said grimly.

"We can make the radio work for you now, if you just want to listen," I said. I tilted my head at Em. *Get down here.*

Em scrambled nimbly down the ladder at the back of the clinic. She was wearing khaki shorts, too, beneath her stately Constellatia robes. I helped the imperial rider tie his horse, so Emmy went in first to warm up the radio.

Inside the stone building, Sinidu was guiding a whooping baby and its upset mother in to Ezra. The baby was alternately coughing and trying to grab at my old die-cast *Spirit of St. Louis* plane, which is now hanging from the clinic ceiling to distract people who are having their broken arm set or their tooth pulled or something. According to Em, Sinidu took one look at her outfit and burst out laughing. Then she ignored Em and took the coughing baby in to Ezra.

The queen of Constellatia tried to tune in to Akaki, which is the only transmitting radio station in the country. But we didn't hear a thing except static, which is most of what we have heard since Akaki was inaugurated. Emmy coaxed and petted the wireless, and then she gave it a whack, and suddenly it bellowed forth an unlikely burst of a symphony orchestra. It was astonishing, but not newsworthy.

The stranger squatted down, bent over his knees with his head in his hands. You could almost smell his frustration. He'd wanted serious information, not European opera.

"What's going on?" I asked him.

"There will be war within a year."

I didn't stare at him, but I can bet Miss Shore will stare at me when she reads this. It is just as unbelievable a package of bundled words as if he'd told me, *Your father didn't die of influenza in 1919* or *There's no such thing as a bird strike* or something like that.

"A war where?" Emmy asked. "Against what country?"

"Here. Against Ethiopia. Italy holds colonies on all our borders, and they want Ethiopia as well." He hesitated and looked up. He considered that I looked like his countryman and that Em, for all her *ferenji* foreignness, spoke Amharic as flawlessly as anyone who belonged here. The soldier added, "Italy against Ethiopia. The only African nation never to be colonized now has invaders on our doorstep."

He didn't know her father was Italian. Or her name—Emilia Menotti.

"How do you know?" I asked. It made no sense.

"It is starting. Small things are going to become bigger things, and they are happening now. I've come from Gondar. I have been two days riding—I will kill my horse if I go faster. But I must waste no time in reaching Addis Ababa."

Sinidu appeared out of nowhere, which she is good at, carrying a jug of water and the big bowl of fried barley, which is usually reserved as a treat for bleeding Tazma Meda kids. "The American children forget you are a guest," she said, blithely giving away the game and revealing us as foreigners. She handed him the water and he drank, and Em switched off the radio, because Sinidu had left the door open and everyone in the clinic was trying to listen.

The soldier thanked Sinidu with a nod. It got so still in the other room that even the baby's coughs seemed quiet.

"Now, play!" Sinidu commanded. "Tell your news or every single ear on the other side of the door will fall off!"

The soldier stole a brief glance at her, and Sinidu's expression changed. Something about him made her serious for once. She listened.

"The police in Gondar attacked the Italian Consulate there. An Italian Consulate guard and three Ethiopian policemen were killed—and what will it achieve except to enrage that grasping Fascist Mussolini, who will use it as an excuse to send in more guards? I was a *guest* there, an envoy from the emperor. Which side should I have defended? And with the standoff in the South, the Italians who will not let the visiting Ethiopian soldiers drink at a well that is theirs by right—"

He paused, glancing up to see if any of us knew what he was talking about, and bit his lip. We do know who Mussolini is, the prime minister of Italy who calls himself *Il Duce*, the leader. He has made Italy one of the Great Powers, along with France and

Britain and Germany. Momma does not like his politics, but she doesn't say much about him because of Papà Menotti.

"I am sorry," the soldier apologized. "I am in haste, and you don't understand. . . . I thought there might be news. If there is none, then I will be the first to tell the emperor about the killing in Gondar. Thank you for the use of your radio. I can't stay here. I'm going on to Addis Ababa—I want to make a report. There is no other way to send word."

Em said what I should probably have told him in the first place. "Our mother can take you."

The poor man glanced at Sinidu—she hadn't been introduced and she didn't look old enough to be our mother, because she isn't, but also now she is getting very big because she is finally going to have a baby, so she was clearly *somebody's* mother. And she is a tiny, beautiful soap bubble of a person who was not likely to be carrying a soldier on her back in place of his horse, which is what Em sounded like she was offering.

The poor man struggled between anger and outright laughter. You could see it in his face. He didn't want to stare at us, and he didn't want to ask embarrassing questions.

"Our mother is a flier," I explained. "She's American and she keeps an aircraft here. She can fly you to Addis Ababa in about two hours."

"Ah!" Understanding and amazement flooded his face. "A woman flier?"

Emmy opened her mouth. "Why not? Sinidu is a woman flier, and she is Ethiopian!"

"Now, you let me speak, Emilia," Sinidu said with grown-up authority all of a sudden. "There is a time and place for every battle, and this is not your battle."

She spoke directly to the soldier.

"You can leave your horse at Beehive Hill Farm and come

back for him later. The American children will lead you. Their mother is working now, but I will send her as soon as she finishes, and she can go with you before it gets dark. Go ask her now, Em."

Em nodded politely, always obedient when Sinidu got sharp. She slipped off to find Momma. We all knew the timing of the flight might be a problem if Momma was supposed to be assisting at a cataract operation or something.

The messenger soldier turned to me and said abruptly, "I have never heard an American accent before. But your Amharic is more fluent than the Italian consul. Were you born in America?"

I hesitated. Of course, I was born in France. "I was in America until four years ago," I offered. It is so darn complicated trying to explain our past.

"What made your flying mother bring you to Ethiopia?"

*Because we didn't expect a war?*

*Because Ethiopia was Delia's dream?*

"My father was Ethiopian," I told him.

He nodded like that made all the difference. Sinidu leaped in to explain exactly what Colonel Horatio Augustus had tried to explain on my first night in Addis Ababa.

"Of course his mother brought him here. The law is that a child born of an Ethiopian father is an Ethiopian citizen."

AND HERE IS A CONVERSATION WHERE I CAN'T REMEMBER what language I was talking in, even though it happened yesterday, the day after the soldier came. I don't think I dreamed it, but it was in the middle of the night, so if I was dreaming, this is the language I would have spoken. Maybe a mixture of both.

"Teo! Are you awake?"

"Of course I am."

It is impossible to sleep in our house when Momma is away. We have a proper round house—not a pretend English villa like the Sinclairs' house or a modern building like the clinic— with walls of mud and sticks and a thatched roof, which some of the coffee cooperative people in the village helped build for Momma. We have got one room, which is divided in three by curtains. When we first came to Tazma Meda, me and Em slept in the same bed and Momma slept by herself. But about two years ago, Momma and I swapped, so now we are divided into girls and boys (I mean, boy) instead of kids and grown-ups (I mean, grown-up). It is sometimes lonely for me and sometimes irritating for Momma, but everybody sleeps reasonably well. Except when lizards go prospecting in the thatch and scorpions jitterbug inside the walls, and if you light a lamp you are sure to attract aerobatic moths the size of bats.

"I'm getting up," Em said. "Coming? I made popcorn." She does all our cooking, which she learns from Sinidu, who worries that we are all going to starve from stupidity. Sinidu used to come up here to make us breakfast every morning; she'd beg and beg Momma to let her niece Hana run errands and cook for us, because anyone of any consequence has a kid working for them, but Momma just will not do it. She will not pay some other Tazma Meda kid to do work her own kids can do, and Hana is younger than Em. So now Sinidu comes up here every other morning to razz Em while Em does it. Em is the only one of us who is interested in cooking, mainly because she is always the hungriest.

Em lit the beeswax taper in the iron lantern and packed up her picnic. Then we took the lamp with us, and a stick in case we met a hyena. We walked the long way around to the airfield, leaving a trail of stinky beeswax smoke. We avoided going near the Sinclairs' Big House because their dogs get noisy if you go too close in the dark.

We stopped at the plane's shed to pick up the empty fuel cans and the plank we use as a bench and carried it out to the middle of the airfield. We set up the bench. Em took off the thick *gabi* she'd wrapped herself up in—like a *shamma* but heavier—and spread it over and around the plank to make it comfortable and give us something to protect our feet from creepy-crawlies. We sat down straddling the bench back-to-back, leaning against each other and looking up. In the dark, it is impossible to tell how wide the airfield is, and the little beeswax light kind of made it worse, so we blew it out.

It was like being in a big black bowl. You couldn't see a thing on the ground—not the shed we'd just passed, not a flicker of light from the Sinclairs' house. Beehive Hill was a bump on the horizon. And above us were a hundred million stars.

Momma couldn't come back till the sun came up at the earliest. It was pointless listening for the sound of the Romeo's reliable engine. But it was comforting to sit on the airfield where she'd land.

*"Shooting star!"* Em cried out.

We'd both seen it. We banged our heads together as we both tilted them back at the same time to get a better view of the sky.

*"Doggone it—"* Em said (that was definitely in English). Then we saw another one, a blazing bloom of gold light brighter than the flame we'd put out in the beeswax lantern. It lasted for three seconds, drifted a little way across the sky, and went out.

"Like rocket ships!" I said (also definitely in English).

"You have to stop basing everything on those Buck Rogers comics Grandfather used to send. They're meteors. The Leonids!"

"There is an American who makes rockets. Real ones. Robert Goddard. He's got a beautiful, big grant and help from

Charles Lindbergh. I read about it in *Popular Science*, the one that had Momma's photo. You know, of the walls around Harar, from a thousand feet up. Sometimes I really wish there was some way I could meet a man who makes rockets."

"You know why people make rockets?" Em said. "Same reason they take photographs from the air. To invade other countries."

"That's not why Momma takes photographs from the air, and it's not why Goddard makes rockets. He does it 'cause he loves rockets."

"Maybe it's not why *he* makes rockets. But it's why people *pay* him to make rockets, and it's why other people take photographs from the air."

Boy, is Em ever cynical, in any language. I am not sure she understands how satisfying it is to make up *anything*, not just stories—to think of new ways to do things. But the soldier's visit was making her worse.

Beehive Hill Farm was incredibly quiet. There wasn't anything there but stars and meteors and trees in the distance, coffee trees and the juniper trees that shade them, and nighttime bugs chirping somewhere not too far from us. Em had one knee crossed over the other and both her legs were jittering, shaking the rickety bench. Her anxiety was contagious.

"What's going on?" I asked quietly.

"You heard him, the traveler. He said, 'Small things are going to become bigger things.' That other argument he mentioned, in the South. He told Momma about it while she was getting the plane ready to go. There is a troop of Ethiopian soldiers asking for water at a well that's controlled by an Italian fort, and the Italians won't let them have any. In our *own country*! That's bound to turn into a fight."

"What's an Italian fort doing there in the first place?"

"They built it five years ago. They have forts everywhere, all along the borders with their colonies, all over Eritrea and Somaliland. But this one *isn't* on a border with an Italian colony! It's inside Ethiopia, by some well in the desert that doesn't mean anything except to a few cattle rustlers out there looking for water. It's sixty miles from the border. The Italians shouldn't be there."

"Well, the Gondar police shouldn't be ganging up on a government office, either."

They all seemed such pointless, faraway squabbles that we normally wouldn't care about. But we'd met the grim messenger, and our mother had flown away with him, and now we were alone with the meteors.

Em's foot, kicking in the dark, drummed against the fuel can beneath the plank we were sitting on. The empty can let out a tinny, hollow echo of protest. And suddenly I realized what was nagging at us both—the uneasy thing that brought these faraway squabbles home to us.

It was the empty fuel can that made me think of it.

"I know why you're scared," I said. "Momma told him he didn't need to pay her for the fuel. He tried to give her ten dollars' worth of bullets, but she wouldn't take them. Remember how mad she was that time we went camping without telling her, and she came looking for us in the plane? She doesn't like wasting fuel. But she took the messenger to Addis Ababa without making him pay. She did it as a favor."

"So she's scared, too," said Em hollowly.

If Momma is worrying about the Italians invading Ethiopia and starting a war, she must be worrying about what that will mean for us—for me and Emmy.

I can't believe anyone would want to come to Tazma Meda to have a battle anyway. But I guess it might affect our fuel supply for the airplane, or the supplies for the clinic or something. Whatever it is, it's enough to make Momma *scared.*

Maybe she is scared we will have to leave. That would scare her to death.

I don't want to have to leave *her.* But I am not sure I want to stay here if I can't go anywhere else—if we get trapped because people are fighting on the borders. I want to be able to *do* things. If Momma doesn't teach me to fly someday, I am going to go crazy. And what is Em going to do in Tazma Meda five years from now, when she is twenty-one? She can't be a deacon up on Beehive Hill.

We didn't go back to the house to sleep. When we got so tired we couldn't sit up anymore, we went and bedded down in the Romeo's shed so that we'd be there first thing in the morning when Momma got back. The shed is bigger than our house but not as solid, because the chinks between the sticks that make the walls are not filled in and the roof is corrugated iron instead of thatch. The iron sheets rattle in the slightest wind and the noise keeps you awake. I don't know when I've ever been so relieved to hear the sound of the Romeo's engine.

There still hasn't been any news about Gondar on the radio, or about the soldiers who aren't being allowed to use the well in the South, so maybe it really isn't important. But Ethiopia is not like Pennsylvania, where there are radios in every house, and the operator listens in on every telephone call, and the mailman and the paperboy come every morning. Here, there are no newspapers and no radios and no telephone. We pick up our mail in Addis Ababa every three or four months. We don't get any mail in the rainy seasons, because we can't fly then.

The answer is, I don't know if what happened at Gondar is important.

I don't know what language I dream in, either.

Theme by Em
Subject: "Ethiopian Culture"
Beehive Hill Farm, Tazma Meda

Jan. 20, 1935 (Ter 12, 1927)

MOMMA IS FORCING ME TO WRITE THIS. BEA SINCLAIR is now old enough to go to boarding school with her sisters, so the Sinclairs have all gone to Addis Ababa to wave good-bye to her on the train, and that awful pill Shore has gone with them so she can escort Bea back to England. Boy, is Bea going to hate having to wear shoes all the time. There's no reason for Shore to come back here except us, so I guess we are done with her. That leaves us without an English-speaking teacher. Momma has been acting a little desperate lately about our lack of what she calls "real schooling"—I think she knows how much Teo minds not being able to stuff his head full of other people's ideas to chew over, and the progressive village school finishes with everybody when they are twelve—so now Momma is going to make us keep up the theme writing to get us to think about other things besides *The Adventures*. Miss Shore left us a boatload of her blue paper theme books. I guess I don't mind *writing*—I *love* writing—but I don't know if I want Momma to read all of it. I bet she won't anyway. She is not patient enough to read two whole theme books full of pencil scrawl and fix the punctuation.

I blame Sinidu—her double-crossing good intentions turned Momma into a schoolmarm. They are both worrying about what Teo and I will end up doing if Italy invades Ethiopia.

Sinidu started on Momma the day after the soldier came to

the clinic to use the radio. "Teach them to fly. Make sure they can write and figure in English. Make them listen to the radio every day."

Sinidu is a pretty good teacher herself, what with the Amharic and the cooking, and anything she does counts as "Ethiopian culture," doesn't it? So I'm just going to pick up writing about Sinidu where Teo left off his last theme for Miss Shore.

As soon as the sun came up the morning after our stargazing, Teo and I were out on the landing strip watching for Momma to get back from her trip to Addis Ababa. We had to wait more than an hour, but she must have left before sunrise, just as it was starting to get light, to make such a speedy trip. We jumped up when we heard the familiar buzz of the Romeo's engine. Each of us grabbed an end of my white *gabi*, and we stood there waving it between us like a flag to welcome her. Momma waved the white end of her own *shamma* from the front cockpit as she taxied past us, the way she always greets us. Then she taxied up as close as she could get to the plane's shed and switched off the engine. The wheels were still rolling, so we pushed her in.

She hopped out lightly and hugged us both and kissed us on top of our heads.

"Oh boy, I thought those Frenchies who do the Imperial Air Force training at that new Akaki airfield weren't ever going to let me leave!" she said cheerfully. "Trying to get me drunk on *tej*"—honey wine, but Momma would never drink wine when she is flying, because alcohol was illegal the whole time she flew in the USA—"and gossiping about the good old days back in France before they came here. One of them trained with my instructor at the same airfield where I learned to fly! Think they'd do just about anything for a lady flier. Look—"

She hauled a five-pound sack of coffee out of the rear cockpit. Teo and I burst out laughing. Momma laughed, too.

"I know. I *told* them I live on a coffee farm, but this is from Harar, and Harar coffee is absolutely the yummiest in the world. Listen, kids, I'm beat—I'm going to take a quick nap before I head to the clinic. Why don't you take some of this coffee down to Sinidu?"

But Sinidu was already in our house when we got there, waiting for us with *fatira* breakfast cakes frying and coffee beans roasting already.

"Beautiful!" Momma exclaimed, and they kissed each other's cheeks, and Sinidu whooped at the five-pound bag of coffee.

"I am not carrying that! I have enough to carry!" She patted her beautiful, big baby bump. "If I thought I had to carry that back to the village, I would make you drink it all up this morning!"

"The kids will carry it for you! Where do you want it?"

"We will take it up Beehive Hill to Kristos Samra for my uncle and my nephew," Sinidu said. "Coffee guzzlers!"

Only a woman can make coffee, so Habte Sadek and Yosef only get to drink coffee when me or Sinidu or her niece Hana makes it for them.

Sinidu turned back to squat by the frying breakfast and added, "Also, my uncle will want to know about the Italian Consulate in Gondar. I will tell Habte Sadek."

Momma squatted down beside her. Momma said, "My sister, you are bringing a baby into a changing world, and I am scared."

"Don't say that," Sinidu said quickly. "You have already brought your own babies into this world, and I think you should do a better job of getting them ready for it. Also, you have not answered my question."

"The emperor is going to offer payment to the Italian government for the man killed. He doesn't want war. There is still a troop of his soldiers waiting for water at the well in Wal Wal, and the Italian fort there still will not let them drink. So maybe a beautiful apology will make them happy. But I am scared. I am scared it will all turn into fighting and people will be killed. I have seen enough death on the ground to last me a lifetime."

She kept her voice level as she said it, and it sounded like she was talking about the Great War.

But I was pretty sure she was talking about Delia.

"If I were you," said Sinidu, "I would teach my children to fly."

Momma swung her head around swiftly to look at her, as shocked as if she'd been slapped. She'd *definitely* been thinking about Delia.

"I am never going to teach my children to fly!"

Sinidu sat back on her heels. She looked shocked, too. "You have taught *me* to fly, you strange *ferenji* woman! Why would you not teach your own children?"

Momma blushed. "You were persuasive," she said.

"Well, let me persuade you some more."

Teo and I listened hopefully and fearfully—worried because Momma was worried, but also pretty sure that once Sinidu got to work on her, she would change her mind.

"You are a fool to keep them on the ground. Make their lying stories into true stories and teach them to fly! If there is war, Teo will be called on to carry a spear. What happened in Gondar— one Italian and three of our own killed, and we must apologize for it? If there is fighting, you do not want him to be an Ethiopian soldier on the ground. Put him in the air, where he'll be safe! Do it now before it starts!"

"Safe in the air!" Momma exclaimed. "Now, that is provincial ignorance."

Sinidu laughed. "And I have already said you are a crazy foreigner! This is not Europe! How do you think the emperor won his last battle over his rival before his coronation? He sent an airplane to drop fire on them from the sky. Teach your boy to fly, and he will be safe from spears and antique rifles."

"I don't want him to go to war at all!"

"When it comes, you will have no choice. The only way to save him is to lift him above the crowd."

"I will think about it," Momma said.

We did not think she meant it. But she did.

ON THE WAY HOME FROM THE CLINIC THAT DAY, WE had to trot to keep up with Momma. She was walking at a determined pace, hands deep in the pockets of her khaki slacks, frowning a little so you could see the dent between her eyebrows. Her *shamma* needed washing. Sinidu had told her so. Sinidu said she would be embarrassed to see "that gray flag" waving in the air next time Momma landed at Tazma Meda.

Momma muttered to herself the whole way. "Old enough to carry a spear! *Jiminy Christmas.* How about a rifle from the last century, like all the other progressive Tazma Meda kids who have spent a couple of years learning to read in the new village school? Shooting up at Italian aircraft with handmade bullets. *What would Delia say?* What would she say *to me?* What would Delia *think* if she knew that's what I'd raised her boy to do? *Over my dead body.*"

She jogged along like it is *easy* to talk and drop emotional air torpedoes and run at the same time.

"Momma, I won't–" Teo panted, jogging alongside her.

I burst out in gasps, "What is—what is all this hokum—all of a sudden—about Teo carrying a spear?"

"You think there *will* be war?" Teo asked. "You think the Italians really are going to invade?"

Momma didn't answer, but she stopped muttering about Delia. I was pretty sure she was still carrying on about sending Teo to war in her head.

"Why are we running?" I panted. It felt like we had hyenas behind us—like we were running away from something.

"I want to be in the air before it gets dark."

"Do you have to go back to the city?" Teo asked, racing alongside her—my legs are still longer than his but he is faster. "How come?"

"I'm not going anywhere. Sinidu is right. If you're old enough to carry a spear, you're old enough to learn to fly."

It was like being struck by lightning—it actually made me shiver all over. I couldn't believe she finally, actually, meant it. I spluttered, "But you—you said—"

"You said *never!*" Teo burst out.

"I changed my mind. Sinidu is right." Momma always repeats things that she wants to believe and doesn't quite. "I'm not watching you march off with a spear over your shoulder as if it is the sixteenth century. If you learn to fly, you will never have to carry a spear."

"You're going to teach Teo to *fly?*" I gasped.

"I'm going to teach both of you to fly, of course," Momma said matter-of-factly. "You are not going to be stunt pilots. You don't need to know how to do loops and rolls and spins. But you are going to be competent, safe fliers like Delia was." She added fiercely, "Yes, she was. She got killed by the worst luck in the world, but she was *safe.*"

"Oh, *Momma!*" I breathed, stunned.

Teo stopped her in midstride and knocked her off balance by throwing his arms around her. It was like the moment when she'd told us we were going to go to Ethiopia—confusing, frightening, but *wonderful.*

"Delia was *safe!*" Teo exclaimed.

Momma stumbled, then regained herself.

"Of course she was safe. Just a damn prairie falcon got in her way."

The thrill of learning to fly went a long way toward making me not worry about war. "You're really going to teach us!" I repeated, trying to make her say it again, just to make sure it was true.

"That Shore woman was hopeless," Momma said chokingly, trying to hide her emotion. "Got to educate you *somehow.*"

"KEEP A RECORD OF EVERY LESSON," SHE TOLD US. She has told us this before, but she said it three times today at least, so I am doing it. We have each dedicated one of Miss Shore's never-ending supply of theme books to keeping a flight log. "I'm not qualified to give you a license," Momma said. "So you need to have a record to show an examiner."

I went first. Momma did the takeoff herself. We haven't raked the airstrip recently, and it is getting bumpy. I watched the farm get small again—it looks so *nothing* from the air, a spilled toy box of little cabins made of twigs and a few piles of matchsticks (the twig cabins are the English-style house and stable, and the piles of matchsticks are the Ethiopian ones, including ours). Then Beehive Hill below us, the slopes dark green with coffee and juniper. Goats browsing in the bush like white bugs—so far below us you couldn't see them moving. Everything is so *little* from the air. On the other side of Beehive Hill was the Beshlo River gorge, and the flat Tazma tablelands all around us and the Simien Mountains in the distance. Momma turned the plane so we were heading south, and the river joined the Blue Nile.

When Momma yelled, "You have control," at first I couldn't even tell she'd let go of her own control column—she was behind me, in the second cockpit, and I couldn't see her. And the Romeo was perfectly in trim, flying itself.

Then I grabbed the control column, but I was so jittery I kept letting go. We wobbled like jiminy. I hated it. I have wanted Momma to teach me to fly my whole life long, and it turns out I hate it. It turns out I am nothing at all like White Raven. It makes me want to cry, but I won't cry. I won't. Through the speaking tube, I heard Momma shouting at me to relax.

"Let go, Em! I'm flying. Just take a deep breath!"

I thought of Delia putting my hands in Teo's. *I. Am. Not. Afraid.* White Raven and Black Dove are always supposed to be in the soup together. But now Teo was a million miles behind me in the third cockpit. I had to do this *myself.* I thought of Momma, letting go of the controls so I could learn, doing the thing she was most afraid of in the whole world. And I ground my teeth together and took the controls again.

I am definitely going to have to write something else for Momma to read. Ugh. I am never going to tell her how scared it makes me to take the controls.

I got to fly for about an hour—just straight. Not up, not down, not turning—just straight and level, halfway to Addis Ababa, following the Blue Nile gorge. If I focused on the river below me, which was beautiful, it wasn't so terrifying. Momma could tell how tightly I was hanging on to the controls—she could feel with her hand on the wheel in the second cockpit. She told me to let go when it was time to turn back.

"Em, just hold on and *feel* what I'm doing, okay? You pull back and the nose lifts and the plane starts to climb. Not too hard—that makes the plane get upset and stall. You push forward, and the nose drops and you go down. Back to go up, forward to go down. Just *feel* it while I fly."

Momma flew up and down in climbing swoops the whole way back to Beehive Hill. It was like being at sea. We landed so Teo and I could swap seats and he could get a turn at the controls. I felt green in a lot of different ways.

Momma climbed out with us and led us from beneath the shade of the Romeo's wings. The sky was fierce and burning blue, and there was a pair of bearded vultures doing aerobatics over Beehive Hill. Momma pointed at them without saying anything.

"They make it look so easy!" I grouched, shielding my eyes against the bright sky to look at them.

Momma shook her head and pulled my hand down with one of hers, and then she took one of Teo's hands, too, so we were all standing there on the airfield holding hands and looking up at the circling birds.

Then Momma swallowed hard.

"You have to be aware of them," she said huskily. "Keep an eye out. You know how small everything looks when you're in the air? You won't see a bird till you're nearly on top of it. But if you *do* see birds—if you think you're going to hit one—pull back. Not so hard you stall, but like you want to climb. A bird'll do less damage if it hits the plane's belly than if it hits the . . . the propeller."

She turned to each of us to look into our eyes.

"Understand?"

We both nodded, once. Her own firm, stern Nod. Then she stood real quiet for a minute, and so did we, thinking of how Delia was missing out on the African sky.

Finally Momma broke the silence. With a shaky little smile, she said, "Birds are better fliers than people. They have a better chance of getting out of your way than you do of getting out of theirs.

"Also," she finished evenly, "you have a better chance of surviving a bird strike than the bird does."

Then she squeezed our hands four times, giving us Delia's secret message.

Then we climbed back into the plane.

I think Momma let me go first to make her brave enough to be able to teach Teo.

## EPISODE FROM "TAMING THE FIREBIRDS"

For the first time in her life, White Raven found that her disguise was not working.

The young firebirds were not fooled. Maybe she didn't smell right or something. The three fledglings made a ring around her and took turns pecking at her wings.

She could hear Black Dove choking a little as he tried not to laugh. He was sitting, invisible, on the edge of the enormous nest.

White Raven turned around and blew fire at him from the tank that was strapped over her shoulders.

"I guess you think this is easy!" she said. "Why do I have to be the one to enter the race?"

"You're the one who can fly like a bird!" Black Dove said as one of the fledglings began pulling the feathers out of White Raven's wings with his beak, one at a time. The young firebird pulled only at the orange feathers— he left the gold and red ones alone.

"You're going to have to bring me some more thread," White Raven complained. "I'm not going to be able to fly with this many feathers missing. This was such a stupid idea."

I AM STARTING AGAIN ON ETHIOPIAN CULTURE IN A new theme book.

We are all staying in the Sinclairs' big British bungalow and looking after it for them while they are away. For the past week, we have been alone in the Big House, and it feels absolutely weird with just us Menottis in it. It is nice of the Sinclairs to ask us to look after it, since they will pay us. It is easier money than helping tourists find things to kill, or guiding them around so they can take pictures of beehives or priests or Teo, which is what we usually do at the festival of Timkat.

Timkat is my favorite holiday even though I missed the parade the first year we were in Tazma Meda. We'd only been here two months, and I was the one who got so many mosquito bites when we first landed in Africa at the port in Djibouti that I had malaria for the whole Christmas season. There we were, back together with Momma for the first time in two years, and all Teo and I did was make up stories or read Vera Sinclair's *Hotspur* and *Wizard* comics that her grown-up brother had sent her from England.

Because of the fever, I spent a lot of time talking to people no one else could see, including Aunt Connie and Delia—and animals! That's what I remember most about having malaria. Sometimes Delia really *was* a black dove, and Teo would think I was talking to him. And Aunt Connie's pony kept tempting me to follow it outside, and the only reason I didn't wander off after it was because I couldn't stand up for more than about five minutes (White Raven was raised by wild ponies and can speak to them). Though once I got halfway up Beehive Hill before I had to curl up under a tree and go to sleep. Teo just waited patiently, drawing pictures in the dirt until I woke up, but I was too loony to find the way back and he couldn't find his way without me, so we had to wait for Sinidu's niece Hana and a bunch of her Tazma Meda friends to find us by accident and lead us home. And that took a long time, too, because Hana's hair is always done in the tiniest braids around the front of her head, and I kept stopping to poke at them and see how they worked and try to do it to my own hair. It was after dark when we got back. Momma was not happy.

After that, she used to carry me back and forth from the clinic in a little hammock slung over the back of a mule so she could keep an eye on me. I got to curl up in a bed of goatskin and thick cotton *gabi* blankets and watch everybody coming and going. Teo supplied me with books from Vera Sinclair's shelf.

At any rate, we did not go watch the Timkat parade that year.

The next year, I put together a truly fabulous outfit in honor of the parade, but Momma would not let me wear it.

*"Take that ridiculous thing off your head right now."*

"It's a *tabot*," I told her, because Timkat is when the priests all over the country take their church's *tabots* out—their Holy Arks, which are copies of the stone tablets that God gave Moses with the Ten Commandments written on them. The priests parade around the town carrying the *tabot* copies wrapped up in silk on their heads.

"I'm a priest," I said. I was a little disappointed Momma hadn't figured that out.

Momma's eyes burned gray fire. "Go put on your Decoration Day dress," she told me. "Don't you dare be so disrespectful to these people and their church! If you ever say anything like that again, I'll wash out your mouth with soap."

Sulking, I said, "You wouldn't waste it if you had any!"

*"Orange-blossom,"* Momma said. "One face bar. Mrs. Sinclair

gave it to me for Christmas, and I am saving it for a very good reason."

Partly it is true she does not want to be disrespectful, which I understand better now than I did then. But partly she is still a Quaker deep down inside, and she doesn't set much store by religious ceremony. Funny how we all see it so differently: Momma doesn't like the ceremony, because it doesn't match how she thinks about God; Teo loves it because in his head it is all connected with God; and I love it without connecting it to God at *all*. But I didn't want my mouth washed out with orange-blossom soap, so I shut my trap like a coin purse snapping and went and changed into my too-short white parade dress, which was boring as well as too small. Momma had never told me what to wear before, and hasn't since.

I still wish I was allowed to dress up like a priest for the Timkat parade. Their outfits beat anything Teo and I can come up with.

Timkat is the Ethiopian feast of Epiphany. It takes place in the middle of January, and it is the biggest holiday of the year. It makes a good replacement for Christmas and the Fourth of July rolled into one, and there is usually a houseful of European tourists staying with the Sinclairs at Beehive Hill Farm—they pay room and board to Mrs. Sinclair and they pay Momma to fly them around and help them take pictures. There are no visitors this year because people are worrying about war. Well, except for the unexpected visitors who arrive *because* of war.

People get more dressed up for Timkat than for anything else in the whole year. The priests are in velvet and silk robes embroidered with gold, and tiered silver crowns that look like wedding cakes, and everybody yodels and shakes bells and beats drums, and there are musicians in white *shammas* with big red stripes around the hem. The priests from the village church, Beta

Markos, carry their copies of the sacred *tabot* around town for everyone to admire (even though you can't actually see it, because it's all wrapped up in silk), and then they take it up to the St. Kristos Samra hermitage on Beehive Hill, because there is an extremely weedy pool cut in the rock there, which they use to re-enact Christ's baptism in the Jordan River. They bring out the *tabot* from the Kristos Samra chapel, too. The churchmen throw the water all over everyone to bless them, and some people get really enthusiastic and jump into the pool. The tourists with cameras *love* all this.

Momma does not love it much, because in addition to not really deep down understanding why they do it, she is constantly campaigning to keep people out of the stinking water of the Kristos Samra rock pool. She grumbles there is always someone turning up at the clinic a day or two after Timkat whose torn toenail is infected after standing in that pool for a couple of hours, or a young deacon with tummy trouble. There is nothing Momma hates to cope with as much as she hates tummy trouble.

Yesterday we were in the Timkat parade at the crack of dawn with Ezra and Sinidu. All the men in the village beat drums or fire their rifles to make a lot of noise while everyone follows the Beta Markos priests up Beehive Hill—the Sinclair girls all used to join in with their guns when they still lived here. Remember how I said everyone gets dressed up? This year I had to wear one of Fiona Sinclair's outgrown party dresses. Tartan silk. What a *girl* Fiona Sinclair is. It is very pretty but extremely tight, and the only way Momma could make me let it out was for Sinidu to sit next to me every morning letting out her own party dress while I did mine.

I am envious of Sinidu's, which is white muslin with embroidered panels up and down the front. She and Ezra are a beautiful couple. Ezra looked young and earnest in his *shamma* that Sinidu had scrubbed white as high summer sun, with a blue and green and silver stripe along the edge. Although I have never seen them touch each other even to hold hands—that would be rude for grown-ups to do in public—he treats her like a tiny, bouncy princess. He watches her with joy. He was sad today because she was grouching about having to climb the hill—the baby bump is enormous now. But mainly she had been listening to the radio too much. Now we were all trying to buck her up.

"Should I stop in the clinic and listen myself?" Momma asked. "Play. Tell me what is happening!"

"Nothing," Sinidu sulked. "There is nothing to listen to."

"I had to switch it off myself, or we would have missed the procession," Ezra said. "It is like watching someone who is drinking too much *tej*. She just gets sillier and sillier."

"What did you hear?" Momma pressed Sinidu. "Anything about the emperor's request for support from the League of Nations? Have they given him an answer?"

That bickering over the well at the fort near the border with Italian Somaliland turned into a fight last month, just like the imperial soldier from Gondar said it would. And a lot of soldiers got killed on both sides, just like Sinidu said they would. But it was all local *askaris*, native soldiers fighting on the Italian side. No Europeans got killed. Just like Momma said they wouldn't.

"Oh, the emperor is polite," Sinidu grumbled. "Haile Selassie wants peace!"

"We all want peace!" Momma exclaimed.

"We don't want to kneel in church praying for peace while the *ferenji* soldiers march in and take everything away from us," Sinidu said fiercely. "Saying prayers is not going to defend our coffee trees and Habte Sadek's treasure and your flying machine. Italian troops are already marching in Somaliland and Eritrea— we know it—but Haile Selassie wants peace. He apologized for

Gondar, and he wants Italy to apologize to him for Wal Wal. And the League of Nations sits in Europe doing *nothing*! Ugh, they are like my mother, like your Teo—polite to everybody."

Momma laughed uneasily. "Haile Selassie is doing the right thing. He's *negotiating*. He is a modern leader!"

"He may as well negotiate with the wind, Rhoda! France and Britain won't defend him. No one dares to offend Italy, none of the Great Powers in Europe want to offend each other. The British want the emperor to pay Italy *again* to apologize for making the Italians have to kill Ethiopian soldiers. Italy's their ally and they think Germany is going to stir up trouble in Europe and they'll do anything to keep Mussolini happy. All these words and treaties and none of them work in the emperor's favor! You know what Habte Sadek says: 'Spiderwebs joined together can catch a lion.' That is what they are doing, those Italians, spinning webs."

Sinidu was getting out of breath. She hugged her arms around her embroidery-covered hidden baby. "I just hope you listen to me and keep your children out of it," Sinidu told Momma ominously. "Don't let that boy of yours get caught in the spiderweb."

"Now, stop talking about war or you will upset the baby!" Ezra warned her.

"Is that what all that European schooling has taught you about babies?" Sinidu grumbled. At least that made Ezra laugh.

We stayed on Beehive Hill until everybody started heading home—and though it is only a fancy show, every single time I watch the Timkat parade, it makes the hair stand up on the back of my neck to see Habte Sadek carry the Kristos Samra *tabot* back inside the rock cave church, where it hides for most of the year.

Finally the Tazma Meda priests carried their own copy of the *tabot* back down to the village. Momma peeled us away from the parade as we all trooped past the track to Beehive Farm. She settled into her long-legged lope, and once again I had to trot to keep up with her and Teo—of course *they* were not trying to run wearing one of Fiona Sinclair's outgrown dresses.

It turns out Momma was determined to get in another flying lesson before it got dark. Sinidu being upset had scared her. Sinidu is *always* happy.

However, only Teo got a lesson, and afterward Momma told him to log his flight as twenty minutes because that is all he actually flew with his hands on the controls. It should have been longer, but we had not been expecting the Uninvited Guests.

Teo is getting very good very fast. I am torn between pride and jealousy. He does it the way he draws, without having to work at it, but also—*he works at it.* Momma let him do the takeoff by himself and yelled at him to head north, following the Beshlo River. Then Momma leveled out high above the gorge but not so high above the flat tabletops of the mountains. She yelled through the speaking tube, "Let's climb!" I was sitting in the back, right behind her, with Teo in the pilot's cockpit. Momma pointed at the sky with both hands. "Up! Up! Pull back the stick!"

Teo did, but not with confidence, and we were *crawling* upward. I started to laugh. Teo glanced back at Momma to get some kind of reassurance that he was doing the right thing, and he spotted me way back in the third cockpit.

I hooked my thumbs together and flapped my hands like wings, trying to remind him he was brave and steady.

*Black Dove!* I mouthed at him.

And that was all it took. He pulled back, as firm and sure as Momma, and pushed power on, and we *soared.* I heard Momma shouting into the speaking tube.

*"That's it, Teo—pull back like you mean it!"*

Then suddenly the plane lurched wildly nose up, which none of us had expected. That was because Momma grabbed the controls away from him without realizing he was still pulling back.

Teo yelled. I couldn't hear what—the sound blew past me like leaves or feathers in a gale. It felt like we were going to stall.

"*Let go!*" Momma yelled, and then she straightened us out.

Teo glanced back at her again in wild confusion, but Momma wasn't paying attention to him anymore. She had turned her head to gaze at something on the horizon, a little to the right of where we were heading. From where I was sitting behind her, it looked as though her body had suddenly become a part of the plane. She wasn't thinking about flying; she was just doing it. It was as natural to her as walking. So I followed her eyes to the horizon to see what she was looking at. I saw a black speck that seemed to hover ahead of us in the middle of the wide blue empty highland sky. Not a vulture.

It was another Romeo.

It is such a familiar silhouette that I watched it coming toward us without realizing how weird it was to see another plane at *all*. How many times have we watched that exact same silhouette floating into the Beehive Hill Farm field, or leaving it behind? A million. A few thousand, anyway.

"*Who is that?*" Teo yelled.

Momma was tense. I could tell. Her head was tilted high, watching the other plane, focused. She gave Teo a sharp thumbs-down to shut him up.

She rocked our wings at the other plane as it got closer, a dipping curtsy, one set of wings down and then the other. The mysterious Romeo rocked its wings back at us, everybody waving. *Selam, selam—peace!*

But Momma still didn't relax. I thought she'd been tense because she was worried the other pilot hadn't seen us, and she didn't want to collide with the other aircraft. But she wasn't worried about having enough room in the enormous sky. She was worried about something else.

She didn't give Teo the controls back after she'd rocked the wings, even though our plane was still flying straight and level, heading north along the river, and Teo is perfectly capable of flying straight and level without running into anything or losing height. Momma kept flying, leaning forward a little bit in her seat, straining to see the other plane as it came nearer and nearer. When the strange plane got close enough, we could see the other pilot waving at us cheerfully. As he passed us, he raised his wings so we could see the Italian flag colors painted underneath.

Momma kept flying, but Teo and I craned around in our seats to watch the other plane. It flew steadily out of sight in a straight line behind us, in exactly the opposite direction—heading right toward Beehive Hill. Toward home.

When the strange plane was out of sight, Momma turned steeply and followed it home.

After a minute or so, she said through the speaking tube, in a normal voice, "There you go, Teo. You can take her for a few minutes. You have control." He did absolutely nothing except keep his hand on the control column. She'd already pointed the plane in the right direction, and we kept going until the dark green smudges of the Tazma Meda juniper and coffee trees came back in sight. Then Momma took over so we could land.

She made a big fuss about how to spot the airfield from the air, which I do not think is awful hard. We are so close to the spot where the Beshlo River and the Blue Nile meet that it is hard to get lost unless you go zooming away over the mountains toward the other side of Wollo Province.

I guess I should put in my other book, the flying log, about all the landmarks and cheats she pointed out, how to work out which way the wind is blowing based on her homemade wind sock, or how to line yourself up with the radio mast in the Tazma Meda village on your port wingtip and the summit of Beehive

Hill straight ahead of you. But actually I wasn't paying enough attention to what she was saying, and Teo confessed to me later that he doesn't remember *any* of it. We were both staring at the strange airplane on the ground below us.

The mysterious Romeo had got there ahead of us, landed, and parked. We could see two men standing on the smooth, trampled dirt in front of the aircraft shed. They were squinting up at us, shading their eyes with their hands.

Momma landed. It was just a normal landing. The two men stood aside as we trundled past them on our way to the shed. We didn't wave the ends of our *shammas* at them like we would have if it were Sinidu or the Sinclairs, but we got a good look at them.

One of them was Papà Menotti. I was surprised at how happy this made me. We hardly know him.

The other was about Papà's age, also a white man, his eyes hidden behind sunglasses with round lenses that made him look like a bug. Both men waved wildly to us as we taxied past, and Teo and I waved back, but Momma didn't.

Momma cut the engine and coasted to a stop just before she reached the shed door. The men strode across to catch up with us, and after we'd climbed out of the plane and taken our goggles off, Momma said hello to her husband.

"Why, Orsino! And . . . is this—"

The other fellow archly lowered his bug sunglasses down his nose for about half a second.

"Not *Capitano Adessi*?" Momma paused as if she was at a loss for words and finally came up with, in English: "Well . . . happy new year!"

Papà Menotti said only, "Rhoda!"

They didn't rush into each other's arms. Instead, Momma held out her hand, and Papà lifted it very grandly to his lips and kissed it. I gaped. Teo whispered to me, "If we ever see Grandma again, I will do that. . . ."

"Ha!" It would melt her. "I can't wait!"

The other man, Capitano Adessi, turned to look at me. He said something in Italian and then followed up in English, "Orsino's daughter? What a lovely young lady you have become, Emilia!"

I took an instant dislike to him. Of all the costumes he could possibly have complimented, not one of them included head-to-toe dust, my hair standing on end, wearing Fiona Sinclair's let-out-at-the-sides, too-short party dress. And I was kind of jealous of his fancy sunglasses, too.

"Yes, this is my clever Emilia," Momma said coolly, turning everything he'd just said right around—complimenting me without mentioning the dust, and pointing out that I am *hers*, not Papà's. "When did you last see Emilia? It must have been in France when she was a baby, when you came to visit us with Orsino's parents. You must have met Delia and Teo, too!" She held out an open hand, gesturing to Teo, her face smooth and neutral. "Well, Delia was killed a couple of years after we went back to the States, and Teo is my boy now. I am teaching him to fly. Teo, this is Capitano Gianluca Adessi."

"Pleased to meet you, Capitano Adessi," Teo said, holding out his hand. Adessi hesitated a second or so—we all saw it. But then he shook hands with Teo coolly. The second he let go, Papà kissed us both, which completely covered up Adessi's hesitation.

Momma gave a brief nod, satisfied with these introductions and greetings. "Please excuse us while we tuck the airplane into bed," she said.

"Let us assist you, of course," Captain Adessi offered, and Papà nodded eagerly, and we all wheeled the Romeo—*our* one, I mean—into the shed. We heaved the doors shut. Then we helped Adessi and Papà tie down their plane.

And then we had to invite them into the house.

"Will you stay for supper?" Momma said.

"We don't have to go back until Monday," Adessi answered for both of them.

"Back to where?" Momma asked politely. "You weren't flying out of Italian Somaliland today, were you? That's much too far to fly in a day!"

"We have been moved to Eritrea," Captain Adessi said. "Orsino is so pleased to be closer to you and his beautiful daughter."

"Eritrea!"

I couldn't tell if she was pleased or angry or scared, since her tone was completely neutral. Well, maybe a little too chipper. But the worried dent wasn't there between her eyes. Since the moment he'd offered to shake hands with Captain Adessi, Teo had been quietly polite. I longed to ask him what he thought was going on.

"You can stay the night, and we can catch up on old times." Momma beamed at Papà. She still hadn't said a word he could understand. He beamed back at her.

Captain Adessi didn't return Momma's smile. "There is some business your husband would like to attend to with you, Signora Menotti. I have come along to help him with the translation."

Momma said something in cool French, something like, *We don't need help communicating.* Papà agreed with her eagerly, and Adessi stood there looking blank.

"Orsino and I both speak French," Momma explained.

"But Emilia does not, so I understand," Adessi said apologetically.

I wanted to paste him.

*"Neither does Teo,"* I butted in.

Momma walked up to the Sinclairs' house with Captain Adessi on one side of her and Papà Menotti on the other. Adessi chattered enthusiastically about the Timkat ceremony he'd seen last year in Gondar, and how sorry he was about the attack on the Italian Consulate in Gondar two months ago, which meant it had been prudent for him to give this year a miss. Teo and I followed behind everybody else. I nudged Teo in the ribs and shook my head in a silent question. *What is going on?*

*Beats me,* he shrugged for an answer.

Papà Menotti suddenly threw a lot of French at Momma. She turned to look at him, startled. He beamed at her like a saint painted on a church wall until she gave him a quick, desperate, frightened grin in return. Then he threw back his head and laughed. Papà glanced around over his shoulder and *winked* at me.

Momma stepped up onto the Sinclairs' big, foreign-looking porch. She turned around and said, "The house is empty at the moment. Everybody is at the Timkat procession. Come up and sit on the porch, and we can have a drink." She glanced at Papà Menotti, who smiled encouragingly at her like he was saying, *Go on!* The little worried dent appeared between her eyebrows. She looked down at me and Teo.

"Kids, can I talk to you for a moment? Excuse me, Orsino."

She marched with determination around the side of the veranda, and we followed her through the double glass doors into the dining room.

"I'm sorry, kids. We'll have to have a quiet supper here tonight instead of going to the Timkat feast."

"Oh, Momma, that's *mean!*" I said.

"Sinidu will be upset," Teo reminded her.

"I know, and I'm not happy about it, either. But Orsino wants to talk and he's only here till tomorrow. He wants to make the Adessi fellow think this is *our house.* That he is coming home here to his family. Jiminy Christmas! How the heck am I supposed to pretend this pile of gingerbread belongs to me?"

Momma is *terrible* at bluffing. She has the worst poker face in the world.

But actually, what I like best about Papà Menotti is his love of dressing things up, and pretending is what me and Teo are best at. There was no way I wasn't going to play along.

I told Momma soothingly, "Me and Teo will take care of everything. You don't have to pretend a thing! Just be yourself. Don't talk about the house. We'll fix up Bea and Vera's bedroom for Adessi. We'll clear out their guns and Vera's comics and borrow some of Mrs. Sinclair's scarves to decorate."

"But we have to figure out supper!" Momma wailed. "Why can't we just all go to the Timkat feast? Sinidu will miss us *and* she will be insulted. And this kitchen is *empty*, and all we have at home is *teff* flour for *injera*, and it won't be ready to eat for *days*."

"We can't take *Italian airmen* from the Regia Aeronautica to the Timkat feast!" Teo exclaimed. Like me, he was tackling this crazy challenge as if it were an episode of *The Adventures*, thinking about what our made-up heroes would do. "What about eggs?" Then with a burst of inspiration, he suggested, "What about Mrs. Sinclair's *tin cans?*"

Mrs. Sinclair's treasured canned food was a beautiful but dangerous idea. You can't replace or pay for her sacred cans, and they only come twice a year, for Christmas and her birthday. But some of them are so old and dusty that she is never going to eat whatever exotic fruit or meat is in them.

"Me and Emmy will take care of *everything*," Teo said. "Momma, all you have to do is talk about flying and look pretty and pilfer some of Colonel Sinclair's whiskey and soda."

Momma has done that before when there are European or American guests staying here, which the American guests in particular appreciate because up until a couple of years ago they could not get whiskey legally back home. She usually pays Colonel Sinclair back one way or another, and he is okay about it. She is not good at play-acting, but she is good at pilfering.

So we got busy digging into Mrs. Sinclair's birthday-food

hoard for supper and her evening clothes to decorate Bea and Vera's room with, and then we had to make up the little girls' beds and hide their shotguns. I made omelets with olives and anchovies (out of very old cans—we picked the dustiest because we thought they'd be the least likely to be missed). By the time Teo and I had finished working magic in the dining room with antique maraschino cherries and silver candlesticks, Momma and Papà and Captain Adessi were sitting on the veranda with cocktails, chatting about coffee prices. And I got Momma all dolled up for supper in a pale blue evening dress of Mrs. Sinclair's that left her back entirely bare. She was nervous as a bride.

"I will tell them where I got it, you know, if anybody asks," she threatened.

"Oh, for gosh sakes, Momma, Mrs. Sinclair let you wear this one last Christmas when you took that senator on a tour," I said. "You act like you own this place anyway. You've been doing all the accounts since Colonel Sinclair's fraidy-cat secretary left. I am not telling them this is *Fiona's* dress I'm wearing."

Momma noticed for the first time that I had changed. "That is one of her good ones!"

"She isn't here and I am!"

Momma wouldn't let me borrow any of Mrs. Sinclair's jewelry, but I found a sparkly rhinestone barrette of Fiona's for her, just to suggest the casual idea of jewels. It was very pretty in the candlelight.

It was beautiful to be sharing this great big secret joke with Papà Menotti. It made him feel less like a stranger. Teo thinks Papà tells everyone Momma runs the place anyway, and he is far enough away that nobody cares whether it is true.

At any rate, Adessi fell for it—or, in fact, he fell for Momma. Everything belonged to Momma last night—the farm, Papà Menotti, the candlelit dining room. We, too, belonged to Momma.

*Teo is my boy now.* And Capitano Gianluca Adessi didn't have any choice except to eat out of her hand. Every now and then she'd pop an olive into Papà Menotti's mouth, like Sinidu does when she's being loving, and then sort of as an afterthought she'd give one to Captain Adessi, too.

Everything was Momma's last night, except her airplane.

That was what Papà had brought Adessi along to talk to her about. It took an awful long time to get around to it, because Papà was embarrassed, and because Momma was being so dog-gone charming. The French doors and the windows were open, nice and airy, and we hadn't lit the lamps, so there wasn't a lick of light apart from the candles—but there were candles everywhere, on the sideboard, all down the table, on the Welsh dresser, and on the windowsills. Momma was talking about photography.

"I used to take pictures at air shows in America—it was a sideline and a much more respectable way of making money than parachuting! And we got such beautiful pictures in the air. My partner, Delia, would do the flying, and I'd do the camera work. I don't do so much of it now, because I haven't got enough hands. Since I came to Beehive Hill, I use the plane mostly for taxiing Dr. Ezra around. We do a flying clinic! And I take tourists game-spotting, and sometimes they take pictures, too. That's what I'd normally be doing this time of year."

She narrowed her gray eyes and said coolly, "But because of the brawling at Gondar and Wal Wal, both my Timkat tourists canceled on me this year. They would have paid well, too. One was an American journalist and the other a Parisian designer."

"I hate to think that my countrymen have caused you any loss of benefit, Signora Menotti," Captain Adessi said. He had a round, boyish face with a crinkly beaming smile that was hard to take seriously—I could see why he tried to hide it. "Perhaps we can make it up to you."

Momma laughed. "You're paying like tourists now?"

"Ah—no."

At this point, Papà Menotti broke the news to Momma in stammering French about why they had come here in the first place.

Momma sat listening like a statue, her face completely blank except for the worry line between her eyes. The only thing about her that moved was the light in the glittering barrette, and the light was only moving because of the faint breeze rippling the candle flames.

Finally, Captain Adessi repeated the gist of Papà's speech in English. But he didn't stammer at all.

"The aircraft you fly belongs to your husband," Adessi said gently. "It is an Italian aircraft. And all Italian aircraft in Ethiopia must be maintained and available to the Regia Aeronautica until relations between the two nations have been mended. Il Duce, Benito Mussolini, the prime minister of Italy, needs your plane."

Momma raised her chin a little defiantly and stared up at some dark place in the ceiling. "Il Duce," she repeated. She didn't look at Papà Menotti. She said quietly, in English, "You mean that pompous, racialist bully Mussolini can't afford his own plane?"

We knew Momma didn't like Mussolini or Fascism much, but we'd never heard her call him a "pompous, racialist bully."

"Mussolini has just launched the fastest seaplane in the world," Momma said. "He has got colonies all over Africa, not to mention toeholds all over Europe, and nobody ever says no to him, because we're all so anxious not to get into another mess of a war like the last one. What does he need my plane for?"

"Oh, Signora Menotti, Orsino was afraid you would take this with a bad temper. The plane is not for Il Duce himself, of course, but for the Regia Aeronautica, the Italian air force. Good, modern aircraft are scarce in East Africa."

"They're a lot scarcer in Ethiopia than they are in Italian Somaliland and Eritrea," Momma pointed out. "Italy's got ten times as many planes here as Ethiopia. Mussolini's already mobilizing his troops in both of those places, and he won't take Ethiopia seriously in the League of Nations. It looks to me like he just wants to show the world what a heavy he is."

Adessi hesitated. Then he took a deep breath and repeated most of their last exchange in Italian for Papà Menotti. Teo and I sat tense and scared. That plane is our link to Addis Ababa. The money Momma makes from her photographs won't be anywhere near as much without it. She'll never be able to buy a plane herself, and she won't admit it, but I'm not sure she can stay in Tazma Meda without one. At least—she's never had to think about staying here without a plane. That plane is our *life*, even if we can't fly it ourselves.

I guess we are not as Ethiopian as we think we are.

"Now, now, now," Adessi said soothingly, like Sinidu talking to a little kid who is having a fit in the clinic. He gave us his beaming grin. "Don't talk as though there will be war! There need not be any aggression. This is the new frontier for Italy—our place in the sun! It is excellent land—you're a farmer; you know how good the land is, and how unspoiled. We are building a new capitol for Eritrea in Asmara, a beautiful modern city, what Addis Ababa *ought* to be if the Abyssinian emperor invested his wealth more fittingly. Addis Ababa is shameful! A modern city without sewers, hyenas eating rubbish in the streets at night? We can complete the work there exactly as we are improving Asmara. And an Italian laborer in Asmara is paid five times what he makes in Rome. Native Eritreans and Italians work side by side. Imagine what these reforms will bring to Abyssinia! You are a pioneer here yourself, Signora Menotti."

"This house is rented from the local landowner, who is

Ethiopian," Momma said stonily. That is true, even if she isn't the one who rents it. "The profits from this plantation are shared among the villagers who work this farm. There are no colonists here."

"And you respect the local population! Of course this is exactly how we approach the hiring of native troops, the *askari* soldiers. You know how hard it is for young men to find work. And how long have the Abyssinians dragged their feet over abolishing slavery? That a man can still be a slave, in a member country of the League of Nations! Appalling! That is one of the first things that would change if there were more Italian control here. This is a situation where everyone can win, Signora Menotti."

" 'A situation where everyone can win,' " Momma repeated. "So what prize will Il Duce award me in exchange for my airplane?"

Adessi glanced at me, then took a longer look at Teo. "Can I count on your discretion?" Adessi asked politely.

I'm kind of making it sound like Papà Menotti wasn't there. In fact, he might as well not have been, because he did not contribute a thing to the conversation except to gaze at Momma with his eyes full of pain and adoration. He'd pushed his plate aside, with half my inventive bootleg olive omelet getting cold, and he was leaning his long torso across the table with his hands clenched in nervous fists against the table, desperate to understand her. In any language.

"I'll say so!" Momma answered. "We're all counting on discretion! Oh, I guess you mean can you count on the *children's* discretion? If we're going to lose the Romeo, they'll be in the same boat as me, so you darn well better include them in whatever you have to say. I was just giving Teo a flying lesson. He'll be disappointed something fierce not to have another."

Whatever else you say about Capitano Gianluca Adessi, you can't say he isn't polite.

"We have not come to take your plane away," he said patiently. "We've come to offer you an exchange. Your husband has shown me some of your photographs from the air—the view of the walled city Harar is magnificent! You are being modest when you say the work is more difficult without your partner. You have an excellent camera mount attached to the aircraft."

"It's twenty years old," Momma said.

"Indeed! Well-made ex-military equipment! I saw the same apparatus mounted on US Air Service aircraft during the Great War. And you are lucky enough to have an unrestricted permit for your air photography. If you could take photographs for us, the Italian government would have good reason to allow you to continue using this aircraft."

You know, when he first said it, I didn't even think there was anything fishy about it. Momma takes photographs for anyone who will pay her.

Momma held her statuesque pose. "'Unrestricted' probably doesn't mean what you think it means. It means I can take pictures anywhere I go, as long as I don't take pictures of trains or government officials or anything in Addis Ababa," she told Adessi. "Also, my permit may be 'unrestricted,' but it isn't *unlimited*. I have to renew it every year. And every time I renew it, they have the opportunity to restrict it. So, what kind of photographs?"

"Reconnaissance," Adessi said. "You are perfectly positioned between the Eritrean border and the Abyssinian capital at Addis Ababa. The *amba* tablelands in the North are inaccessible from the ground, but many of them would make ideal airfields. Scout for us. Make suggestions. There is nothing sinister in it."

Momma turned to Papà Menotti quietly. "When, Orsino? *Quand?* How long will we play this game until they take the plane away? How long have I got?"

He answered her in French. She told us later that his answer was, more or less, till May or June. Sometime between the rains. Not this season, but either after the little rains or before the big ones, when it is easy to fly. Nobody goes anywhere when it's raining.

"Does that mean Italy won't move until summer—just gathering weapons and information for when the big rains end?" Momma asked Adessi.

"You must not talk like that," Adessi said. "You must not *worry* like that!"

Then Momma collapsed across the table and reached for Papà's hands. Mrs. Sinclair's pale blue silk cast shadows down her décolletage and the candlelight sparkled in Fiona's rhinestone barrette. Momma said something to Papà, ignoring Papà's friend.

"Of course we will bring you warning again closer to the time," Captain Adessi said smoothly.

After a moment, Momma shook herself a little. She straightened, but she was still holding on to Papà Menotti's hands. She gritted her teeth and then said evenly, "Be an angel, Em, and clear the table. Take care of Fiona's dress, sweetie pie."

*Oh, whoops, Momma.*

She really does have the world's most terrible poker face.

I glanced at Adessi. He didn't know who Fiona was, and I realized he might not have even thought Momma was talking about the dress I was wearing—she could have meant, "Go pack up a dress to send Fiona" or even "Go finish your sewing project." So I did what White Raven would do: I just brazened it out. I completely ignored the Fiona comment. "Gimme a hand, Teo," I said.

The grown-ups were back on the veranda by the time we'd finished the dishes, trying to act like Europeans. They spent the evening cordially admiring pictures of me and Teo that Momma has taken over the past couple of years. In the morning, they all acted like nothing uncomfortable had happened. They are on the veranda now, recovering from their tourist trip up to the St. Kristos Samra hermitage this morning.

Maybe Capitano Adessi is right about the good intentions of the Italians. He *gave* Habte Sadek his dark glasses—just pressed them into the old priest's hands, and patted them, smiling his beaming, crinkly smile. (Habte Sadek thanked him coldly. He is suspicious of foreigners giving him presents.) Adessi and Papà Menotti will leave pretty soon because it is about a three-and-a-half-hour flight back to wherever they came from in Eritrea. Teo and I have not heard Momma say, "Yes, I will take your pictures for you," but we are both pretty sure she will do it. She will do whatever it takes to hang on to the Romeo.

Doggone it, I don't think I *will* let her read this, either. It will just make her mad. And I have been scribbling here for *hours*. I am going to give up.

I don't think anyone has told Papà Menotti I am learning to fly, too. But he gave me and Teo both tiny French glass compasses for Christmas, so he must be hoping, or expecting it to happen soon. I don't think I'll tell him. Well, I can't tell him. I guess he'll find out when he sees me flying.

The compasses are beautiful. Like something out of *The Adventures*—each one is only as big as a shirt button, a clear glass disc set in a brass ring, a sky-blue arrow like an eyelash in each rose. One for each of us. I love that they are exactly the same.

Date: Feb. 5 and 7, '35 (Ter 28 and 30, 1927)

Type of Machine: Romeo Ro. 1

Number of Machine: I-STLA

Airfield: Tazma Meda to Akaki, Addis Ababa (and
    back)

Duration of Flight: about an hour and a half both
    times. Momma is annoyed that I didn't keep
    track.

Character of Flight: cross country

Pilot: Momma

2nd Pilot or Pilot Under Training: me (Teo)


Remarks:



WOW, I AM TIRED OF HAULING FUEL—NOT FIREWOOD,
but aircraft fuel in kerosene cans. The Italian pilots made off
with all the fuel at the aircraft shed, so we had to carry down
more from the Big House. Sinidu's niece Hana helped us, but
Momma wouldn't let Sinidu because of the baby. Papà Menotti
paid for their fuel, but we have burned a lot ourselves since
then, and we owe Colonel Sinclair for it, so I'm writing it down:
35 gallons owed = 105 Maria Theresa dollars.

I shouldn't complain about hauling fuel, because that's what
is keeping me in the air, and I will do anything to stay in the air.
I can't believe it is finally real—I am finally learning to do something that will get me somewhere.

But I am not happy about the chain of events that is driving
Momma to turn me and Emmy into pilots.

Since the Italians left, Momma has spent every single spare second teaching us to fly. Possible invasion and a deadline have really changed her tune. By the time we'd finished fueling up that Sunday evening, it was getting dark and she *apologized* because she couldn't get us in the air right away.

"It's back to work tomorrow as usual, but let's not tuck our baby to bed," said Momma. "We can tie her down outside on the field, and then she'll be all ready to go tomorrow morning."

"Where are you going tomorrow morning?" Em asked.

"I'm not going anywhere. I want to bring you both up to scratch with landing this kite before those clowns come back and try to take her away." Nobody wanted to admit it wouldn't matter whether or not we could land if we didn't have a plane anymore. "Ezra's expecting me at the clinic first thing, and no doubt all the Timkat casualties will start turning up, but we'll get in about an hour of bumping up and down on the airfield before I have to go. When I can trust one of you to nail it every time you land, I can sit in the back and you can take turns at the controls without us having to swap places every half an hour. And then we can really get to work on navigation. The Sinclairs will not be happy about us using so much of the farm fuel, so we better make sure we put their house back together."

"When do they get back?" I asked.

"It'll be this week, but I don't know when. Wash the sheets after I go to the clinic tomorrow, all right, Emmy? And, Teo, don't try to put the empty cans back. If you stack her shelves with empty tin cans, she'll find them someday. But if you make them vanish, she might not ever notice. They'll make beautiful buddy burners for camping if we fill them up with beeswax."

We spent the evening after the Italian pilots left covering our tracks—Momma pressing gowns (pressing is not a skill she has ever thought about passing on to either of us), Em and I making up beds and moving furniture back into place. We couldn't do a thing about the burned-down candles in the dining room, but it was Timkat and we did have unexpected visitors, and it's not the first time we've used Sinclair stuff when they left us in charge of the Big House. We filled all the wood boxes. And— this is lucky—Papà Menotti gave Momma a bottle of Chianti, which she left on Colonel Sinclair's desk. The Sinclairs never ask any questions about where Momma's thank-you presents come from, European wine being rarer than fuel around these parts.

Then we spent the next three days working on landing. Neither me nor Em has satisfied Momma's high standards for solo flight, but she's let me land by myself (and she hasn't let Em, which Em is surprisingly stoic about). I can land now with Momma's hands completely off the controls. At first she had to prompt and coax me every second—"Little bit more power, sweetie pie—little more power there—hear the wires singing? That's the right note for landing—" Em watched it all from the backseat and said that Momma was holding her hands up in the air over her head the whole way down. She never touched the controls. After we were on the ground, she and Emmy both burst into applause, clapping like crazy. And the next time, Momma didn't say anything, just let me do it by myself.

Now we are here in Addis Ababa so Momma can renew her photography permit. It was the Italian pilots' visit that made her think about it. She dug it out and discovered that it had expired about six months ago. Getting any kind of paperwork done is always a pain in the neck, and nobody ever checks for permits in Tazma Meda, which is why she had not done it sooner.

I got to fly the whole way here, with Momma sitting behind me, telling me what to do, and Em will get to fly back. I have a feeling she's not going to like it. She is surprisingly crabby about flying. She makes a big fuss about the checks and the fuel and the oil and stones on the runway, putting off takeoff as long as she can, then hanging on to the stick for grim life (I know 'cause I have to sit in the back and it *is* scary when she lands). And two solid hours of flying *is* exhausting. That's twice as long as any lesson Momma's given either of us up to now.

Apparently Em did find the way here herself, though. She was giving Momma directions from the backseat, and Momma was passing the headings on to me. I didn't realize it till afterward. I must have made Em work *hard*—I kept forgetting to watch my heading and I drifted off course about twenty times. Every time, she had to put me right.

The most panicky thing about landing at the new airfield at Akaki, which is about a dozen miles outside Addis Ababa, was how many people were watching. A strange airplane always attracts hordes of people. I kept thinking of Colonel Augustus, back when we were first here for the coronation, and what a fool he made of himself with everyone watching. So then I got nervous and circled the field about four times to check the wind—of course that was just long enough to give everybody within about a mile a chance to come out and stand there, staring up and wondering who in the world would be flying into this new Imperial Ethiopian Air Force field in an Italian aircraft without the Regia Aeronautica flag painted underneath its wings.

Eventually Momma yelled at me, "If you don't line up and land this time, I'm going to do it myself."

I glanced back, and, right behind her, there was Em smiling encouragingly and waving her hands with her thumbs linked together to make wings—our secret greeting. Momma gave me her firm Nod.

So I lined up and came floating down.

Momma sat there absolutely silent—she didn't say a thing to me as I landed. I wasn't using any power, and all you could hear was the sweet song of the wind in the wires. The wheels just kissed the ground in a cloud of red dust, and we all coughed and spluttered. Of course I had to weave back and forth to see around the Romeo's high nose as we taxied to the aircraft sheds at the other end of the field, and Em waved at everybody on both sides of the plane more like a strutting rooster than a White Raven.

I have got the hang of it. I really do. It is the first time I have landed anywhere but Beehive Farm, and it was *perfect*.

The problem with being a crackerjack is that you cause just as much of a sensation as you do if you are a clown. I caused more of a sensation when I climbed out of the cockpit than even Em and Momma did. They are white women—but now I am a flying Ethiopian.

And no one flies in Ethiopia except the Italians patrolling the borders, and the French instructors at Akaki, and the five dozen young Ethiopians they are training.

I think all the flying Ethiopians in Addis Ababa were there at the same time. The French instructor Pierre Ferrand came shoving forward to shake my hand. "Beautiful!" he cried out in Amharic. "Ready to join us?"

Momma laughed. "Not till he learns to find his way here himself," she said firmly.

Everybody helped us push the plane across the airfield, and we were all coated head to foot with dust by the time we'd finished. The plane, too.

Momma and Ferrand had a very serious conversation in French, which Em and I couldn't understand. Then we took all our gear—me with our clothes in a bundle on a stick, Momma with her German camera over her shoulder and a water skin on her head, and Em with the maps and compasses and china pencils and all the other equipment that you need for a long-ish flight, and we set out to walk the twelve miles to the city because there is only one train a day, and that came and went a long time ago. Fortunately, that is all we had to carry, because most of our cargo on a long flight is just extra water, in case we have to land in the middle of nowhere for some reason.

It was dark before we got to the middle of the city, but in spite of everything being covered with dust, it was cool. There are actually *more* trees closer to the city, because the emperor Menelik started planting them in the nineteenth century when Addis Ababa was first built, to make up for them cutting down all the native trees in the first place. The eucalyptus trees smell beautiful. So did the smell of cooking we passed every now and then—*berbere* spices and coffee and *injera* bread frying.

"Were you talking about fuel with the Frenchman?" I asked. We are supposed to put in an order of fuel for the Sinclair farm while we are here.

"We were talking about you," she said, sounding grumpy. "Ferrand wanted me to leave you there to do some ground school with the Imperial Ethiopian Air Force while I go into the city."

"Wow," Em and I let out in one breath. *Ground school with the Imperial Ethiopian Air Force.* That just doesn't sound real.

"You should have let him!" Em said, always loyal.

"Maybe I would have, if they would have taken you, too, Em," Momma said crossly. "But I didn't even ask. You're a white girl. I can't leave you there alone with a couple of French soldiers of fortune—ooh la la—not to mention dozens of young Ethiopian fliers. Can't expect Ferrand to take that kind of responsibility."

"How old was Delia when she went to France with you?" Em asked boldly.

Momma didn't answer right away.

Finally she said, "You hush up. Older than you. Okay, not much. Only a couple of months older than you. But she'd already been working in her momma's beauty parlor for two years. I'm not saying I don't trust those young pilots. They are from the best families, and they are the most educated young men in Ethiopia. But I *don't* trust those Frenchies. I know them too well myself, and you have no experience of men outside Tazma Meda."

"Well, what about Teo?"

"He is not joining the Imperial Ethiopian Air Force!" Momma said explosively. "That is not what we're here for."

She hitched the water skin more comfortably on its pad on her head. I could see her long white fingers tightening in the fold she used to hang on to it. She can do it as easily as Sinidu now. Part Ethiopian countrywoman and part *ferenji* flier.

"I didn't have any trouble getting that permit in the first place because of Ezra, but now that people are talking so much about war, I am worried I will have trouble renewing it because of being called Menotti, and also . . . *Gosh darn* those Italians."

She trailed off, shifting her grip on the water skin again. We waited, walking through the unfamiliar dog barks and murmurs of the scented city darkness.

Emmy exclaimed, "Jumping cats, Momma, are you going to renew your Ethiopian photography permit so you can take pictures for the Italians? Someone is going to accuse you of spying! How are you gonna get away with that? You have the most terrible poker face in the world!"

Momma laughed. "It's just pictures of mountains." Then she added, "The Italians aren't paying for them, though, so I thought I would sell them."

"To the *Ethiopians*?"

"Sure. Then everybody will be happy. It's not like I ever get my salary paid at the clinic. I bet they are more likely to pay me under the table for photographs that give them a jump on Italian military strategy than for my legitimate job. No official paperwork involved except the permit renewal."

"Wow," Emmy breathed.

"I don't like to do it," Momma admitted. "But we're burning too much fuel and I can't afford to take pictures that I'm not being paid for. Between your flying lessons and those double-crossing Italians, we need somebody to pay us for something."

It was a terrifically long walk after that. The cooking smells began to drive us insane after about ten miles.

Emmy finally broke Momma's sober silence with, "I am praying that Mateos still has the same cook."

"Mateos doesn't even know we are coming," Momma pointed out reluctantly.

Addis Ababa is a sprawling camp, a city of mazes, thousands of them, and they *change*. In Tazma Meda, you always know where everybody lives—people always come back to the same house eventually, even if they are out among the coffee trees or up Beehive Hill with the goats or hunting all night. But in Addis Ababa a lot of people move around, looking for work or following some noble in the hope that he needs another retainer, and so people's makeshift houses move around, too.

In the dark, among a thousand half-made huts, it started to feel dreamlike—unfamiliar but familiar in its own way—and it smelled so good, of eucalyptus and pepper and manure. Em grabbed my hand. I knew we were all worrying a little about hyenas.

It is a real shock the first time you figure out that some grown-up can't always be relied on. That you have to do some things for yourself.

I squeezed Em's hand three times the way Delia taught us when we were little. *Are you scared?*

She squeezed back bravely: *I am not scared.*

I whispered in her ear, "Momma's lost. Can you find the way?"

Oh, Momma would have *done* something—she would have

asked someone for shelter or led us to the American Legation eventually. But she was not going to find Mateos's house that night on her own.

Em stopped walking. She said in English, a little loudly, "Momma, I know how to get to Mateos's house from the spice market."

Momma stopped. She hitched the goatskin up again. "We will have to go back out to the main road."

"But I can find it."

Momma sighed. By now we were all ready to fall over and go to sleep right there, starving or not.

"That's what you said to do in the air, right, Momma, if you're 'uncertain of position'? Go back to the last point where you knew where you were. You get me to the spice market, and I will get us to Mateos's house."

She laughed softly. "Right, Em! Okay. Better late than never. Back to the main road this way. How the heck did you know I was lost?"

"I didn't. Teo knew."

I don't actually know how Em does it. She must have a little collection of landmarks stored in her head somewhere. We haven't been to see Mateos for about a year and a half. But she got us there right away once she'd oriented herself in the right direction.

I have *never* been so tired. And I never slept so well anywhere as on the floor next to Mateos's fire pit last night.

We made our real greetings in the morning.

"Ah, Teodros, my brother's son!" Mateos held me by the arms and flashed his bright, earnest grin. He kissed me on both cheeks. "You are so tall—old enough—"

"—to carry a spear," we all chorused, and then we all laughed nervously.

"Yes. Are you worried about it? Do not worry!"

Mateos was glad to see us, but soberly quiet, even for him. We don't see him very often, but he knows us well, and he started setting out all the food he keeps in the house. His house is even smaller than ours—maybe if he had a wife he would live somewhere more substantial. As it is, he has practically nothing but his sleeping mat and one *mesob* basket table for storing *injera* bread. He sleeps in his *shamma* and carries his spear and rifle with him when he goes out in the morning. He does still have the same cook, but she hadn't turned up yet the next morning when we all woke up ravening over last night's leftover soggy *injera*. But she got a beautiful meat feast of *sega wat*, chicken and lamb both, all ready for us the next evening—probably the last lamb we will get before Lent. It was a real treat after an unholy day hanging around waiting for someone in a new government building to put a stamp on Momma's photography permit.

Momma got the permit, though she didn't seem very happy about it afterward. The worry line was there between her eyebrows the whole way back to Mateos's house. But then she brightened up when Hirut, the cook, jumped up from where she was frying *injera* to welcome us and kiss everybody. Momma had brought honey and *tej* from Beehive Hill as presents, and Hirut ate with us. After supper, when things were a little calmer, Momma asked Mateos in a low voice, "Is Ras Assefa going to be all right?"

Ras Assefa is Mateos's boss. He is the younger brother of the man who was my own father's boss: Mateos worked for one brother; my father worked for the other. Ras Assefa, Mateos's boss, is a very highly placed railway official.

"Of course he is all right!" Mateos answered in surprise. "Why are you worried about Assefa?"

"We had to do a lot of waiting in the Parliament building

today, and that means we did a lot of listening. People say that in the last League of Nations meeting, the French gave a big chunk of the Ethiopian railroad over to Italy. So what does that mean for people who work for the railroad? Maybe Italy will come and ask if that pompous, racialist bully *Il Duce* Mussolini can borrow their trains."

Mateos laughed. "Ras Assefa will be all right. He is a landowner, a *ras*, a lord. Words on a page three thousand miles away are not going to make a difference to his status in the emperor's eye. It is kind of you to ask."

"Well, here is a question for you, then." Momma took a deep breath, hesitating. The worry line suddenly got deeper. She dropped her question like a bomb falling from an airplane.

"Could Teo come along with you and meet Assefa tomorrow?" Em and I stared at her.

Mateos looked at me thoughtfully. "Ras Assefa can certainly give your boy work, Rhoda. You're lucky you're here this week— for Timkat last month, we were in Aksum, Assefa's home."

"Oh, I do not want to leave Teo here, but maybe if he could meet Ras Assefa himself—" She cut her words off, going red. Em is right about her terrible poker face. Not one of us had any idea what she was getting at, but Em and I both knew she was not trying to get me a job as a foot soldier.

"Let Teo come with me tomorrow and he can have a taste of a soldier's work," Mateos said agreeably. "There are boys his own age in Assefa's guard. It will be a better afternoon for him than filling out forms."

At this point, Em exploded, "*Momma!* That is *not fair!*"

I was more baffled than outraged—*now* what was going on? "But you wouldn't let me stay with the Ethiopian pilots!" I pointed out.

Momma leaned over to me and said sharply in English,

"Listen, Mr. Invisible, I have a mission for you. And I am not talking about it in front of the cook. So just smile and say yes."

I glanced over at Em, begging her silently for her opinion on this strange suggestion. She had her lips pressed together like she didn't trust what would come out if she tried to say anything.

"Emmy!"

Her hands were in her lap. She twisted her thumbs together and made wings. It was an invisible push.

"Well?" Mateos asked. "Will you come with me tomorrow and meet Assefa's soldiers?" His quick, bright grin is hard to resist. I wonder if I do that—suddenly make people notice me by smiling at them. I will have to watch it.

Em's hands closed and spread open again in her lap, daring me.

"All right," I said.

MOMMA EXPLAINED WHAT WAS GOING ON AFTER WE'D gone to bed, whispering low in my ear once we were all snuggled down on the carpets behind a curtained-off partition of Mateos's tiny house.

"I got my permit back *because of* those pictures I took for the Italians. The Ethiopians want them, too, so I am going to give copies of everything to Haile Selassie, and the Ethiopian government will pay me for them. And I think that's fair. I said they could pay me through Ras Assefa, but they said *you* have to deliver the pictures, because I am too conspicuous. We don't want the Italians to notice anything. So that's what I want you to do tomorrow."

"I'm not really invisible," I protested.

"You mostly are," she said. "You are quiet and polite, like Mateos."

"She means you are clever about reading people's minds," Em translated. "Like Mateos."

"So why can't Mateos do it?" I demanded. I was not sure how seriously to take these compliments.

"Mateos doesn't know about it, either. And I don't want him to get in trouble for sharing Italian military photos."

"What about *you* getting in trouble, Momma? What about *me*?"

"The photos are *ours*, so it's all right. You were flying the plane when I took most of them."

Em was a bundle of excitement over me doing a real, live Black Dove mission, and she is also consumed with envy.

But it was easy—I just had to do what everybody told me to do and go where they took me. That is pretty much what I always do.

Before Mateos and I left in the morning, Momma slid a slim cardboard envelope into the front pocket of my khaki shirt as she kissed me good-bye.

Mateos gave me his extra spear so I would not look like an idiot. Or you could say it was to make me invisible. Following Mateos through the paths between the maze of huddled houses and shacks, I watched his feet, trying to move as quickly and quietly as he does.

Everything in Addis Ababa is new, and in the blue light before dawn, it looks like nothing real—a jumble of shapes thrown together, packed tight, and none of them matching. And then you get to the Parliament and government offices and . . . you *still* feel like you are in a dream. These buildings are all European and they are beautiful, but they are *so new*.

The emperor's palace was glowing as rosy as Beehive Hill in the early sun as we came close. Outside the gate were a thousand people waiting for jobs, as always. It is fooling yourself to pretend they are doing anything else. It is still a poor country and we are always forgetting how lucky we are in Tazma Meda.

I got to walk right through this crowd on our way to meet Ras Assefa's personal guard because Mateos brought me. And also because I am dressed in respectable khaki shorts and a shirt, almost like a uniformed soldier. It feels a lot like pretending to be Black Dove even if I'm not pretending on purpose—it feels like I blend in, but I don't really belong here.

That set me a little bit on edge. With Momma's photographs in my pocket, I couldn't help feeling apprehensive. And I worried about what I was going to say to people, and not being able to hide my accent.

I know Mateos is supposed to be Ras Assefa's advisor, but as far as I can tell, his work is just to make Ras Assefa look important. That is also what his personal guard does. The guard, the people I spent the day with, is a crowd of young men who are trained like soldiers and act as Ras Assefa's escort. I got a glimpse of him as we escorted him to the Parliament buildings, and he just looked like an ordinary railway official, a little heavy, in a dark European three-piece suit and glasses. Mateos carried his sunshade for him—a white umbrella, also European. After Assefa and Mateos had gone inside to various meetings, the rest of us had to hang around most of the day waiting for them to come back out.

Mateos had told them I was his nephew and might be able to join them as a guard someday soon. I tried to keep my role simple and play "Goatherd Visiting His City Uncle." I got away with the accent, too, by being from a highland village no one had ever heard of. But three of Ras Assefa's retainers were about my own age, and I could not shake them off.

"New boy! Play! Tell us a story!" demanded one.

"A battle adventure," said another.

The oldest, whose name was Sergew, came to my rescue. "What do any of you children know of battle?" he scoffed. "You were all herding goats just like this fellow when the emperor squashed the coronation-year rebellion."

"I am no goatherd!" argued one of the others. "As you know, Sergew, I can throw a spear farther than you."

"Don't listen to the boasting," the youngest of them said. "None of us has seen battle. But you should have been with us last month, when we went up to Aksum. We felt like real soldiers, even without a battle. We marched forty miles a day!"

"We gave demonstration drills in all the villages in the Takazze Valley—"

I felt my shirt pocket to make sure I hadn't squashed the photographs yet. I could guess what was coming.

"The story can wait—let's see if the country boy can throw a spear."

So then we had to have a contest to see (1) who could throw the farthest, and (2) who was most accurate. Yosef and Habte Sadek's lessons came to my rescue. I was able to throw farther than some of them, which was respectable, but I was at the bottom of being accurate. The sun got higher. We took turns making a protective wall around two or three of us at a time playing games of *gebeta* with pebbles in the gravel. You couldn't be seen to be loafing, but there wasn't much of anything else to do.

"So, country boy, will you join Ras Assefa's entourage?" Sergew asked me. "Or the imperial guard?"

A few of them laughed. My spear-throwing skills are not up to imperial guard standards.

At that exact moment, a plane motored overhead. It was one of the biplanes from the Akaki airfield, probably training.

We all looked up. People pointed and exclaimed. People are amazed by airplanes, even in Addis Ababa.

"Imperial Ethiopian Air Force!" Sergew said.

"Air Force!" everybody clamored. "Beautiful! That was how Haile Selassie finished the coronation-year rebels—he sent in aircraft to shoot them down from the sky! Remember that?"

"How fast can the planes fly? What do you have to do to join the Air Force?"

"Do you know anybody who can get you in?"

I didn't say anything. They weren't aiming these questions at me anyway, but at anyone who would answer them, and I was working at being invisible.

"How long did it take us to march from Aksum—ten days? And that was fast going," said one who looked younger than me. "An aircraft would take you ten hours."

"Less," said Sergew. "An aircraft travels five times the speed of a train."

"Take off just after dawn and arrive in time for dinner!"

Sergew seemed to know what he was talking about. Or know more than anybody else there, anyway.

So I asked a test question.

"Do you know what the plane was? The one that passed over us?"

"Potez. Built in France. The emperor has three of them."

"How can you tell?" That was an honest question, because I can't tell one from another when they're flying over. Except for a Romeo, of course.

Sergew laughed. "It's the easiest. Our boss's brother, the general Amde Worku, took flying lessons in one of those. He has pictures of them in his house up north in Aksum."

It took me a moment to realize that the man he was talking about, Amde Worku, had been *my* father's boss—Gedeyon, my real father. The brothers Mateos and Gedeyon had worked for the brothers Assefa and Amde Worku, the emperor's loyal advisors and soldiers. Too bad I didn't have *this* to write about when I had to do that stupid theme about fathers for Miss Shore.

My father and Amde Worku must have taken lessons at the same airfield—maybe even flown in the same plane.

It made me *shiver*. To come all this way, to be among strangers, and to learn something like this.

"You should learn to fly," I said to Sergew, who was obviously interested in planes. "You should go join the Imperial Ethiopian Air Force."

"I'd join if I could, but I was born a slave to Ras Assefa and was bound to his service before I came with him here to the capital."

At the time, I really couldn't believe it. I mean, I *did*, but I *couldn't*. Stupidly, I had to make him spell it out.

"You were born a slave?" I repeated.

"Born before 1916," he told me. "That was the year of the reforms to gradually bring an end to slavery. The reforms started so we could join the League of Nations, long before Haile Selassie became emperor."

I was born in 1919. Sergew, born a slave, is only a little older than *me*.

Of course I know that slavery has not been completely outlawed here. It is one of the things that Grandma complained about when we got here. It is something that Momma insists is changing. And we don't see it, because the only wealthy Ethiopian person we know—Ezra—doesn't have any slaves. Or if he did, he freed them a long time ago. I can't imagine Sinidu keeping slaves. I really can't.

So hearing Sergew say that he was born a slave was like being punched.

He must have seen that in my face.

"Don't worry about working for Ras Assefa," Sergew assured me. "I have been free since I was a child. Ras Assefa freed all his slaves when the reforms were announced, and gave them work, too. I have made a contract with him and will not leave his service for gratitude. The air force is elite—I could not learn to fly without a sponsor or my own income."

"Ras Assefa is a good man to work for," someone else added. "You're with Mateos, country boy? He's your uncle? He is highly placed."

"It's true—when we're traveling as soldiers, Mateos is Assefa's closest advisor," Sergew said. "And we are lucky, too. At the festival of Timkat, when we were in Aksum, we had the honor of standing guard at the gates to Maryam Seyon. That's where they keep the Tabota Seyon, the sacred tablet that is the true Ark of the Covenant."

"You stood guard at Mary of Zion during Timkat!" I exclaimed. That really is an impressive honor. "What a blessing!"

I got to meet Ras Assefa himself right at the end of the day, when we escorted him back to his own house. At the gates of his compound, our troop melted away—some of them went to guard the house, and some of them were dismissed. When it was just me and Mateos left standing there, Ras Assefa clasped Mateos's arms and kissed him on both cheeks. Then he turned to me and did the same thing. Like the emperor, his European suit and glasses made him look as if he'd just come from a visit to the League of Nations in Geneva. Or like what he was: a railway official.

But I knew he was also an Ethiopian lord. A former slave owner. Someone who had made a decision to change things. Someone who was working on reform and modernization, probably harder than most people. He is old and new Ethiopia all in one.

I really noticed it in his house. He invited us inside. The stone walls are completely covered with Ethiopian paintings and woven decorations from top to bottom, and the thatched roof is completely hidden by European chandeliers. I think there must be hundreds of them, Venetian glass and Irish crystal, like a cave of ice. There is no electricity, but they are beautiful in candlelight. It has given me a fantastic new idea for a story: "The Land of Glass."

"Sit," Ras Assefa said to me. "I want to hear about airplanes! Mateos, go ask Efram to bring us tea."

Assefa and I were alone for about two minutes, and he didn't waste any time. He said simply, "Pictures."

I reached into my shirt pocket and gave him Momma's photographs of mountaintops. He slipped them out of the cardboard sleeve and leafed through them quickly. I couldn't see the pictures, but I could see that she'd labeled them all with their geographic coordinates so you could tell exactly where they were taken.

"Can these pictures be made bigger? Will she take more?"

"I think so," I answered cautiously.

"Very good," said Ras Assefa. "Please ask her to scout Tigray and the Eritrean border. She can stay with my brother, Amde Worku, in Aksum, when she is in the North. He can get her fuel." Seemingly out of nowhere he handed over a soft, heavy bag on a long cord.

"Under your *shamma*—quickly," he directed.

Even without looking I could tell the bag was full of Maria Theresa dollars, at least a hundred. Each one of Momma's pictures is probably worth Mateos's wages for a month.

But it will pay for the fuel we owe Colonel Sinclair.

"Thank you, Teodros. The emperor is indebted to Woyzaro Rhoda for sharing these," Ras Assefa said.

When Mateos came back in, soft-footed as a hunting lynx,

we'd already made the exchange and he didn't see any of it. So I guess Ras Assefa doesn't want to involve him any more than Momma does.

"Tea is coming," Mateos said.

"Do you like yours sweet?" Assefa asked me. "Coming from Tazma Meda, you must have a taste for honey!" He was so jolly and friendly that it seemed impossible we'd just done this shady deal. Or that he'd ever been a slave owner.

I wondered if Mateos, too, had been born Ras Assefa's slave. Probably not, though, because my father did not work for Ras Assefa, and Mateos was my father's brother.

"So you are learning to fly!" Assefa said to me. "My brother Amde Worku flew when he was in Europe. Amde Worku has been waiting for years to meet Gedeyon's son, and what wonderful news to tell him that you are learning to fly! An Ethiopian pilot is a rare thing. Mateos, see that Amde Worku knows Teodros will soon be a licensed pilot."

This is the kind of grown-up talk that always makes Em start squirming.

"I'm not old enough to be licensed yet," I said cautiously.

"You must meet Amde Worku soon," Ras Assefa said, ignoring my protest. He patted my shoulder, and I realized it was an order. He was reminding me he wanted Momma to photograph the Eritrean border. "Please, take more tea."

THE QUESTION OF WHETHER OR NOT MATEOS HAD EVER been a slave kept nagging at me. I didn't dare ask him about it. But I couldn't stop thinking about Aksum—the Eritrean border, Ras Amde Worku, the young soldiers who'd marched there on foot at the rate of forty miles a day. I could keep pace with Mateos as we loped home through the rough paths of Addis Ababa, but I couldn't have kept it up for forty miles. Or been able to walk forty miles again day after day for a week or more.

"When you were in Aksum for the Timkat festival, guarding the church of St. Mary of Zion, did you get to see the *tabot*—the Ark of Zion?" I asked. Habte Sadek would love to hear about this when we got home.

"They never take the true one out, not even at Timkat. The only man who can go near it is the Guardian, the holy man who cares for it. Anyone else would be blinded on the spot if he saw the Ark of Zion!"

It is hard to get Mateos to talk about himself, but I could not help wondering about his opinion.

"Do you believe that?"

Mateos fell silent for a long time.

"I believe you would not survive an encounter with the Ark," he said finally. "It might not harm you to see it any more than it would harm you to see a priest in his full rich finery, but you would be killed if you touched it. You would be killed before you got close. Someone would stop you. It is a treasure too holy to be made light of, and that gives it power—even if it is only the power of men acting on its behalf. With war looming and the Italians in Eritrea so near our border and Aksum, you can see why the priests at Maryam Seyon might want a military guard."

"Is there really going to be a war?"

It was worth asking Mateos—I bet he knew more than Momma.

"I hope not. If there is, it will not be the emperor's fault. He begs and begs for peace, for assistance from the League of Nations, for a treaty, for a solution."

Mateos suddenly stopped walking, and turned to me in the

dark. I could only see his profile, not his expression. "I hope not," he repeated. "But I am afraid anyway. In Aksum, so close to the border, we saw aircraft overhead all the time—giant things with three engines, playing in the sky like well-fed lions in open country. They are safe enough at a distance, but what will happen when they get hungry? And how can anyone with a spear protect himself from cannons in the sky? Aksum's priests and treasures and monuments will fall when the invasion comes, however hard the local warriors fight."

He paused.

"What will you do, Teodros, if we take up spears? You will have the advantage of flight. Will you fight for us? Will your *ferenji* mother stay here?"

"She was a nurse in the Great War. She believes in peace. She will fly to aid the wounded in battle. Maybe I can help her."

You know, that almost sounds like I am talking about St. Kristos Samra—*she flew to hell. She is the mother of peace.*

If we can keep the plane, it is not too crazy to think that Em and I could help out in a field hospital if there is a war. I wish I had some kind of real training. Ezra and Assefa had to go to Scotland to learn their doctoring and accounting skills. Em and I will never learn anything more than what's on Vera Sinclair's bookshelf unless we leave Tazma Meda. Momma is right that teaching us to fly is the only education she can give us.

I WAS EXPECTING EMMY TO BE LIKE A HUNGRY LION herself after her day of hanging around with nothing to do except to be jealous of my adventure, but she surprised me.

"Momma and I went to make sure that the Sinclairs' fuel was

going to be delivered—we walked to the depot and nagged and bribed them, and told them four hundred times where to leave the cans for the mules to pick up, and Momma even bought them food for the journey. And then we rode with them in the truck to the edge of the city and waved good-bye as they drove off. Walking home, we were so hot and tired that when we came to St. George's church we went inside just to sit down and cool off. The palm matting under your feet always feels like silk after you've been trudging along the road all day! We went and knelt on the women's side, and you know what . . . It was *so nice* just sitting there with Momma, being quiet. Like being in meeting. But nicer, 'cause we were just doing it for fun."

"When did Momma ever come along with us to meeting!" I laughed.

"Huh." Em thought about this. "You're right. She was always in bed."

"I know what you mean, though. It's like being in the chapel at Kristos Samra. Close to something you can't explain."

"I know the churchmen look at us and think, *Ferenji heathens!* But nobody kicks you out. They welcome you anyway, and let you think in their beautiful places."

"Like—"

She knew exactly what I was going to say, and laughed. "Like being in the sky."

Date: Feb. 7, '35 (Ter 30, 1927)
Type of Machine: Romeo Ro. 1
Number of Machine: I-STLA
Airfield: Beehive Hill Farm, Tazma Meda
Duration of Flight: 20 min.
Character of Flight: Disastrous
Pilot: Momma
2nd Pilot or Pilot Under Training: Emilia Menotti

Remarks:

I STILL CAN'T LAND. UGH. I JUST WORRY ABOUT birds *all the time*. And I'm not likely to make a successful landing anytime soon for two reasons: (1) I tore the tire, so now it needs patching, and (2) the little rains are about to start.

After Teo flew back here and did another of his beautiful slow-floating-ibis–like landings while I greeted Ezra and Sinidu from the back by waving my *shamma*, Momma wanted to give me a chance to practice, too. On my very first touchdown, I was in such a panic about hitting a bustard—which wasn't even in my way—that Momma snatched the controls away from me at the last second. Then I tore the tire when I did manage to land.

I HATE LANDING.

It is nice to be back in Tazma Meda—nice to be back on Beehive Hill Farm, where everything feels so safe. We went up to the Big House to make a triumphant presentation of the receipt for the fuel delivery that is on its way (we beat it here because we flew), as well as the accumulated money we owe the Sinclairs for the sundry things we have borrowed, and everybody was feeling so relieved and pleased to have our good relations (and fuel) restored that the Sinclairs invited Momma to stay and share Captain Adessi's Chianti with them. Afterward, we had supper with Ezra and Sinidu.

"That is the worst landing I have ever seen you make!" Sinidu teased Momma.

"That was Em," Momma said, shaking her head.

Teo said quickly, "There was a bustard on the field. We had to go around to avoid hitting it, and ran over its nest on the landing run."

"Poor thing!" Sinidu said. "But silly of it to nest before the rains!"

So I had an excuse. But I know I am bad at it all on my own without help from bustards flapping around all over the airfield.

This is one time when White Raven is not going to help me one bit. White Raven taught herself to fly by watching people land on the beach where she grew up being raised by wild ponies (Delia and Momma did a flying show on Chincoteague Island for the firemen's carnival in 1926, and me and Teo *loved* the swimming ponies). Okay, those White Raven details are pretty far-fetched. But until now I actually thought that White Raven teaching herself to fly was more realistic than her being raised by a herd of swimming ponies. Now I am not so sure.

# EPISODE FROM "THE STORM BIRDS"

### (1932?)

The strange plane struggled and fought to land on the dark beach, but the rising wind blew it out to sea. The best it could do was to put the wheels down on the sandbar. It got there just as the light faded. The tide was rising with the wind. Soon the sandbar would be covered.

White Raven could not see the pilot, but she knew there must be someone flying the plane. He might be all right if the plane did not float away or the water did not cover it completely.

"No one but us can save that plane," White Raven said to her friends.

Hurricane and Seagrass and Willowbark stamped restlessly in the sand at the edge of the waves. Seagrass whinnied a sharp question.

"I don't need to ride—I will swim with you," White Raven answered. "Save your strength for the trip back."

Hurricane tossed her head defiantly at the storm, and they all pushed forward into the rising waves at the same time.

They could only see the sandbar when the lightning flashed, but finally they made it. The wheels of the flying machine were already underwater. Seagrass pushed his strong back beneath the aircraft's wing on one side, and Hurricane and Willowbark took the other side.

When the water rose high enough, they would be able to swim the plane to shore safely on their backs.

White Raven climbed up to look for the pilot. There was no one in the cockpit. She pulled herself up through the wires until she got to the top of the upper wing. There was the strange pilot! He had climbed up to get away from the waves. He was almost invisible against the dark sky, perched above his aircraft like a nesting bird.

He held out his hand for her to shake. *"Selam!"* he cried. "Peace! My name is Black Dove! What are you doing out here in the ocean with this terrible storm coming? Looks like we are in the soup together!"

"I'm White Raven!" she answered as she shook his hand. "This island is my home, and I am here to help!"

"Thank you," he said. "Did you notice that our names are a perfect match?"

Just then, the plane floated free of the sandbar. Hurricane brayed a warning from underneath the wing she was helping Willowbark hold up.

"Hang on tight!" White Raven yelled. "My friends are going to save your flying machine. But it might be a bumpy ride!"

Date: April 15, '35 (Miyazia 7, 1927)

Type of Machine: Romeo Ro. 1

Number of Machine: I-STLA

Airfield: Tazma Meda to "Delia's Dream"!
   N 12° 58' 10", E 38° 50' 29"

Duration of Flight: 1 hr. 30 min.

Character of Flight: navigation training

Pilot: Momma

2nd Pilot or Pilot Under Training: Emilia Menotti

Remarks:

I STILL HATE FLYING.

No amount of pretending I am White Raven is making me like it. It is only the thought of White Raven and her bravery and her adventurousness, etc., etc., that makes me able to march out to the stupid plane and climb into the stupid cockpit and take the stupid controls. I am disgusted with myself. But I am scared of it. How can I love being in the sky so much and be so scared to do it myself?

I am not even any good at driving the plane to the end of the field on the ground. I keep trying to go in a straight line, but of course I can't see where I'm going, because the nose is so high up. You're supposed to weave back and forth. I nearly killed us all today, and it was *on the ground.*

I am good at finding my way across long distances. In that, I am exactly like White Raven. I am good at it on the ground and I am good at it in the sky, too. In flight it is all about timing and mental arithmetic. You get to use all the things you think you're never going to use—the compass Papà gave me for Christmas and the silver stopwatch he gave me for my twelfth birthday, and all those hours of Miss Shore torturing us with geometry and algebra and slide rules. Although, boy, am I glad she has flown the coop even if it does mean we never get another lick of education.

Today was the first morning after the rains when the sun came up and everything was suddenly green, and Momma came springing into the house to wake us up with so much bounce I thought it was Sinidu.

"Teo, race down to Ezra and tell him we're going away for a couple of days. I warned him I'd have to make this trip as soon as the rains were over. I have photographic work that's already overdue and today's the day!"

"For a magazine?" I asked.

"If I'm lucky, some of the pictures might end up in a magazine. Teo, for goodness' sake, don't let Sinidu come hiking up here with that new baby to make us breakfast when Emmy can do it herself. Emmy, up and at 'em, *breakfast.* And then I need you to plot the trip with me."

"Where are we going?"

"Aksum! Ras Assefa asked us to come. The holiest city in Ethiopia! And you two are coming with me. I have to take photos, but we'll make it into a holiday. We'll see the standing stones and the chapel where they keep the *real* Ten Commandments. Isn't that where Habte Sadek's brother ended up? And we'll visit Ras Amde Worku. Ras Amde Worku is the one who was helping to establish the Ethiopian Legation in France, the one who Teo's father worked for. Mateos told me he wants to meet Teo."

Teo and I glanced at each other, wide-eyed. He pulled on his shirt in about a second and took off with Momma's message for Ezra.

159

"I'm going to let you work out the whole course, Emmy," said Momma. "I'll check it, but I want you and Teo to do as much of the work as possible, since this is our first really big flying trip together. It'll be good practice for you, and it'll free me up to do the camera work."

Normally we *love* going on trips with Momma. This time I was worried about having to do the flying myself. "How far is it?" I asked.

"About three hundred miles. We could easily do it in one long flight, but I think it would be fun to make an overnight stop on the way," Momma said. "That way you two can take turns flying. And we'll camp, like I do with Ezra and Sinidu when we make our flying clinic visits."

"Don't we have to give the plane back to the Italians?" I asked.

"We're in the clear as long as they still want us to take pictures for them. And we'll be practically on the border anyway, up in Aksum. We can fly on to Eritrea and visit Papà Menotti."

"Momma, you have got a screw loose," I said. Because the last thing we need to do is make anybody think we are running errands for the Regia Aeronautica or conspiring with them or something. Even if we are. "Don't you listen to the radio? Every time there is news it is about the Italian soldiers piling into Eritrea and Italian Somaliland. Waiting. It's like the way those kids in New Marlow used to hang around outside the school just *waiting* for me and Teo to come out so they could take our pencils and pelt us with spitballs. The Misses Larson were just as useless as the League of Nations when Haile Selassie asks them for help."

"We have friends on both sides here." Momma smiled her most fantastic and enthusiastic smile. It is darned hard not to be infected by her excitement when she is looking forward to something.

Momma is not very patient with me, and we argued a *lot* over the wind-speed calculations when we figured them out this morning—I know she knows more than I do, but she is so darn ambitious. She wants to go this wiggling, slow scenic route over the Simien Mountains, but she also wants me and Teo to take turns flying the plane, and neither one of us is really up to what she calls "canyon flying," where you go scooting low and close to the sides of the mountains. I am especially not up to it. I am too jittery about the unpredictable wind that mountains make.

Actually, I am too jittery about the whole airplane even when the wind is steady. That is the part Momma doesn't really seem to understand. It is true she was scared about letting us take over the controls in the first place, but she still seems to think it will all come naturally once you've done it a couple of times. The fact that it is coming naturally to Teo is not helping me at all.

You'd think she'd *remember* how hard she had to work just to get someone to give her a lesson.

You know she hasn't forgotten how Delia died.

We have come halfway to Aksum today, and that is where we are now—camped on top of a tableland high in the Simien Mountains. It is all grass, very narrow, and completely impossible to reach on foot. There aren't even any goats up here. The only living things are bearded vultures nesting in the crags of the cliff. There were a lot of them soaring below us as we came in, but they were interested in wildlife down where the ridge isn't as steep and they didn't get in our way as we floated down from above. Up here, there are no trees, no nothing, just flat grass on a plateau exactly the length and width of a runway.

It was one of my best landings ever. I was so relieved to be done and not to have hit a vulture and not to have to fly the rest of the way, because it is Teo's turn tomorrow. I let the plane putter along across the plateau, and I didn't realize how narrow it was. I was *trying* to weave back and forth so I could see where I was going, and I didn't realize how close we were to the edge until Momma suddenly yelled at me and stomped on the right rudder, shoving the power on at the same time to make the turn tighter to get us away from the edge. I was about to take us right over the cliff at about five miles an hour.

Momma took over taxiing and parked the plane right in the middle of the ridge. I sniffed quietly to myself for being such a stupid fraidy-cat. Momma turned the engine off and then stood up in her cockpit and leaned over to give my shoulders a squeeze.

"Come on, sweetie-pie. That was a beautiful landing you did! I'm not mad at you. Let's get out and look around."

Momma put her arms around our waists, and we walked from one end of the ridge to the other before we set up our camp.

This tableland is empty and perfect, and it is completely ours. There is no way anyone else in the world could have ever set foot here. We are the first human beings *ever* to be here. Like explorers discovering America.

"We can name it," Momma said.

"Italy-Doesn't-Know-It's-Here," I said in Amharic.

"Shangri-La," said Teo, which is a made-up paradise out of *Lost Horizon* from Vera Sinclair's bookshelf. "Or Solomon's Temple."

Momma said firmly, "Delia's Dream."

Teo and I glanced at each other quickly and away again before either of us giggled, because Delia's Dream is kind of corny. But we let Momma name it. Because that is why we're here and that is what this place is. A place in the African sky that doesn't belong to anybody. A place where war will never come.

It is incredibly quiet here. The Sinclairs have sometimes got the generator going at night, or their dogs bark, or hyenas hoot in the bush, or there are bugs singing, but here there is no noise at all. It is too cool for bugs because it is so high up. All I can hear is Momma breathing. She is lying on her back, very quietly looking at the sky, and Teo is lying on his stomach next to me, reading what I write.

I'll have to stop writing when it gets dark because there is nothing to build a fire with up here. I know what he means now about how tired he was after he flew to Addis Ababa, because I am absolutely beat.


Hey, White Raven.

You want to write, Teo?

I want to tell you those vultures scared me more than when you nearly drove over the edge of the cliff.

Me too. I hate flying.

Really? Really really? Or just for today?

I hate it all the time when I'm doing it.

Wow, don't let Momma read that.

She'll just think we're working on *The Adventures* if she sees us taking turns with the pencil. Anyway, look at her: she is way up in the clouds with Delia right now.

Yeah.
Hey, Em, you know all that stuff you wrote about this place being empty and being ours? Explorers discovering America? You sounded just like Captain Adessi. "This is good land and it

ought to belong to people who know how to appreciate it." You make it sound like we colonized this place.

Well, we did!

We didn't. It doesn't belong to anyone. You don't know who owns this land. Maybe they have never been up here, and maybe they never will. But just because you got to it first doesn't make it yours.

You mad at me now, Em?

Stop pestering me when I am trying to write a flight log entry.

Ha-ha—this is one more flight log entry you will *never* let Momma read.

I'm not mad at you. I am thinking about what you said.

Flight Log Entry

Date: April 16 & 17, '35

Type of Machine: Romeo Ro. 1

Number of Machine: I-STLA

Airfield: Takazze Valley to Aksum/Aksum to Amba
    Kwala via Debre Damo

Duration of Flights: 1 hr. 50 min., 1 hr. 25 min.

Character of Flight: cross country

Pilot: Momma

2nd Pilot or Pilot Under Training: Teodros Gedeyon

Remarks:

MOMMA SAYS KEEP A LOG, EVEN WHEN YOU DON'T
want to.

Em spent so long after supper curled up in a corner crying,
as if it was *her* and not me, that Momma finally told her to go
take a walk and cool off. And Em just *went.* She won't get lost,
and if she does she can always ask anybody to direct her to Ras
Amde Worku's house, which is where we are staying. Momma
did say he wanted to meet me.

I would have gone with Em, but we are not sure I am
allowed to.

So I'm just going to sit here and write about the last couple
of flights till she gets back. There are plenty of candles.

Ras Amde Worku is the wealthiest man I think we've ever
stayed with. His house is stone and flat-roofed, three stories
high, like an old church. It is surrounded by gardens. He has

got a collection of European glass and crystal chandeliers just like his brother Ras Assefa. I am writing beneath them, and the candlelight is being thrown back and forth in them like shooting stars. It is like being in a crystal cave. As though we have walked into a scene from *The Land of Glass*.

And guess what—there are pictures of Potez biplanes all over the house. Sergew was right.

Here, if I were being Black Dove, I would take a deep breath and make myself invisible so I can make a cool and clever escape. But I am not really Black Dove. No chance of going invisible now. I'll take a deep breath anyway and write carefully, as if Miss Shore were going to read it. I will *try* to be organized.

THERE IS NO AIRFIELD IN AKSUM. THERE ARE PLENTY of fields outside the city where you can land a plane if you feel like it, and I guess most people choose the same one we did if they come here in a plane.

Aksum is as beautiful as we thought it would be, mysterious and a little strangely creepy. When we got here yesterday, we flew all around the city—*I* flew all around the city—looking for a good place to land. Aksum is very easy to find because everything nestles in the fold of two hills at the edge of a wide upland plain, and right at the point where the hills come together is the two-thousand-year-old graveyard full of standing stones seventy feet tall. We saw them for the first time from the air, and Momma got me to fly pretty low overhead. People came out and waved. Momma took pictures.

"Partly I am documenting," she said importantly, after we landed and Em and I were tying down the plane. "In case there is looting." She unfastened the camera so she could take it with us.

"What looting?" Em exclaimed. "You mean if Italy invades, they're going to run away with a bunch of standing stones? I'd like to see them try!"

"What do you think Cleopatra's Needle is, in Central Park in New York City? Egyptian loot. They took one just like it to London, too. And that was more than fifty years ago; it would be easier to transport them now. But you know—" Momma sighed happily. "I like taking pictures of things no one else has photographed before."

There was a crowd of people who'd seen us overhead and had come to watch us land, and they were eager to help us find a place to stay. When Momma mentioned Ras Amde Worku, we got guided to his house right away. He came into the garden to greet us. Wearing a *shamma* edged with gold thread and a short leopard-skin cloak, he looked like a prince out of a story. And he kissed me and cried when Momma told him who we were.

I'm not going to write about that. This is a flight log.

Aksum is not as big as Addis Ababa, but it feels more like a real place. It is so much *older*. And even though it is in a different kind of landscape and the houses are different, and the people on the street and in the market mostly speak Tigrinya and you can't understand them, it feels more like Tazma Meda than Addis Ababa. It feels like a real home to the people who live here.

This morning, we walked back to the plane while it was still dark so we could be ready to take off right at sunrise to get pictures of the monuments from the air with the light all slanty and the shadows long. I volunteered to fly, just to get Emmy off the hook for the time being. I have not figured out what's going on in her head about flying. She is the one who got all the

Tazma Meda kids to play tag on the radio mast. She is not afraid of heights or of being in a plane. I know she is as daring and as talented as White Raven. So how can she be afraid to *fly*?

I don't think about Black Dove in the air. It is just me being Teo. What makes me good at it? The Delia in me, maybe? Or just me wanting to prove to Momma that she doesn't need to worry? It is like that time she let me ride bareback with her, but better, because I can do it again and I can do it myself.

Today I got to circle around and around the ancient grave-yard in Aksum, very low over the standing stone monuments. Then we made a low pass over Maryam Seyon Church—Mary of Zion, where the real Ark is kept, the Tabota Seyon—which is kind of cheating, since women aren't allowed inside the walls around the church. If we'd been on the ground, neither Momma nor Em would have been able to see over the walls.

The churchmen came out and waved at us (everybody always waves at us). I thought of Habte Sadek's brother. Amazing to think we might *know* some of these people, or know people they knew. But I guess none of these connections are coincidences—they all trail back to Ras Amde Worku. It is because of Ras Amde Worku's brother going to university with Ezra that we ended up in Tazma Meda. Spiderwebs joined together.

Momma says she didn't take any pictures of Mary of Zion—that *would* have been cheating. Nobody cares if you take pictures of the ancient gravestones, but Mary of Zion is alive, and it is a private place. Taking photos without asking would be like looting it.

We flew west, over Yeha, and Momma took pictures from the air of the temple that is two thousand years old. Em says she didn't know where we were going—Momma was making her take notes so Em could find our way back without Momma's help when we turned around. We crossed weird humpbacked mountains and then we were in drier country among high, wide plateaus, which are called *ambas* around here, most of them as bare and empty as the tableland where we'd camped the night before. Then, ahead of us in the middle of nowhere, there was an *amba* that was full of houses.

As we got nearer, it started to look like a real village—all high and remote on the *amba*, with goats and a stone reservoir like the one at St. Kristos Samra on Beehive Hill, and vegetable gardens—very green because the rains only just ended.

"How do they get up there?" I yelled through the speaking tube.

"They climb up a rope," yelled Momma. "Follow the cliff around; you'll see."

So we did, and not only was there a rope but there was also a stone gatehouse at the top of it—carved into the rock like the St. Kristos Samra chapel, except this one was stuck halfway up a sheer cliff side.

"This is Debre Damo—a monastery!" Momma shouted. "Like the hermitage at home. But here, no girls allowed, like Mary of Zion in Aksum. Not even girl goats allowed here. Not even chickens!" She shouted something else that I didn't hear all of, but it was about how much Delia had wanted to see this— how the idea of it being banned for girls drove Delia crazy.

I was beginning to think the photos were just an excuse. This whole trip was just a Delia pilgrimage—the monastery Delia had wanted to see, my father's old boss from their days in France, Delia's Dream in the empty sky. Momma was all happy and excited. You can tell by the tone of her voice, even distorted and shouty through the speaking tube over the roar of the engine. She was here because this was a thing she had wanted to do with Delia, and now she was doing it with us. Delia is in her head, running the show, the way White Raven runs the show for Emmy.

Momma said afterward that she hadn't told us about Debre

Damo ahead of time because she hadn't been sure she'd be able to find it. She wasn't worried about getting lost—she just knew that finding this one tiny monastery on top of an *amba* plateau would be a little like looking for a needle in a haystack.

She got me to fly in a circle around the edges of the *amba*, very close. We could see *everything*—a boy wearing a thin *shamma* pulled over his face like an Egyptian mummy, taking honey from a beehive hung in a tree; two other boys drawing water from the big green stone cistern, and a very old stone church that looks a lot like the house we are staying in—like the carvings on the ancient pillars in Aksum. That church on that *amba* is supposed to be almost as old as the standing stone pillars in the ancient graveyard.

Everybody stopped work when the plane flew overhead, except one old man we decided was deaf and couldn't hear the engine, and they all came rushing out to get a look. I don't think they knew, or even guessed, that Em and Momma were forbidden women—of course they couldn't see anything about us but our goggles and waving arms.

But I felt guilty. Like a colonist again. It *is* a kind of looting, being able to nose down on things from the air. A kind of invasion. Like—like poking through Aunt Connie's drawers when she told us not to. Like pilfering Mrs. Sinclair's tinned cherries. We haven't set foot there, of course. But we've *seen* it.

On our second pass around the *amba*, a tall man loped calmly across from the old church carrying a spear. He didn't hurry, but he timed his pace so his path crossed ours. Then, just ahead of us as we passed low, waving at everybody along the edge of the *amba*, he threw the spear at us.

Em and I agreed afterward that it was the most beautiful throw we've ever seen. The spear soared high in a perfect arc, out over the edge of the *amba*, and passed us about fifty feet ahead of the Romeo's nose. If I'd been flying a couple of seconds faster, we'd have hit it—or I guess it would be right to say it would have hit us. That was how close to the edge of the *amba* we were.

But the spear missed us, and I watched it fall away to our port side, over the edge of the *amba*, down, down, down toward the valley floor until it was a black speck lost against the yellow stone and gray-green shrubs of the landscape.

It seemed to fall forever.

I thought of Habte Sadek, younger than me, rescuing his church treasures from the British army, his spear against their rifles.

I pulled the nose of the Romeo up and slowly turned back the way we'd come, calm as anything.

Behind me, I could hear Momma laughing her head off.

"Guess he told us!" she yelled.

*"He could have taken our propeller off!"* Em screamed at her from the rear cockpit.

"He wasn't trying to hit us," Momma said. "Or he would have. He was just telling us to get lost! Bet they don't get many air shows around here! Put Teo on track for Asmara, Em! Don't worry, we're not going all the way into Eritrea, but it makes a good place to aim for on the map."

That was how close to the border of Italian territory we were—we were using their new colonial city as a navigation point. I love Momma and will follow her anywhere, but I am beginning to . . . *worry.* I think she is too sure of herself and of her ability to charm people. I think she is ignoring too many rules about diplomacy. I am not sure she even knows what they are.

And the local laws. Do they apply to Momma? Or to Em? Because they seem to apply to me.

Em yelled the heading for me to take, and I think we crossed the border into Italian Eritrea anyway.

It is impossible to see where the border is. It's just more of the same yellow and brown mountains, dusted with green, seeming like they go on forever—there's no fence, no road—no *boundary*. It's like crossing from Pennsylvania into Maryland—nothing changes. I don't get the navigation, because there doesn't seem to be anything to navigate by, nothing but *ambas* and valleys in between with temporary green river bottoms. Sometimes little villages clustering together. We weren't flying very high, and from time to time we'd see the terraced fields of farms, or goats high up the sides of the valleys or on top of an *amba* that wasn't too steep to climb.

The world is too huge to find your way in from three thousand feet above the ground. Em keeps telling me it is easy if you do it accurately, even if you don't know what you're looking at. "Teo, don't worry about matching everything up. All you have to do is follow the compass heading."

It is true that accuracy is not my strong point.

The landscape below us was all so same, same, same for a while that one strange difference stood out like a scrawl of red crayon in a black-and-white newspaper.

The strange scrawl was an airfield.

Not just a flat place where the grass has been scythed, like at Aksum. Not just a landing field with one plane in it and a shed made of sticks with a corrugated iron roof like at Beehive Hill Farm. This was a real airfield with more planes than there were at the new Imperial Ethiopian Air Force base at Akaki the last time we were there. This was a real airfield, and it was right on top of one of the empty *ambas*.

The *amba* was wide and flat and grassy, much bigger than the tiny ridge we'd landed on in the Simien Mountains and named Delia's Dream. Unlike that ridge, this *amba* wasn't empty. There were wooden huts all along the edge, and there were planes parked everywhere—smart rows of Italian planes of the Regia Aeronautica with the Italian flag painted on their tails.

So this was where Papà Menotti was stationed—on an *amba* airfield on the Eritrean border, half an hour's flight from the holiest city in Ethiopia. If there is a war, Aksum has not got a chance of protecting itself.

"How do they get there?" I yelled, which was a dumb question—obviously they *flew* there. "I mean, how can they manage to stay there . . . ?"

It was one of the sheer-sided *ambas* you couldn't have scaled without ropes and picks. You couldn't have climbed to it without cutting stairs into the side of the cliff. They couldn't take trucks full of fuel there, or even carry it on muleback.

I glanced over my shoulder at Momma. She was calmly unfastening the camera from the mount.

"Go on. Fly closer! Right around the *amba*!" Momma yelled. "Beautiful!"

She'd come here on purpose. She'd known what she was going to find.

She didn't seem worried about it, so I tried not to be worried, either. I pushed the nose down and cut the power a bit and glided lower.

The top of the *amba* was as green as the lawn at the British Legation, since the rains had just ended. There was a great big water tank, and goats like they had at the *amba* monastery we'd just seen, except that the goats were penned so they wouldn't get in the way of landing aircraft. By the time we'd finished our second circuit around the *amba*, there were a couple of dozen people running around and waving and pointing.

"Go ahead and land!" Momma yelled. "And we'll refuel! This is Orsino's air base, and we have photographs to deliver!"

So I started to circle around again to get as long a landing run as I could. As I was leveling out the plane lurched in a heart-stopping way it wasn't supposed to. I glanced back over my shoulder again and thought my blood was going to freeze.

*"Fly the plane!"*

Momma shouted the order in the voice that *no one* disobeys, and I whipped my head around forward and steadied the plane in level flight.

Behind me, Momma was climbing out of her cockpit. When I looked over my shoulder at her she was on her feet. She had unbuckled her harness and was standing on her seat, bracing herself upright by holding on to the sides of her windshield. Her getting up had made the plane jolt.

*"What are you doing?"* I screeched into the wind.

She didn't answer. I glanced back at her again, holding the plane as steady as I could, and saw her step up out of her seat and set a foot calmly onto the body of the plane. She wasn't wearing a line or anything—she wasn't even holding on to one of the straps from her seat. I ground my teeth together, aware of her reaching up into the wires that crisscross between the lower wing and the upper wing. I snatched another glance backward and she was standing on the fuselage behind me, hanging on to a wire with one hand and waving at the men below with broad, happy sweeps of her other arm.

It is true that we have written about Black Dove and White Raven doing exactly this in the air. But writing about it is not the same thing *at all* as trying to fly a plane while your mother is standing on top of it waving at people.

I couldn't see her face, because she'd turned it away from the wind. But she was absolutely calm as could be. I imagined her beaming smile.

*"Jumping cats! What the heck, Momma!"* came Emmy's scream through the speaking tube.

But Momma couldn't hear her with her head up there in the wind. She was busy waving to her audience, who must have seen the Italian registration on the tail by now. Maybe they even knew who we were. I could see them cheering and waving handkerchiefs.

I flew like I was balancing egg crates on the wings. I didn't dare turn. When we reached the other end of the *amba*, I just kept flying straight ahead.

I felt the faint shifts of weight in the airframe as Momma climbed back down into the middle cockpit. And then I heard her voice through the speaking tube, as if everything was completely normal.

"Gee whiz, this is fun!" she said cheerfully. "You can turn around now. I want to land there and pick up some fuel. They're bound to have a good supply! Jiminy Christmas, if I thought it would get me wing-walking again, I'd have taught you both to fly a long time ago! Barnstorming in Ethiopia—"

"*Why*, Momma?" Em yelled.

"Just wanted to make sure they recognized us before we landed—" She cut herself off with a laugh. "Teo, you fly *just like your mother*," she said warmly.

All I really wanted to do was put my fingers in my ears so I could concentrate on landing without having to listen to her babbling. But I needed my hands to fly with and my ears to hear the wind in the wires.

Date: April 17, '35
Type of Machine: Romeo Ro. 1
Number of Machine: I-STLA
Airfield: Amba Kwala to Aksum
Duration of Flight: 40 min.
Character of Flight: cross country
Pilot: Momma
2nd Pilot or Pilot Under Training: Me (Em)

Remarks:

MOMMA PRATTLED AWAY, SOUNDING VERY HAPPY and pleased with herself. Every now and then, Teo glanced back to make sure she wasn't about to do another crazy stunt. But she was fine—she'd even strapped herself in again. I saw Teo's shoulders relax a little.

I am getting very good at reading Teo's shoulders.

I *saw* why Momma decided to show those soldiers she was a harmless barnstorming lady pilot and not an Ethiopian spy plane. And that is pretty much what she thinks she is, a harmless barnstorming lady pilot, scraping a living so she can keep herself in the sky.

I didn't think Teo saw what Momma and me had seen, though, the thing that made her scared. The Italians should have known who we were, and they didn't recognize us at first and it scared her. I didn't want to tell Teo. Not until we got out of there safely.

He did another of his beautiful bumpless touchdowns. Momma told him to cut the power, and he did, and soldiers came running up to greet us—all white. Momma asked in Amharic, "Can we buy a full tank of fuel from you?"

We can only talk to the Italians in Amharic!

Papà Menotti wasn't there. He was switching back and forth between bases. His friend Captain Adessi wasn't there, either, but apparently we'd just missed him. When we realized that we might get stuck with Adessi and not with Papà, we decided not to hang around there too long.

Momma gave them greetings from Ras Amde Worku and told them that he would pay for our fuel.

Ras Amde Worku owns that *amba*. It is called Amba Kwala. The Italians pay him *rent* for it.

"Doesn't it bother him that there are possible enemy aircraft parked so close to his hometown?" I asked Momma while the soldiers were filling our fuel tanks. "He is an Ethiopian general!"

"He seems to think that it will keep him safe. Not because they are on his side, because they are not, but just because they have a business deal. Kind of like me giving the Italians photographs of possible airfield sites so they let me hang on to my plane!"

So Teo turns out to be right about people owning land that looks like it doesn't belong to anybody.

Momma is also right—she is not so different from any of them. She is taking pictures for the Italians and selling the same pictures to the Ethiopians. She doesn't think of it as double-crossing in the least. It is just more of the sharing she does wherever she goes, making everybody love her when she lands on someone's doorstep, showering people with smiles and beautiful Tazma Meda honey and coffee.

After today, I understand how our ties to this country are tighter than I knew.

Teo won't write about it, so I will.

MOMMA IS GETTING WISE TO ME TRYING TO AVOID flying, and as soon as we were off the airfield she just *let go*. I don't think she would have let the plane fall out of the sky, but I wasn't brave enough to find out. I took the controls in a hurry.

I landed at the same field in Aksum where Teo landed yesterday. Momma did a lot of yelling at me: "Back! Back—pull 'er up! *More! Listen to the wind!*" et cetera, and it was not my worst landing ever. Ras Amde Worku had come out to the airfield to meet us. He wanted to see Teo flying, so he had to be disappointed.

Serves him right, too.

It was only midday and he took us riding. I think he is older than Momma, but it is impossible to tell. He is *kingly*. That is the right word for him in his leopard skin and cloth of gold. Hard to imagine him as a diplomat in Paris, or to remember that his brother Ras Assefa is a railway official in a suit. Ras Amde Worku brought horses for us, and he was standing there at the field where we landed, waiting like a lord in a medieval painting with a bunch of other men holding the horses.

We were all buffaloed into thinking this was going to be a real treat. We rode a couple of miles out of town where there is a rock with a thousands-of-years-old lioness carved on it. Momma and Amde Worku kept riding ahead so that Teo and I couldn't hear them chatting.

"You'd think they were old pals!" I grumbled.

"Aw, they are old pals," Teo allowed. "They were both taking flying lessons at the same airfield, weren't they, back in France."

We watched Momma and Ras Amde Worku riding a little ahead of us. They were both wearing white *shammas*, but she still looked like a tourist and he looked like the king of Constellatia. I had to remind myself that he wasn't any stranger to foreigners and that he got paid rent by Italian pilots.

Remembering about the Italian pilots helped me make up my mind about telling Teo what had happened earlier to frighten Momma.

I asked, "Remember the priest who threw a spear at us at the first *amba* we buzzed this morning?"

"I'll say so!"

"Well, remember when Momma climbed out of the cockpit while you were flying over the Italian airfield? She wasn't doing it to show off. That was what she made it sound like afterward, and that was why she tried to fool us with all that silly chattering. She got out of the cockpit because one of the soldiers was pointing a gun at us. She got out so he could see she was a white woman. So that he wouldn't shoot."

"But our plane is Italian!" Teo said.

"But it's not one of theirs."

"I sure hope she knows what she's doing," Teo said ominously.

We caught up to the others when they stopped to look at the carved rock. Momma was busy with the camera, so I didn't notice how her mood had changed. She let me take pictures of her leaning against the rock alongside the lioness. Then she showed Amde Worku how to frame the picture. She got it set up and focused for him, and he took a photograph of all of us standing there.

"Family group—with ancient Tigrayan lioness!" he joked in Amharic. "You are tourists today. Where did you go after you left Aksum this morning?"

"We circled over the ancient graveyard and the church of Mary of Zion here in Aksum, and then we went to find Debre Damo, the monastery on the cliff-top *amba*, where they only allow men," Momma answered. "I have *always* wanted to see Debre Damo!"

"You saw it from the air?" Amde Worku asked skeptically. "Did you photograph Debre Damo?"

"I did not photograph Debre Damo or Mary of Zion," she told him, sounding shocked. "I don't take photos of churchmen without asking for their blessing. I am not a real tourist!"

"They might think of you as an invader, however," Ras Amde Worku said, smiling so it didn't sound exactly like criticism. "But you are not the first. About a thousand years ago, Debre Damo was invaded and looted by a woman soldier called Judith."

"Really!" Momma exclaimed. "Well then, I am twice as glad I didn't take any pictures there. That *would* have been like a woman looting the place all over again."

Amde Worku laughed. He put Momma's camera carefully back into her hands and said, "You will take me to see it tomorrow."

"I owe you a flight," she agreed.

"You are indeed in my debt," he said calmly.

There was an awkward silence. For a moment, everybody stood around saying nothing, and Teo and I exchanged looks and wondered what was going on.

Finally, Momma said, "You can go ahead and tell Teodros what you have to tell him." With her voice still quiet and even, Momma added, "You have to tell him yourself, Ras Amde Worku. You have to tell him yourself, because I will not ever do it."

I didn't hear him say it. But I am going to write it down.

Ras Amde Worku walked away with Teo for a little while. They disappeared around the other side of the big rock with the huge ancient lioness carved on it. Amde Worku walked with a confident hand set on Teo's shoulder, guiding him, while Momma and I held their horses for them.

"What the heck?" I asked Momma, not for the first time that day.

"It's Teo's business," Momma said, her tone still so level and careful it sounded like she was trying not to move her mouth. "It's about his father. Something Teo has to hear about Gedeyon Wendimu. He can tell you himself if he wants to."

HE DID TELL ME HIMSELF, ON OUR WAY BACK TO Aksum. We rode a little bit behind Momma and our host, just the way we had on our way to see the rock lioness.

Teo looked different. You could see instantly. He looked like Momma looked in the first couple of weeks right after Delia died. Like someone had pumped all the life out of him, all the light out of his eyes. Like he had his eyes open, but he was sleep-walking.

"My father wasn't just Ras Amde Worku's secretary," he told me hollowly. "He was his slave."

I was so flabbergasted that for a moment I couldn't say anything. Then I just burst out with, "Didn't Delia *know* that?"

Teo shook his head. "I don't know. If she did, it's the one thing she never told Momma. Momma didn't know it till today."

"The French let Ras Amde Worku bring a *slave* with him to help them set up their foreign office?"

"They didn't tell anyone in France he was a slave. There are all kinds of ways you can be freed. As a gift. Or you can earn it. Amde Worku was going to free my father for the work he did in France, but Gedeyon died first."

"Wow," I said. This was shocking news for sure.

"Wow," Teo echoed bitterly.

I had a feeling there was more. I waited for him to say something else. I wanted to grab his hand and squeeze it four times, but we were both on horseback and he was too far away, and the look in his eyes was a little too private.

I knew he would tell me sooner or later, because he always does. So I waited.

Teo continued suddenly, "When I was talking to those soldiers in Addis Ababa, when we went to see Mateos before the little rains, one of them told me that if you were born to a slave before 1916, then you are automatically a slave, too. They are still a lot of old laws in place."

"Good thing you were born in 1919," I said.

He turned to look at me, and *he was crying.*

"1916 is the Ethiopian date," he said. "You know how the Ethiopian calendar is a little over seven years behind? You know how we always used to put the Ethiopian date on our themes for Miss Shore, just to annoy her, as well as the English date? The English year of the reform was 1924."

For the next couple of seconds, I could only stare at him in horror. Then I started crying, too.


I BET MATEOS KNOWS. I BET HE KNOWS AND NEVER said anything to Momma in the whole seven years she's been here. He is such a polite and private person—he wouldn't ever have mentioned something like that unless she mentioned it first. Probably he doesn't even find it shocking. Probably *he* was somebody's slave once, too, and it is just ordinary life for him.

Haile Selassie is trying to get rid of slavery gradually because he needs rich generals like Ras Amde Worku to give him loyalty without reservations. When people don't like his reforms, they rebel against him. The emperor can't risk offending his aristocracy with new laws they resent, and a sudden ban on slavery will leave a couple of million people with no work and no place to live. He can't do that when the whole country is about to be invaded.

How could Delia *not* have known? She must have known. But how could she have known *that* and never told Momma? How could she have wanted to go to Ethiopia *anyway*? Delia is the biggest dirty double-crosser of the bunch.

Teo stopped crying before we got back to the house, before anyone could see him. But I have pretty much not stopped.

Ras Amde Worku owns that Italian airfield, and he *owns* Teo, too.

Em, can I write on your paper? You okay? You were gone a long time.

*I am fine.*

I am worried they will make me stay here.

*Oh.* I was being selfish. I am sorry I went without you. It was just a stomp around the ruins. Trying to think. I won't leave you alone again, *I promise.* If they make you stay, I will stay, too. We are in the soup together. They can make you stay, but they can't make me go.

They might not let you stay with me.

———

Em? You okay?

*Damn. Damn. Damn.*

They can throw me out of the house, but they can't make me leave. They can't make me leave Aksum if they keep you here. They will have to tie me up and drag me out of town.

I think Ras Amde Worku is too polite to throw you out of his house, Emmy.

Black Dove, let's write. Let's work on a story. Let's work on Glassland.

Make me a prisoner in the Fortress of Clarity.

Got to rescue you.

## EPISODE FROM "THE LAND OF GLASS"

The entire Fortress of Clarity was made of the clearest glass, from the dungeons to the highest tower. White Raven could see the whole way through every room. She could see soldiers marching in a column down a glass corridor, and she could see a row of miserable-looking people sitting about ten feet apart from each other, not talking. Those were the prisoners in their cells. Clear glass walls separated the prisoners.

White Raven was sure they must have brought Black Dove here when they captured him. She could not see him in that cell block, but maybe he was invisible.

She looked again at the row of prisoners. She was too far away to see their faces, but they all glimmered with the iridescent luster that was ground into the skin of all Glasslanders. So none of them was Black Dove.

Because White Raven could see into the Fortress of Clarity, of course anyone inside could see her, too, but she was disguised in the uniform of a Glassland cavalry girl. White Raven had dusted her face and arms with powdered silver to imitate the Glassland luster. Nobody cared that she was standing beneath the big glass stronghold gate. She looked like she was reporting for duty or delivering a message.

She counted the prison cells, using the prisoners to mark them.

There was a gap. There was a space between Prisoners Number Three and Four, a space wide enough to hold another prisoner in a cell. From where White Raven stood, it looked as if the cell was empty. But there was no other gap in the line.

The high gate in front of her was barred. But the line of marching soldiers was coming in her direction, and soon they opened the gate and began to file through. They all nodded politely at White Raven as they marched past her. She smiled back and walked boldly into the fortress before the last soldier came out.

She headed straight for the cell that seemed empty. Her Universal Single Key would only work once. It was a risk to use it if her guess was wrong.

But when White Raven got close, she had no doubt she was right. Black Dove was waiting for her, watching through the clear glass door as she approached. She could tell because he was bleeding. He had left a smear of blood against the back wall where he had been sitting, and when he saw his partner he had stood and paced across the small cell to the clear door. He was standing there now. A single drop of blood suddenly appeared in midair and splashed to the clear floor, the only color in the room.

Now White Raven did not need to worry about wasting her one use of the Universal Single Key. She felt for the lock, found it, and fitted the key inside. The glass key shattered as she turned the handle, just the way the locksmith had explained would happen.

"*Tafash!* You've been lost! Don't hug me," she warned softly as she pushed open the smooth, heavy door. "You'll smear my phony luster. It comes off much too easily. Are you okay? You're bleeding!"

"It's just a little cut." Black Dove's voice was reassuringly familiar. "My arms are cuffed behind me."

Now that he pointed it out, White Raven could see the outline of the thick glass manacles he wore, stained with another pink-red smear of blood.

"I tried to smash the handcuffs," he said. "They're chipped now—that's how I cut myself. The hurt is nothing, but I can't break the chains."

"You'll leave a trail for the guards to follow," White Raven said. Fear and worry gave her voice a sharp edge of anger. "Every speck of dust or loose thread shows up against the glass."

"Then let's get out of here fast!" he said fearlessly.

She hooked her arm through his to help him balance. Then they ran together to escape the Fortress of Clarity. The whole way out, White Raven worried about how they were going to get rid of Black Dove's invisible chains without hurting him any more.

MOMMA TOOK RAS AMDE WORKU FLYING THIS morning, like she promised. When they came back, they were both very calm and polite. They'd worked out an agreement. He was apologetic without actually giving an inch. He has known this since the day Teo was born because he'd registered Teo. Registering slaves is *also* part of the reforms—it is supposed to make the legal requirements harder for slave owners. Amde Worku showed us a copy of the official document that is kept in Addis Ababa. He has just been waiting for us to turn up freely on his doorstep, because otherwise we could have argued that Teo had run away, and the 1931 Emancipation Law would have protected him. But here he is in Amde Worku's house and the registration has never been in dispute.

*Spiderwebs joined together can catch a lion.*

Amde Worku has sat here like a spider, a big, rich, elegant, friendly spider, waiting for us to fly into his web.

But he is not going to let go now, because now he *wants* something from Teo—or Momma.

She took him to see his Italian airfield. They landed there and shook hands and drank *tej* that Ras Amde Worku had brought with him. I don't know what he talked about with the Italian airmen, but after they got back, he made us all sit down together and talk about war. There is obviously going to be a war, even if only about ten people outside Ethiopia and Italy are paying attention.

"You are going to have to choose sides, Woyzaro Rhoda," Amde Worku said.

"I am a Friend," said Momma, which for sure meant nothing to Ras Amde Worku and doesn't normally mean much to Momma, either. "I am a conscientious objector. Do you know what that is? I am a Christian, a follower of Christ like you, but I do not believe in making war. How can I choose a side! I have an Italian daughter and an Ethiopian son, and their fathers have left them both a worthless legacy, and you are all going to try to kill each other inside a year! The Italians will dive on you from the air, like eagles hunting. They will do it as soon as the big rains end."

"They will not attack Aksum with air fire. I have seen to that in my dealings with them."

"They may honor their contract with you yourself, but it will not stop them from laying waste to all those around you."

"And we will fight back," Amde Worku answered calmly. "With men, and with mountains. Mile upon mile of the Simien Mountains, where we can beat them back like we did before. They are ill-supplied, and they don't know how to use the land. Distance and earth are our weapons. We beat them at Adwa nearly forty years ago and we will do it again."

Momma shook her head. Her lips were pressed together tightly.

After a moment, she said, "Don't you see? Don't you see what I showed you today? Your brother is a modern man—he works for the railway! You have been to France. You *know* that distance and earth are *nothing* to a man in a flying machine. We can fly from here to Addis Ababa in six hours. It takes your retainers ten days on foot. The Italians have hundreds of planes. The emperor has only a dozen, and they are not armed. Don't you see?"

"I do see," Amde Worku said. "I see very clearly how I can use Gedeyon's son and his flying skill in service of his country."

*In service of his country*—ugh. I can see why it brings out the Quaker in Momma.

"He is not old enough to get an international pilot's license," Momma said. "Not for another six months."

"Then I will expect him back in six months," Amde Worku said. "At the end of the big rains. When the war starts."

Oh, what difference does it make—any of it? When war is declared, Amde Worku says, there will be a conscription call for all Ethiopian men, and if they do not join, they won't be put in prison, which has happened before to so many Quakers who won't fight. No . . . they will be *executed*.

Delia didn't want us to go to *war*. She didn't want her boy to have to *fight*.

We have written down everything about our agreement with Ras Amde Worku and made copies of it so all of us can have one. We all signed everything (I signed as a witness). These pieces of paper have no legal meaning in any country, but making a thing like a treaty made us all feel a tiny bit less hollow. You can see why the emperor does it. There was that friendship treaty between Italy and Ethiopia in 1928, and it is just as much of a joke.

The title was Momma's idea.

# TOWARD EMANCIPATION

*(April 18, 1935/Miyazia 10, 1927)*

1) The law forbids Christians to sell slaves. Ras Amde Worku will never negotiate a financial or trade transaction that involves Teodros Gedeyon Dupré.

2) The conditions of the relationship between Teodros Gedeyon Dupré and Ras Amde Worku are void beyond the borders of Ethiopia.

3) Teodros Gedeyon Dupré will not cross those borders without first notifying Ras Amde Worku. In exchange for this trust and for Teodros's continued freedom of movement in Rhoda Menotti's household, Teodros will not attempt escape from Ethiopia.

4) A requested act of recompense, to be required in the event of war with Italy, may nullify this relationship.

5) All other current law (including the legislation of 1923, 1924, and 1931 in the Gregorian calendar, Ethiopian years 1916, 1917, and 1924) and future Ethiopian law will apply.

Amde Worku

Rhoda Menotti

Teodros Dupré

Witnessed by Emilia Menotti, April 18, 1935

Date: June 10, '35
Type of Machine: Beechcraft B17L
Number of Machine: NC 14405
Airfield: Akaki, Addis Ababa
Duration of Flight: 1 hour 10 min.
Character of Flight: Training
Pilot: Billy Cooper
2nd Pilot: Teodros Dupré

Remarks:

SINIDU HAD THE MOST SENSIBLE REACTION—AT LEAST we thought it sounded sensible: "Why did you even come back to Tazma Meda? Go straight to the American Legation!" she scolded Momma. "Go right away to the Americans, and they will defend you!"

Momma was snuggling baby Erknesh while Sinidu made us breakfast. Momma has finally given up trying to stop Sinidu from cooking for us—when Sinidu comes bouncing into the house in the morning, it is impossible to stop her. But Momma will not let Sinidu do it with the baby tied up on her back, even though that is what Sinidu does in her own house. (She also does it when she is working in the clinic, and in fact, Momma sometimes works in the clinic with the baby tied up on her own back. Everybody fights over who gets to snuggle Erknesh.)

"Ras Amde Worku is one of the last respected slave own-ers, and Haile Selassie will not dare offend people like him. A good general on the Eritrean border is more valuable than gold and salt. But America is the land of the free! Slavery there was abolished nearly a hundred years ago!" Sinidu insisted. "They will take care of you!"

"Oh—" Momma blew her breath out of her lower lip so that the hair on her forehead trembled with the wind of her disgust. "It was not ended that long ago and we were the worst slave traders the world has ever known. And we have other problems now." She gave another angry sigh and bent over, holding Erknesh lying between her knees and cupping the baby's head between her hands. "But you are right. It's a good place to start. It's nearly five years since the kids got here, and Em and Teo need their passport endorsements renewed. They're listed on my passport, which is good for ten years, but their endorsements only last for five because they were under sixteen when I put them there. Em's expired when she turned sixteen. I should get it fixed before those Italian clowns take the plane away. I don't think they'll do it as long as I keep bringing them pictures of goat tracks where maybe they can drive an armored car across the Simien Mountains, but I don't know how long I've got."

"As long as the rest of us. The Italians will wait till the big rains are over, and then they will attack. You should leave before the big rains."

"How can I leave Ezra alone with the clinic?" Momma said. "And you, Sinidu? Because if there is war, you will need me to help." She stared into the quiet baby's eyes and said sorrowfully, "Anyway, we can't just up and *leave*. We can't fly out, because Ras Amde Worku has deals going with all the Italians on the Eritrean border, and they would take the plane away the second we landed and send us back. Plenty of people in Eritrea have slaves, too—they know how it works. And we can't even take the train out of Addis Ababa, because Ras Assefa works for the railway, and he is Ras Amde Worku's brother."

We have been to Addis Ababa three times since then, and we still have not got the passport issue figured out.

Momma has not dared bring up the other issue—the slavery issue—because without the first one being solved, we do not have a leg to stand on.

Getting paperwork done is just as much of a pain with the Americans as it is with the Ethiopians. The first time we went to the legation, they told us we needed to make an appointment ahead of time, so we planned to come back and see them again in two weeks. The second time, Momma filled out a lot of forms, and then they told her to come back in another *three* weeks. That brings us to *now*. And Emmy's endorsement expired back in February, when she turned sixteen, so she has no legal document saying she is allowed to be here. I don't know which of us is in bigger trouble. (She thinks I am.) The only good thing about it is that we are in the soup together.

I have never seen Momma come so close to punching a civil servant in the nose as she did today.

"You can't validate these endorsements." The clerk was thin and sweating, and kept glancing over his shoulder out the window as if he expected the Italians to start bombing the city at any moment. "These are not renewable."

"But they have been valid for the past five years!" Momma spluttered. "October 1930 to October 1935! I have already filled out the forms, and now you just have to renew what's there!"

"The endorsements are only available for children under sixteen. Emilia's expired on her birthday in February. You can't carry an endorsement for another adult on your personal documentation. Emilia will have to submit an application for her own passport."

"But I—I already tried—it's *your fault* the endorsements haven't been renewed! Okay, not *your* fault, mister, but the fault of *this office. Now* you're telling me these kids need their own passports, not new endorsements?"

"If you want passports for both of them, you'll need to provide supporting documents for Teodros Dupré. His name isn't the same as yours. He's not your son."

Em and I stood shoulder-to-shoulder, an inch apart. We didn't dare grab each other's hands in a government office—boys and girls don't do that in public. I have never seen Ezra and Sinidu hold hands, and they are married. *Not your son.* It felt like I was hanging on the edge of an *amba* cliff, and neither one of them had a rope to throw me. All they could do was watch.

"He's a US citizen. He's here on my passport!"

"A birth certificate?"

"He was born in France. His mother was American."

"Documentation from his mother or father?"

Em and Momma both sucked in their breath at the same time. "His mother died in 1927!" Momma said. "His father—"

"Is his father American, too?"

"His father is dead, too," Momma said flatly.

"Was he American?"

I clenched my teeth. Emmy sniffed once and rubbed at her nose. Momma didn't answer. She looked away. We all knew what we'd get if she told him my father was Ethiopian.

"Do you have a birth certificate for him? A marriage certificate for his parents? A letter from his father? Something with his name on it?"

"You are pussyfooting because my boy is a Negro," Momma snarled.

The clerk turned away and coughed. "Excuse me." He mopped his streaming forehead with a gray handkerchief. "I am following regulations because he is clearly not *your boy*," the clerk said. "If you want my honest opinion, Mrs. Menotti, you shouldn't have brought someone else's child into a foreign country in the first place. We'll let you know when Emilia's passport is issued, and you can leave before the endorsement for Teodros expires."

Momma's eyes burned gray fire.

"How long will it take?" she asked through her teeth.

He shrugged, avoiding her flaming gaze.

"A couple of days?" Momma pressed. "A couple of weeks? The rains are going to start, and you won't be able to get a message through to us in Tazma Meda."

"Then you'll have to come back after the rains."

Momma was seething with the effort of remaining civil. But you have to. *You have to*, if you want to get anything done without a battle. That is why Haile Selassie still hasn't given up on the League of Nations.

So I asked carefully, "If it's not too much trouble, would it be all right if we fill out the new form for Em today?"

The man looked at me in surprise. I don't know if he was surprised because he hadn't realized I was able to speak English, or if he hadn't expected me to be so polite to him, or even if this was the first time he realized I'd been standing quietly against the wall with Emmy waiting for him and Momma to finish arguing.

"Well, I guess so," he said, mopping his brow again. "If you have a photograph with you."

Of course that is the one thing we are always able to provide.

They let Momma fill out a fresh passport application for Em. They would not let her apply for a passport for me. There is nothing to prove I am a US citizen.

When she'd finished, Momma herded us out of the office without smacking anything except the stack of papers on the desk—she kicked the desk, too—and she slammed the European-style door behind her so hard it rattled the walls. Then she took two steps down the hall before she sat down and pulled her arms up around her knees and burst into sobs.

Em and I stood like guards in front of her, trying to hide her. We didn't look at each other.

There is only one official document in this country with my name on it, and that is the registration that Ras Amde Worku filed when I was born.

Em turned around suddenly and bent down to hug Momma around the shoulders. I knelt beside Momma and grabbed her hands and held them tight. But she didn't squeeze them.

"What am I going to do?" she choked wildly. *"What am I going to do?"*

"THEY MAKE ME FEEL *SO DUMB*," SHE LASHED HERSELF as we straggled back to Mateos's house, where we are staying in the city. "They make me feel like such an *idiot*. Oh, it isn't *fair*. The emperor's closest advisor is American, that Everett Colson—so why is it so hard for us to get help from the Americans themselves? All I've done—"

"Why the heck didn't you try to get the passports fixed as soon as we got back from Aksum?" Emmy joined the wailing. "Now Teo is stuck here—"

"I did try!" Momma said, wiping her nose. "Anyway, we are not leaving Tazma Meda without Teo!"

"I don't mean I want to leave," Em said. "I love Tazma Meda. But I want the *choice*. And whatever Teo wants—"

She trailed off. I love Tazma Meda as much as Em does, but she and I both know that no one is ever going to let me build airplanes or fly around doctoring people without some kind of education, which does not include being registered as a slave to a prince in a small highland city on the Ethiopian border with Eritrea.

Momma cut Em off. "I don't want to leave Tazma Meda, either," she admitted unhappily. "I guess that's why I dragged my feet. We are safe in Tazma Meda."

It's true that in Tazma Meda nothing has changed. Not even anything in *my* life has changed. But for the first time ever, I am ready for the big rains to come and never stop. Always before I have nearly gone crazy when the big rains come. It is why I have read everything on Vera Sinclair's bookshelf ten times. It is why I have translated nearly half of the Romeo's maintenance manual into English using a pocket Italian dictionary. It is during the big rains that I always start to wonder if I could possibly ever go to France to learn to design aircraft.

But this year I want to stay stuck in the mud for the rest of my life and never turn sixteen and never have to go back to Aksum to fulfill that undefined thing called a "requested act of recompense" in our agreement with Ras Amde Worku. None of it touches Tazma Meda.

We are all in Mateos's house in Addis Ababa now, deeply uneasy and in a panic about official documents—the ones we have and the ones we don't have—and we are so determined to keep it nobody's business that we haven't even asked him if he knows about Ras Amde Worku and my father. It doesn't make a difference, and no one wants to talk about it anyway.

In her disgust at the Americans, Momma has gone back to the Ethiopians. We don't know what she offered them or what they told her. We don't know when or if she has to give up the plane. She spent the whole day at the Parliament building today. I think they might have paid her in person this time.

At any rate, it meant she left me and Em alone for the day by ourselves in Addis Ababa.

We probably should have stayed in Mateos's house playing *gebeta* or working on *The Adventures*. We have written a *lot* of episodes in the past couple of months. In the Buck Rogers comics, Buck is always rescuing Wilma—the hero rescuing the girl—but in *The Adventures* it is always the other way around, White Raven mostly rescuing Black Dove. I know she will make it come out all right—I mean, *we* will make it come out all right— but the episode where they get lost in the Maze of Mirrors and Black Dove keeps running into dead ends because he can't see his own reflection is spooking me.

Also, Mateos's small house is very dark, which makes it hard to write. Meanwhile, you can almost *feel* the city around you rumbling with unease, like a storm that hasn't broken. There is a reddish dust cloud hanging over the line of the main road in and out, because so many soldiers are coming and going. All morning there were two boys our own age wrestling wheelbarrowloads of rifles back and forth along the narrow lane outside Mateos's compound. There was a circle of tailors sitting in the square at the end of the lane with sewing machines, their *shammas* propped up with sticks for shade over their heads like little tents, and they were fiercely stitching up real tents.

"I'm not staying here," Em said. "Let's go find someone who can tell us news."

It was hard walking around Addis Ababa with Em. She is more obviously foreign now than she's ever been. Em's current disguise is an aviator outfit. She is always asking herself *What would White Raven do?*, and she says she is trying to make herself feel braver about flying by playing the part. I don't know if it makes her braver, but it definitely makes her conspicuous, partly because it is so outrageous to see a girl wearing slacks here.

She is a convincing aviatrix in a white blouse of Fiona Sinclair's and Fiona's abandoned riding breeches. It is the goggles hanging around Em's neck and a long white scarf of Delia's that really complete the costume. The American girl flier Emilia Earhart! Ha ha ha. Americans—not just us—are being warned to get out of Ethiopia. Mrs. Sinclair left, and Colonel Sinclair went with her, although he swore he would come back when he got her settled because he doesn't want to abandon Beehive Hill Farm.

Of course we *can't* leave.

Em and I ended up lounging on the steps of the Hotel de France looking pretty much like an idle Ethiopian youth waiting for a chance to carry somebody's bag (me) and an extremely youthful and equally idle airwoman waiting to take someone on safari (Em). There are still loads of foreign journalists and photographers everywhere you go, so we didn't notice the genuine airman until he was standing right next to us. He, too, blended in—he blended in the way *I* do, except for the shoes. Not even the emperor's personal imperial guard wear shoes. Otherwise, this fellow was dressed like the French airmen out at Akaki. But he was a Negro, so we just assumed he was one of the very high-up official types who have been educated abroad—someone like Ras Assefa in his well-tailored European suit.

The black man stopped on the stairs to take in Em and her outfit. He had a narrow stylish mustache that bunched up like a caterpillar when he grinned, and he gazed down at Em with amusement and surprise.

After a moment, Em said boldly, in Amharic, "You must be looking for help."

Because Ethiopians don't stare. Nobody can help looking at Em, but people usually do it sort of sideways.

"Pardon me?" the stranger said in English.

We both straightened up.

"You're American!" Em and the stranger both accused each other at exactly the same time.

"What in the world is a little white Yankee girl doing here on the steps of the Hotel de France in Addis Ababa, dressed up like Amelia Earhart?" the man asked. He squatted down on the steps next to us. "May I join you?"

Em said, "We don't own this porch."

She didn't sound very welcoming, so I squeezed over closer to Em to make room for the American.

He looked down at Em's feet.

"Do you fly barefoot?" he asked.

"I do everything barefoot," she said offhandedly. "You ever see an Ethiopian kid wearing shoes?"

"You an Ethiopian kid?" he teased.

Em glared at him.

"But you do fly?" the airman pressed her.

"Maybe," she said. "Maybe I just like dressing up like Amelia Earhart." She gave me a push in the shoulder to make me speak up for myself. "This is Teo Dupré. He's a pretty good flier if you're looking for a pilot."

The American laughed. He had neat oiled hair and fine white teeth. He was good-looking and conservative and careful.

"I wasn't looking for a pilot. I *am* a pilot. Sort of takes one to know one." He offered Em his hand. "Colonel Billy Cooper."

"Miss Emilia Menotti," Em said pompously.

Colonel Billy Cooper shook hands with her and turned to me to shake hands with me, too.

"Pleased to meet you," I said, and like most people, he did a double take when he heard me talk.

"You're a Yank, too! I thought—"

"You thought he was my bodyguard or something?" Em guessed. I ribbed her with my elbow, but she didn't shut up. "Or maybe my hired boy? We're not in the USA here. It's not a *free country.*" Her voice rose a pitch, going dangerously cold. "Maybe you thought he's my—"

*"Pipe down, Em,"* I said through my teeth.

We both sat there, breathing hard. It was like poking at a sore that wasn't healing. For a moment we glared hatefully at the black American pilot, basking in official independence, while we sat freezing in our invisible glass prison.

"You thought what?" Em pressed Cooper, with her eyes narrowed. She looked like a honey badger going after a hyena.

"I thought he was from around here," Billy Cooper answered her with easy cool, and I could tell he was a smooth customer, and I liked him. "You must be the last pair of American kids in Addis Ababa. What are you doing, loafing in front of this den of thieves? You waiting for the next train home or something?"

"Our momma isn't going anywhere," Em said. "She gets paid to take aerial pictures for people, so she's still getting plenty of work."

*"Oh!"* The man's face lit up as he put a bunch of jigsaw puzzle pieces together in his head, and suddenly he knew more about us than we knew about him. "Your momma's a lady pilot? Is that her Romeo out at Akaki? The one with the bust tire?"

Em froze up again.

"Maybe," she allowed coldly. "Say—what's your business?"

He smiled. "I'm in flight training. Trying to help out with the emperor's air force."

Em leaned forward a little, curious and hostile. Now she reminded me of a lion or leopard inching up behind its prey, hiding on its belly in long grass. "Like Horatio Augustus?"

"Not like him."

"But you're doing his job?" Em asked. "Let me get this straight—you're another American pilot hired by Haile Selassie to train Ethiopian pilots? Doesn't the emperor *ever* give up?"

"Don't think he does," the American said, smiling. "Yeah, that's me, another *ferenji* hired by the Ethiopian emperor to train his pilots. You know his financial advisor is American, too? Everett Colson? I'm not as official as Colson, but I'm a little more official than Augustus. I'm here with Colonel Johnny Robinson, the Brown Condor. You heard of him?"

"Who's he?" Emmy asked.

"Why, he's the man responsible for putting the Challenger Air Pilots Association on the map! He's the man responsible for turning Harlem Airport in Chicago into the center of Negro aviation! Just this year, we got a state charter from Illinois to form the first Negro Military Order of Guard, Aviation Squadron. They don't allow us in the state National Guard, but we have our own Aviation Squadron, thanks to Johnny Robinson. And a crowd of us signed up to come out here to beef up the emperor's air force. American Negroes are behind the emperor's fight one hundred percent. Ethiopia is the last and only independent black African nation."

That made me guess that no one back home was paying any more mind to slavery in Ethiopia than we had, and I ached for Delia and her ignorance.

"There's a crowd of black American pilots here?" Em asked, wide-eyed. "Things have changed for sure since we left the States."

Billy Cooper gave a soft and bitter laugh. "Oh, not so much. Only me and Robinson actually made it out here. They wouldn't approve passports for anyone else. Didn't want to violate the US government's Neutrality Act. I already had a passport. So I've been here two weeks now."

We knew all too much about the Americans not approving passports.

"So what do you think?" Em asked evenly. "What do you think of Ethiopia, now you're here?"

"Bigger challenge than we expected," the airman answered cautiously.

"Yeah," Em agreed in a grim voice, and she and I exchanged that quick, dark, knowing glance, which was like our way of poking at the sore.

"Your momma used to be the White Raven, right?" Cooper asked next. All those barnstorming pilots back in America in the 1920s—everybody knew everybody. "Didn't she used to be a double act? Black Dove, White Raven?"

It sounded strange to hear it in its original context, since those names were so connected with us by now.

"Yeah, that was Momma and Delia," Em said. "Delia Dupré."

"I remember. Bird strike. Terrible accident. I'm sorry."

We both nodded.

"Which of you actually flies?" Cooper asked.

I glanced at Em. She was the one who looked like a pilot, after all.

"Teo flies," she said. "He can land a plane in his sleep."

In fact, I often do when I'm dreaming. Usually after hitting a flock of invisible glass birds that tear my face and the fabric of the wings apart as they shatter. I have started to dream extremely creepy Glassland nightmares that I have not told Em about. I am often Black Dove, in trouble, in my dreams.

Even if she won't admit it, Em *can* land the darn plane, too, awake, although she is unbelievably heavy-handed. She tore up the patched tire *again* after Momma came back from her air clinic tour last month. Getting the tire fixed properly is another reason for us to be here in Addis Ababa so soon before the big rains.

"You Delia's boy?" Billy Cooper asked me. "How many hours you got?"

"Fifty-some," I answered.

"You sixteen yet?"

I hesitated. It was as though I had invisible bruises that he couldn't see and that he kept bumping into without meaning to. I took a deep breath and said carefully, "I'm not sixteen till October."

"Come back in October," the American offered, grinning. "I could license you."

Em nodded, still eyeing him suspiciously.

"Sure, thanks," I said with hollow enthusiasm. Because who knows where we would be in October—where our plane would be—where I would be.

"You kids staying here in the Hotel de France?"

"We stay with my uncle," I said.

"We're out here looking for trouble," Em said drily.

Right on cue, there was a big slamming of doors and shouting and carrying on from inside the hotel.

A lot of the yelling was in French, but some of it was in English and it was orange-blossom-soap-type stuff. Then, storming out onto the veranda burst Horatio Augustus—the Ebony Eagle himself, after all these years—cussing out the French hotel owners and the Italian air force and the Ethiopian government—and he'd just moved on to the American people when he saw us mooching around there with Billy Cooper.

"Why, you and your pal Robinson are the *very punks* to blame for it all—" he snarled at Cooper explosively.

He was still dressed in his sky-blue pilot's uniform, but the gold thread of the epaulettes was fraying.

Cooper stood up. "Hey, I don't know what you're talking about—" he started to say.

"You're trying to muscle in on my act, you and your boot-licking boss, taking my job—"

They faced each other at the top of the steps—two *ferenji* fighting over how to run their host country. One of them had his face twisted up with rage, and the other just looked astonished.

"I'm not here to muscle in on anything! I'm here with the Military Order of the Guard, Aviation Squadron! Shoot, don't we need all the men we can get?"

"You don't know this place like I do," Augustus snarled. Then, as though he just wasn't in control of his own body, he pulled back his fist and let it fly forward right into Cooper's jaw.

Suddenly, they were slugging it out like a pair of boxers, raining blows into each other's faces and stomachs, until they locked together and rolled, thumping and clattering, down the stairs and into the dusty road. They bowled over Em on the way down, just catching the edge of her leg so that she tumbled down the steps behind them. But while they stayed down, rolling around and trying to kill each other, Em jumped to her feet.

Her costumes sometimes have little finishing touches that no one can see. She hadn't told me about this one.

She raised her arm straight up at the sky, like the Statue of Liberty holding up her torch, and suddenly the world seemed to explode around her with an earsplitting bang.

*"Em Menotti!"* I yelled. "Don't you dare—"

She shrugged. "Everybody else has a gun."

She was holding a small revolver, a lady's revolver, not much bigger than her hand. She'd fired it over her head to get the fighting men's attention, and now that she had it, she stood pointing the little gun in their direction.

"The nifty thing about this one," she said, talking over her shoulder at me rather than at the two grown men she was aiming at, "is that it came with ammunition. It's not as big as those antique Italian rifles the other kids carry, but I can shoot mine."

She held the little gun in both hands. It glinted, engraved

nickel and mother-of-pearl. Augustus and Cooper stayed still. And then, about half a dozen foreign reporters came tumbling out of the hotel.

"Put down the gun," everybody said at once.

"It's Mrs. Sinclair's," Em told me. "She kept it with her costume jewelry, and she left it all behind. She only took her good stuff with her."

"Pilferer," I said.

Em laughed. Then she made the gun disappear back into whatever part of her outfit she'd hidden it in in the first place.

"Fellas, I want you to get up and shake hands. Act like there's a war about to start and you're both here to help us win it. Okay?" Em directed.

Cooper got up at once. Augustus got to his feet slowly. In a million years, I do not ever want people to look at me the way the European journalists were looking at that man today.

I came down the stairs to stand next to Em and hissed in her ear, "Don't you ever do that to me."

"You know you'll never make as much of a fool of yourself as Horatio Augustus," Em whispered back. "So I won't have to."

THE TWO MEN STEPPED AWAY FROM EACH OTHER, their backs turned a little, aware of the small crowd that was watching them. Some of them were taking notes. One of them was taking pictures. Someone came running out of the hotel, demanding to see if he had a permit.

"Smoke?" Cooper asked with patient generosity, offering Augustus a cigarette. He murmured, "Better make it look like we're old friends." I knew exactly what he was doing: trying to rescue the reputation of America's Negro pilots in the eyes of the press hyenas.

Taking the hint, Augustus accepted the cigarette and said quietly, "Thank you."

They bent over Cooper's lighter and turned their backs on the reporters, shoulder-to-shoulder. Cooper rubbed at his jaw.

Horatio Augustus said, "It is the grand disappointment of my life that I will not be flying for the emperor anymore. I fear I should have deduced that before I returned here. But he has given me a regiment of foot soldiers to run up north."

"It all counts," Cooper said quietly.

Augustus nodded, smoking. "I have contacts in the northern provinces anyway."

For a little while, the two American pilots stood so still and quiet that most of the crowd got bored watching them and went back inside. Em and I both sat down on the steps again. You wouldn't have guessed they'd just tried to beat each other's brains out over someone else's war.

"I am about to give you some celestial advice," Augustus said suddenly.

"Yeah?" Cooper was cautious.

"That boy there—" Augustus waved his smoke in my direction. For a moment he forgot to talk like a poet. "You got the lowdown on him?"

For the last ten minutes, both men had been acting like we weren't even there, and now they were suddenly talking about us.

"Yeah, what's the lowdown on *him*?" Em repeated, leaning over my shoulder.

"It is advice from a higher authority," Augustus told Cooper loftily. "Test that boy and bestow an international aviator's license upon him. *That* will make an impression on the emperor.

Teodros Gedeyon Dupré is his father's son, and he is destined to fly for Ethiopia. The law that applied to his father applies to him."

Em's mouth dropped open. She suddenly gripped my shoulder with fingernails that were like little daggers. Horatio Augustus sounded like he *knew*. He'd said the same thing when we first met him. And he'd just said he had connections in the North—he could mean in Aksum. He might know about Ras Amde Worku and his outmoded aristocratic ways.

Em swallowed. She let go of me, stood up, and dusted her hands on the seat of Fiona Sinclair's riding breeches. She smiled the starlet smile that she'd inherited from Momma and learned from Delia. I knew there was only one thing on her mind now, and that was how to keep Augustus from saying anything else to Billy Cooper about us—about me. If Momma wasn't going to tell the passport office about it, we sure weren't going to tell some American stranger we'd only just met.

But Cooper was curious now. "When's your momma coming back?" he asked us. "You really know how to fly a plane, huh? You got time to come out to Akaki with me and strut your stuff?"

I glanced desperately at Em.

"Teo doesn't show off," she said. She let the smile land on Augustus. "Not like some."

Cooper laughed. "Well, I didn't ask the right way, then. How would you like to try out an Imperial Ethiopian Air Force Potez? Or maybe the new Beechcraft? Staggerwing'll do over two hundred miles an hour. Faster than the Italian Fiat fighters—"

"Like fun!" Em scoffed.

"No kidding. Sweet little plane. We ordered it for the emperor and got one of the Frenchmen to fly it down here from Europe. It still has its American registration. My boss, Johnny Robinson, is supposed to be the main pilot for it, but he broke his arm right before he came out here, so I get the lion's share of the flying until he's mended."

Somebody makes you an offer like that, out of the blue, and suddenly you forget everything else.

*Faster than the Italian fighters.*

This was why Momma and Delia learned to fly—in the sky, there are no boundaries.

"Yes!" I said. "Now?"

*"Teo!"* Emmy was scandalized. "Are you *plumb crazy? The emperor's plane?"*

Neither one of us knew, till that moment, how easily I could be bribed.

Cooper laughed. "It's got dual controls—I'll be the chief instructor. Come along with us! It's got an enclosed cockpit, and there's room for a committee!"

"How are we going to get out there?" Em protested. *"What are we going to tell Momma?"*

"You'll be fine," Cooper assured us. "I have a car."

That means he is incredibly important, or his boss is, anyway. Not even Ras Assefa, the railway official, has a car.

Em tried not to act impressed. She jerked her thumb over her shoulder, pointing to Horatio Augustus, who stood sulking at the backhanded reminder of his coronation rehearsal crack-up, even though everybody had been tactful enough not to mention it.

"Is this fella coming along?" Em said brazenly. " 'Cause he still owes our mother twenty-five dollars."

Boy, do I ever wish we had documentation to prove *that.*

Sanni 3, 1927

TEO IS SCRIBBLING AWAY ABOUT HIS BEECHCRAFT flight. Like me, he has started to use his flight log as an excuse to complain about anything under the sun, but eventually he will get around to raving about speed and power and how tight that plane can pull a turn. Whatever he writes about the actual flight will hardly be worth the pencil stubs he is writing with.

The plane *was* fabulous. It is true. White with dashing streaks of red and a gold Lion of Judah painted on the fuselage. It is the first time either one of us has ever been in a closed cockpit! So easy to climb into, and so easy to see out of, and we were all together in one cozy little cabin, like a car, with Teo and Billy Cooper side by side up front, and me behind them. We could actually hear each other without having to scream. And there is no wind in our faces.

Augustus did not come—he was not even allowed on the airfield. Not after his coronation disaster five years ago. Poor guy, stuck on the ground. You have to admire him for coming back to Ethiopia at all.

But maybe he feels the same way about it as we do.

It was a strange flight. At first, we circled the city and the Entoto Hills, over the empress Taitu's palace and Haile Selassie's new palace, but we stayed high. When we got back to Akaki, we didn't land; Cooper made Teo climb up to four thousand feet above the airfield and try out tricky aerobatic maneuvers—not just emergency recovery like Momma makes us do, but air show stunts that she would never have let either one of us try in a million years. And, boy, was Teo game for that.

He is so *confident* in the air. Even in a plane he'd never flown before, even when he's trying something new—he is so unhurried and unfussy that it was almost like being in the plane with Momma.

Actually—this is so strange—strange that I can even remember. But the steady way he flies reminds me of *Delia*.

I know Momma has said that before. But this time I thought of it all on my own.

Teo landed back at Akaki just as smoothly as he'd flown. I don't know how he did it, either, because it is so different being *inside* the plane.

So—why did Cooper decide he had to see Teo fly *today*? What was so important about that flight that Teo was allowed to take off in *Haile Selassie's new plane*? We are going home tomorrow, and we will be stuck in Tazma Meda till the big rains are over and Teo isn't sixteen yet. And Cooper doesn't know about Amde Worku's horrible *requested act of recompense*. It was like he had to get this flight in as soon as he was able, in case he didn't get another chance—as though it meant something.

I think Horatio Augustus knows about Amde Worku's racket and that there is something fishy going on that no one is explaining to us.

Gosh, Teo is a good pilot. And now everybody knows it. He *loved* trying out those aerobatics. Momma is holding him back. I bet he is a better navigator than he thinks he is, too.

I am scared he is going to end up shot out of the sky by an Italian fighter plane before the next Timkat.

———

"MOMMA DOESN'T KNOW I HAVE MRS. SINCLAIR'S gun," I told Teo as we walked back alone through the dim streets to Mateos's house. It was nearly sunset when Cooper dropped us back at the Hotel de France. That is the closest you can get to Mateos's house in a car. In most of Addis Ababa, you can't even drive.

"I figured she didn't," he said. "I'm worried she's going to beat us home. What's our story for her going to— *Oh!*"

The gasp came out of Teo like an eruption, and I gasped, too, as a heavy arm clamped down across my shoulder. A man had come up behind us and now held us fast, both of us at once, one of us on either side of him.

"Hush, Teodros—Emilia," he said gently.

It was Mateos, of course, but he scared the pants off us. He is *unbelievably* quiet. Even by Teo's high standards of invisibility, Mateos is hard to beat.

"Hush," he said again, like he was telling us a secret, so we shut up.

He steered us. He turned us sharply to the right, and zig-zagged down pathways even I didn't know were there. He got me lost in thirty seconds. I was *mad.*

"Mateos! What—"

Then he was wrapping Teo's *shamma* around my shoulders and up over my head like a veil—I hadn't even noticed when he made Teo take it off. Mateos hissed in my ear, more urgently this time, "It's all right, just be *quiet.*"

He'd followed us from the steps of the hotel where Billy Cooper had dropped us off. I had no *idea* Mateos could be so secretive. Teo was behaving himself, so I did, too.

We passed a house full of barking dogs—more barking dogs than should have been in a strange house. There wasn't any other sound, or any light. Mateos hurried us past, absolutely calm, absolutely silent. And fast.

For half an hour, we wove through streets where we'd never been before, one of us under each of Mateos's arms. I felt safe and yet completely at sea all at once. And then we were turning the corner around the stick fence into the little garden of his house, with the white goat like a ghost nestling under the dark curtain of the flowering banana trees. There was a yellow flickering light waiting for us and Momma drinking coffee, without a ceremony like the ignorant American that she is, by boiling up leftovers on the brazier.

She'd heated supper for us, too.

"I flew a Beechcraft Staggerwing today," Teo announced, taking off into the wind, which is usually the safest thing to do.

Momma looked up at us, but in the light of the brazier and the one lamp you couldn't see into her eyes. I think we were both a little scared of her reaction.

Then she gave Teo the Nod. All right. Ready to go.

She turned to Mateos.

"They okay?"

"Your truants are fine." His bright smile came and went, and then he was serious again.

"Kids, you can't wander around Addis Ababa on your own," Momma said quietly. "I didn't really think you needed *telling*."

She wasn't angry. She was just still and serious, as though the cloud of silence that surrounded Mateos was contagious and she'd caught it.

"Momma, we wander *everywhere* on our own," I pointed out.

"Not at night in Addis Ababa. Hyenas! Anyway, now the Italians are evacuating their legation," Momma said. "You hear me? The Italians are leaving the city. That's so they don't get attacked by Ethiopian soldiers. Everything's a mess. You two are *ferenji*. And, Emmy, you are an Italian flier's daughter, and anyway, you stand out like a sore thumb. Use your heads!"

"You have to assume the streets are safe for no one at the moment," Mateos put in calmly. "*Ferenji* more than *habashat*, foreigner more than Ethiopian; and I have been ordered by Ras Assefa to give you his protection."

"Protection?" I said bitterly. "Ras Assefa is Ras Amde Worku's brother."

"Protection and guard."

"Don't," Momma warned wearily. "Just stop."

"Are we *important*, or just *valuable*?"

"*Emilia, stop it!*"

"Both," said Mateos.

So he did know.

THE BIG RAINS HAVE COME TO TAZMA MEDA.

There are different ways of being a prisoner. I've been think-ing about it since that Glassland episode where I had to rescue Black Dove from the Fortress of Clarity. All these invisible pris-ons. Us being stuck here because of the rain—it is the wettest rainy season Momma says she has ever seen since she came here. About an inch a day falls, according to the rain gauge by the Romeo's shed, and there have been rock slides mile after mile on the Gondar road and another on the track up to Tazma Meda, so no one can get in or out. So that is one kind of prison.

But I also feel imprisoned by things like having to wear Fiona Sinclair's hand-me-down girly dresses. I bet Bea Sinclair feels like she's in prison in an English boarding school without her gun, having to wear shoes all the time. Baby Erknesh tied on Sinidu's back stares longingly at Teo's die-cast *Spirit of St. Louis* hanging out of reach from the clinic ceiling. Me in the pilot's cockpit of the Romeo. When I climb out of that plane after I've landed, it always feels like I just made a jailbreak.

Not that anyone has been flying the Romeo since the big rains started. And Habte Sadek is a prisoner, too. Incredible to think that he has been sitting in that same shady cave and on the same narrow ledge in sun and rain for nearly seventy years. And he is still sitting there, but now it feels like he is a prisoner, and it didn't used to feel like that.

Habte Sadek fell and broke his collarbone just after the rains started, and Ezra thinks he also cracked something in his pelvis, but of course no one can tell what's wrong inside him. The big slab of rock in front of the door was wet and slippery, and he missed his footing coming out of the St. Kristos Samra chapel and just fell down the step. Now he can't lift his arms above his head and he is obviously in a lot of pain when he tries to walk. But the worst thing is that he has got these scrapes on his legs that won't heal.

Ezra said to Momma: "Rhoda, I love you and I love your children, but you are raising Teodros to be the most idle young man in the nation. You can love and pamper children without making them lazy! I want Teodros to go up to the hermitage and change the dressing on the old priest's wounds morning and evening. I can't trust the deacons to do it well, and your boy is not doing anything else worth doing."

This is unfair to Teo, who attacks projects he cares about with the power of a steam roller and who is never idle inside his head even when he's asleep. But Ezra does not think much of filling empty school notebooks with comics and made-up stories, or sitting in the rain on Beehive Hill watching birds for a whole morning and then spending the whole afternoon sketching different wing shapes. Teo and I have also been helping Momma with the Romeo's annual beauty treatment, which involves an unbelievable amount of fiddly knot-tying where the canvas needs replacing. (Though Momma complains Teo is too artistic with his bows and she has to check everything twice because he is careless and leaves them out here and there.) We are repainting the plane, too—ochre, which is all there is, the most boring color in the world. And Teo has his usual rainy-season writing project, which is to keep going on his translation of the Romeo's dang maintenance manual with the help of an outdated English-Italian dictionary that does not include any aviation terms.

I am not accused of being lazy, because I've been helping Sinidu and Hana take turns with the sewing machine to stick gigantic red crosses onto canvas tents in case we have to become a field hospital. But nothing Teo does counts as *work*.

"It will spare the rest of us for other tasks," Ezra continued. "And Habte Sadek likes Teodros."

That has a lot to do with it—us being Sinidu's special friends. Habte Sadek would not let just any old foreigner mop up his legs. I am not allowed to do it anyway, because I am a girl and Habte Sadek is a priest, and getting your oozing wounds mopped is a private thing for anybody.

So we have been going up there twice a day so Teo can scrape off the gunk and dab on iodine. It is *awful* seeing Habte Sadek becoming so frail. He has always been fierce and proud and strong. His wounds haven't gotten any bigger, but they don't get smaller, either. They are just *there*, festering, making everyone miserable. They have been there for six weeks. Maybe when the rains end they will get better.

We go up in the early morning, when it is misty but not raining, and again just before sunset. You can't see more than a hundred feet down the mountain because it looks like everything is draped with one of Delia's gray silk scarves. The mist gets in your hair and even clings to the little hairs on your arms and legs, until you feel like a sponge—not dripping wet, just saturated. Every now and then, the big rains remind me of spring in New Marlow, Pennsylvania. It *smells* like spring in New Marlow, PA.

After Teo has finished playing doctor, I make coffee, because that is something that only a girl can do, and it is a good way to make peace. I do this almost every morning. The first couple of times nobody drank any—Habte Sadek tried, out of politeness, but the doctoring made him so whacked he could hardly sit up, and Teo absolutely didn't eat anything for about three days in the beginning, and I don't blame him. Now they are both used to the awfulness of the cleaning routine, and they look forward to coffee and popcorn afterward.

One of my jobs is trying to get Teo to learn to read Momma's maps, and that is one of the things Habte Sadek is, in fact, very good at. Who says you can't teach an old dog new tricks? Habte Sadek is *passionate* about Momma's maps, now that he knows they exist.

"Had I this knowledge all those years ago—" he says with anger in his voice, then stops and laughs. "But no matter. It would have made us faster, perhaps, but no more determined. You are lucky to live in this age of shared knowledge! Look—here is the way we came from Magdala," he tells us. "And here, the way through the mountains. And here is why no one followed us—"

One time Teo complained, "I can't picture it. That's my problem with maps. I don't understand why a painting makes sense to me and a map doesn't!"

"Think of it in a different way," Habte Sadek told him. "Here is how we made a map, when we were traveling from Magdala so many years ago. You see these lines on the page? You can build this shape with your hands."

Sitting on the stone step in front of the carved cave chapel, Habte Sadek scooped together a pile of damp earth and modeled it into a miniature Beehive Hill. His hands are bony and dark and still strong—they don't shake at all.

"If you do it enough with your hands, you'll learn to see it in your head," he suggested. "Look! I'll make a map with my hands and you put it on paper. That will help. There is always another way of making a map."

We talk about what we hear on the radio. One of our patriotic chores is to carry the accumulator for the clinic radio up to Beehive Hill Farm so we can charge it by hooking it up to the battery in Momma's plane or the Sinclairs' generator, since there is no other electricity in Tazma Meda. It is not like last year, when there was nothing to listen to. Now Haile Selassie talks to us on the radio almost every day. We hear about Mussolini telling his

Fascist Blackshirts that he will conquer Abyssinia *totally*—not even pretending to introduce colonial reforms anymore. Partly he wants to show off how strong he is to the rest of Europe. Partly he says it is the "new frontier" for Italy, like the Wild West, "a place in the sun" for Italian pioneers to move in and take over the abundant farmland. It will bring them jobs and prosperity. He does not mention what will happen to the farmers who live here already.

Then we get more polite and pointless wrangling in the League of Nations. Tekle Hawariat, who is Ethiopia's League of Nations delegate, says that all we want is to be able to defend ourselves, and then the Americans make themselves a law that means they have to stay neutral on anything to do with international conflict. So they won't sell us any weapons. But they'll still sell *fuel* to anyone who wants it, ie. the Italian army. Everybody in Addis Ababa is buying guns like they are all the rage.

This morning Habte Sadek said to Teo, "When the rains end, and the emperor announces his call to arms, I will find myself cleaning my own wounds."

"We're not going anywhere," I told him firmly.

"Teodros is old enough to carry a spear, and I have seen to it that he knows how to."

Teodros is not going to walk off to war carrying a spear. That just will not happen. But there is that "requested act of recompense" hanging over our heads. So Habte Sadek is probably right—sometime, soon, Teo will not be here to clean his wounds.

I wish everything would go back to the way it was two years ago.

Habte Sadek can hobble about now, but he can't reach down to his feet. The rains are going to end in less than two weeks. It is already the new year, 1928. The Ethiopian new year, I mean. It is September 1935 in the United States.

Teo swallowed. "Ezra will show Yosef how to change the bandages."

"Yosef and the other young deacons will go off to war along with you. I would go again myself if I could walk."

"Oh, you must not do that," Teo exclaimed. "You are a man of peace! You have dedicated this chapel to Kristos Samra! Who would guard the treasures you rescued from Magdala if you left?"

The old priest grinned. "All is safe here. Why did we bring it to this place of all places, if not to keep it safe? My brothers and I saw to that when we first arrived. There will always be peace and safety here."

*She flew to hell to make peace between God and Satan.* That was what Habte Sadek told us about St. Kristos Samra when we first met him, when he told us how he renamed the hermitage when he first came here.

I picture St. Kristos Samra as a sort of cross between Sinidu and my own made-up White Raven. It makes more sense to me as a story than as religion. None of those Friends meetings with Grandfather ever made me realize the beautiful *adventures* connected with God. Flying to hell! Rescuing treasure from an invading army! Now I want St. Kristos Samra to fly back here and get to work on a new peace negotiation between Haile Selassie and Benito Mussolini. Nobody else is going to do it.

## EPISODE FROM "THE LAND OF GLASS"

They had not reached cover when the rain began.

At first it felt like fine, cool mist. The glass drops were so tiny you could not see them, but the sun was still shining at the edge of the storm, and the glass mist made the air glitter with a million rainbows. It was too dazzling to be beautiful. Black Dove hid his face in his arm, and White Raven pulled him forward, using the homing skills she had learned as a child growing up on Wildmare Island.

Then the sun was hidden by clouds, and the rain started falling harder. Now it felt like hail, stinging their arms and faces.

"Let's stop!" Black Dove murmured indistinctly, trying not to open his mouth. "We need to build a shelter!"

"Our tent will be buried when this starts to pile up," White Raven panted. "We'll be crushed! Come on. There's a cliff ahead—I can feel the mountain wind and I can smell a spring. We can find a cave. We'll be safer in a cave, and we need water."

The smooth glass plain beneath their feet was worse than a frozen sheet of ice. Its clear surface was slippery and tricked them, growing more treacherous as the hard rain fell. White Raven felt a sharp pain as something pierced the skin at the edge of her forehead. She gasped, and Black Dove said urgently, "How far? The raindrops are breaking up."

He didn't mean the rain was stopping. It was much more frightening than that. The smooth glass raindrops were falling with such tempestuous fury now that they were smashing each other. Instead of heavy, round crystal pearls, the sparkling rain was falling as deadly sharp-edged jagged chips of broken glass. That was what had cut White Raven's face.

She didn't try to talk anymore. She linked arms with Black Dove, and they slid and fought their way through the fearsome rain until they reached the tall green glass shelter of the Emerald Cliffs.

They collapsed, torn and bleeding, inside the mouth of a shallow cave and huddled against the back wall with their faces buried in each other's shoulders, not daring to raise their heads until the crashing, clattering clamor of the glass storm died.

---

Date: Oct. 11, '35/Meskerem 30, 1928

Type of Machine: Romeo Ro. 1

Number of Machine: I-STLA

Airfield: Tazma Meda/Takazze Valley/Aksum

Duration of Flight: 3 hr 35 min total

Character of Flight: transport

Pilot: Momma

2nd Pilot or Pilot Under Training: Teo

Remarks:

I DON'T KNOW WHY I'M WRITING THIS. TEO SHOULD do it himself. He probably *is* doing it himself, in his own flight log, wherever he is. He will be writing exactly the same thing, and that makes us *close*. We're doing it *together*. Now we are big enough nobody can actually tie us down; we get tied down in different ways. And this is one.

The whole village was glued to the radio in the Tazma Meda clinic all last month. I am sure we know more about what is going on than most of the rest of the country does. And *everyone* is going to fight—married men are supposed to take their wives to cook for them. (Not that Ezra would ever go anywhere without Sinidu anyway.) "All boys old enough to carry a spear" are supposed to go. If you don't fight—"Anyone found at home after receipt of this order will be hanged."

Loads of people have left to go to Addis Ababa and join the emperor's army. Ezra has not, because he is officially working for the Ethiopian Red Cross now. When the time comes, he will go wherever the soldiers go, and Sinidu and their baby will go wherever Ezra goes, and I guess we will, too. Colonel Sinclair is not back yet, so Ezra has been trying to rally everybody else—mainly, unmarried girls younger than me, like Hana and the rest of the crowd of Tazma Meda kids we sometimes run around with—to shoulder the coffee harvest. But who cares about the coffee? Who is going to buy Ethiopian coffee now? The Italians?

The Italians came back to Adwa exactly a week ago—the place where the emperor Menelik II led the Ethiopians to defeat them in 1896. The Italians were not defeated this time. They came with planes, just as we knew they would, and this time they bombed Adwa. When all the Ethiopian soldiers had retreated, the Italians marched right in and shook hands politely with the local priests.

We were going to go to Addis Ababa ourselves to pick up my new passport, which is supposed to be ready now, and to try again for Teo. But three days ago, before the airfield was completely dried out, a plane came and circled low over Beehive Hill Farm until most of the village came running out to see what was going on.

Teo and I were there before Momma, who had to come up from the clinic. She thought the same thing we did—that someone was finally coming to take our Romeo away. When our plane goes, we really will be trapped. We've been dreading it all year, then dreading it even more when it stopped raining, and then when we heard that Ethiopia really had been attacked and invaded. Nobody trusts an Italian airplane anymore.

But it wasn't an Italian airplane. I couldn't tell, but Teo knew right away.

"It's the Staggerwing," he said. "It's the emperor's new Beechcraft Staggerwing, the one Colonel Robinson ordered from

America. The one Cooper showed us—the one I flew. *Beautiful!*"

"What's it doing, then? Why's it circling like that? It's not going to bomb *us*, is it?"

"Em, you goof. The field is soaking. Whoever's flying it is looking for the best wind direction and the least puddles."

It took the pilot so long to decide that it gave everybody time to gather a big crowd to welcome him.

The white-and-red Staggerwing landed and everybody could tell it was an Ethiopian plane because of the Lion of Judah painted on the side, so everybody cheered—except me and Momma and Teo.

Cooper sat in the front of the cockpit. But the engine kept running while he got out, and we realized that he was flying as the second pilot—Johnny Robinson was flying as pilot-in-command. Robinson didn't get out, and he didn't look at us. He was focused on two things: holding the brakes while Cooper did his business with us, and leaning back in the cockpit to talk to the two passengers sitting behind him.

Billy Cooper stood outside the plane now, waving widely and beckoning to us. Momma loped across to meet him, and Teo and I followed more slowly. The engine idled the whole time we talked. These visitors weren't here to stay. They were on some other important imperial mission, and Tazma Meda was only a detour for them.

Cooper shook Momma's hand and then beckoned to her again. She stuck her head in the plane's open door, half kneeling, and spoke to the two passengers sitting in the back of the plane. When she stood up again and backed away out from under the wing, Cooper shut the door to give the passengers privacy. I heard him ask Momma, "You still got your own plane?"

"Yes! We thought at first that you were the Italians, come to take it away!"

"Can it fly? You got fuel? Is she ready to go?"

"Yes, but—"

"That's great. That's really great. I thought we were going to have to take the kid back with us to Akaki and let him fly one of the Potezes—"

I wanted to grip Teo's hand, but we are too old to do that when people are watching. This was it—we were pretty sure. This was Teo being taken away from us as a soldier—as a slave? To shoot at Italian aircraft? To be shot at by them? To do *what else*?

DAMN. DAMN. DAMN.

"Well, this is better, anyway," Cooper went on. "Your own plane is an Italian design, and maybe it will go unnoticed. Teodros has to go north to Aksum to get his marching orders. You can fly him there yourself. That's a command from the emperor to his subjects, okay?"

"The emperor already told me himself where he wants Teodros to go, and I'm not his subject," Momma said coldly.

Cooper nodded in apology. "I mean your boy is his subject. Your boy's an Ethiopian citizen, right? He's being mobilized to Aksum—" All the color had leaked out of Momma's face by now. I've never seen her look so bleak and defeated. It was the way he'd said "mobilized," like Teo was already enlisted in some military outfit.

"—That's where his father comes from," Cooper went on. "He's been called up by one of the emperor's generals who's based up there, so that's where you have to take him. And when he gets there, he's got a job he'll need a plane for. If he can use your Romeo, that'll be the best camouflage he can get. They say you agreed you owe the fella in Aksum—"

Momma sucked in her breath between her teeth as Cooper finished the sentence.

"—you owe him a—a 'requested act of recompense.'"

227

"*I know what I owe him,*" Momma said.

"I'm sorry, Mrs. Menotti," Cooper said, ducking his head again in embarrassment toward the cockpit of the Staggerwing and its passengers. "It's not my agreement."

"Do you *know* what the agreement is?"

"Of course not!" Cooper sounded shocked. "Military intelligence, right? How would I know that?"

Momma chewed her lip. Then she burst out angrily, "Would you work for a slave owner, Colonel Cooper?"

"You know Haile Selassie is not a slave owner!" He glanced quickly over his shoulder at the passengers. "Mrs. Menotti, this isn't the time or place—"

I could see the other American pilot, Colonel Robinson, up front, and I could see the two passengers in the back, side by side. The one nearer to us was a white man, a lot taller than the other. The shorter man was in the shadow of the enclosed cockpit, and his face was hidden by his sun helmet.

Momma let out an angry, defeated sigh. "Yeah, I can see that. I'm sorry I said anything."

It was Haile Selassie sitting in that plane—the emperor himself.

I don't know why it took us both so long to recognize him. Momma had known him right away. That was why she'd knelt by the door. She'd spoken to him. She wasn't going to take on the issue of Ethiopian slavery reform here on the Tazma Meda airfield—none of us were. I guess I have discovered another limit to my own so-called bravery.

I gasped aloud to Teo, "*Don't look him in the face!*"

Teo looked away quickly. Then he slowly bowed his head three times, just like we'd done at the coronation rehearsal. I started to kneel, but Teo pulled me to my feet.

"You'll make people notice him," Teo hissed. "He's trying to stay invisible."

The emperor looked away from us then and said something to the white man sitting next to him. But he'd seen us. He wanted Teo to do something for him. He knew who we were.

Cooper handed Momma a little cardboard envelope. She backed off like she was expecting a viper to shoot out of it and sting her to death.

"It's your boy's pilot license," Cooper said. "I tested him when I met him in Addis Ababa in June. I know he won't turn sixteen till next week, but no one's going to care." He held out the cardboard envelope.

"It's a command from the emperor," Cooper repeated softly. He gave a nod over his shoulder at the people in the plane. "His Imperial Majesty Haile Selassie I, Conquering Lion of the Tribe of Judah, King of Kings, Elect of God."

Cooper glanced back at Teo.

"Your boy is one of maybe fifty licensed Ethiopian fliers, and the only one with his own aircraft available. Let him decide for himself if he wants to take your plane or borrow one of ours."

"Momma," Teo said as quietly as he could and still be heard, "don't make me have to fly on my own from Addis Ababa to Aksum in a strange Potez. Fly me up to Aksum, and let's find out what I'm supposed to do."

TEO'S LICENSE IS AN ACTUAL FÉDÉRATION AÉRONAU-tique Internationale license issued by the United States of America. That doesn't mean he is a citizen of the United States of America—it just means that whatever he is, the USA issued his license, and he can fly as a pilot anywhere in the world. As well as being signed (I guess before it left the USA) by the chairman and executive vice chairman of the National Aeronautic Association, it is also signed by Johnny Robinson. Billy Cooper's word is the only thing that anyone has to go by to tell them that Teo is a competent pilot, but obviously Billy Cooper's word counts for a lot. We had to stick a photo in ourselves. Momma put in a copy of "Abyssinian Shepherd Boy." It is ridiculous.

So now Teo has actually got an official identity document with his name on it. At least one of us does.

MOMMA MADE ME DO THE PACKING. SHE TOOK TEO up to the Big House so they could use the Sinclairs' dining room table for planning our flight to Aksum. She made him do it all himself so he'd get practice in case he had to do the next leg without help. She is trying desperately not to show us how scared she is, but that worry line is making a trench between her eyes. Her face is going to get stuck that way. Maybe mine will, too.

Is this why she didn't want to teach him to fly? So he wouldn't have to go soaring off into the blue on his own and maybe never come back? But this is why she *did* teach him to fly, so he wouldn't get thrown into a battle as a foot soldier. I can't decide which is worse.

When we set off from Tazma Meda, when we were still together, we were all trying to make the best of it. We wanted to land back on the ridge Momma named Delia's Dream, but there was such a strong crosswind we couldn't. It is so narrow you can only land along it when the wind is blowing straight from the north or the south. We found it all right—it lay below us tantalizing and beautiful, ours, and we just couldn't land there. Teo was flying, and Momma was in the middle cockpit—she took over the controls for a second attempt, but only got down to about a hundred feet before she shook her head and put the power on and soared away. I heard her shouting at Teo what to do next, but I couldn't tell what she was saying.

I wriggled around to watch Delia's Dream get smaller and smaller under the tailplane, feeling like the Delia-shaped hole in my heart was so impossibly big now it was going to swallow me whole.

I wish you could go through life without ever caring about anything, without ever getting attached to people and dreams and inaccessible places. It just makes you sad when you can never go back. White Raven never looks back—she just moves from one adventure to the next, as if nothing that happens ever changes her. The Buck Rogers comics Grandfather sends are like that, too. But real life is not like that. Look at Momma. She was the original White Raven once, in a bathing suit and a silver garter, hanging by her knees from the undercarriage of a Curtiss Jenny. Now she is something less showy but a lot more complicated.

I wish I could be more like Habte Sadek. He is not sad. He is proud of his past and unafraid of his future.

After all that fooling around over Delia's Dream, we landed in a valley of the Takazze River near a village, where we spent the night. We had to shoo a bunch of little kids away from the plane in the morning. Even with a paid person standing there "guarding" it, there was still a little kid sitting in the middle cockpit yanking the controls around. Momma spent a long time checking to make sure everything still worked—she even took off on her own to do a flight test, leaving me and Teo standing in a crowd of people who didn't speak any language we could understand.

"Did you ever tell her about the loop you flew with Cooper?" I asked Teo.

"It would have just scared her if she knew I tried stuff like that. She was already fit to be tied after that trip to the legation, without me telling her some strange fella was teaching me aerobatics in the emperor's new plane."

We watched the Romeo as it turned into a struggling dot against the blue, then flipped over backward on itself and came screaming earthward at two hundred miles an hour.

Everybody cheered.

"If she crashes and goes up in a ball of flame, we will be stuck here," Teo said.

"Yeah, and then you won't have to go work as a slave pilot for Amde Worku," I answered.

Neither one of us said anything as we watched. Now we were holding our breath, worried that Momma might actually be *that* desperate.

I heard Teo's long sigh when she landed safely.

"Are you relieved or disappointed?"

"Oh, *Em*." It was halfway between a sob and a laugh. "What do you think? Someone would have tracked us down eventually."

Neither one of us is ready for Momma to go up in a ball of flame. Especially if it is pointless.

Momma hopped out of the plane to fend off a couple of kids who were getting too close to the propeller. She looked wind-blown and exhilarated. She must have enjoyed that.

"Get in, quick, before anyone gets in the way," she ordered. "I'll get her started again—" That is how we happened to end up with Momma riding behind us in the third cockpit when we set off on the final leg for Aksum—me in the middle behind Teo, and Teo with the map in the front. Momma was more anxious about taking off without slicing anybody in half than she was about figuring out who should sit where. She stood guard while Teo and I climbed in. She would have been more careful about where she put us if she hadn't been happy with the Romeo when she tested it.

Teo let me take off. The wind had died in the night and there wasn't any drift. It was *perfect* for flying.

Teo was concentrating hard on getting the navigation right. We were high, about four thousand feet above the ground—you can't go much higher than that over the highlands in northern Ethiopia, because even on the ground in the valleys you're at six thousand feet above sea level. It is freezing cold up in the air at ten thousand feet above sea level, and you can't breathe if you go much higher. But it's easier to read the map up there because the scale makes more sense when you're that far away from earth. Also, you can make the fuel last longer, and you don't have to worry so much about the wind over the mountains. So being that high was all to help with Teo's navigation.

We were only about half an hour away from Aksum when we saw the other Italian planes, a dozen of them, like a swarm of flies in the distance. Teo spotted them first and pointed. They were lower than us and flying in more or less the same direction. Momma sat behind me staring at them through the binoculars.

"Caproni bombers—wow!" she yelled at last. "Three engines—huge! *Not a fair fight.*"

Suddenly Momma cussed under her breath. I don't know what she actually said. She probably didn't mean me to hear—it was low and private, and I only know it was bad language because of her tone.

Then she yelled gently, *"Emmy."*

Honest—she yelled gently. She made it sound like it was just supposed to be an ordinary conversation. "Hey, Emmy, look around at me."

I craned backward in my seat. Momma was leaning forward intently. We stared at each other for a moment eye-to-eye through our goggles.

"Downwind, straight and level," Momma yelled at me. "Tell Teo turn downwind, fly straight and level."

"He is level!"

"Downwind!"

She pointed in the opposite direction of the wind.

"She wants you to fly downwind! Straight and level!" I screamed at the back of Teo's head.

"Okay," he said, and his shoulders went all tight and hunched, like he knew what to expect but didn't want to look behind him to see whether he was right. I bet we were thinking the exact same thing: *Those bombers are following us.*

Teo turned the plane downwind. With the wind behind us, we were going a lot faster.

"Em!" Momma called to get my attention again. I looked back. She pointed one finger at herself and then at me. "Swap you!" she yelled.

I shook my head. I didn't know what she was talking about.

"Swap seats," she yelled. "So I can fly." She pointed to her eyes one at a time. "Watch. I'll show you how."

Teo glanced back at me, not sure what was going on behind him.

"*Straight and level,*" I screamed at him, and hoped he didn't look back again.

Calmly, Momma unbuckled her straps. Then, carefully like always, without upsetting the balance of the plane, she pulled herself up on the windshield of the third cockpit. When she had her feet on the seat, she climbed out, one knee on either side of the plane, hugging it like a horse. She kept her head tucked low to protect her face from the wind. It is absolutely freezing flying at ten thousand feet above sea level.

Momma didn't talk anymore—just pointed at her eyes behind the goggles. *Watch.*

She crawled over the front of the windshield so she was sitting behind me. Then she crawled backward, back into the third cockpit, and lowered herself into her seat again to show me how to do it when it was my turn.

And then she climbed out again, fast, no fooling this time.

She paused behind me before she climbed over my head—she rested a hand on my shoulder and squeezed four times. *I am not scared.* Then she scrambled over top of me and perched on the fuselage behind Teo like an owl while she waited for me to give up my seat for her.

I knew she wasn't doing this for fun, not with Caproni bombers after us, if that was what was going on. Teo couldn't help but be aware of her behind him. The balance of the plane's weight shifted as she moved from the back to the front, making us nose-heavy, and we began to sink a little. Teo glanced around wildly and Momma yelled firmly at his ear, *"Fly the plane."*

He held steady, straight and level, speeding along with the wind behind us. So it was my turn.

I put my hands on the sides of the cockpit to push myself up, just like she had—just like climbing out of the plane when it was on the ground.

This sounds stupid, but I had not realized how *windy* it was going to be.

That was why Momma had told Teo to turn downwind—to balance the wind behind us with the wind of the plane's own movement—to make it a little easier for her and me to climb out of the plane. But when I got up there, sitting on the back edge of the cockpit, my whole upper body just felt battered by the wind. I hung on to the cowling. I still had to get my legs out and then—and then *crawl backward* along the fuselage and over the windshield into the empty seat behind me?

It wasn't *anything* like being on a horse, whatever Momma made it look like.

Momma glanced back at me and gave me a thumbs-up. I thought of the four hundred times I'd made White Raven do exactly the same thing.

If I'd known *why* Momma thought it was so important for us

to *swap seats in midair* I'd have tried to do it faster. But I was so darn scared that the only thing that made me move was knowing that if I didn't, and Teo crashed, it would be all my fault.

I got my legs out and began to crawl backward.

It is *nothing* like a horse.

This is kind of embarrassing to admit, but I did it with my eyes closed. I couldn't see where I was going anyway. I kept my head tucked in, like Momma did, trying not to catch the wind full in my face. It felt like it took forever because I was so worried about running into the windshield of the rear cockpit and getting knocked off balance. I felt for it with my feet, kicking behind me—I couldn't believe it was so far away! But it wasn't as high as I thought it would be, and I got to the windshield in such a mess of gratitude and relief that I just kind of poured myself over it and into the third cockpit.

I sat on the binoculars. Momma had left them there for me on her seat. That meant she wanted me to be the lookout.

Doing the thing you are scared of is much harder than not being afraid of anything. It is easy to be *brave*. It is not so easy to be scared and do a brave thing anyway.

I opened my eyes.

I could see the back of Momma's head safely in front of me— she'd climbed into her seat while I was climbing into mine. She beat me to it and she'd already taken over the controls from Teo. She was flying while I was still strapping myself in.

I started to scan the sky outside the plane.

I spotted the Italian bombers. They were a lot farther away than they had been before we'd turned away from the wind and sped up. They were still on their way south, and I made a little mental calculation in my head about which direction we were going and what we needed to do to get back on track for Aksum. Of course I'd left my map and china pencil in the middle cockpit, but I had the stub of another china pencil in my blouse pocket like a good little aviatrix, and Momma had left her own notebook shoved down the side of the seat. I grabbed it and let it fall open across my knees to a blank page.

I wrote down what I thought our heading was. There is a compass on the dashboard of the middle cockpit but not in the back. Luckily my one from Papà Menotti was in my skirt pocket. I struggled around in my seat to get it out, and when I found it, I looked out at the sky again, and that was when I saw the two Italian planes that were racing after us.

They were as high as us and smaller than the big triple-engined Caproni bombers, which were disappearing in the distance. Momma must have seen those fast little planes as soon as they started chasing us—the time it took for me and her to swap seats.

The last time we'd met a plane in the sky—less than a year ago—it had also been an Italian plane, and we'd waved our wings at each other. *Selam!* Everybody friendly, and the pilot, it turned out, was my own father. So I didn't expect there was anything different going on now, until those planes started firing their machine guns.

They were Fiats—Italian fighter planes—faster than us. They should have recognized our plane as Italian, too, but we had just finished giving it a fresh coat of paint and the I-STLA is painted over and hard to read. The plane looks like it is in disguise, and Romeos are built to the same design as Fokkers, which are Dutch. We could have been *anybody*. Those Fiat pilots thought we were their enemy. Scouting or taking pictures or something. Not that we'd ever do that, right?

"Hang on—" Momma gasped, and lowered the nose. We dove so fast my stomach seemed to leap into my brain. It was worse than Billy Cooper's aerobatics.

The two Italian planes came diving after us. They kept firing, and you could *feel the sound*. It rattled in your blood. But we kept on flying smoothly and I only knew we'd been hit when I saw the edge of the upper wing burst into flower in three places as the bullets and wind tore through the canvas above Momma's head.

The fuel tanks are hidden in the upper wing.

I stared at the bullet holes, trying to see if anything was leaking, trying not to think about what would happen if the fuel tanks caught fire in the air.

"Keep your heads down!" Momma screamed.

But I wanted to see what was going on. She knows me so well that she checked over her shoulder.

"Em, you're a *target*. *Get down!*"

Then I realized what she meant—I was all alone in the back with my head sticking up. The rear cockpit is the only one not under the wings.

I ducked down.

My windshield shattered.

I was still clutching my pencil in one hand and my compass in the other, and Momma's notebook was lying open on my lap, wedged against my stomach. Now the pages were covered with splintered glass.

Momma swooped lower. It felt like we were falling. She's never thrown the plane around like that with us in it, not even making us practice emergencies. I thought we'd been hit and we were dead. I turned my head a little and saw a rocky mountainside rising above us, tinged with fresh green, and I was sure we were about to crash into a mountain.

But the engine roared into life again and Momma leveled out, tearing through the sky, hugging the side of the mountain.

She was barnstorming—stunt flying. It was what she did best, or nearly what she did best, and the Regia Aeronautica fighter pilots weren't flying-circus veterans and they'd never done any canyon flying in Idaho, and they couldn't keep up with her.

I had to look. I risked losing the top of my head and peeked over the edge of the cockpit. In front of Momma, Teo kept his head down obediently.

The Italian Fiats were overhead now. But they weren't as close to the steep mountainside as we were.

Momma dove again, following the side of the mountain to the valley floor. We were harder to see against the land than against the sky, with our fresh coat of ochre-colored paint. Now I am grateful it is such a boring color.

I wondered where we were. I pressed my little glass compass into the ball of honeycomb wax that Momma keeps on the dashboard so you can stick things there and not lose them. The compass needle was still spinning—it wouldn't calm down till we flew straight and level for a while. The fighter pilots were in just as much danger of getting hopelessly lost as we were, maybe more.

"You up, Em?" Momma called. "Watch them for me. They stopped shooting—they're faster than us, but they're not getting closer. They might've lost us. Don't want to go too far off course—"

The Fiats were getting farther away. If I looked through the binoculars I couldn't see them at all, because I couldn't find them through the narrow tunnel of the distance lenses.

"Did we turn around?" I asked. "I bet they don't know where we are heading!"

"Can you get us back on track?" Momma said.

"You have to give me the map."

"*Good girl!*" She reached up to the torn canvas of the wing and felt around for leaking fuel, though I don't know how she'd have felt it in that wind—it evaporates so quickly. But she gave me a thumbs-up, so I guessed she thought it was safe. Then she handed me her map, rolled up like a scroll. Her mouth dropped open when she saw the remains of my windshield.

"I'm okay."

I saw the back of Teo's head come up in front of her. We were all okay. The plane was okay.

"Hang on—" I said. "I need a minute to figure out the heading—"

I got us back on track. Finding my way in the air is the one thing Momma has taught me how to do that I am really good at.

Teo isn't, though. Even when he needs to be.

I am not going to think about it.

WE WENT THE REST OF THE WAY TO AKSUM WITH-out seeing another plane in the whole sky, which is—if you ask me—exactly how it should be.

Aksum is beautiful right now. It is always beautiful, but right now the fields all around are like lakes of gold. The Meskal daisies are in bloom, tall yellow asters blanketing the high savanna with sunlight. They grow all around the landing field, too, clouds of gold among the gray-green acacia and candelabra trees.

Just as we reached the edge of the gold where the grass of the landing field was scythed short, we passed right over a group of people who ducked and cringed as we purred groundward. I noticed them because they *glittered*. And nothing glitters here, except water sometimes right after the rains. I thought these peo-ple must have new rifles or spear points—why else would they be carrying anything that reflected so much sunlight? Of course they had to be armed. Adwa, which the Italians took last week, is fifteen miles away. *Fifteen miles.* It is *nothing*. Between the planes patrolling the air and the army on the ground, it is a miracle we got to Aksum before the Italians.

The people below us didn't wave, and I spent the whole of the landing run worrying that they were going to try to blow my head off.

It was a typical smooth Teo landing—at least, I think Momma handed over the controls to him for the landing—but the airfield is in a dip in the lea of a broad hillside, and after we were down, we couldn't see the glittering people anymore.

"Switch off!" Momma yelled.

Teo stopped the engine.

"Out you get, kids. Bet there's a reception committee waiting for us."

Momma paused, perching on the edge of her cockpit, and pulled off her goggles and helmet. She looked exhausted. She glanced up at the torn fabric of the upper wing, and touched the jagged edge of my broken windshield. "Careful climbing out, Em."

Teo saw them first—the people crossing the airfield.

"There they are," he said quietly. He didn't point.

Maybe we were supposed to turn away. Maybe we weren't supposed to watch. You're not supposed to stare at people, and it wasn't Timkat.

But it looked just like a Timkat procession. Coming out of the brush at the end of the airfield, emerging from the savanna grasses like a herd of shy mountain nyala, was the group of people we'd passed over as we were landing. There were definitely soldiers with them, but that was not what made them glitter, and they were not the fighting force we were expecting.

Four of them were priests in their full robes, wearing crowns. Another was dressed like a deacon, just a white robe and a *shamma*, but he looked like he was about a hundred years old. All these people had boys walking next to them, carrying gold-fringed silk umbrellas to shield them from the sun. There were half a dozen soldiers flanking them, four carrying rifles and the two at the front carrying spears. It was the crowned priests who glittered, not the armed soldiers.

In between the soldiers and the priests walked four more deacons, these carrying a shapeless something shrouded in white canvas. They carried it on a litter on sticks over their shoulders. They walked proud and reverent as if they were carrying the emperor himself across the field.

It was like seeing the painting on the walls of the chapel in the cave on Beehive Hill come to life. It was like watching Menelik and his royal attendants marching with the Ark of the Covenant, straight out of a church decoration and onto an airfield. Straight out of how many thousand years ago and into *now*.

I glanced at Momma, just one quick glance. She watched them with a perplexed frown. The hair around her face was standing on end.

"Keep an eye on those fellas," she said. "Here come folks we know from the other direction."

She pointed. From across the landing field came another group of men, and this time it *was* a troop of soldiers.

I looked through the binoculars. Leading the soldiers were Ras Amde Worku and *Horatio Augustus*. Horatio Augustus was still in his pale blue air admiral's gear or whatever he thinks he is. Ras Amde Worku looked like a prince again, wearing the smart khaki uniform that makes the Ethiopian officers look like they are working for the British army—and a lion's mane headdress and collar over a silk cape. He was the most splendid person there, more regal even than the priests.

I turned back to see where the priests were headed. They'd been really easy to spot from the air, but you wouldn't have seen them on the ground unless you'd known they were coming, because they hadn't taken the road.

If you lined everybody on that airfield up and tried to figure out who was the most important person there based on their fancy outfits, you would not have guessed it was the barefoot boy dressed in someone else's hand-me-down shorts.

Typical Black Dove.

"Why didn't they all turn up together?" I wondered aloud.

The priests didn't come anywhere near the plane. They made their way purposefully around the field, keeping their parade as far away from us as they could. It *was* a parade; it was like Timkat—but at the same time, creepily, it wasn't. There were no bells, no drums, no chanting. There was no noise. It was the same procession, important churchmen carrying something as carefully as they'd carry a *tabot*. But it was the wrong day of the year for a *tabot* to be taken out, and there was no festival to go with it, and we were the only ones who saw.

On the far side of the field, where the road was and the ground started to climb steeply, there was a little hut made of stick walls, with a corrugated iron sheet for a roof. It is all new—none of that was there the last time we were here. The shed is like our aircraft shed at Tazma Meda but a lot smaller. While we watched, Augustus and Amde Worku and their soldiers and the priests all met in front of this little building. Two of the soldiers with rifles stood at the door, and the deacons with their strange *tabot*-shaped cargo and one of the priests went inside. Only the deacons came back out. Then everybody except the priest in the hut and the guards at the door came trooping toward us across the airfield.

Teo and I inched closer to each other, making a flimsy rampart in front of the plane. Momma planted herself squarely in front of us. Our protective instincts are pretty ridiculous.

The ancient person in white seemed to be as important as the priests. The soldiers laid down a carpet right there on the airfield next to the plane. Then they set out a chair for the old deacon or whatever he was, and laid a piece of brocaded silk over the top of that, and he sat down and someone held a parasol over his head with one hand and waved away flies with a horsetail fly swatter with the other. The priests stood next to him under their own parasols. All the soldiers stood silently at attention while this was going on, even Horatio Augustus, who seems to have learned a thing or two about keeping his mouth shut since he has come north to lead a bunch of real soldiers carrying real guns and real spears.

Momma stood and watched with one hand holding the blowing hair away from her eyes. She looked absolutely cranky, like a little kid waiting for a grown-up to give her the go-ahead to talk.

Teo bowed.

Teo—

It was the right thing to do. He always does the right thing. Even when he was a little kid with his sweater on backward or inside out, he'd always know when to shake hands or take his cap off. He does it without thinking. I can't ever do the right thing without *hating* people for having to do it. Is that the difference between Momma and Delia, too? I can't remember Delia well enough to know whether she was as good as Teo is at making herself invisible. Maybe that was why she liked France—she could be beautiful and invisible at the same time.

Oh, *where is he?*

I WILL JUST KEEP GOING AS THOUGH I AM WRITING a story. *The Adventures of Black Dove and White Raven*, "Episode 432: The Battle of Aksum."

Teo bowed. After a moment, so did Momma, so I did, too.

The sitting old man in white didn't look at us. He just nodded, looking bored and somehow oozing disapproval at the same time.

I still wonder if he could have been Habte Sadek's brother. He was old enough to be. Maybe he was. It doesn't matter.

Ras Amde Worku made the next move.

He made a beeline for Teo and clasped Teo's arms and kissed him on both cheeks.

Then the old man said something, but it was in Tigrinya, which they speak up north here and in Eritrea, and we couldn't understand it. He was obviously not greeting us, and he was obviously not happy.

I think he was complaining about there being so many girls around.

Amde Worku answered him reassuringly, dragging Teo forward to make a formal introduction. Teo bowed again.

*"What is going on?"* I demanded in a whisper.

*"Shhh!"* Momma hushed me.

I considered what I'd risk by throwing a fit. Or even just by asking a lot of questions. Maybe Horatio Augustus would have jumped in to answer them. But I didn't know what I was risking. So I shut up.

I am kind of glad I did, in fact, thinking back.

Ras Amde Worku said to Momma, "Only the boy may go."

"He can do the flying. But I need to go along as his navigator."

*Is she bluffing?* I wondered. And then I realized she couldn't be bluffing. She is no good at bluffing. She was *still* panicking about Teo not being able to find his way.

"He will go without you. He has his own license," Amde Worku said placidly. "So Horatio has assured me, and I have seen a copy of the text. Teodros must be the pilot, and the aircraft will only accommodate one passenger and cargo. We can supply fuel—"

Momma argued tensely for a little while with Ras Amde Worku, with the old man in white making comments in Tigrinya every now and then, and Momma looking increasingly worried, and Ras Amde Worku translating everything the old man said with extreme politeness.

Momma stood unyielding, the wind ruffling her wild hair so that it stood up golden brown as the shock on top of an ear of corn. Then she tried to lay down her own terms, which I thought were pretty reasonable under the circumstances—the circumstances being that she was supposed to give them her plane and her kid to go do some errand which they wouldn't explain to her, leaving her and me stranded three hundred miles from home and not knowing when Teo was going to come back for us.

"I have two conditions for you," Momma said. "The first is that Teodros Gedeyon is not going to take this plane anywhere unless you paint me a couple of giant red crosses on the wings and the tail. Ethiopia has its own Red Cross unit now—they got their League approval in July. So you have to make the plane look like an ambulance—neutral. We were fired on by the Italians on our way here."

Amde Worku relayed this to the priests, and they argued and argued and argued. Finally Momma got out the first aid kit and gave a medical demonstration until they finally figured it out and nodded in agreement. Everybody ended up exhausted with relief when this argument was over.

See, we can be reasonable when we try.

"The second condition?" Amde Worku asked at last.

"You play fair and tell us what's going on."

I couldn't stand it anymore. I had to butt in. "Let me plan his route!" I begged, and everybody frowned at me. Even Augustus shook his head gravely, as though he understood Tigrinya and was best friends with the priests.

The churchmen talked quietly to each other for another endless amount of time. It was like waiting to be eaten alive by bugs. Ras Amde Worku listened, and finally he turned to us and said, "Woyzaro Rhoda, though we understand and agree to your request to paint the aircraft for its onward journey, neither you nor any of this party may place conditions on Teodros's service."

Momma sat down on the ground and pulled me and Teo down beside her.

"What are we delivering and where?" she demanded.

"You may not know either."

"The plane's not going, then. Teo's not going."

Very slowly, Amde Worku repeated to the others what Momma had said. You could see his reluctance in his whole body as he talked.

The old man said something. Ras Amde Worku answered him. Then he said something to one of the soldiers. It was a quiet command, made grimly. The soldier shifted his grip on his spear so that it was aimed at Teo. He moved fast, but Momma was faster.

"*Hey!*" she shrieked, and launched herself straight off the ground at the spearman.

She was fearless. You know what she was like—she was exactly like a leopard mother. She grabbed the staff of the soldier's spear with both hands—she couldn't wrestle it out of his grip, but she wrestled *him* away from us, and he couldn't get her to let go. Horatio Augustus himself, and I have to give him credit for this, grabbed the guy Momma was struggling with in a bear hug from behind. Another soldier dropped his own spear so he could grab Momma's arms. But what really froze everybody in their tracks was a sharp command from Amde Worku—and one of the other soldiers, I guess following orders, jammed his rifle against Teo's head.

Momma went limp. She couldn't fight them all at once.

There aren't enough words in the world to tell how much I hate that man.

They didn't pay any attention to me. I scooched toward the spear that the other guard had dropped.

"*Emilia!*" Momma roared at me in a whisper.

So then we all just froze where we were for a few seconds.

Momma let go. She held up her hands.

"Don't hurt the boy," she gasped. "You won't get anywhere without the boy—"

Ras Amde Worku quoted the mobilization announcement we'd already heard the emperor read, more than once, over the radio.

" 'All boys old enough to carry a spear. Anyone found at home after receipt of this order will be hanged.' Teodros is in my service, but the order comes from above me and is out of my reach." That snake was just trying to pin the blame on someone else. "He serves or he dies. He has no choice."

"You're not asking him to carry a spear!" Momma cried. "Another boy can choose whom he'll serve!"

At this point Teo fell flat on his face.

I thought about producing Mrs. Sinclair's revolver, which was tucked inside the waistband of my skirt, and decided that one more gun was not something that was going to improve the situation. So I fell flat on my face next to Teo. I didn't care who saw. I leaned my head against his shoulder. If they really were going to shoot him, they could shoot me with him.

The ancient man said one word in Amharic.

"*Peace.*"

He was talking to Momma. He was apologizing.

I felt Momma's hand on my shoulder. She knelt in front of us.

"*Selam,*" I heard her repeat in a whisper. "*Peace.* Oh God, Teo."

"I'll do it," he muttered into the ground, in English.

Then he lifted up his head.

"I'll do it," he said in Amharic, his voice quivering with defeat. "Please tell them to take the guns and spears away."

We heard them giving the orders. We heard the soldiers moving away from us. Momma was still kneeling over us with a hand on each of our shoulders. She was crying now.

"Some lousy Friend I make," she gasped in English. "My grandma ran a station on the Underground Railroad and here I am, selling my best friend's boy down the river. I'm sorry. *I'm sorry!* But I can't—can't let—"

"I'm going to come back, Momma," Teo said gruffly. "Cut it out."

Oh boy, what do you do when you realize your mother can't save you or help you or *anything?* That she can't even give you a rousing battle speech to make you brave because she is just so darn scared herself?

"*Coffee,*" I interrupted rebelliously. "Let's make peace with coffee. We have to remind them they don't completely rule the roost. Only girls can make coffee."

WE DIDN'T HAVE ANY THINGS FOR A COFFEE CERE-mony. All we had was camping equipment. But me and Teo are good at this kind of magic. Teo cleared a spot in the grass, and I set up the buddy burner, in one of Mrs. Sinclair's pilfered cans, and Momma got out the coffeepot. We'd brought coffee that was already roasted and ground, like the terrible Americans we are, for camping with. While the water was boiling, I picked an armful of Meskal daisies, summery gold everywhere, and spread them all around the burner and the edges of the ancient guy's rug.

Then—I thought this was really good—I got all the little things out of Momma's flight bag. I got her set of screwdrivers and her rulers and china pencils and all our compasses and watches, and I arranged them in a gleaming circle of shining science around the edge of the burner. And then we shared out tiny sips of coffee to everybody, in our blue enameled cups from Momma's camp kit.

Things became more civilized all of a sudden. Coffee does that. Or maybe it is *women* who do that.

Ras Amde Worku squatted on his heels, looking untouchably, medievally majestic in his lion fur. In his apologetic steamrollery way that gets me so het up, he gave us this much explanation: "The Italians are a day's march away. They will take this city for its holy and symbolic significance. We have evacuated our own force from Aksum, and they will find no resistance here; the bishop and other important holy men who can travel on foot have gone with them. But one of these remaining churchmen needs to hide. There is a place we want him to go, and we believe the fastest and most secret way will be to take him by air. It will be as if God had sent angels to fly him to safety."

"Well, it will be fast," Momma admitted, her face still looking kind of gray. "But for sure you know we're not angels. A human hand needs to chart the path as well as fly the plane. We need to know the destination ahead of time so we can figure out how to get there. You flew yourself, once or twice, Ras Amde Worku. You *know*. We have to know where they want Teo to go."

"They will only tell the pilot."

After a bit more wrangling Momma persuaded them to take Teo aside and spend a sensible amount of time planning the route with him. So when we'd emptied the coffeepot, the ancient person stood up, still with the younger boy holding the silk umbrella over his head, and beckoned to Teo.

Teo got slowly to his feet as if he had great big sacks of coffee tied to his joints. Momma handed him both of the maps and her notebook, and all his previous flight plans. He turned and bent down, full of ceremony, to select a collection of rulers and pencils. He picked up his glass compass that Papà Menotti had given him. I watched him drop it in his shirt pocket. He looked at me.

"Hey. You were going to plan my route."

I felt like my heart was being torn out of my chest.

"The route back to Tazma Meda is marked on that map," I told him urgently. "You did all the calculations for this trip yourself and it worked. Just check *everything* against what's there on the charts. Use it as a guide. Follow the heading and check your compass every five minutes. You'll get it right."

We couldn't hug each other. We couldn't even hold each other's hands anymore, not a grown boy and girl in front of priests.

I linked my thumbs together to make wings, White Raven's secret greeting to Black Dove.

He gave me a pained, quick grin. Then he turned and followed the soldiers and the old man across the airfield and into the shed.

I sat down on the grass and covered my head with my arms. I wanted to wail the way the Tazma Meda women do at a funeral, except I didn't want to upset Teo. So I just ground my teeth together and sobbed quietly to myself.

Momma started cussing. She had the sense to do it in English, so nobody could understand her, but she still sounded like she was cussing.

"Rhoda." Amde Worku said it calmly, with certainty. "This is important."

"What is it? Why won't they tell me? Why *Teo?*"

"He is a pilot. He is my servant. And he is a man."

"A *man!*"

"And you are not," Amde Worku pointed out.

Momma killed the flames in the buddy burner by upending her cup over the tin. Defeatedly, like she didn't care who was watching her or what they thought, she gathered up the rest of our equipment. Ras Amde Worku started giving Horatio Augustus instructions about their next move.

"I want the same soldiers to escort the holy men back the way they came. Let no one see them from the road. Two must carry old Kasa so it can be done quickly. The deacons will keep pace with the rest. Your other men must make this place secure for Woyzaro Rhoda and her daughter, and you must be ready to evacuate this field if the Italian force arrives—"

"Retreat?" trumpeted the Ebony Eagle. "*Run away?* Never—"

"Evacuate," said Ras Amde Worku calmly. "Yours is the only fighting force left in this city, and you are not here for defense. You have forty men and one cannon under your command, and that is enough to protect an American woman and her daughter. When you have made sure they are safe, you are to follow my force south. We will not fight the Italians so close to their supplies in Eritrea—we will lure them into the mountains and exhaust them there."

After a couple of minutes, I got up and just walked away.

Nobody ever stops me.

I didn't go anywhere. I just wandered around the edge of the landing field. There wasn't any fence; it wasn't a real airfield yet, but it was turning into one. There were soldiers along the road, who didn't seem to have anything more to do than I did, and they were just standing around gabbing with their rifles across the backs of their shoulders and their arms hanging over the rifles like shepherd boys do with their sticks. The sun was high and there was a faint breeze ruffling the gold Meskal daisies. It was absolutely *unbelievable* there was supposed to be a war going on, or that we could *possibly* be near the front lines.

Momma came to get me after a while.

"How's Teo supposed to find his way to their mysterious location?" I wailed. "And what'll we do, just sit here and wait for him to get back?"

"I guess we'll have to."

I felt my lip wobbling again. We just keep sliding deeper into this pit of nightmare, the ground crumbling beneath us. *What would White Raven do?* I need a quiet place to think about it.

"Come on, Em. You and me got to make sure the Romeo is ready when Teo is."

There is no quiet place.

We refueled the same way we do at Beehive Hill Farm, making forty-two trips back and forth from a couple of barrels left by the road, carrying cans of fuel on our heads. Somebody turned up with brick-red paint so they could get big red crosses slapped up on the Romeo's wings and the tail. Momma bandaged up the torn wing and the jagged windshield in the backseat with surgical tape from the first aid kit, and crawled over every inch of the plane yet again. After she'd done it herself she made me double-check everything, too.

"Em, your hands are smaller than mine. Reach in there and tell me if you feel anything wet. Reach down there and tell me if you can find *anything* that moves. Stick your finger down this tube—"

The plane is fine. I heard Ras Amde Worku's men laughing about painting red crosses on the aircraft and saw one of the churchmen giving them thunderingly dirty looks. A red cross on a house here means something else (it means the same as "red light district" in the USA), so now that there is an actual Ethiopian Red Cross Society it makes some people confused. At any rate it will disguise the plane.

Then I had to sit in the cockpit for twenty minutes with my

feet on the brakes while Momma got Horatio Augustus to prove he knew how to swing the propeller so he could start the engine for Teo.

Momma did not seem scared when Italian fighter planes were shooting at us—at least, she hadn't acted like she was scared. She had taken the controls and got us out of a tight spot. She is fine as long as she is flying. But now she can't take the controls. That's when she gets scared—when she can't do anything to fix things herself.

I wish I didn't know how scared she is.

We did all the tinkering she could possibly think of and then we had to leave. They made us get out of the field—we had to stand in a dip on the other side of the road and we couldn't see Teo when he crossed the field with the mysterious priest who'd been in the shed the whole time. It felt like waiting while your house burns down. We heard the Romeo's engine start. We heard the rise and fall of its familiar hum as the plane taxied away from us, heading downwind. There was a pause—I imagined Teo down there by himself, checking at the last minute to make sure he was heading the right direction for takeoff, that the oil pressure looked normal, noting what time it was.

He had four and a half hours before it got dark. He couldn't fly without refueling for much longer than that anyway, though, so whatever happened he must have landed before it got dark.

Suddenly we could see the Romeo again. It rose from the air-field like a moth. The new wet paint seemed to gleam in the sun. The arms of the crosses belled out wider at the tips than in the middle, like the crosses carved in the window holes of St. Kristos Samra. There wasn't anybody sitting in the windy rear cockpit with its smashed windshield, because that was where they'd put the cargo, whatever it was. You could see the top of a shapeless bundle that was wrapped up and strapped down, the thing the churchmen had been carrying in the litter over their shoulders. A little tail of the cloth that covered it flapped wildly in the wind. The plane was waving good-bye to us.

"*Oh—*" Momma breathed. I locked my arms around her neck and we watched the Romeo with its weird cargo bumbling slowly but steadily away from us to the south.

We watched until we couldn't see anything.

AFTER A LITTLE WHILE I SAID, "WHERE ARE WE going to stay?"

"We can stay here. Ras Amde Worku's trying really hard to make us happy. It's half killing him that we're not staying in his house, but he understands how much I want to be here when Teo gets back. They'll let us use the shed to camp in. Augustus's soldiers are about half a mile away, on the edge of the city. They'll send a patrol to guard us, and water and carpets and a cook. Oh, Emmy—" She gave a bitter bark of laughter. "Bet you can't imagine the American Legation giving us cooks and an honor guard! And that dang Horatio Augustus has given me a couple of gas masks he brought over from the States—tells me he can sell them for twenty-five dollars apiece in any market in Addis Ababa, so he's paid off what he owes us with interest."

"No one can afford that!"

"Yeah, it makes you wonder. But a secondhand rifle costs two hundred dollars. Someone's paying."

I couldn't believe it. "What're we going to do sitting around in Aksum with gas masks?" I asked.

"Well—"

Momma was awful serious.

"I told you about gas. I would not be alive today and you wouldn't be here if it wasn't for my boss Dr. Mackenzie making us all wear gas masks and rubber raincoats, when I was in Belgium during the war, before I met Papà Menotti."

She is always very serious about the Great War.

"Listen, Emmy," she went on, "you know they bombed Adwa last week. Well, Augustus heard something about burning yellow smoke pouring out of Italian planes over troops in the south, near Wal Wal, about the same time last week when the fighting started. I don't trust him farther than I can push him, but I won't say no to a couple of gas masks."

Ras Amde Worku came to get us when the coast was clear and the priests had all left. Momma and I had already divvied up the camping equipment so that Teo would have the best of it, which meant we were low on things like matches and water and now we had no coffeepot or groundsheet. We went to take what was left into the shed and get ready to play house there.

Gosh, it was bleak when Ras Amde Worku first showed us inside. Augustus had his men build it to be an operations center for the airfield, hopefully expecting some aircraft to turn up there and need an operations center, but there was nothing in it but a rickety handmade wooden table for modern airmen to spread their charts on. There wasn't anything on it now. It felt like nothing had ever happened there or would again. The floor was packed dirt, still a little bit damp but not muddy. Whoever built the place had cleared the undergrowth, but there wasn't a rug or a mat. There weren't any windows, either, just the light coming through the chinks between the sticks that the walls were made of.

"I have asked my men to erect a thorn fence around this place against the nighttime hyenas," Ras Amde Worku told us. "I will leave you a guard, as well."

"Thank you," Momma murmured. She wasn't really paying attention. She bent over the table, looking closely—looking for *anything*. She moved on from the table to the back of the shed. "Here's where the cargo load was resting," she said, kneeling in the light coming in through the open door and rubbing damp dirt between her fingers. "You can see how the ground's pressed flat. Ras Amde Worku, give me *something*."

"Secrets rest in Aksum," Amde Worku said. "There is a great treasure kept here. Surely you know what that may be, if you put thought to it. Maybe the Italians know, too. We cannot risk them coming here as an invading army and taking what they find."

Suddenly he sounded like Habte Sadek.

There is only one great treasure in Aksum that Habte Sadek has ever talked about, and that is the Tabot of Zion.

Did Teo have *any idea* what he was doing?

It makes *The Adventures* feel so babyish.

I squatted down beside Momma, staring at the voiceless markings on the dusty floor.

"Have they taken it to Debre Damo?" Momma asked. "To the monastery there, the one on top of the cliff? Ras Amde Worku, they should have asked my advice! There are Italian aircraft on Amba Kwala within a twenty-minute flight of Debre Damo. They will fly from Amba Kwala to Debre Damo with bombs and guns if they think it is worth it. You saw the planes *yourself* when I flew you there."

Amde Worku assured her again, soothingly, "Our boy is going to be safe, Rhoda."

That was when I saw it—Teo's picture in the soft earth.

He'd drawn it under the table.

Even with the door open it was in shadow—I can't believe he'd been able to see what he was drawing. He must have done it blindly. But he'd used big, bold strokes—he could have felt them in the earth, like a sculpture. Like Habte Sadek showing us how he made maps for his friends when he was a boy. And I could tell what Teo's pictures made.

There was a hill with trees on it. He'd done two trees, quick jagged lightning sweeps across the ground with the flat of his hand for treetops, crooked trunks, and a rounded handful of earth for a hive dangling by a thread from each tree. Just below the top of the hill, set in the hillside, was the arched door and window of a chapel.

At the bottom of the picture was an airplane—a biplane with three cockpits. Our Romeo Ro. 1. Outside the plane were two faceless figures. One of them wore a crazy hat that might have been a flying helmet. The other wore a priest's crown, like the ones Habte Sadek rescued from Magdala. And between them they were carrying a *tabot*, heading away from the plane.

So he did know what he had taken with him.

And *I knew where he'd gone.*

Down at the edge of the drawing, outside the rest of the picture, was a thing that looked like a big bowl with two little people in it.

*We are in the soup together.*

It was a message to *me.* I couldn't let Ras Amde Worku see it.

I leaned against the table and swooshed one foot back and forth across the drawing. The damp ground was cool and smooth against the sole of my foot. It felt exactly like the smooth packed dirt floor of the chapel at St. Kristos Samra.

FORTRESS OF CLARITY

I'm sick of it. *I hate it.* Fortress of Pitch-Darkness. Fortress of MUD.

I CAN'T WRITE A STORY WITHOUT TEO.

I keep trying, but it feels so petty. Real life is ruling me. I want to escape it by writing, but all I can write about is what just happened. And up until the god-awful battle yesterday, the past three days have been unbelievably, unbearably boring—boring and upsetting at the same time, just waiting and waiting for Teo to come back, but he never does. No news from anybody about anything. We get our meals cooked by a girl named Miniya, who is younger than me. She drops her face into her shoulder with absolutely unbearable shyness when we talk to her. Nobody has *ever* made me feel like such a crazy *ferenji* without even trying.

So I try to think about *The Adventures*, try to think about me and Teo *being* Black Dove and White Raven and how it all comes out right in the end of every episode, but I *just can't do it.* I can't even *think* about it. It feels so *wrong* to try to make up these stupid, pointless stories when real people are dying all around us. When our real life is like that last episode of Buck Rogers that Grandfather sent us last year, where Wilma is stuck being lashed three times a day in the beryllium mines on Jupiter and we *still* don't know if Buck gets out of prison so he can rescue her. I mean, I guess he does. He always does. But I don't know how this time. And we'll never know for sure.

I didn't write that whole so-called flight log entry on the date it happened. I wrote it over the past three days because nothing else was happening and I had to do something or shoot myself. The first night of waiting—the first night on our own in the shaky, little not-a-house shed, lying there with Momma rolled up in our *shammas* on Amde Worku's fancy rugs, everything crisscrossed with shadows and moonlight through the thorn barrier and the gaps in the stick walls, listening to the hyenas yipping in the distance—it was like that first night she came back from the hospital after the Bird Strike. She was just like that. She lay with her back to me, and she didn't even cry. It was like I wasn't there.

"Momma, I know where Teo went," I whispered to her back.

After a moment or two, she rolled over to face me. I couldn't see her in the dark.

"How?" she whispered back.

"He drew a comic in the dirt under the table. I rubbed it all out so Amde Worku wouldn't see it. He's taking—"

She shot her hand up fast and clamped it over my mouth. "Don't tell me! For God's sake, don't tell me."

"But—?" I thought she'd be overjoyed.

She took a deep, shaking breath, and rolled onto her back this time, staring up at the tin roof in the dark. "When the Italians get here, they might go looking for whatever he is supposed to be hiding. No one can get it out of me if I don't know. Don't let anyone know *you* know." She took another deep breath. "You think he'll be okay?"

"If he doesn't get lost, I'm *sure* he'll be okay," I swore.

I believed that when I said it three days ago. I am *sure* I know where Teo went. But I don't know why he hasn't come back for us yet.

———

RIGHT SMACK IN THE MIDDLE OF BREAKFAST YES-
terday, we heard engines. It was a distant sound at first, like a
swarm of bees. A long time ago, when we first came to Tazma
Meda, the bees did swarm once, and it sounded like that—a dron-
ing hum that grew slowly louder and louder, and Momma made
us all lie under our *shammas* for an hour even after the noise
stopped.

This only sounded like bees for a moment or two, and then
we knew it was airplanes. Not just one airplane, not the plane we
were hoping for. This was so many planes roaring closer that we
couldn't tell how many it actually was.

We were sitting outside our hut watching Miniya fry *injera* for
us. Momma tilted her head, listening. I could see the little dent of
alarm between her eyes getting deeper and deeper.

"Oh, jiminy Christmas," she gasped. "That is the Italian air
force coming to invade Aksum."

She stood up in the sunlight, shielding her eyes with one
hand as she scanned the sky.

"Maybe nobody will speak English, and we won't have to talk
to them," I said hollowly. "Momma—did you do *anything* for them
besides take pictures?"

"Nothing! *Nothing*, Em. I took pictures of mountaintops, just
what I've always done. That's what they asked for, and they let me
keep the plane. I made sure the emperor got copies of every photo
that I took for them. The Italians never even paid me!"

"The Ethiopians did! You are a dirty double-crosser!"

It was as close as I could come to saying, *Everything is all your
fault. You are our momma, and you are supposed to protect us.*

"*I never double-crossed anybody*," Momma snapped. "I am just
feeding you kids."

That's the other thing mothers are supposed to do
instinctively—feed their kids.

I can still remember Delia saying exactly the same thing.

"*Cross my heart*, Emmy," Momma added, sounding kind of desperate. The noise of the planes was getting louder. Momma gasped in frustration, "Oh, where are they coming from?"

She spun in a slow circle, using one heel as a pivot, trying to figure out the direction of the sound. Horatio Augustus's men heard the noise, too. We hadn't seen much of them over the past few days, but we knew they were close by, working on building the thorn fence around us, patrolling the landing site under cover of the candelabra trees on the other side of the field. In the distance, we could see barefoot men in white *shammas* carrying rifles and spears and all their gear and dragging an enormous gun on wheels, gleaming new and probably German, since Hitler is the only European leader who hasn't come up with some diplomatic excuse not to sell us weapons. Horatio Augustus had forty men with rifles and one big field gun, but that was it. There wasn't a darn thing he could do to protect Aksum from an air attack. Ras Amde Worku had already told him *not* to. But he was doing it anyway, hiding with his men in the low ground cover across the field, waiting for the planes to arrive.

Momma suddenly called to Miniya.

"Go! Go home! Run *now*," she ordered her. When Miniya hesitated, Momma did the unthinkable, and gave her a light slap across the back of her shoulders. "*Go home.*"

Miniya ran.

Momma stood still, watching the whirlwind around us and listening to the horrible insect drone of the approaching swarm of aircraft getting nearer.

"Momma—" I hesitated. "Should we leave, too?"

My brain hummed, *What would White Raven do, what would White Raven do?* She'd disguise her reason for being here. . . .

"We need Meskal daisies!"

Momma shot me a sidelong glance.

"We have to make it look like we're expecting them—we have to welcome them!" I said. "You take their reconnaissance photos for them. We have to fool them into thinking we're on their side. Let's decorate!"

There were golden asters blooming as high as my hips all around the back of the hut, and I started pulling them up in armfuls.

"Em, you loony—"

"Help me, Momma! We'll tie them around the door—make it pretty—make it *girly*. People *love* that. Remember how Delia tied all those red-white-and-blue ribbons on the Jenny for the Fourth of July when that one fella wasn't going to let you fly, and the crowd booed until he did? Remember how you'd wear those matching feather boas when you passed around the hat after a show? And your white carnation wreaths on Decoration Day? That's what girls are supposed to *do*—make things pretty."

"I am not that kind of a girl," Momma grumbled.

"That's why you need folks like Delia and Sinidu and me to help you. I'm not girly, either. I just like dressing up. You do, too! You wore Mrs. Sinclair's blue silk dress when Papà Menotti visited."

Momma threw heaps of gold blossom over the trampled ground around the entrance to the hut and stuck flowers through the chinks in the walls around the doorway. "If they don't think we're poor, defenseless, neutral American women, they're going to think we're a couple of prostitutes," Momma muttered grimly under her breath.

It was *so much better*. I almost wished Papà Menotti would turn up just so he could appreciate the effort. I started braiding flower stems together to make a wreath for me to wear just in case he did.

"You want one, too, Momma?"

"I don't want a wreath. You have to help me think. We need a story for the Italians when they land. We can't tell them any of the real reasons we're here—why are *you and me* here and not Teo? Where's our plane—how did we get here, how are we getting back, and where did Teo go?"

She really couldn't be a spy, or she'd absolutely be the dumbest spy in the world. She can't make anything up or pretend to be anyone else except herself to save her life.

But making up stories is what I do best.

"Momma, it's *easy*!" I said. "Tell them Teo brought us here and then—" I took a deep breath. It was okay to say this. "Tell them he brought us here and then flew back to Addis Ababa. He wants to be a pilot with the Ethiopian Air Force. He *is* a pilot with the Ethiopian Air Force. He's old enough to carry a spear, right, so isn't that just the most obvious? But we got Teo to bring us here because we want to go back to Papà Menotti. Teo wouldn't take us any farther, because he didn't want to fly in Eritrea."

The first airplanes appeared over the hill that cradled the airfield.

"But when he comes back they'll—"

"They'll take the plane away from us now anyway, right? He'll have to pretend he changed his mind and brought it to them on purpose. And that'll be okay."

I grabbed Momma's hand, because over the hill came three of the enormous Regia Aeronautica Capronis flying in a neat V formation. They roared like big cats in the night and passed us, making a long turn back to the field because they needed so much space to land in.

"Momma!" I yelled. "My story makes sense, right?"

"It makes sense!" she yelled back. "Except we don't want to get whisked away to Asmara or somewhere—out of the line of fire."

I saw the flaw in my beautiful fish story. We were going to have to find a way to stay in Aksum so Teo could come back for us. We had to stay in Aksum to make sure no one tried to shoot him out of the sky when he did come back.

I stood clutching Momma's cold hand and trying to imagine how we'd fake it.

The three Italian planes were in line one after the other now so they could land. Up close they were the scariest things I have ever seen. They had great big black skull and crossbones paintings on them like pirate ships. Just as the first one touched down, another two appeared over the hill.

Momma squeezed my hand three times.

*Are. You. Scared?*

And I realized, when she did it, that she was also telling me: *I. Love. You.*

We'd have a little while before Teo came back. I'd have time to think of a good cover story for him.

I squeezed back.

*I. Am. Not. Scared.*

Or it could also mean: *I. Love. You. Too.*

We watched the second plane taxi and the third plane land.

More were still flying in. There are ten now in all—the three big triple-engined Capronis, five Fiat fighters, and two Romeo scout planes. Aksum already has as many aircraft at its brand-new airfield as Haile Selassie's Imperial Ethiopian Air Force has in Addis Ababa.

Momma pointed toward the place where the road curved around the hill. "*Listen.*"

I stood still.

There was a different terrible noise over there—the roar and rumble of motors on the ground. Hearing it made me think of American cities and at the same time made me realize what an utterly weird and alien sound it is to hear in highland Ethiopia. While we stared, the first light tanks came wallowing up the road to the new airfield, with open trucks behind them full of white soldiers, all in uniform, all carrying the same new rifles. And more cars. The big, ugly tractory things at the front began to make their way across the field, bulldozing the yellow Meskal daisies in their path.

Over where the procession of priests had gone three days earlier, people began unloading barrels and crates from the three huge planes that had already landed. They were setting up a big canvas tent for storage. The men beneath the planes' wings scurried like frantic bugs in an anthill that's got stepped on, and you could faintly hear shouts across the field.

"What's going on?" I asked.

"They've run into Augustus's men, I guess," Momma said. She stared through the binoculars. "Why couldn't he just wait, or follow Ras Amde Worku into the mountains like he is supposed to!"

You could only sort of hear the shouts. But we heard the gunfire like it was right next to us.

Momma threw herself flat on the ground. That was self-preservation taking over from maternal instinct. She'd been fired on in Belgium and Italy in the Great War, and throwing yourself on the ground is what you do when you have heard gunfire and you know what it means. But *my* instinct was not to save myself. It was to try to see what was going on.

"*Get down*, Em!"

In about ten seconds, I dragged the table out the shed door and used it to boost myself up onto the roof.

"*Em Menotti!*" Momma roared, jumping to her feet, maternal instinct trumping self-preservation once again.

"Gimme the glasses, Momma!" I lay on the warm corrugated

iron roof and stretched my arms down to her. She heaved the world's most defeated sigh and threw me the binoculars.

I lay flat. I felt pretty sure nobody would shoot at *me*, even if I stood up, but the whole hut was incredibly shaky with me on top of it and I trusted the roof less than I trusted the Italian and Ethiopian soldiers wrangling on the other side of the golden savannah field.

Probably I was stupid to look. I didn't think about what I might see.

I saw the Italian men with their rifles. I saw them kneeling, professional soldiers, trained, cold. At first I couldn't see who they were shooting at. But then came a man out of nowhere, like a medieval painting, in a white cloak and with a spear, charging like a mother hippo protecting its young. He ran straight at the line of rifles, put his spear into one of the kneeling men like he was killing a lion, and fell in a fountain of his own blood as everybody else gunned him down before he could even pull his spear out of the man he'd killed. He fell over on top of the other dead man, blood spouting out of him like a burst water skin.

I dropped the binoculars and buried my face in one arm, clinging to the edge of the roof with my other hand.

"Em! Em? *Emmy!*"

But I couldn't look down or answer. I was pretty sure I'd be sick if I moved my head. So I just lay there on the shaking iron sheet until, after what seemed like a year later, I felt my momma's lean, warm body pressed close against mine and one of her strong, thin arms holding tight around my shoulders.

The battle only lasted half an hour. That is when Augustus got smart and retreated, I guess. I don't know how long it will take the emperor to find out about it, if he ever does. And if it doesn't even get reported in Ethiopia, it will never get reported in an American newspaper. How long will it take before anybody outside Aksum finds out? Before anybody else in the world ever gives a damn?

After a little while, Momma let go of me and shifted around so I could squint up at her from beneath the crook of my arm. I saw that she had rescued the binoculars.

"Listen, Em," she said softly. "In a minute, when you get your breath back and we climb down from here, you and me are going to be Red Cross nurses. This will *really* make it easy for us to be here. It doesn't matter how we got here or where we're going. That's what we're needed for and that's what we can do. *That's* what girls are supposed to do. Fix things. Clean up mess."

"Sooner make things pretty," I choked.

"That's *why* we like to make things pretty; it's just 'cause we're so dang sick of cleaning up horrible messes. Same instinct. You going to be okay?"

"I'll be okay," I gulped.

And of course I've helped out enough in the clinic that I've seen plenty of ugly stuff. I had to hold down a little kid while Ezra shoved his dislocated arm back in place, and there was that woman who nearly cut her foot off chopping wood. I sat there for about four hours in the middle of the night telling stories about Connie and her ponies in Amharic to Sinidu while Momma stitched up the places where her new baby had torn her coming out.

But I'd never seen a man get exploded by a rifle before. Or have a spear planted in his chest.

"Good girl."

After a couple more minutes, I realized Momma was waiting for me, and that if some wounded person on the other side of the airfield had already bled to death because there was no one leaning on his severed artery, it was going to be my fault. And anyway, White Raven wouldn't be lounging around feeling sorry for herself if there were bleeding soldiers to rescue.

I lifted my head.

"All right, we can go," I whispered.

"I'll climb down first. Then I can help you. This shed's going to fall apart if we're not careful."

Now the Fiat fighters were lining up and parking neatly along our side of the field below the hill, and men were climbing out. A handful of officers had banded together and were heading toward us. One of them waved up at us, and Momma waved back.

"Signora Menotti!" the airman called to her. He was wearing round, dark sunglasses that made him look like a bug.

It wasn't Papà. I knew I recognized him, but it took me a minute to figure out why. Of course there are not too many Regia Aeronautica officers I know by name, but the dark glasses tipped me off. He must have a supply of them, because he gave his other pair to Habte Sadek. It is Captain Gianluca Adessi, the one who visited us with Papà Menotti at Timkat last year.

"Signora Menotti and the lovely Emilia!" he called up to us.

That made me remember how much I didn't like him the first time. Calling me lovely when I am lying on a dusty roof, trying not to throw up. He is phony. He does not love play-acting because it is fun and beautiful, like Papà Menotti. Captain Adessi is just insincere.

"Crowned with flowers!"

I reached up to touch the Meskal daisies in my hair—I'd forgotten all about them—and I thought, *I am White Raven, the master of all disguises.*

"You welcome us more kindly than the local population—" Adessi began.

Momma glowered down at him. "Is anyone hurt?" she interrupted.

"There is one, I know. Can you help?"

Momma slung the binoculars on their leather strap over her

back so they wouldn't get in the way as she climbed down from the iron roof. I thought about lying up there forever—maybe everybody would feel so sorry for me, in my wreath of Meskal daisies, that they'd realize they were being stupid, pack up, and go home. But White Raven nagged at me, and Momma did, too.

"Come *on*, Em," Momma called, with irritation in her voice. So I came down.

Captain Adessi showered my hand with kisses. "A thousand apologies to Orsino's lovely daughter! It is a tremendous and pleasant surprise to find you here! And after you have made this place so gracious, for the soldiers to frighten you like this—"

He suddenly reminded me a *lot* of Horatio Augustus.

"What's going on here?" Momma asked.

Adessi let go of my hand so he could make a broad, sweeping gesture with his arm, showing off the airfield. "These are aircraft of La Disperata—*the desperate* squadron. You see how the skull and crossed tibias is our symbol!" He had it on a patch on the breast of his flying suit. Suddenly the round black lenses hiding his eyes seemed sinister and creepy, like he was trying to make his boyish face look like a skull with empty eye sockets. "Those who are here have come to occupy this airfield while our soldiers occupy the city. You heard—I fear you saw—that we have had an incident with bandits. Mercenaries. No one from the locality. They have retreated, perhaps to join the fighting forces farther south, but we will not press on the attack until we have established our base here." Adessi pointed to the thorn barriers that those mercenary bandits had *put there themselves* for us. "You were wise to barricade yourselves against them," he said.

Well, at least Augustus got away. I glared at Captain Adessi, feeling triumphant. *Master of disguise*, I reminded myself. *You're just a helpless* ferenji *girl looking for her father.*

"What in the blessed name of our Lady are you doing here?"

"Where's my father?" I interrupted. "We came here to find him! If it's going to be all so dangerous, I want to be with my father—"

Captain Adessi turned to Momma, silently asking her to verify what I was saying. I just *long* to have somebody take me as seriously as they take her. How many people do you have to charm and how many aerial photographs do you have to take and how long do you have to be married before anyone begins to take you seriously?

"My son brought us here," Momma said.

"Your son?"

"Teo," she said icily. "My foster son. His father was Ethiopian."

"Where is he now?"

Momma's worry line deepened, and she hesitated. I jumped in to rescue her. "He's gone back to Addis Ababa to fight for his country."

"You are a family divided," Adessi observed.

Momma gave a brief nod. I could tell she didn't trust herself to answer aloud.

"I do not know what to say," Adessi apologized. "Orsino flies far to the east of here. We will get news to him somehow—or when an aircraft is free, take you straight to Asmara, where our main squadron is based and you will be safe—"

"*Thank you,*" Momma cut him off firmly, because we sure didn't want to end up in Asmara. "We're not going to Asmara without Orsino. But since we're here now, put us to work."

Oh—I am so glad I have still got Momma. Even if she can't control what happens, she *still* tries to fix things. We don't think the same way, not like me and Teo, but we are still partners. I am so glad I am not alone.

———

THERE WERE A DOZEN MEN HURT. NOT JUST SPEAR wounds. Some of Augustus's soldiers have rifles, too.

I didn't have to do anything messy. Partly I think it was because I am a girl with flowers in my hair. There was a military doctor who didn't speak English, but Momma is good at taking orders from doctors, and he liked her right away—he could see she knew what she was doing, and he'd just point at gauze or tweezers and she'd do what he needed. They got me to run errands between their impromptu field hospital tent and the supplies they were unpacking. More soldiers turned up in trucks with more stuff. The doctor would write a note and give it to me, and I'd run it to someone else forty yards away, and the next fellow would pry open a bunch of crates and trunks till he found a bottle of morphine or whatever it was I'd been sent for.

I did a lot of standing and waiting while they hunted. I felt sort of stunned. But I know the exact moment I woke up.

I'd been reading the labels on the boxes they were unloading, and they were all meaningless, and then suddenly they made sense again. There are always things that make sense even when you don't know what the words mean in a different language. A white cross or a rod and snake mean a box of medical supplies. An arrow shows you which way up something is supposed to stand. The skull and crossbones warns you when something is dangerous.

I wasn't really thinking about it, the moment I woke up. Everything just suddenly came into focus, the way it does when you adjust the lens on a camera.

People were taking crates out of one of the trucks. One of the Disperata pilots was directing. He had a patch on his flying suit with the skull and crossbones—what did Adessi call it, skull and crossed tibias? It was white on a black patch, like the one

Capitano Adessi wears, like the pictures on the Capronis, with the words LA DISPERATA painted underneath.

The crates the men were unloading weren't labeled with the squadron symbol. They just had ordinary skulls and crossbones stamped on them in black. And though I didn't know what the symbol meant when I saw it on the planes, I knew what it meant on the crates.

They were full of poison.

There were fifteen of these poisonous crates. They'd all come out of the same truck. A couple of men were examining a shell they'd lifted out of one of the open crates, checking it for damage. They were wearing heavy gloves and gas masks that made them look like giant bugs. The masks made Capitano Adessi's round black sunglasses seem like ordinary sunglasses, which of course they are. The masks these men wore were attached to hoods that came down over the backs of their necks.

I never saw anything so ugly that anybody would wear on *purpose.*

I don't think I've ever seen a real shell before, either, but it was exactly the long bullet shape of a Buck Rogers rocket, and I knew it was a weapon. If not a shell, maybe an actual bomb.

I am pretty sure that no Ethiopian soldier I have ever met has got a gas mask in his kit. Not even the Imperial Guard have gas masks.

They are brave enough to run in with spears against men with rifles leaping out of airplanes. They are brave enough to fight them in hand-to-hand combat. But bravery is not going to make a difference if they can't breathe.

*It isn't fair.*

Even if they do still keep slaves.

*None of it is fair.*

———

I COULDN'T TALK TO MOMMA ALONE TILL AFTER
sunset. After supper. After a long evening around a bonfire drinking unceremonial (but delicious) coffee with Captain Adessi. I
hate his coffee. I hate how good it is, how *nice* everybody is to us.
I was ready to explode by the time Momma and I were finally by
ourselves.

They are letting us stay in our camp in the operations hut—we
are the only women on the airfield, and it is a little bit private.

Since we'd climbed down from the roof about six hours ago,
Momma hadn't said anything to me that wasn't "Pass the iodine"
or "Isn't it lucky Gianluca speaks such good English!" After we
went to bed, we lay side by side on our tummies looking out
toward the bonfire, which was still going—they'd hacked down
an acacia from the edge of the airfield to feed their First Night of
Occupying Aksum celebration.

"The party's for morale," Momma said. "They weren't expecting that attack. They weren't expecting resistance out here—their
soldiers who came on foot didn't have to fight their way into the
city. Gianluca's official line is that no blood was spilled in taking
Aksum—a bloodless victory."

"Not counting any fella fighting with Horatio Augustus, I
guess?"

"No civilians ended up bleeding. I don't know. Don't know
how the Italian soldier with the spear in his chest doesn't count.
Maybe it only counts as a bloody battle if more than five people
get killed."

I shook my head bitterly. She couldn't see me, but she felt it.

I said softly, "Did you see them unloading?"

"Yes," she hissed under her breath.

"Did you see what it was?"

"Looked like shells. But that's what the big guns on the trucks
are for, Em. And the big planes are bombers. They've got to have
explosive attached to them."

"It's not explosive. I watched them unloading," I said. "It was poison gas. They were lifting the shells out of the crates and checking for leaks, and they had to wear gas masks to do it."

"Em—that's not—"

I don't know what she was going to say—*That's not true? That's not funny? That's not very nice?*

But anyway, she cut herself short and didn't say anything for a moment or two.

"I saw what the boxes had written on them," I whispered. "*Iprite*. Do you know what it means?"

"*Iprite!*"

It was a completely strange word and maybe I wasn't pronouncing it right.

"Momma?"

"*Iprite*—are you *sure*? But that's against—" She cut herself off. "*I can't believe it*—" I could tell, despite her outrage, that she did believe it—whatever it was. "How much?" she whispered at last. "You have any idea how much?"

"A whole truckload."

"Em. I want you to show me. We'll have to wait till they settle down—"

"We don't have to wait," I said. "We can go out any time we want and we don't have to sneak. We're *girls*. We're *harmless*. And also, we go to the bathroom a lot, and not in the same place as a bunch of soldiers. And if I had to go, you would come with me, because you are my mother and you wouldn't want me to go find a place by myself. You would want to make sure no one took me by surprise."

"Oh, *Emmy!*" she laughed breathlessly.

I had got all wrapped up in my *shamma* to go to sleep. Now I rewrapped it ever so modest and demure, practically like a veil across my face, so I was covered head to toe. All that white would be very showy in the dark.

"They won't think we're trying to hide," I said.

And no one did. We walked straight across the airfield with Momma's big flashlight lighting up the grass in front of us. Other people were walking around with flashlights, too, and some with flaming torches, so no one even bothered to ask who we were until we were practically right on top of the evil pile of crates.

They did have a couple of fellows standing there to guard the stuff, and Momma had a polite conversation in French with one of them, sharing cigarettes while I splashed the beam of her flashlight all over the crates and the carefully lined up shells the men were guarding so that Momma could read the writing on everything.

At last, Momma turned away from the crates, and by this time everyone was laughing like they were at a party.

"Seen enough, Em," she said to me in English as we headed back to the hut.

She didn't go back to bed.

"Hold my flashlight for me," she said.

She began sorting through her satchel, dividing everything up into two piles. After a couple of minutes, I realized one pile was for her and one was for me.

"We're splitting up?" I asked, alarmed.

"Just in case we *get* split up. Just in case. Now, listen. I know it'll be awkward, but hang on to your bag any time you go outside. Just take it everywhere. Then you can take the gas mask with you without it being too obvious. Promise you'll always take it with you."

She waited.

"Okay."

"Say you promise."

"I promise! Jumping cats, Momma! Grandfather says Friends don't swear oaths!"

"Because we don't need to. We're supposed to be truthful all the time, but you are not, and I am not taking a chance against mustard gas," Momma said, her voice low. "That's what that stuff is. Sometimes we called it *yperite*—must be the same word as *iprite*. It is absolutely the nastiest weapon anybody knows how to use. Even if you have a mask on it'll still burn your skin—it gets in people's clothes; it poisons the ground and everything it touches. We had to wear rubber gloves and rubber boots when we were stripping anyone who'd been exposed to it or we'd end up with the most god-awful burns on our own hands. The Germans used it in Belgium, and the Italians used it in Libya, and I am grateful to God that Orsino only ever killed people with machine guns."

She paused for breath.

"I thought it was illegal! I thought they said it was illegal to use in war, when they laid down the Geneva Protocol in '25! They better not be planning to use it here. God, Emmy, all our barefoot soldiers—!"

"You said *our*."

"We live here." She was silent for a moment, then added, "Teo is ours."

So that was it. At last I knew for sure whose side she was on. I was so relieved—it felt so *right*—that I started to sniffle.

"We'll be okay, Em," Momma said hollowly, pulling me close with one skinny, strong arm. She even tried to joke to cheer me up. "It smells like garlic. Mustard gas, I mean. I thought I'd never eat garlic again for *years*, but who can resist anything swimming in Sinidu's clarified butter? So you smell garlic in the air, you put on the gas mask."

"But—Teo! But—"

I wanted to say, *Habte Sadek! Sinidu! Erknesh! Mateos!* And all the other people who didn't have twenty-five-dollar gas masks.

But if I'd said another word, I'd have burst into sissy tears, so I just sniffled and didn't say anything.

Momma understood. "We won't stay here forever, but we need to give Teo the time he needs. A month, maybe? If he doesn't come back in a month, we will leave. We will walk home. If Ras Assefa's retinue can do it in a week, so can we."

I am not sure I believe that. But I have trouble imagining portly Ras Assefa in his business suit doing it, too, and I know that he did (probably not in that suit). Maybe we can follow the Italian soldiers some way south when they go after Ras Amde Worku and Horatio Augustus.

Today, Momma confronted Capitano Adessi about the mustard gas, and this is what he said: "Oh, we would never use that in combat. It is against the Geneva protocols for war. But the *iprite*, this gas, is so difficult to dispose of that we have to guard it carefully, which is why we have brought it to Aksum, where there is so little resistance to our occupation. Please do not judge diplomatic policy by the evil weapons you see stockpiled on the ground."

He paused, lowered his buggy black glasses so we could see his eyes, and beamed at us.

"Listen! Here is better, happier news. *Il Duce* Mussolini announces today the complete abolishment of slavery in Abyssinia. As an American, you will be overjoyed to hear such progress, not two weeks since the occupation began!"

I DON'T KNOW HOW MOMMA REACTED, BECAUSE this time I couldn't sniffle the tears back. I burst out crying and ran away.

---

I STARTED OUT TRYING TO ESCAPE INTO WRITING *The Adventures* and wrote all this instead.

I should be happy, I guess. The Italians have arrived, full of good intentions, and Teo is no longer a slave. That was easy, right?

Except he is already gone. He doesn't know it. He is doing whatever he has to do because he missed the announcement by three days. How can it make any difference now—especially if he is working for the emperor? Just because Mussolini has made some proclamation after invading Ethiopia doesn't mean he can change the rules here. Although maybe it will help Teo if he gets made a prisoner by the Italians—maybe they will forgive him having to do something that he was forced to do as a slave. Unless, of course, they want to figure out what he *did* do. Then what?

Oh God, oh God, I can't think about him being a real prisoner. It makes me *sick* to think about the Black Dove prison stories I have made up.

Waiting for Teo is terrible. The longer we wait, the more I am sure he has been hurt or killed. But the longer we wait the more I hope he *won't* come back. More and more, I think the Italians will just shoot him the second he climbs out of his plane. There are two Romeos here, two-seaters that they use for reconnaissance, and they have been going off on their exploring missions and coming back again all day. Every time I hear one flying in, my heart soars for a second because I think it might be Teo, safe and alive. And then a moment later, I start to pray that it *isn't* Teo.

It never is.

Amba Kwala, or should I call it the Fortress of
   Clarity ha ha, Day 3

I AM GOING A LITTLE CRAZY NOW. AS FAR AS I CAN tell, my father is *not* as important an officer as his friend Capitano Gianluca Adessi, and he has *not* been able to take a vacation and spare fuel from his invasion activities to take me somewhere safe, as if I were an airmail package. In fact, I think I am pretty safe *here*, in terms of not getting shot at or taken prisoner or whatever else happens to an American girl who is supposed to be neutral but who is caught up in the spiderweb of someone else's war. In real life I think I am already a prisoner.

In fact I am trying to escape. There must be a way down over the side of the *amba*. The goats do it—a few of them are not penned and they disappear over the edge and you never see them again, but there aren't piles of dead goats lying around at the bottom of the cliffs, so they must go somewhere (although now that I have followed one of them all day, I know it just came back up in a different place). I have found a bearded vulture's nest big enough that I could hide in it if I needed to. Papà Menotti has *no idea* how far down the side of that cliff I have made it.

But I am going to have to pilfer some rope if I want to get any farther. I am scared to do it. I mean I am not scared of pilfering things—I pilfered binoculars from Adessi's plane and he didn't even notice it, because I was using them like they were mine. And I pilfered his map by accident because I was holding it as I got out of the plane when he stuck me here—but I am scared of climbing down the *amba*. Without rope I can get a short way down and back up, but *with* rope I am pretty sure I will only be able to get a long way down, and if I get stuck halfway down, I won't be able to get back up.

I guess I should be scared of what will happen to me once I *do* get down and am on foot in the middle of nowhere. But that doesn't scare me so much because I like being on foot in the middle of nowhere. And I still have Mrs. Sinclair's revolver, and the compass Papà Menotti gave me.

I was not *worried* to begin with—I never thought I'd end up stuck here. But now I am beginning to think that they did it on purpose. I have been kidnapped.

That sounds ridiculous, but I bet it is true.

Three days ago, back in Aksum still waiting for Teo, Capitano Adessi lured Momma away from me by asking if she'd like to try flying one of the Fiat fighter planes.

Of course she said yes. Any flier worth her salt (except me) would have said yes. I am sure Teo would have said yes.

The Fiats only have one seat, so she couldn't take me with her, and Adessi must have felt pretty sure that if I was on the ground without Momma, she wouldn't try to steal the plane. He must have been pretty sure that not even Rhoda Menotti would be batty enough to leave her sixteen-year-old daughter alone on an airfield full of Italian soldiers in a remote city in the African highlands. I never for one second believed she'd be batty enough to do that, either.

What she did do was take the plane so high into the blazing blue sky that we couldn't see her, and then came roaring earthward in the most incredible display of aerial daring that I am sure most anybody on that airfield had ever seen. Even though I never believed she'd fly off without me, *again* I started to worry that she was going to kill herself. Accidentally if not on purpose.

She threw the plane over and over itself and then she came plummeting toward us in a dive, but she straightened up about twenty feet above the ground and screamed away into the sky again. Everybody, including me, stood there with our mouths hanging open, gaping as she climbed.

But instead of coming back for another dive or loop, she suddenly leveled out, three thousand feet above us, and tore away toward the south.

Capitano Adessi put his hand on my shoulder, and I jumped about a mile.

"Shall we chase your mother, Emilia?" he asked. "Shall we take a Caproni and go after her?" And I said yes.

The thing is—I knew what she was doing. She was taking the opportunity to do a little scouting. If she flew for twenty minutes in the direction of the first heading Teo took, she might see if he'd landed or crashed along the way. Of course we both knew he was more likely to do either of those things later in the trip than in the first twenty minutes after taking off, but I didn't blame her for wanting to *try*.

So I knew she'd come back—if she didn't spot our wrecked plane lying on a mountaintop somewhere—but also, I wanted to chase her. I wanted to ride in a Caproni bomber. It is true that I hate landing so much that my fear of it has spread like poison into all the other things that go into taking control of the Romeo, but I still love being in the air. And when am I ever going to get another chance to fly in a Caproni bomber? I imagined waving to Momma out the paneled glass window of the huge, enclosed cockpit. She'd be proud and a little jealous.

It took us twenty minutes to get going, check the fuel, and make sure nobody cared if I came along. The *waste* of fuel should have made me wonder, I guess, but it is hard to think of everything, especially when your mother has just disappeared into the sky and you are alone with the skull-and-crossed-tibia Desperate bugs.

So we got strapped in, with me in the navigator's seat in the most gigantic plane I'd ever climbed into, and we took off and roared away south in Momma's direction. Capitano Adessi handed me a map. It was in Italian, but mountains are mountains.

Adessi didn't talk much. It was too loud to gab anyway, and my helmet doesn't have an intercom connection in it. After a while he leaned over, peeled back the side of my helmet and shouted into my ear, "Want to fly?"

I thought he really meant it! I thought he was going to show me how to use the three tall throttle levers between our seats and how to make the three massive engines purr in a trio!

I knew that he'd grab the controls right back if I did anything wrong, and he'd just laugh it off and it wouldn't matter. And then I could tell Teo I'd flown a Caproni.

Captain Adessi lifted his hands from the flight controls—the plane was in trim, so of course it just kept flying itself. He didn't realize I had the first idea of how to fly a plane—he was just being nice.

I nearly said yes.

But then he took the map out of my hands and turned it around.

"Wrong way up," he yelled jovially.

I had it upside-down on purpose. I had flipped it so I could follow our course. I hesitated, because it was hard to explain how I read a map, let alone shout it to someone who was flying a plane with three engines over wild mountains.

He pointed to a place in exactly the opposite of where we were heading. "Turning here!"

Then he turned the plane in a completely different direction to either the way we'd started out or the way he'd told me we were going.

"But—"

I wasn't really scared when he set off in the wrong direction without explaining what he was doing. I figured he had a reason for it. It was incredibly loud and hard to talk. Maybe he'd spotted another plane out there and he thought it was Momma—after all, that was why we were up here. Maybe he hadn't finished telling me something about the map. Maybe he had some other errand he hadn't told me about, like refueling or bombing the ancient temple at Yeha. Maybe he wasn't trying to confuse me on purpose.

So when he asked me again if I wanted to fly, I just shook my head and gave him a thumbs-down. If we were detouring to bomb the ancient temple at Yeha, I didn't want anything to do with it.

We passed over Yeha. I spotted the golden temple walls through the binoculars. We kept going and I pretty much knew where we were the whole time, and through the binoculars I spotted the airfield at Amba Kwala long before you could see it without them, and when Adessi lined up the plane to land I was interested in spite of myself. I held my breath as I watched him smoothly balancing all those gigantic engines against each other. And then, when he shut everything down and climbed back and opened the door, there were all these joyful, happy people racing out to the plane from all over the *amba*, and one tall and slow-moving, slow-smiling person in the middle of them was Papà Menotti.

And you know what? I was so happy to see him. I was really, truly *happy*.

I leaped out of the big plane and he swooped me up in his arms—"*Mia bella cara!*" And then in Amharic, "*Selam! Tafash!* Peace—you've been lost! Beautiful!" He speaks a little bit of Amharic now, and a darn good thing he can, too, or we would not be able to talk to each other. His Amharic is terrible. But it is better than nothing.

So then he wanted to give me lunch. I still can't figure out how important he is, but if he didn't have his own tent before, he has definitely got one now that I am here, a good one with two partitioned rooms and a porch and plenty of folding furniture like a little European house. Half a dozen very excited and helpful people all in uniforms helped set us up a really beautiful lunch and then just left the two of us alone so we could have an awkward half an hour of reunion time.

While we were eating farfalle drowning in olive oil (delicious, *delicious*) I heard the Caproni's engines fire up.

I jumped to my feet and spun around to see if it really was the plane I'd come in, taking off without me. It really was. Then I ran about fifty steps across the *amba* toward the plane before I realized I'd left my satchel and flying helmet hanging over the back of my camp chair. I stood for a moment panicking, then ran back for my bag. Momma had made me promise never to go anywhere without it. It had the gas mask in it and Capitano Adessi's binoculars, and the map he'd given me to look at in the plane.

But I'd never have caught up with that plane even if I hadn't gone back for my bag.

As Adessi took off without me, I stood there waving—*still not worried!* I thought he was going to do an aerobatic show or something, like Momma. I was *sure* he was going to come back for me. Sure.

Then, as the hours passed—when it got dark and that stink-bug Adessi still hadn't appeared—I knew he must have dropped me here to stay on purpose. But I still believed he was going to come back in a day or two, bringing Momma with him. I was sure she'd come when she knew I was waiting here for her. I am *bait*.

Now three days have gone by, and she still hasn't come for me, and I am not so sure what is going on.

I can see out. I can see for miles all around me, across the *amba* plateaus. I can see all the planes that come and go. They go out carrying bombs and come in empty. Other planes come in and deliver fuel and more bombs.

Everybody knows I am Capitano Orsino Menotti's daughter.

Everybody is very friendly. One or two of them are horribly friendly. But it is such a small place that there is nowhere for them to hide away with me, and everybody always knows what everybody else is doing.

I am with my father and I am safe. And I am miserable. I don't know what to do. I don't know how to pick up the pieces. I don't know how to get away from this war—to get back to Tazma Meda—to get back to Momma. To get back to *Teo*.

It *really is* like being a prisoner in the Fortress of Clarity.

YOUR MAJESTY, I HAVE TORN OUT THE PART OF MY flight log that I kept while I was imprisoned on Amba Kwala. I was kept there with my father for four months. More than once he took me with him on bombardment missions. I did not have to go, but I wanted to—because it was the only way I could find out what was happening in the war. I knew when your army pushed into the Italians at Christmas because I saw it from the air through my stolen binoculars. And I knew that La Disperata sometimes landed and refueled at Aksum, because it is easier to bring fuel there than to the Amba Kwala airfield. I thought that maybe if my father and I touched down in Aksum sometime I could sneak off—find my way home—ask help from Ras Amde Worku's household. Anything other than being stuck on Amba Kwala. But my father never landed anywhere else with me.

One time, when we'd run out of bombs, we flew daringly low over a battle, and I saw our soldiers—I mean your soldiers—charge into an armored tank with their spears. I didn't see blood; I didn't see anyone fall. But the tank stopped, and our warriors in their white *shammas* swarmed over top of it. And that was the way the whole battle went that day, and for many days after Christmas, and my father would fly home with his ammunition spent and no one on the *amba* would talk to each other, because they couldn't believe it. Except me, elated with hope and secret loyalty.

One time my father's machine-gunner opened fire on a Red Cross hospital tent set up nearly ten miles away from the fighting. It was flying a British flag, and clearly marked with a giant red cross on top of it. It was ridiculous to pretend that the gunner mistook it for any part of anybody's army. I don't know why he did it—maybe he doesn't like the English? I am mad at the English, too, because they still let the Italians bring ships full of guns and trucks through the Suez Canal to get here, *and*, like the Americans, they won't help arm us. But what does Papà's gunner have against hospitals? Papà was very angry with him after we landed.

The last time I flew with my father, you shot at us.

I don't mean your gunners or your army shot at us. I mean you yourself, Your Majesty. You, the *negus*, one man alone, Haile Selassie—*you* shot at us.

Ordinarily we do not get fired at in the big Caproni with its three roaring engines, because your army has so few antiaircraft guns. La Disperata rules the sky alone. But when La Disperata attacked Dessie, you had that single cannon in your headquarters, and as my father dove toward the round, thatched roofs and green terraces, I watched you through my stolen binoculars. One solitary brave man against the world, running up the hill to the gun platform—

I knew it was you. You were already legendary. I'd *heard.*

*You hit us.* Did you know that? Because if you know that, if you saw, you'll know which plane I was in. A Caproni bomber with the middle engine out. A direct hit, in fact—a piece of the propeller cracked off and came flying through one of the glass panels in the windshield right past my head. I thought—if you've read this far, I bet you can guess exactly what I thought. I thought it was a bird.

But it wasn't, and it didn't hurt anybody, and Papà Menotti calmly shut down the middle engine and flew home steadily on the other two with the wind howling around us through the broken window panel.

Would you have fired on us anyway if you'd known that Teodros Gedeyon's sister was in that plane?

Papà tried to give me the piece of the propeller to keep as a souvenir. But I could not touch it.

After you shot at us, my father wouldn't take me on another bombardment mission. But it is not because of being shot at that he stopped taking me. It is because the bombers have started spreading *iprite*.

It started about a week after Christmas. I recognized the canisters. They fixed some of the planes so that the gunners would be spraying mustard gas instead of bullets. There was always at least one plane loaded with gas in the group that went out—it was not my Papà's plane, but he was still flying with them and he had his own gas mask and he did not want to take me along in case something went wrong.

In case *I* got gassed.

And I did not want to go anyway.

Papà explained to me why they are doing it. There was a change of command in the Italian army—Mussolini thought the old commander was moving too slowly. The new one is more ruthless. And they are angry about an Italian airman who was brutally murdered by vengeful villagers. The things that were done to him are terrible, and it is true that some of your warriors cut ugly trophies from those they slay in battle. We both know this. I can't imagine anyone in Tazma Meda doing what was supposed to have been done to that unlucky fellow, so I am not sure I believe the report. But that is why they are using gas now.

I began to be afraid that one day Papà would not come back to Amba Kwala and I would be alone with the strange, ruthless pilots of La Disperata, coming and going from their poisoning missions. I had to get away before my father was lost.

I knew what White Raven would do.

I realized I was going to have to pilfer a plane.

THIS IS WHERE MY FLIGHT LOG BEGINS AGAIN.

HERE I AM ALONE ON DELIA'S DREAM. I PLANNED MY flight here on purpose, knowing it would be a good place to split the journey. Here I am, alone in the Simien Mountains with the bearded vultures circling overhead. The strangest thing has just happened. I landed here all by myself. (That is not the strange thing, though it is a beautiful thing. I landed here *myself*, safely. Oh, the sweet song of the wind in the wires, when you know it is right! Now it is getting dark. I will have to stay here tonight. It is the first time I have soloed. This was my first flight all by myself and I am still alive and I am not lost. But that is not the strange thing.)

You know what I keep thinking? I am *so mad at Delia*. I am so mad at Delia I want to cry. *Mustard gas!* Fire in the thatched roofs, bombs exploding in people's gardens, dead goats and shepherd boys. *Mustard gas!* Delia sent us here because she wanted to live in a place where black kids didn't get lynched. Oh *God*. I am so mad at Delia.

And at Momma, for falling for Delia's dream.

And at me, for believing any of it could be true.

And yet the strange thing happened. It really happened. I am holding it here in my other hand, while I'm writing.

The wind was straight down the ridge, the opposite of where it was blowing the first time we came here, which is actually better because the ridge is a little wider where you touch down from the opposite direction and I didn't nearly blunder over the cliff this time. I didn't hit any of those danged bearded vultures, either. I parked right in the middle of the tableland in case the wind changes overnight, then sat down on the grass next to the lower wing, feeling very happy and grateful to be back on earth.

So I was sitting here, happy, and I patted the ground next to me to say hello to it. Tafash, *ground, you've been lost.* Selam.

*Peace, peace, peace.*

My fingers touched a smooth, round, familiar shape—I picked it up. Round like an eye, two clear glass discs set in a brass ring, a sky-blue arrow like an eyelash in the rose. I held the compass in my palm. I thought it must have fallen out of my blouse pocket when I climbed out of the plane. I'd put it in that pocket because the slacks I am wearing are much too big for me and I was worried it would get lost.

So now I dropped it back in my blouse. There was a *click*.

It was such a little sound. Such a tiny noise—that is the strange thing, that such a tiny noise, with no danger attached to it, could have made my heart leap into my throat the way it did.

I knew what I'd heard. I knew what the sound meant. It was the sound of the compass I'd just picked up hitting *the compass that was already in my pocket.*

I almost was afraid to look. I sat frozen for a moment, feeling my heart beating against the two compasses.

Finally I fished them both out.

They are exactly the same: identical round glass compasses the size of a button. They are the compasses Papà Menotti gave me and Teo for Christmas a year ago.

I have picked up Teo's compass. In all the wilderness of Ethiopia I have come to the pinpoint place where Teo left his compass.

A dozen wild explanations zoomed through my head: he dropped it when we first landed here? That couldn't be; he had it with him in Addis Ababa when we went flying with Billy Cooper. Then I must have picked it up at the nameless landing place in the Takazze Valley, or back in Aksum—right? Is there any other way to explain it?

The only other way to explain it—

He picked it up and put it in his own breast pocket when he walked away from the coffee ceremony in Aksum. I remember him doing it. It was the last thing I saw him do. His dark brown fingers slender like Delia's, closing over the round glass and golden brass, the quick, careless way he dropped it in his shirt pocket just like I did a second ago.

The only *possible* way to explain it is that he landed here.

And took off again safely.

Date: Mar. 2, '36 (Yekatit 23, 1928)

Type of Machine: Romeo Ro. 1

Number of Machine: 15-22

Airfield: Amba Kwala to uncharted mountaintop,
    somewhere between Aksum and Lalibela,
    N 12° 58' 10", E 38° 50' 29" (Delia's Dream)

Duration of Flight: 1 hour 35 min.

Character of Flight: still alive.

Pilot: EM (ME)


Remarks:




I GUESS THIS WON'T COUNT AS REAL FLIGHT TIME or a real solo since the plane is stolen.

It is the fortieth anniversary of the victory at Adwa. Forty years to the day since we pushed the Italians out of Ethiopia. The only African nation never to have been colonized.

*Oh*—I can't think about it. I am going to write until it gets dark because otherwise I will have to think about everything. I will have to be here in the dark looking up at the deep starry sky and worry about the wheel chocks holding while I get the engine started tomorrow, and where Momma is, and Teo, and where he went next after he lost his compass here . . . although of course he would still be able to find his way, because there is a compass on the dashboard of our own Romeo Ro. 1. There is one on the dashboard of this one that is mine now, this Romeo Ro. 1 with its black-and-silver skull and crossed tibia, as Gianluca Adessi says, standing out against the yellow grassland camouflage paint.

I keep thinking about how upset Papà will be. How he made me that little Christmas tree with an acacia branch and decorated it with brass bolts hung on threads so that they twinkled as they turned, with loops of copper wire to make shining garlands around the twigs. He fixed beeswax candles in the twigs and lit them all. It was just exactly the kind of thing I'd make. I keep thinking of how pretty it looked, twinkling in the shadow of the canvas awning when we crawled out of the tent on Christmas morning. And how pleased and anxious he looked, waiting for my reaction, and when he held out his arms I hopped into them—

"Oh, Papà! *Grazie, grazie! Bella, bella!*"

I guess I didn't say "beautiful" the right way, but he knew what I meant. For the hundred most important seconds of our lives together, we totally understood each other.

It isn't just from Delia that I get my taste for pretty, sparkly things.

And then he gave me this tie clip—the little pearl tie clip that he always wears, the one that Momma gave him when they were married. Because he hadn't realized I was going to be with him on Christmas Day, and it was the first Christmas we have been together since maybe *ever* (I can't remember another one), and he had nothing else pretty to give me. And I tried not to take it. And then I realized that I *had* to take it—that it would hurt him more if I didn't take it than if I did. And now he hasn't got Momma and he hasn't got me and he hasn't even got the stupid pretty little tie clip.

*Stop, White Raven.* Just stop thinking until the stars come out. Write about the flight.

How did I do it? I don't know how I did it. I mean—I do know *how.* I just can't believe that I did.

Now that I know I can steal a plane from the Italian air force, I am brave enough to do almost anything.

I got the idea of how to do it by thinking about White Raven. Not Momma, I mean, not Rhoda Menotti the wing-walker, not the crazy flying woman trying to raise her American kids in Ethiopia. I mean White Raven the adventure hero in our stories. What would *she* do if she wanted to steal a plane?

She'd disguise herself as a Regia Aeronautica pilot, of course.

(I imagined myself making a false mustache out of a centipede or something, squinching it between my upper lip and my nose to hold it in place.)

I wanted a Romeo. I didn't want one of the zippy new Fiat fighters—I wanted something I knew how to fly, and I only know how to fly a Romeo Ro. 1.

They don't take them out as often as they take the others. When they do, it's usually just one of them going along with a group of bombers and fighters. The Romeos have cameras mounted in the back instead of guns, so I guess they go along to take pictures or notes or count the troops or something. They only have two cockpits (ours with three is not normal), but sometimes only one pilot goes alone with no observer. I know all this because I have been watching and watching and watching.

At three o'clock in the afternoon today, three Italian pilots walked out to the parked Romeos lined up on the edge of the *amba*. I walked along with them. The *hardest* part of the plan, though not the scariest, was keeping my disguise secret until I needed to use it, then putting it on at the last minute. I thought I'd only get one chance. This was it.

There was one fellow on the *amba* who spoke a little English, who is friendly with Papà Menotti and helped us talk sometimes, and I pestered and vamped him into giving me his flying jacket, crossed tibia and all (and he has done a lot of pestering *me* because I do not wear it). Captain Adessi, that stinkbug, turned up on Christmas Day and gave me a white silk aviator's scarf, useful for wiping dead bugs off your goggles. Little does he know he contributed to my escape plan. I pilfered one of Papà Menotti's maps.

I have a pilfered pair of sunglasses so that I, too, can look like a Disperata bug. I have my own water bottle and my own goggles and my own flight bag. The hardest thing was to cover up my legs. They all wear flight suits and I am in a skirt. And I am barefoot. I pilfered Papà's socks and a pair of his trousers this afternoon—the trousers are held up with string. All planned ahead of time. All thrown on in about two minutes when I saw the pilots heading to the Romeos.

When two of the three Italian airmen climbed into the Romeo at the end of the row this afternoon, and the other man climbed into the plane next to it, as they sat there waiting to get their engines started, I climbed into the third plane in the line and waited to see what would happen.

I think I didn't really expect anything to happen. I'm not sure I would have done it if I *really believed* anything would happen.

But it did—the guy swung the propeller of the plane I was sitting in, and the engine started.

I was completely camouflaged with my goggles on, invisible—more Black Dove than White Raven, for sure. The fact that I knew what to do with the plane—feet on the brakes, waiting for them to move the wheel chocks out of the way, set the engine idling at the right speed—no one knew now that I wasn't just part of the lineup. *No one knows I can fly.*

When the other two Romeos began to taxi across the *amba*, I just followed like a baby goat following its mama—no hurry—I left the same amount of space between me and the second plane as he left between himself and the first.

The thing is, it's easy taking off.

In the air, I left a great big gap between me and the other two planes. I followed them at a distance for a little while—only for a few minutes, because I figured they knew what they were supposed to be doing and they didn't expect me to tag along. Then I turned south. I'd planned my route ages ago. That was the easiest part of my escape.

I guess it was not just convenience that made me land here on Delia's Dream, though it is about halfway to Tazma Meda. I always meant to come this way. I thought about it while I was flying—this is the sky Delia wanted to see. This is the sky Momma sees when she is flying alone with her memories of Delia and Delia's dream of an open African sky.

I am mad at Mussolini; and at the French, who won't stand up to him; and at the British, who won't let anyone arm us; and at President Roosevelt, who is too wishy-washy to send the help he knows we need. I am mad at the slave owners who are so important Haile Selassie won't risk offending them. I am mad at Delia and Momma for falling for the dream. I am *so mad* at everybody else for ruining it.

FROM TEO'S FLIGHT LOG. THERE IS NO DATE, BUT HE *wrote this before he left Aksum. I think this is safest in your own hands, Your Majesty.*

I WISH I KNEW SOME BETTER CUSSWORDS. *GOSH DARN it* does not feel strong enough. Or I wish I knew how to pray properly. I am sure I have sat through 150 Friends meetings and never said a single prayer. All the beautiful church services in Tazma Meda are in ancient Ethiopian Ge'ez, the church language, and not even Ezra and Sinidu can understand it. I love listening; I love being there. I wrote all that stuff for Miss Shore about how it makes me believe in God to be there. But how do you learn to pray?

I am supposed to be FLIGHT PLANNING. I asked all the Aksum guards and priests to go away and leave me here to do it myself. And it is true they were giving me a headache and— well, I am scared. I would rather make up the adventure story than have to do it in real life.

I don't actually have to do much flight planning—just reverse the headings and change the wind direction. Emmy was right. I did all the hard work back at home, myself, under Momma's watchful eye. The maps and calculations are all ready to go, and I will check them before we take off. I am so lucky that I can use them. I will be *careful.* Because these guys—these crazy people I am supposed to be helping—they think we are going to be able to follow some goat path for three hundred miles. They do not know anything about flight, or air navigation. It is up to me to get it right.

I have spent the whole day being scared—from the time Momma was doing the aerobatics in the Takazze Valley and we thought she might kill herself on purpose, to being hunted and shot at by the Italian fighter planes, to being threatened with a rifle up against my head, to being led away into this shack with the guards standing outside.

When I first came in, I couldn't see anything for a moment, because there was such a contrast between the bright daylight and the shadowy inside of the hut. There were two big lumps of darkness in the gloom. One turned out to be a table, and one was the box-shaped thing they'd been carrying on a litter made of sticks across the airfield when we landed, like a small case wrapped in gauze and strapped with leather cords. Pacing between them, fiercely covering the ground there and back, was a boy my own age, dressed like a priest. He glittered faintly when he walked.

When I came in, he threw his arm up against his eyes to block out the brightness of the light in the doorway, but he didn't stop pacing until they closed the door behind me. Then we stood still, facing each other, both of us blinded for a minute.

We let our eyes adjust to the gloom and he stared at my feet. I wondered if I was supposed to bow or something. I took a step forward with my hand out, and he stepped back quickly, then checked himself and stood his ground. But he didn't hold out his hand.

He was scared, too.

Nothing makes you brave like knowing you've got the advantage of fear. I said in Amharic, "I am Teodros."

He kept on gazing down somewhere around my knees. His

hands were clenched in fists. I took a step toward the wrapped-up box and reached a hand toward it. "This is your cargo?"

He leaped in between me and the box, holding up his hands in protest. He gestured firmly in the air, blocking my way. *Don't touch,* he said with his body, though he didn't utter a word.

"Do you speak Amharic?" I asked.

He didn't respond at *all*—just stood protecting his box and staring at my knees.

"Okay," I said in English . . . resorting to talking to myself for reassurance, but also kind of hoping that my voice would sound so calming and full of authority that it would reassure this kid and also, maybe by luck or magic, make him understand what I was saying.

How was I supposed to plan a route with someone who couldn't or wouldn't tell me where he wanted to go?

*"Teodros,"* I said again, pointing to myself. I could see all right by now by the light coming in through the chinks in the walls. I moved slowly and purposefully, hoping I wasn't going to upset my passenger or make some stupid error to offend him. I unfolded the chart with the route from Takazze drawn all over it and spread it over the table. I patted the map.

"Please tell me you know where you're going," I said without hope, pointing to the page to tell him to come and look.

He crossed over to the table. He moved slowly and purposefully, as though we were getting ready to fight a duel.

"We're here," I said, pointing to Aksum.

He didn't touch the map. He looked at it with fearful interest, but I could tell he didn't know what he was looking at.

It doesn't *look* like a landscape—if you've never seen a map, how can you know what you're looking at? Habte Sadek figured it out so easily, when we tried to cheer him up with Momma's maps during the big rains.

*There is always another way of making a map,* he'd said.

I chewed my lip and scratched the base of my skull, trying to be a genius. What did this guy actually know? Had he ever been out of Aksum in his life? Probably not—Habte Sadek had modeled landscapes with his hands because he'd traveled through them. But this young priest had most likely never seen anything but Ethiopian ecclesiastic books and church paintings—

"Look, this is Aksum!"

I grabbed a china pencil and drew the giant stone monuments of the necropolis on the map, in the gap where the hills meet. I drew the pool above the city at Mai Shum. I sketched in the church of Mary of Zion.

I drew a little square for Aksum's airfield, with a tiny Romeo, and me standing next to it. I made it all look like a church painting—bold, curved, simple lines, like a cartoon, myself with a round face and a stubby robed body, standing stiffly by the plane like I owned it—like it was my mule. I put a tiny flying helmet on me.

The boy priest leaned over the map next to me, watching, quizzical, figuring it out.

"Aksum," he said quietly, in recognition.

When I finished drawing my own feet, he reached out and touched the pencil.

I looked up—straight into his face. He looked away quickly but closed his fingers around the pencil, tugging at it.

I gave it to him.

He leaned over the map, and very carefully, studiously, inside my small sketch of Mary of Zion, he drew a *tabot*. It looked just like the picture of the Ark of the Covenant in the comic strip paintings on the walls of St. Kristos Samra at Beehive Hill.

Then I realized that if it was the *tabot* in St. Mary of Zion in Aksum, it *was* the Ark of the Covenant.

The real one. Or as good as. *As good as.* Because that's what people think it is.

The boy patted his picture gently with the tip of his finger, like he was telling me I shouldn't have left it out.

But also, he was showing me that he understood what I was telling him. He knew I was showing him Aksum and its place in the world in a very tiny picture on a piece of paper.

Then he started drawing again. Inside my little chapel, next to the *tabot* he'd drawn, he made a little cartoon picture of himself.

He was copying the figure I'd made of me—he drew a robed figure of a boy staring out of the page, as if we could look at each other on paper but not in real life. The figure of him was just like the figure of me, except that instead of a flying helmet the little person wore a priest's crown. And instead of standing next to a plane like he owned it, he was standing next to the Ark of the Covenant.

When he'd finished, he tapped the end of the pencil against the priest in the picture and then tapped it against his chest. *Me,* the picture said, in picture language. *That's who I am,* he was telling me. Maybe he didn't speak Amharic. Or maybe he just didn't dare to say this out loud.

I looked at the picture and took a long, deep breath.

This boy was the Guardian of the Tabota Seyon, the Ark of Zion.

I STILL DIDN'T KNOW WHERE WE WERE GOING. AND I didn't know how to ask.

But the guardian of the *tabot* was one step ahead of me.

He held the pencil in a funny way, but he knew what to do with it. First he scratched out the picture of the *tabot* in St. Mary's. Then he drew a new *tabot* on top of my little plane, right on the nose in the front—like a figurehead on the prow of a boat.

I sighed in frustration. I knew that was what I was supposed to do—carry his treasure in my plane—the problem was that I didn't know where to go.

But then he began to transform the landscape around the plane. I watched, frowning. He is *good.* You don't get that good without practice. He must do a lot of drawing. Maybe he doesn't have much to do with himself most of the time—pray, burn incense, watch over the nation's treasure, draw pictures in the dust and on the walls.

He drew a wavy line underneath the little airplane I'd sketched. Now the plane was sitting on top of a hill. He drew a door with a window beside it, both arched with crosses on top, into the curve of the hill beneath the plane. It looks *exactly* like the front of the chapel on Beehive Hill.

Then next to the plane he drew a tree, a quick outline of a crooked, flat-topped acacia. And hanging by a thread from the tree he drew a beehive.

Below the crest of the hill he drew another tree, with another beehive hanging in it. Then he drew the same thing next to the door of the chapel.

My map was covered with blue bee trees now.

Then finally, beneath everything, he drew the patterned cells of a honeycomb. He drew them to fit exactly in the contours of the hillside.

Then for the first time, I understood that Beehive Hill is not named for the beehives hanging in the trees.

When Habte Sadek and Sinidu talk about "the honeycomb," they don't mean what's inside the hives.

They mean the hill itself.

Beehive Hill is *itself* a honeycomb of cells, and golden treasure hides in the hollow hill like honey in the hive.

The boy put down the china pencil and waited.

His directions couldn't have been more obvious if he'd told me in English—*Take me home with you.*

Well, maybe he doesn't know I live there. Maybe he doesn't know where it is, but just knows *what* it is—a place of peace and safety and secrecy. But there is no doubt about where he wants me to take him.

When he first told me, I was so flabbergasted I couldn't take it in. I stood shaking my head in bewilderment. How could he know?

But of course, Habte Sadek's brother had told the priests at Aksum about Beehive Hill, nearly seventy years ago.

The boy tapped the page with light fingers, then raised his hand and tapped me gently on the chest, just over my heart. He'd told me again, given me a clear message I couldn't fail to understand—*Take me home with you.*

I turned around to look at the cargo he was bringing with him.

I think it will fit in a cockpit. It can't be that heavy, but it is an awkward shape. I want to wedge it in the back and strap it down. It sure isn't going to be stuck on the nose like a figurehead. The plane will still be flyable.

I am still staring at the box-shaped thing sitting there in the gloom. Now that I think I know what it is, it spooks me a little. How old is it? Older than the skulls of the priests in the cliff walls on Beehive Hill. Older than the crumbling monastery on Debre Damo. Older than the mysterious grave markers in the Aksum necropolis. *Thousands* of years older.

The boy is drawing again.

*Spiderwebs joined together can catch a lion.*

———

NONE OF THIS IS COINCIDENCE. I AM HERE *BECAUSE* I am from Tazma Meda. That is where the only church treasures rescued from Magdala ended up. That is where Habte Sadek, Sinidu's great-uncle, the soldier deacon from Magdala, grew old. There is an airstrip there, and I am the Ethiopian boy who knows how to fly there. I am the legal property of the richest man in the district, and I have been given a pilot's license so I can take my nation's holiest object to the perfect hiding place. It is not destiny, but it has all been planned. It's like the *tabot* itself: it doesn't matter whether any of this is true or not, destiny or not. Maybe it *isn't* the real *tabot*. Maybe it's a decoy. What matters is what people *believe*.

I am still scared—scared of being in charge of the plane, scared of the priest and the Ark of the Covenant or whatever it is—and I still have got to find my way back to Tazma Meda on my own. But at least I know where I am going now.

I HAVE LANDED AGAIN ON DELIA'S DREAM. IT IS ALMOST halfway between Aksum and Tazma Meda. I knew it was going to get dark before I made it home, and I didn't want to waste fuel looking for a place to land. And I didn't want to land any place as public as that airfield in the Takazze Valley. The wind was in the right direction this time—so I landed here. I am parked right in the middle in case the wind changes overnight. We are sleeping beneath the wings of the plane, one of us on either side of it.

I dreamed the damn Ark sprouted legs, scaly bird legs—chicken legs, not anything beautiful. They were kicking and struggling against the ropes tying it into the plane and I knew I couldn't fly with that thousands-of-years-old creepy thing wriggling around right behind my head in the plane, so I cut the ropes. It hopped out of the cockpit on its scrawny bird legs and went scampering away across the ridge and disappeared over the edge.

I woke up with my teeth chattering.

But we are safe here. *We are invisible.* That's what Black Dove does best, right? No one can see us here. No one can come up here. I guess now I'm feeling responsible for this fellow.

And the *Thing* he's guarding. Although I kind of hate it. It scares me and spooks me. I *hate* being responsible for it—the greatest treasure in Aksum. Maybe in the world. I'm pretty sure the Italians would agree with the Ethiopians about this one thing.

But I don't mind being responsible for the Guardian. Isn't that weird?

After I woke up from that horrible dream, I moved to be on the other side of the Guardian so I could put him between me and That Thing. After all, he has learned to live with it. It doesn't bother him.

I wonder if he has a name.

I landed here about an hour and a half before sunset, and there really hasn't been a thing to do except write. We couldn't build a fire—there's not a stick of wood up here. So once it got dark, we could only go to sleep. I am writing now with the flashlight, but I'm worried about the batteries, so I guess I'll stop in a minute. I can't even take a walk—it's so dark that I'd risk walking right over the edge.

But then I'll have to think. The stars are beautiful, but no more beautiful than at home when all the lights are out. I am hiding from them, under the lower wing of the Romeo because I don't want to think about space. Or rockets. I don't want to think about why I'm here, what I'm doing, what I'll do next. If I really were Black Dove, I could count on White Raven to come and rescue me. But Em is stuck in Aksum till I get back. I am on my own. I will have to figure out a way to rescue *her* when I'm finished with this.

I don't know if my mother—I mean Delia, my real mother—would be proud of me for doing such an important job, or devastated that I owe anyone such a debt. I guess I don't care what Delia would think anymore. She is dead, and Momma and Em are alive, and they are the ones I care about. They are the ones it is agony to leave behind.

Until I got here and lined up to land, I'd forgotten how the sides of this ridge are covered with birds! The bearded vultures all came in to roost just as it was getting dark—they are absolutely the biggest birds I've ever seen. They seem bigger than the ones at home. The ol' Ebony Eagle ought to change his name to the Bearded Vulture. It would be more original, and it would be *Ethiopian.*

Date: Mar. 3, '36 (Yekatit 24, 1928)
Type of Machine: Romeo Ro. 1
Number of Machine: 15-22
Airfield: Beehive Hill Farm
Duration of Flight: 1 hour 15
Character of Flight: home
Pilot: Em Menotti (me).

Remarks:

IT IS SO REASSURING TO FOLLOW LITTLE RULES, LIKE sticking the flight log details in, as if someone like Miss Shore was going to check what I've written and give me points out of ten. "Very careful work, Emilia." I wonder where Miss Shore is and what she is doing. I wonder if she reads the British newspapers to her fresh victims and tsk-tsks over the "war in Abyssinia" and shakes her head and remarks, "I had a very narrow escape there!"

Lucky her.

No one else I know is escaping. When I flew along the Takazze River gorge this morning, I kept passing over scattered people and animals and automobiles and tents—not an army, but people on their way to join the fighting, which is farther east. I stupidly went low, risking being shot at (or speared at), but I wanted to *see*. And what I saw was that everyone was scared of me—scared of my Regia Aeronautica plane. It was very strange watching the shadow of my wings pass over everybody. People ran, and it was like ants swarming below me in the valley, only I knew it was people, and I wanted to go home.

And eventually I was home. I was flying over the Beshlo River. The closer I got to Tazma Meda the more I recognized the shapes of the mountaintops because they were *familiar*. A year ago I learned to fly here. For a moment, in a flash of warm pleasure, I was proud of myself. *Look what I've done, all alone!*

And also—you know how sometimes when you come home and you haven't seen a place for so long that it seems unbelievably beautiful, and you want to cry because you love it so much you think it's going to break your heart? I felt like that, too. I am *home*.

Beehive Hill looked ordinary as I flew in over the ridge. It was comfortingly familiar—the hives hung in the trees like giant cocoons, the uneven rows of the little coffee groves in the shady woods behind people's houses. Smoke rose lazily here and there, curling into the sky, making me realize how hungry I was for real food, *injera* and something peppery, Sinidu's *wat* with loads of *berbere*. I had been eating nothing but stale, stolen La Disperata bread for two days. I wondered if I was brave enough to wave the end of my *shamma* to greet everybody while I was flying in, like we always do when we land at Tazma Meda, and decided firmly that it was a bad idea to try to do anything else other than concentrate on landing safely. I looked for the Tazma Meda radio mast to position myself for landing at Beehive Hill Farm.

And the radio mast was not there.

There is nothing but a pile of timber and rubble where the clinic was.

It was just like looking through the lens of Momma's camera and changing the focus. Suddenly it all looked different, and everything was clear.

They bombed our clinic. They must have done it to knock down the radio mast. It is the only radio in the district, the only source of news for a couple of hundred miles in any direction. There isn't any other reason why they'd bomb Tazma Meda.

It happened three days ago. The smoke is people's houses that are still burning. Tazma Meda is ruined just like Delia's sky. There isn't anywhere else to go now.

Now I know what they do when they drop bombs, and if they used gas here, they would have killed everything—mules, goats, chickens, coffee trees, not to mention people. But I was too high to see how bad it was. There wasn't anything to do except land anyway. I couldn't go back, so I just had to keep going. So I lined up with the ruined clinic on my wingtip and the solid lump of Beehive Hill ahead of me, and got ready to land.

I am sure my heart actually stopped when I saw the sooty shell of Momma's Romeo, like the black skeleton of a tree destroyed by lightning, tipped up on its nose right in the middle of our airfield.

Honest, my heart stopped.

I couldn't land. Even if the field had been clear, I was so shaken I couldn't do it. I had to shove the power on full and soar back up into the sky and do a long, wide circle around all the wreckage of my home—the smoking houses, the pile of stony dust that used to make Tazma Meda special, and then I was back to the beginning of the circle, and it was still there, the plane Teo took off in from Aksum, here at home *dead*. Utterly destroyed, nose down in a pile of ash on the yellow grass.

I hadn't cut the power or started to descend or any of the things you're supposed to do to get ready to land, so I was way too high to dive down safely. I had to make *another* circle.

And this time I noticed everything that was *alive*. There were goats ambling like ants below me on the hillside like there always are; the coffee trees are ready to harvest; and the bearded vultures were doing their slow spiral dance over Beehive Hill like they always do, getting in my way. I wasn't scared of them anymore.

Not after being shot at by Haile Selassie. And when I thought of this, I felt strong enough to concentrate on just the plane, on just the things I have to do to land safely. Because whatever was waiting for me on the ground couldn't possibly be any worse than that terrible moment in the air when I first saw our plane and knew it would never fly again.

I had to land beside it.

IT HAD COME DOWN NOSE FIRST SOMEHOW IN THE middle of the airfield, and by the time I'd put on the brakes and come to a stop and switched off the engine of my own plane, the wrecked Romeo was a ways behind me and I couldn't see it anymore. I took off my helmet and goggles and sat listening to the very eerie quiet of Beehive Hill Farm. None of the usual sounds of everyday life. No dogs. No people calling to each other while they worked. Only bugs and birds twittering.

Finally I gave the control column four firm squeezes. I kind of love that little Regia Aeronautica plane now. It has taken me safely home, and it did not try to run away or kill me when I had to start it myself this morning.

I thought that was the most frightening thing I ever had to do, when I did it this morning. But that was before I had to get the courage to climb out and walk back to Momma's charred and wrecked Romeo to see what I was going to find there.

The plane had been sitting there for *ages*. There are bird droppings all over it and three silvery abandoned sunbird nests, like juggling balls of grass and cobwebs, hanging in the snapped wires beneath what is left of the wings. There weren't any bones or decaying bodies lying around, but someone could have hauled off the dead pilot to be buried—it happened a long time ago.

Probably about four months ago, when the sunbirds were nesting.

So then I was afraid to go home. I was afraid to cross the airfield and go into my own house and find . . . my head ran wild with the horrible things I might find. An empty house would be the least horrible, and I didn't like the thought of an empty house at all. So I thought I would go find Sinidu. But then I thought about the bombed clinic, and I didn't want to go looking for Sinidu, either.

The safest thing to do was to try the Sinclairs' house.

The Big House was standing there with the French doors of the veranda wide open and stuff pulled out of drawers, like someone was trying to pack and couldn't figure out what to take along, and then decided to run away without taking anything. I don't know what happened there, because the Sinclairs left months and months ago. Probably people hunting to see if there were any useful guns left behind—everyone knows the Sinclairs' house is full of guns. People on the farm, including us, have been using the house since they left, but no one has been living in it.

"*Selam!*" I yelled. "Peace! Hello! Where are you?"

There wasn't anybody there. I checked the girls' rooms and it felt like nobody had been there since Bea Sinclair rode off on a mule to go to boarding school in England a year ago. But I guess the last people there were us. Momma's boots are dumped on the floor of Fiona's bedroom, the soles completely worn through. I couldn't figure out what that meant, but I didn't like it.

I quickly got spooked by being in the abandoned house. So then I spent about an hour trying to pull and push my stolen plane into the aircraft shed. I am not sure why I thought this was such an important thing to do, but I was very determined.

Guess who came to my rescue? Tazma Meda kids.

They turned up out of nowhere.

"*Tafash*, crazy *ferenji* girl. *Selam*, peace, peace! You want help getting the plane in the shed?" asked Sinidu's niece Hana, the one Momma never lets do any work for us. Her beautiful, tiny braids were frizzing out around her forehead like she hadn't bothered fixing her hair since the village had been bombed.

That was when I started to cry.

"Come on, everybody. Em is tired. Help her out here."

There were six of them, four girls and two little boys. The boys had spears twice as long as they were tall. *Hana* had a rifle over her back. They all lined up with me, three on each side of the plane, and boy, was it easier to push with their help.

"My father left the gun for us when he went to join the emperor's army," Hana told me. "He took spears and a knife but said that we could have the gun. Did you see me shooting at you when you came around Beehive Hill the second time? We thought you were the Italians coming back with more air fire. Why are you flying an Italian plane?"

"I stole it," I said proudly, wiping my nose.

Hana shook her fist at the sky. "Beautiful!" She gave a ululating cry of triumph, and me and all the girls joined her. The boys shook their spears. It felt good to be with people again. It felt good to know I'd taken down the Regia Aeronautica by one plane *myself.*

"What happened when the planes came the first time?" I asked.

They told me about the bombing.

Hana's mother and her grandmother were killed. Her *mother and grandmother* were killed here in Tazma Meda, by bombs being dropped on the clinic. Hana did not tell me this. She walked a little way away from us and wailed while the others told me what had happened. They still have not dug them out from under the rubble.

"Anybody who has no other place to stay has gone to St. Kristos Samra," Hana told me afterward. "You can stay there, too."

"What happened to my mother's flying machine?" I begged them to tell me. "What happened? What happened to my brother? Please—"

I waved at the crisped Romeo full of empty birds' nests, feeling like I was about to suffocate with panic. *What happened?*

"Teodros is fine. He came back here four months ago, long before Woyzaro Rhoda. But now they have both gone with Ato Ezra to be battlefield doctors. They transported all the Red Cross equipment to the northeast, where the emperor is gathering his army."

I started to cry again.

*Teo and Momma are both all right.*

This time the kids all piled around me, squeezing my hands and stroking my hair.

"Hush, hush," Hana crooned, and then I felt terrible, *terrible*, that she had to comfort me when my mother was *alive* and hers was *dead*. And also, I realized suddenly, Hana's mother is Sinidu's sister. That means Sinidu's sister and mother are dead too, and she doesn't even know it yet.

But when Hana told me about Teo and Momma, I was so overcome with relief that for a few minutes I couldn't do anything but sob.

When I'd stopped being a baby, I tried to get the Tazma Meda kids to tell me more about the crash, but none of them knew what had happened. No one had come running up to Beehive Hill Farm to give Momma's Romeo a reception the way they did with my Disperata Romeo, because Momma's plane is ordinary and they see it flying in all the time. Zere says he heard the explosion, but he is very little and was scared to come and look. Much later, Sinidu found Teo sitting on the airfield staring dazed at the smoking shell of the plane, and took him down to stay with her and Ezra and the baby.

That was a long time ago. Long enough that Momma gave up

on waiting for anyone to come back for her in Aksum and *walked back to Tazma Meda*. I can't believe she *walked here*. But she said she would, and I guess if Ras Assefa's soldier boys can do it and Habte Sadek could do it when he was twelve, there's no reason Momma can't do it, either. That explains the worn-out boots in Fiona Sinclair's bedroom! Momma must have pilfered Fiona's riding boots to replace them. She will never speak Amharic without an American accent and she will never master the Ethiopian art of going barefoot.

Hana and the other Tazma Meda refugees are staying in the shallow caves up on Beehive Hill, just around the corner from the entrance to the St. Kristos Samra hermitage. I came up here with them for tonight. The only place I could bear to think of sleeping in Tazma Meda is the aircraft shed, but it is standing out there in the open next to the airfield and could make a good target if the bombers come back. Up here, we are hidden away invisibly.

I won't stay, though. I am going to suffocate here. The only reason I did not already take off and go after Momma and Teo is that it is about to get dark. The kids are going to go with me to help get the plane out first thing tomorrow morning. We siphoned all the fuel out of the Sinclairs' generator to fill it up. Also, we raided Mrs. Sinclair's tins with complete impunity. I don't think she is going to care this time. Honestly, that empty house gives me the willies. The piles of skulls in the cliff walls next to me are less creepy, and I can understand why no one is staying on Beehive Hill Farm even though it is huge and completely empty. I don't want to stay there, either.

In the little rock crevasse on the other side of me is the mother of that baby who had whooping cough last year. She is part of the coffee cooperative. Her face was gray, literally gray—covered with dust, with her eyes red and wet in the middle. She sat up straight when she saw me and reached out an arm—too stunned for a hug.

She didn't have her toddler with her, and I didn't ask why. I just kissed her. My lips left a wet print in the dust on her cheek. Everything about her fills me with despair.

I wonder if Momma and Teo came up here—if they had to burrow away in this haunted honeycomb of a hill, like me, before they left to go to war. I guess they didn't, though, because they'd have been in our house together, and it wouldn't have felt so full of ghosts to them.

My house, *my house*, our beautiful stick-and-thatch house that the coffee cooperative people built for Momma when she came here, my home is lost to me. It is standing there whole and unharmed, but I can't go back to it. It will never be home without Momma and Teo in it.

So I have to leave, too.

But also I am full of hope. Because Momma and Teo are together and alive. They are doing something important now, really *helping*. The sun is setting now, but I will fly out to find them when it rises again tomorrow morning.

YOUR MAJESTY, THIS IS THE LAST PART OF THE STORY
I have to write. I haven't got an ending yet, and Teo is not going to
come up with one for me. So maybe you can do it yourself.

I am writing it from the Red Cross field hospital here in
Korem—or what is left of it.

The sun came exploding straight into my face in the Beehive
Hill cliff side on my last morning in Tazma Meda. It is unbelievable how well I slept in that hermit's hole next to the skulls. Four
months' worth of exhaustion plus a small dose of hope and confidence are a good way to knock yourself out, even when your bed
is haunted and uncomfortable.

So it was broad daylight by the time I took off.

I headed back north, but I hadn't seen any fighting on my
way to Tazma Meda, and I wasn't seeing any now. After about
half an hour, I started to zigzag off my planned route; I had an
*idea* where to go, but I didn't *know*. After an hour and a quarter,
I started to get anxious about the pointlessness of flying around
trying to find two people somewhere in the whole of Ethiopia. I
hadn't started with full fuel tanks, and there wasn't any more to
raid from the Sinclairs' if I went back.

I flew higher, up where it was cold and the air got thin, trying
to get a better view.

That was when I saw the Disperata planes, coming toward
me at an angle.

Oh God!

I was high above them. Maybe they didn't see me. I couldn't
climb any higher and still be able to breathe. If I turned around,

I'd lose the distance I'd made and I wouldn't have enough fuel to do it over.

Then I realized that they were heading exactly where I wanted to go.

I made a decision I didn't want to think about too hard. I figured I would look suspicious if I followed them from a distance. So I joined them.

I set my course to meet them, hoping they were from the Asmara base and not the Amba Kwala one, hoping that radio between airfields is as much of a sorry excuse for communication as it is anywhere else in Ethiopia, hoping they would think I was just another Disperata Romeo tagging along.

I didn't get too close. I don't know how to fly in formation. One of the Fiat fighters broke away from the rest of them to check me out. He gave me a friendly wave, and I waved back.

Well, what else was I going to do?

They weren't flying very fast—just taking their time and saving their fuel, knowing they had the total advantage of anything on the ground. It was easy to keep up with them—easy to fly with them, as long as I didn't get too close. Well, I didn't want to get too close anyway—I didn't want them to pay too much attention to my stolen plane's markings. They knew where they were going, and I went with them.

When I saw the tens of thousands of soldiers gathered at Korem, the first thing I thought was, *How could I possibly have missed this?*

It went on forever. It looks like Addis Ababa from the air, like a city, without the new government buildings that don't seem to belong there anyway. I hope that isn't rude. This is how it used to be, in ancient days, when the capital moved around wherever the emperor was. That's almost how it is now. Back then, though, the sky was safe.

I was so focused on *getting* here that I kind of forgot what the other planes had come here for. They didn't forget. They moved in lower, without even speeding up, and before I realized what was going on, I saw the scurrying ants all over again as the Fiats opened fire with their machine guns. You could easily make yourself believe there weren't any people down there—that nobody real was getting hurt. I think that's how you're able to fire a gun or drop a bomb, just pretend it will never hit anyone real, anyone you know. Only I *knew* Momma and Teo were probably down there somewhere, or somewhere nearby just like this, and all I wanted was for it to stop.

I couldn't even take them away with me if I landed. We can't all fit in this plane.

But I was determined to do something. Korem is on a wide plain, with Lake Ashenge spreading silver and glorious to the north, and mountains all around. I spotted our tents near the British Red Cross camp, in the open near the lake a little away from the fighting, and I was almost a hundred percent sure they were the same tents I'd helped sew the big red crosses on while the rains hammered down on the iron roof of the Tazma Meda clinic. You don't spend half a month working on something like that and not be familiar with it for the rest of your life.

I didn't want to land too close to the troops. It was hard to find an open space there anyway. I landed close to the Red Cross tents, in the flat grassland by Lake Ashenge.

I knew I was flying a Disperata plane, and I knew people were going to hate me. I was pretty much expecting to be shot at and have spears thrown at me. But nobody even tried. Everyone just ran away from me, scrambling to get away as I came lower.

The other planes had sped off—I was flying the only Italian plane in the sky. I wound the end of my *shamma* around my hand and held it up out of the cockpit so that a tail of it streamed

behind me like a little white flag—*Please don't attack me. I surrender.*
I passed low and slowly over the place where I wanted to land,
checking the ground, and wanting to let them see I wasn't going
to shoot at them. I'd have to go around a second time before I
could land—I can't land and wave a white flag at the same time.
I need both hands to land. I have to *concentrate* on landing. But
I hoped *someone* would know what I meant on the first pass.

And someone did.

There was one small, slender woman who hadn't run. She
had a baby tied to her back and was carrying a fuel can on her
head. I could see her clearly as I passed about fifty feet above her.
She stood all by herself, shielding her eyes against the bright sky
as she watched me. She seemed completely unafraid. She seemed
*curious*. After a moment or two, she started to wave wildly.

It was Sinidu, *Sinidu*. She knew it was me because she was
*Sinidu*! She didn't recognize my white flag as a sign of surrender—
she recognized it as our Tazma Meda landing greeting. She
recognized *me*.

I shoved the power on and my heart soared aloft with the
plane. The stolen Romeo roared back skyward so I could get in
position again to land.

The second my wheels touched the ground, Sinidu was running toward me. By the time I'd stopped rolling, she was beneath
the wing. The second the propeller stopped turning, she was
reaching for me. I pushed my goggles up onto my head and scrambled out into her arms. Little Erknesh was laughing her head off,
that crazy baby. She loves it when you run with her.

"*Tafash! Tafash!* You've been lost!"

Sinidu and I both reached up to wipe tears off each other's
faces at the same time. Then we both laughed. Then we both tried
to ask questions. She put her arm around my waist and started
pulling me toward the tents, and—this is true—she had not even

had time to tell me where my mother was before we heard the roar of more Regia Aeronautica planes, flying low.

They were flying ahead of a swelling bank of yellow cloud that fogged the entire horizon, the ugliest thing I have ever seen. It blotted out the green of trees; it blotted out the sandy stone walls and the gray-green mountains ringing the plain. Sinidu and I grabbed each other's arms again and froze.

She turned to me and said wearily, "Our soldiers will run now. The gas destroys our ranks, every time. And then, *ai*, so many burns and no clean water—poor Ezra has burned his own hands just by touching the wounded—" Sinidu broke off in frustration and despair with a keening wail, like no noise I'd ever heard out of her in my life.

The roaring grew louder, and we both watched, open-mouthed, as the planes headed straight for our field hospital on the outskirts of the plain where the troops were gathered, still pouring foggy yellow destruction.

It smelled faintly of garlic. Just how Momma had told me mustard gas would smell. So then we both knew what it was.

I don't know how long it took me to get out my gas mask and put it on, but I did, because Momma had warned me and made me promise, and that was what I'd told her I would do.

After I got it on and I was looking at Sinidu and Erknesh through the glassy aquarium goggle eyepieces, I panicked all over again. I remembered all in a rush that there were other people in the world besides me, and if they got killed by poisoned gas, it was going to hurt me worse than if I was killed myself. Beautiful Sinidu and her beautiful baby standing right next to me—Teo and Momma and my heart out there somewhere underneath the cloud.

All I could hear now was Erknesh screaming. I couldn't even hear the airplanes anymore. When Sinidu let out that strange yodeling wail, her baby joined in screeching at the top of her little lungs.

It was just like she was yelling to me for help.

It was hard to see through the strange glassy windows of the mask, and stuffy breathing through the filters. I knew that even with the mask on, the mustard gas would still burn my feet and any other skin that wasn't covered. And Sinidu and Erknesh didn't even have masks.

I couldn't run into that hell to save Momma and Teo. Momma knew what to do. Right? She'd survived the mustard gas attacks in the Great War.

But Sinidu and Erknesh—

"Get in the plane!" I yelled at Sinidu. I grabbed her arm and pulled. "Come on!"

"The water!" Sinidu gasped, struggling out of my grip and grabbing up the fuel can she'd put down when she hugged me. And I knew that mustard gas would poison any water it came in contact with, too, so it was worth us dragging this one can along with us—

I boosted her up onto the lower wing, and she climbed into the front cockpit, baby and five gallons of water and all. She shuffled everything around so that Erknesh was wedged in next to her and Sinidu was *sitting* on the water, which gave her a better view, while I scrambled into the cockpit behind her. The sky was full of noise and boiling cloud. I realized I hadn't started the plane and I couldn't see anything through the mask if I was going to fly.

Sinidu yelled back to me, "I will hold the brakes while you swing the propeller!"

Of course she would. How could I have forgotten that she has been flying for longer than I have? Of course she could hold the brakes for me, while she sat on the only clean water in Korem with her baby squeezed into the cockpit beside her.

I jumped out again and started the engine on the first try. I came running back to the cockpit and yelled through the roar and wind of our own engine, "I have to get the mask off—I can't see to take off!"

Sinidu yelled back, "Get in. I will take off."

So I did. Sinidu taxied with confidence, turned us into the wind, and shoved the power on. The stolen Italian plane lifted over the glittering silver of Lake Ashenge and soared over the low forest and the rocky tops of the surrounding hills.

I ripped the stupid mask off. I was embarrassed that I'd put it on so selfishly. My face was all sweaty and teary, and I couldn't breathe anyway, and it didn't have anything to do with the gas. I wiped my eyes with my *shamma* and pulled my flying goggles into place while Sinidu flew steadily up and away from the destruction.

For what seemed like ages, neither one of us looked behind us.

Finally Sinidu yelled to me, "Can you take us back? I am not so good at landing." She turned the plane in a long, slow curve again over the lake.

We hadn't gone so far we couldn't still see the pall over the land we'd left behind. I took over the controls with shaking hands. Somewhere down there were Momma and Teo and Ezra—all the pieces of both our hearts.

I almost didn't want to go back. As long as we were up here, we didn't know the worst. Until we landed, there was still some hope that everybody was okay.

And also, I didn't want to land until the yellow fog started to clear.

I circled and circled over the lake, the Romeo making a distant dark reflection in the blue of the reflected sky on the surface of the water. It looked like Teo's die-cast *Spirit of St. Louis* where it hangs, remote and untouchable, from the clinic ceiling. After a while, I didn't have a choice about landing, because I was about to run out of fuel.

I landed closer to the lakeshore than I had the first time. There were dead people half submerged in the reeds or just lying with their faces in the water, fallen where they'd tried to drink or to wash the burning poison from their skin. There were other people lying in agony at the edge of the lake or staggering toward it, more than I could count, who were not dead. I climbed out slowly. Sinidu didn't say anything. When I got up onto the lower wing to see if she was okay, she handed Erknesh up to me. The baby knew me. She reached for me, doing her baby vamp act, and pulled at my goggles. Sinidu climbed out.

The yellow fog had drifted away; the air was clear around the Red Cross tents, and the Regia Aeronautica planes had left before we'd even touched the ground, ignoring us because we were a La Disperata reconnaissance plane.

Babyish sobs slipped out of me.

"Hush, Emilia, we are going to find your momma. Hush." Sinidu was fixing Erknesh more securely on her back again. We didn't go very fast—we were cautious, worrying about burning our feet, trying to stay out of people's way. The noise they made—

Well, you have no doubt heard it, Your Majesty. But I had not heard men screaming before. It is the most terrible sound I have ever heard.

We found Ezra first. He had not been gassed. He had been shot. He must have been shooting at the planes himself—he was still gripping a rifle, not his own. His face, his hands, all his skin was covered with dust. I ground my teeth together, sucked back a sob, and grabbed Sinidu around the waist to hold her back.

*"Don't touch him!"*

She didn't struggle. *She let me* hold her back when we found her adoring husband's body. Oh God, we were both so *careful*; even in grief, we *knew* how careful we had to be. I held on to

Sinidu and she wailed up into the sky, her eyes closed. Erknesh joined in, and then I did, too. For a minute or two, there was nothing any of us could do but cry.

We weren't the only ones. The mourning wail was a steady, throbbing background beat to the moaning and screaming. It is worse than any nightmare horror ever made up in a story. It has died down now but does not stop. None of it has stopped. I keep wondering what White Raven would do, and then I want to smack myself in the face for ever making up stories about people getting hurt and killed. *I* have killed people in stories.

Sinidu rested her forehead against my shoulder. I leaned my head against her hair. I could hear Erknesh snuffling and for a moment caught the sunny, sweaty smell of the top of her head. Then it was all faint, ominous garlic again.

"Come," Sinidu croaked quietly at last. "Let's go find your momma."

I nodded but didn't lift my head.

"Gloves," Sinidu said, rousing herself. She took hold of my hand and gently guided me to take a step forward. "We need gloves. There are rubber gloves we can wear. We must not touch anything without gloves. The medical stores are in the canvas tent, the one the Swedes gave us—we must wrap our feet—"

We tore my *shamma* into strips to cover our feet. There were people everywhere, lying, sitting, dead and alive, coughing and weeping. A few were staggering around like us, trying to help.

We got to our supply tent. The flaps were tied tightly shut from the inside. This time we tore a piece off Sinidu's *shamma* to wrap around my hands and arms because I had to shove them inside the poisoned canvas so I could untie it.

Inside, we found Momma in Teo's arms, Teo wearing her gas mask.

———

SHE'D WRAPPED HIM IN ABOUT FIVE LAYERS OF *shammas* and blankets. They both had gloves on, and on top of everything else, they'd wrapped themselves together in a tarpaulin.

This time Sinidu held me back, just the way I'd held her back when we found Ezra.

"Gloves," she said quietly, pointing.

Teo raised his head when he heard her talking.

"*Gloves*," Sinidu commanded in a whisper, and led me, shaking, past what was left of my family. "There is water here, too. In the sealed cans it should be all right. Don't touch the goatskin bags. Don't try to wash anything. Save it for drinking."

I pulled the rubber gloves on and turned around.

"Teo," I said.

He turned toward my voice. I didn't know if he could see it was me. It is horrible trying to look through those lenses. He reached an arm toward me.

I grabbed his hand and squeezed it three times.

He squeezed back, and we both started to cry.

MOMMA WAS CONSCIOUS BUT COULDN'T TALK. HER eyes were swollen shut and her breath came in shallow, gulping gasps. She gripped Sinidu's hands like a lifeline, just the way I was hanging on to Teo's.

"Hush, hush, we will clean everything up," Sinidu crooned. "Would you listen to that baby telling stories to herself! I want to be a baby on someone's back with nothing to worry about! Ai, Rhoda, it is you and I and our children alone now—Em and I will make you comfortable, and then we have to help the wounded—"

Teo took the mask off as Sinidu and I untangled all the wrapping.

"Emmy," he whispered.

"I'm here! I'm here!"

"I can't see!" he said.

Momma made a strangled noise of despair, and I think I did, too.

"We weren't together when it started," he told me. "I came running here to find her, and she made me take her mask—then it took us a while to get barricaded in."

Momma's hands fumbled for me and Teo. The four of us hung on together for a few moments while Erknesh babbled blissfully away to herself. That undamaged baby is like a little star of hope to every single person here tonight.

IT IS NIGHT NOW.

The blisters have started coming up. They come up hours after the stuff touches you—you don't realize how bad it's going to be. I have a big one on the back of my leg from something I brushed against, and I don't even know how it got there. Little ones on my feet where I wasn't being careful. Teo's feet are all right—Momma wrapped them up in a rubber sheet. Momma's feet are all right, too, thanks to Fiona Sinclair's pilfered riding boots. It is her face that is burned. We have put some petroleum jelly salve on and tried to wash her eyes, but it is like she has stuck her face into a frying pan full of oil. Her whole forehead is one huge blister the size of my hand. Another big one across one cheek, swallowing part of her mouth. She still can't talk. Sinidu has made her drink by dripping water between her swollen lips through an eyedropper.

326

She is awake. She can't see or talk, but she has been writing us little notes.

*EM TAKE TEO HOME*

"Tazma Meda has been bombed," I whispered. "We can't go home. We have to stay with you."

She shook her head and wrote:

*TAKE TEO HOME TO P.A.*

"Rhoda, the emperor Haile Selassie, the *negusa nagast* himself, is here," Sinidu told her. "He is ready for battle, camped in the mountain caves above Korem. Just like us on Beehive Hill. You are American, you are a pilot—you should appeal to him to get your children out of this country. Aim for the sun!"

A strangled gurgle of bitter frustration from Momma—as if she could move or talk or make a polite request for a personal favor from anyone, let alone the emperor of Ethiopia. I bet she was thinking of that damned civil servant in the US Legation. She wrote:

*EM YOU MUST DO IT*
*TAKE TEO HOME*
*TAKE TEO HOME TO USA*

HOW AM I SUPPOSED TO TAKE HIM HOME TO THE USA????

Since when is the USA *home*?

But where else are we going to go?

"Okay, I will, Momma," I whispered. "I will."

I GAVE SINIDU MY REVOLVER.

She took it without saying anything. She kissed me on both cheeks.

"Do you know how to use it? *Would* you?"

"Yes and yes," Sinidu said.

"I figured."

Sinidu is beautiful. She has always been beautiful, of course, but she is like what I made up White Raven to be. Much more than I am.

She is running our field hospital. People listen to her because she is Ezra's wife.

She has no formal training, but she has been working for Ezra for ten years and she is as good as a doctor and knows better than Momma how to convince people that she can help them with Western medicine. She is the most sensible and most senior person here who is not hurt. And she is doing it all herself with a baby on her back when she is working and the same baby on her breast when she is resting, but she will not eat anything, because she is fasting, on account of we are going to bury her husband tomorrow, and her sister and mother are dead.

"Our soldiers are too honorable," Sinidu said with fury in her voice. "Pulling down tanks with a dozen men and their knives, throwing spears at airplanes! The only weapon we have in abundance is Ethiopia itself. We need to change the way we fight. We need to sneak up on the enemy in the dark and *set them on fire*."

It made my heart ache to hear her joyful voice filled with such bitter anger.

It is quiet now, apart from the moaning and the wails of grief. No one fights at night, because that's not what warriors do.

"Emmy," Sinidu told me, "you know about the pictures your momma has given the emperor—you know how Teo's served him. He knows who you are and he will want to help you, but you have to get his attention for a minute or two. That will be the hard part, because he is here for a hideous battle and it is breaking his heart. You need to make him *see* you. I know a beautiful present you can give him that will get his attention."

She took off the canvas satchel she was carrying over her shoulder. I hadn't even noticed—she is always carrying a ton of stuff, including Erknesh and five-gallon cans of drinking water. But the satchel was Momma's flight bag.

"Look behind the maps," Sinidu said.

Between Momma's maps and the back of the bag was a pretty woven mat made of red-and-green-dyed straw, and it kept the back of the canvas stiff and flat. Behind it was a pile of paper. I pulled it out sheet by sheet.

It is a stack of things that Teo and I have written. Momma has been carrying Teo's and my drawings and stories around with her in her flight bag, all folded up neat and flat, everywhere she goes. *Adventures* we wrote when we first started school, and ones we sent her when she went away to Italian Somaliland and Ethiopia without us for two years, and stories we wrote after we came here, and some of our essays.

Sinidu thinks that you will like to read it. That it will tell you about *us*. I'm not going to send you all the dumb comics we drew when we were little, but I have tried to put our themes and things together so they make sense.

These are just stories, you know. They are part of what we are, but they are not the real thing. All this year I have been thinking, *What would White Raven do?* And today, every time I thought it, I just didn't care what White Raven would do. So today I've just done what *I* would do. I've just done what I think is right.

I'm not going to stop making up stories. But I'm thinking they are not always just a maze to get lost in so you can run away from real life. They can just as well be maps to help you navigate.

I've been thinking about it so much tonight—about Momma carrying these pieces of paper around with her, and about all of us being on our own. Our momma carries us around with her in her heart wherever she goes. But we learned to live without her long ago, and I think we can now, too.

You know what Sinidu said to me when I took these from her to give to you?

She said, "If you take care of Teo, I will take care of your momma."

Momma isn't going to leave Ethiopia. She isn't going to leave Sinidu. Momma is still the crazy *ferenji* flying woman here, but you know what? I saw what happened to her when Delia died. It might kill her to stay here, but it will definitely kill her to leave. She needs what is left of Tazma Meda more than she needs us. She needs to fly here again, if she ever gets better. There is no other sky for her.

But Teo and I are different. We can fly anywhere.

It will save us to leave. And maybe then we can come back.

We are on our own—Teo and I. We always have been, ever since the first Bird Strike.

There is one more thing I want to tell you. It is about Teo. So I am sending you one more section from his own flight log, which he probably shouldn't have written anyway. It will be safer in your keeping than out in the world, where someone might find it and make guesses about things that are supposed to be sacred secrets.

He is sleeping now, and I honestly don't care if he gets mad about me ripping pages out of his flight log, because Momma told me to save him, and I am going to.

"Emmy," Teo said to me, "do you think God blinded me on purpose?"

"*What the heck*, Teo? You got a boatload of mustard gas dropped on you! That wasn't *God!* God isn't like some mean airfield owner's kid kicking over your Lincoln Log house or scribbling on your drawing because he doesn't like the color of your skin! God doesn't go around lynching people—why would he bother to blind someone? What does *God* have to do with it?"

"I saw the Ark of the Covenant," he told me.

Date: Oct. 11, '35/Meskerem 30, 1928
Type of Machine: Romeo Ro. 1
Number of Machine: I-STLA
Airfield: N 12° 58' 10", E 38° 50' 29" (Delia's
    Dream) to Tazma Meda
Duration of Flight: 1 hr 25 min total
Character of Flight: transport
Pilot: Teodros Gedeyon

I DID NOT LOOK. NOT ON PURPOSE. I DID NOT TOUCH IT, and I did not look. The Guardian knows I did not touch it.

And maybe Habte Sadek would think this was wrong, but in the moments after the crash, it was only the Guardian who I thought of. He was slumped forward behind me, and for a moment it looked like the control column of the middle cockpit had been shoved into his chest like a spear. (It hadn't, though he is badly bruised and I think his ribs are cracked. There is nothing I can do about it, but he is stoic and I think he will be all right.)

The impact sprained his ankles. I am not sure how that happened. I am so thankful they're not broken! It was the bustard that nests on the runway, the one I used as an excuse for Em's bad landing when she tore the tire. It really does nest there, and it really does nest there before the rains. It happened *exactly* as I touched the ground. The bird just came flying up as though it had been spit out of the earth. I saw it and remembered instantly that Momma had told us to raise the nose, to get hit underneath instead of head-on, but of course she meant if it happened *in the air.* When I raised the nose, the plane tried to take off again. We bounced, and there was a terrific *bang* as the big bird whacked into the Romeo's belly. We would have been okay if it had happened higher in the sky. But with the bounce, and the nose high at such low speed, I went straight into a stall. I didn't have *time* to go for the power, even if I'd had the extra height.

So we bucked and nose-dived straight into the ground. I can remember every second of the fall. *This is how my mother died.* I didn't have time to go for the power, but I had time to think, over and over, *This is how my mother died,* and *This is going to kill me,* and *This will kill Momma.*

But I wasn't hurt. I wasn't even bruised. So after the engine stopped and the noise and the fear stopped and everything was still, I realized after a few seconds that I wasn't dead. And then I looked back and saw the Guardian, hanging in his harness straps behind me, very still. And then I was more frightened than I'd been before. Habte Sadek told us a church is nothing without its *tabot.* But surely a *tabot* is meaningless without the heart and mind that give it meaning.

He just seemed *so important.* His warm hands that keep the incense lit on the altar also drew the pictures to show me where to hide the heart of his church.

That was also when I realized that I would have done this job even without being forced into it at gunpoint and spearpoint and the harness of slavery. They should have just asked me. If Habte Sadek had asked me, I wouldn't have thought twice about it. I would be *proud* to do what Habte Sadek did. I would be *honored.*

I untangled myself from my own harness and scrambled back through the wires between the wings. I thought the other boy was unconscious, but that was only because he was all scrunched down in his seat. He was cowering forward with his arms over his head. He didn't have a flying helmet, so I'd kind of wrapped him up in his own *shamma* before we set off, to protect him from the wind, and it had cushioned the blow to his face.

He fought a little, flailing, while I unbuckled his harness.

Words spilled out of me. "Peace, peace—"

I saw the lick of flame curling from the crushed engine, over the nose on the other side of the windshield.

*"Stop fighting me! Come!"* I yelled at him, and hauled him half out of his seat. He groaned and grabbed at his ankles. *"Get out!"* I got him under the shoulders somehow and gave him another huge heave backward, and that got him out of the plane. I tipped him face-first over the edge of the cockpit and jumped down after him.

*"Get away from the machine—"*

He did not need to be told that, because he'd seen the little flames, too, by now. And also, he hated the machine. I'd had a hard time earlier, bullying him to get back in when we set off from Delia's Dream.

He struggled away as fast as he could, crawling on his hands and knees, me pulling and pushing to get him to move faster. We made it about twenty yards before he lurched back in the direction of the plane.

"The Tabota Seyon!" he gasped. They are the same words in Amharic as in Ge'ez, the ancient language of the church.

We both looked up. The *tabot* was still strapped in the backseat.

I can't explain why I went back for it. I really can't.

But I did go back for it.

I didn't get hurt doing that, either. The fuselage was only fabric, so it wasn't hot, not like metal would have been—the flames were licking at it like a fire that won't get started, one you have to keep blowing on to get it to catch. I tore at the ropes and straps until the package fell out of the cockpit and hit the ground. I threw myself after it, bundling the wrappings into my arms with whatever was inside them, an awkward, heavy, shape-less lump of mystery. I ran back to the Guardian and shoved it at him and turned back to the plane to watch as it burned to a crisp. There was a roar as the flames found the fuel tanks in the wings. We were close enough that the heat felt like it was burn-ing our faces, although it didn't. There was hardly any smoke. The air above the inferno was a writhing column of clear heat.

The Guardian looked down at the bundle in his arms. There was a corner of something poking out—a corner of smooth black stone, rough and glittering, like the deep sky above Delia's Dream last night. He swiftly gathered up the cloth to cover it.

But I saw.

*Anyone else would be blinded on the spot if he saw the Ark of Zion,* Mateos had said.

I saw it. I looked away, too, when I realized that I should, to be polite. My eyes were stinging with the heat of the fire behind the *tabot.* But it was just an old stone.

I CARRIED THEM BOTH UP TO ST. KRISTOS SAMRA, HIM on my back, the *tabot* in my arms. I did it in relays so the *tabot,* all carefully wrapped up again, didn't go out of his sight. It took me three hours. Habte Sadek welcomed me with tears.

TEO TOLD ME HE'D SEEN THE ARK OF THE COVE-nant, and I shook my head without speaking. I swallowed and opened my mouth and shut it again. After a moment, I said, "Who told you that would make you go blind? The priests at Aksum? Ras Amde Worku? Habte Sadek?"

"Mateos said so, the day I went to the emperor's palace with him in Aksum. He said I'd be killed if I touched it. I didn't touch it, but I saw it."

"You mean that? Some superstitious legend from someone who isn't even connected with it, and you'd give that a second thought? Teo! You said yourself it was just an old stone! And even if it was the most magical thing in the whole world, do you believe God would do that?"

"I saw it," Teo said, "and now I can't see. God's vengeance."

"Are you *crazy*? That's not how God works! What makes you think you're so special, anyway? What about Momma? *She* didn't see the dad-blamed Ark. How come *she* got a bucket of *iprite* in the face? What about Ezra? What did he do wrong that he got gunned down, being a doctor for the Red Cross, trying to protect Sinidu and his baby girl? What did *Erknesh* do wrong that her father is dead? People go right ahead and hurt each other all the time! Don't blame *God*!"

"So *how does God work*?" he demanded furiously. "Are you going to tell me how God works? All you believe in is White Raven!"

"Yes, because White Raven is *inside me*!" I was furious, too. "So, yeah, she is sort of like God, guiding me, helping me figure out the right thing to do! Isn't that what you told Miss Shore in that stupid essay last year? 'God is in you, waiting for you to feel him there.' *You* said that! God works through *us*. Through people doing the right thing. Through you. Through Momma giving you her gas mask and covering you up!"

He didn't answer right away.

Then he whispered, "I am so scared."

"Well, don't blame that on *God*! Least you're not by *yourself*. I'm *here*," I vowed. "We are in the soup together. And I have an idea."

YOUR MAJESTY, I PRAY TO THE GOD WHO GUIDES you that you will choose to help us.

SS *Earl of Craigie*
Port Said, Egypt

March 31, 1936

Dear Momma,

We are on our way.

I don't know if you will ever get a chance to meet Haile Selassie again or to take him a message. He must know by now that he cannot win on his own. The Italians want him as a prize, dead or alive; so he has to get out, too, while he can, in order to live free and be able to return someday.

Maybe I will come back with him. For him.

Here is what happened after we said good-bye to you and Sinidu the morning after the attack.

Emmy spent two hours helping people drink and trying to clean burns, and asking anyone who could talk where to find Imperial Ethiopian Air Force planes. She knew Haile Selassie wouldn't be far from his Beechcraft, or the place where it landed. She said she wanted to deliver her captured Italian aircraft to Haile Selassie. She found out how to get there.

She took me with her—guided me into the front cockpit. I couldn't see a thing, because I couldn't open my eyes.

"Let me sit in the back! I can't fly!"

"I'll fly," Em said with total confidence. "You sit in the front, where I can see you. I like flying from the second cockpit because that's where you and Momma always put me! There isn't a lot of fuel left, but we only have to go about ten miles—the ridge on the other side of the plain. Up there where the caves are, like on Beehive Hill. I'll land as close as I can get. We are going to ask the emperor for help—I know the plane will get us an audience—"

I let her strap me in.

I could see light, changing shades of red and orange and pink behind my swollen eyelids. The plane lifted off the ground, and I could feel the sun on my face and the shadow of the upper wing crossing the cockpit as Em turned carefully away from the field hospital. I could feel her straightening out again. I couldn't hear much, though, over the roaring of the engine—until I heard the cannon fire.

"Dang it! That is the emperor shooting at me again," Em yelled through the speaking tube.

*"What?"* I nearly laughed, except that she sounded serious. My stomach swooped as she pulled back on the control column and shoved on power, and we soared steeply upward.

"It is the same old German antiaircraft gun he had in Dessie! Teo—" This time her yell was hesitant. "Teo, can you fly?"

*"I can't see!"*

"Yeah, but can you *fly*? If I set the trim, can you just keep us level? Because I have a plan—"

Yes, Momma, she did what you would have done. No secret greeting or disguise—just herself and her crazy, beautiful ideas.

"I'm going to aim for the sun!" she yelled.

I felt the machine turn, felt the sun on my face, the warmth and the light. I took the controls and held the plane steady. Then I felt Em climbing up onto the fuselage behind me—felt the shift in weight and the increase in drag. I inched power on. If we weren't level, I wasn't going to be able to see us going out of balance and you really can't always feel it.

She leaned in close to my head and yelled into the wind at my ear, "Hold her straight like that! Real straight, we're only about five hundred feet above the mountaintop! I'm going to stand up and wave as we go past. He might shoot me, but I don't think he will." She squeezed my shoulder four times and stood up.

I flew that stolen plane blind for probably not more than a minute. It felt like hours.

I could feel Emmy's weight close behind me, the unnatural balance of it as she clung to the wing struts over my shoulder. Eternity went by. I flew by color, trying to keep the light inside my eyes an even shade of orange, keeping the sunlight on my face. I felt Em carefully shifting her weight again. Suddenly her voice came through the speaking tube, sounding normal.

"I got her, Teo. Ready to land now."

"You okay to land, Em?"

She gave a choked gasp of laughter. "Ready for anything now!"

The American pilot Billy Cooper, right-hand man to the emperor's personal pilot Johnny Robinson, met us on the field.

I sat still in the front cockpit. I didn't dare move without help. I heard Emmy climb out behind me, I heard her bare feet hit the soil, and I heard her give a little grunt of pain. I don't know how bad the burns on her feet were, because I never saw them. They are healing now.

"Lord!" Cooper exclaimed as he recognized her. "I didn't realize you could fly!"

"I have a new plane for the emperor," Em said. "And I want him to pay me for it."

---

Momma, we met him. We met Haile Selassie himself.

Someone escorted us. I didn't realize Em was leading me into the cave where the emperor was camped until I felt the silk carpet under my feet. The second I stepped onto it, the strange, unreal kiss of smooth, soft silk against the soles of my bare feet instantly exploded into memory—of the rehearsal for Haile Selassie's coronation and my foot on the smooth red carpet behind the rope barrier, and how I looked up and saw him standing there—a small man in a black silk cape and white sunhat, and how Emmy and I both bowed, and how he'd laughed at us.

I was so sure he was standing at the other end of this carpet under my feet now that I bowed three times.

Then I knelt the way I'd knelt on the airfield in Aksum, expecting to be shot.

The emperor said in Amharic, "Tell the American pilot he may sit."

He meant me. I didn't realize it at first. But, of course, he wasn't talking directly to me.

Someone else repeated to me in Amharic, "You may sit."

I sat on the thick silk. There was a short, awkward, strange period of silence. Then the emperor said in Amharic, "You may go."

This time he wasn't talking to me, either.

Em says he made them leave us alone with him.

When we were alone, he spoke to us in Amharic, directly to us, as though we were his advisors or his own children. I don't think he'd have done that back in Addis Ababa. But here on the eve of battle, with his field hospital half-destroyed, after he'd tried to shoot us down and we'd brought him a captured enemy aircraft, he made an exception.

He said, "Emilia, forgive me the number of times I have fired on you in flight."

He'd read her letter by then, though not everything else, of course.

Emmy answered graciously, "You didn't have a choice. You did what you had to do."

Momma, she sounded *just like you*. I mean, her *voice* sounded just like you. I hadn't noticed it in the plane, because of the speaking tube and the wind and the engine noise. And I'd never noticed it until I couldn't see her talking. But she sounds exactly like you.

The emperor spoke my name.

"Teodros."

Suddenly I wasn't afraid of him—or of saying or doing the wrong thing. I knew we didn't matter to him much—he had more important and terrible things to deal with. I thought he'd probably forget about us as soon as we were out of his sight. But I also knew that right now, he cared enough to try to help.

There was a little silence. Then he said my name again.

"Teodros. I owe you a debt of gratitude."

"Your Majesty," I told him, "you don't owe me anything."

"I owe you your freedom, if nothing else, because your military service affords you your freedom. Did you not know this? It is one of the measures in place to finish slavery in this kingdom. All those who serve in my militia are free men. I am ashamed no one has told you yet—all the more so since you are named for Teodros, who first outlawed slavery nearly a hundred years ago."

I opened my mouth and couldn't think of an answer. Not even *Thank you*. No sound would come out. If I had picked up a spear in Tazma Meda and walked to the front with Ezra's Ethiopian Red Cross unit, or joined Ras Assefa's personal guard like Mateos suggested, I would have automatically been free.

You can see why Amde Worku didn't mention it.

Momma, you taught me to fly so that I wouldn't be forced to become a soldier. But knowing how to fly forced me to become a slave.

I still can't really believe that *any* of these laws could ever apply to me, just because of who my father is. But I guess it makes as much sense as that I should have the right to an American passport just because of who my mother is.

"I am going to dismiss my American advisors and command them to leave Ethiopia," the emperor said, and his even voice was heavy with disappointment and weariness. "Some will go before the others. You must travel with one of the American airmen. John Robinson will take you to Addis Ababa today, and William Cooper will escort you from there."

He paused. I didn't know if he was gathering breath to speak again or waiting for a response from me, and after a moment it just felt natural to protest:

"I don't have to leave. I'm Ethiopian as well as American."

"And you can prove neither nationality on paper, in the way of civilized nations," he reminded me gently. "I have thought about what will be best for you. And I have asked William Cooper to adopt you as his American son. Your fellow American, the statesman Everett Colson, will sign the necessary papers."

That is how Haile Selassie solved the passport problem for me. The emperor more or less *ordered* Billy Cooper to adopt me. I don't think it makes the faintest difference in the world to either one of us, since I am sixteen now. But it sure did make it easier for us at the passport office. Of course it also made it easier for us that Colson, the emperor's financial advisor, sent an official letter telling them what to do.

And as for Emmy—her new passport was waiting for her in the US Legation when we got to Addis Ababa! All thanks to you filling out that application last June, Momma. Em says she is never going to let it expire again.

I can see, Momma. I can see well enough to write this letter and I am getting better and better every day. I hope you are, too.

When you are back in Tazma Meda, please tell Habte Sadek that I am safe and well. I hate how quickly pain is aging him, and I know there's a good chance I will never see him again. The day I crashed in Tazma Meda, he gave me his blessing and we made promises to each other. Please tell him I will not forget.

This ship is going through the Suez Canal just now. It is marvelous—a giant work of civil engineering that just goes on and on. Em is a little bored by it, but mainly she is grumpy because she is full of gloom anticipating when we will have to change ships at some point, to get across the Atlantic. She still remembers how they wouldn't let you and Delia sit on the deck together on the American ship when we crossed from France when we were three years old. All I remember is the hammock Delia made out of sheets in the cabin for me and Em. Em is dreading that we will have to stay inside the whole time.

We can't share a cabin on this ship anyway, because Em is a girl. She is sharing with an Englishwoman who reminds us a lot of Miss Shore. I am with Billy Cooper. He has had a couple of dirty looks at the bar, but no one has refused to serve him. It will be strange and hard coming back to the USA. But we have a plan.

We have a plan! I have four, count them, *four*, written recommendations to enroll as a design student at the Curtiss-Wright School of Aviation in Chicago—one from Everett Colson, one from Billy Cooper, and one from Johnny Robinson, which is just a single scrawl of a sentence but is also *signed by the emperor himself.* That counts as the fourth, if you ask me. Curtiss-Wright is where Cooper and Colonel Robinson both got their training.

And I'll be able to continue flight training with the Challenger Air Pilots Association at Harlem Airport in Chicago. I could be an instructor, Momma, or *an aircraft designer.*

Things have changed since Bessie Coleman had to go to France because no one in the USA would teach a Negro woman to fly. I don't think they've changed a lot, but they've changed a little. They train men *and* women at Harlem Airport now—whites *and* blacks.

Momma, just the way you had to decide what you wanted to do, Emmy is going to have to decide what she wants to do next. I know she is thinking about it. Grandfather sent us a telegram to welcome us home before we even get there—he wants to send us to high school at Fox Friends in Lambstown, where you and Connie and the aunts went to school. I am not going to do that. I am not going back to a white high school in Pennsylvania after being a slave and an air force pilot in Ethiopia.

I don't think Emmy will go back, either.

Maybe she won't want to do the same thing I'm doing. I guess we won't be together forever. . . . People grow up and leave home, and they make new homes. Em and I both know we can go it alone if we have to. Whatever she does is up to her.

I hope she comes with me.

Your loving son with a new name,

Teodros Cooper
(Still really your Teo.)

## AUTHOR'S NOTE

My author's note for *The Lion Hunter* begins with an Ethiopian proverb: *To lie about a far country is easy.* I feel the pressure of this proverb even more acutely now than I did then. Dr. Fikre Tolossa, who generously offered his expertise and encouragement in checking this novel for accuracy while it was still in manuscript form, asks the question "Can fictional writers retract, make up, or distort history to achieve their goal or prove their point, when they deal with historical situations?" In my earlier books set in Ethiopia, the events of fifteen hundred years ago were so murky that I did not worry too much about playing fast and loose with them. Since I've started setting my stories in the twentieth century, I am less comfortable with this juggling of reality. I try hard not to make up or distort history. I see myself as slipping plausible characters and situations into a historical setting without changing the actual facts—a bit like a discreet time traveler. It is true that the very nature of historical fiction lends itself to factual error. I try to avoid errors, and I hope I am not so much distorting historical events as drawing attention to them.

The heart of any novel, for me, is the characters who inhabit it, not the historical details that adorn it. Rhoda and Delia are both riffs on my own mother (again, fast and loose); I got the idea for Teo and the Guardian communicating via pictures from my own experience of drawing with Tigrayan children at the foot of the *amba* at Debre Damo. These emotional connections are the real truths of this story.

So with that disclaimer, here are a few notes about what's real and what's fictional in *Black Dove, White Raven*.

—The Ethiopian calendar runs a little over seven years behind the Gregorian calendar. The extra few months means that sometimes the conversion makes the date appear to be eight years behind instead of seven. Megabit 22, 1916 is the Ethiopian date of Haile Selassie's slavery reform act of March 31, 1924.

—Haile Selassie didn't actually acquire his Beechcraft airplane until November 1935. I had it arrive a few months earlier so Teo could take his flight test in it.

—I made up the battle of Aksum and the occupation of the airfield there. Most Western accounts take the line that there was no bloodshed when Aksum fell to the Italians in October 1935; I've taken my line from reports in contemporary Australian newspapers that there was "a short attack in which aeroplanes participated."

—I made up Amba Kwala and its hidden airfield, mainly because I made up all the pilots who are stationed there. But Amba Kwala is not unlike Mai Edaga in Eritrea, where the Regia Aeronautica based a number of Romeo Ro. 1s for terrestrial reconnaissance.

—I also made up the character who appears as the Guardian of the Ark, an individual who must have had a real counterpart whose history I do not know.

This raises the whole issue of mixing up invented characters with people who really existed. In my earlier books, my imaginary hero Telemakos interacts extensively with two important real historical figures, the Aksumite emperor Gebre Meskal and his contemporary Abreha, the elected king of Southern Arabia. In

*Black Dove, White Raven,* it feels almost sacrilegious to introduce the emperor Haile Selassie in a speaking role; yet his involvement in the Italo-Ethiopian War of 1935–36 is so integral to the historical situation that I felt it was impossible to tell the story without making him a character in it, particularly since the Imperial Ethiopian Air Force at the time was so very small and so very close to the emperor.

In addition, several of the pilots mentioned in this book were real, or were based on real people. John Robinson, often credited with being the man who provided the initial impetus for the piloting program at Tuskegee Institute, was in fact the only American pilot of the Chicago-based Challenger Air Pilots Association to make it to Ethiopia (a passport issue, of course). Robinson's dedication to the Ethiopian Air Force is astonishing—as well as training Ethiopian pilots, he was essentially the emperor's private air chauffeur throughout the war until Haile Selassie went into exile in Europe. After World War II, Robinson returned to Ethiopia where he continued to train pilots both civilian and military, and helped lay the groundwork to establish Ethiopian Airlines. In *Black Dove, White Raven,* his imaginary colleague and second-in-command, Billy Cooper, is loosely based on Robinson himself.

My invented Horatio Augustus is based on Hubert Julian, a flamboyant figure who is only thinly disguised in this book. It's impossible to write about Julian, even under a pseudonym, without making him recognizable; he really did jump out of a plane over New York City playing the saxophone, he really did wreck the Ethiopian emperor's private plane in the coronation rehearsal, and he really did provoke a fistfight with John Robinson on their meeting in Addis Ababa. The contrast between Robinson's steady dedication and Julian's flair for the dramatic was as evident in real life as it is in my fictional portraits of Cooper and Augustus.

Julian constantly risked reinforcing the minstrel show stereotype of the black man as a buffoon; Robinson was so self-effacing in his quiet persistence that few whites took public notice of his achievements. The rarefied air of early aviation, not to mention Imperial Ethiopia, turned both men into innovators and high achievers. I have tried to sketch them sympathetically.

The pilot Bessie Coleman, Rhoda and Delia's early mentor, really was the first black woman to earn an International Pilot's License—indeed, she was the first American of any color or either sex to do so. It is true that no one would give her flight lessons in the United States. Determined to get in the air, she took a language course and went to France to learn to fly. It's no secret that I take my inspiration from early women pilots, and increasingly I'm intrigued by those who had to overcome barriers of color as well as of sex. More even than Bessie Coleman, I'm fascinated by Willa Brown, another founding member of the Challenger Air Pilots Association. She held a master's degree in business administration and was the first African American woman to earn an American private pilot's license, the first to become an officer in the Civil Air Patrol, the first to become a commercial pilot, and the first to run for Congress. She was one of the eight black aviators who intended to come to Ethiopia as military support during the Italian invasion. I am in awe of such courage.

Sinidu, my own Ethiopian aviatrix, has her inspiration in Mulumebet Emeru, who trained to fly in Addis Ababa in the early 1930s. Mulumebet had soloed but had not yet been licensed at the time of the Italian invasion. I know little about this progressive and daring pilot, but Sinidu also represents many gallant Ethiopian women who served as combatants, medics, and camp followers during the Italo-Ethiopian War—such as Lekyelesh Beyan, who fought at her husband's side under Haile Selassie at the battle of Maychew on March 31, 1936, carrying her father's rifle and her four-month old daughter on her back.

Like John Robinson and Willa Brown, American blacks knew what was going on in Ethiopia in 1935 and desperately wanted to send them support. In the early 1930s there were about a hundred African Americans and West Indians living in Addis Ababa, some of them in official positions: John West, a graduate of Howard University, worked for the Ethiopian Ministry of Education, and Dr. Reuben S. Young for the Ministry of Public Health. American newspapers, black and white, almost universally detested Italy's leader, Benito Mussolini. But antiwar sentiment prevailed, which is why no passports were ever issued to the brave men and one woman in Chicago who'd planned to offer their services as pilots to the Imperial Ethiopian Air Force.

Historians view the Italian conflict in Ethiopia as the opening gambit of World War II; the unwillingness of the League of Nations to take sides in Ethiopia mirrors their reluctance to antagonize the growing threat of Nazi Germany. Britain and France dragged their feet at interfering because they didn't want to lose Italy as an ally against Germany (remember, Italy had been their ally against Germany in the *first* world war). Hitler, for his part, watched the scenario with growing confidence. Italy's advance on Ethiopia proved the powerlessness of the League of Nations, which could not control its member nation Italy nor support its member nation Ethiopia; it proved that the United States would not interfere in global conflict; it proved that the Great Powers of Europe didn't want to engage in battle. In 1935 Germany had already withdrawn from the League of Nations, yet even as Britain refused to give aid to the Ethiopians it negotiated the British–German Naval Treaty, in violation of more than one international agreement, which pretty much allowed Germany to build a navy superior to any in Europe. And by observing France's response to Mussolini's bullying manipulation, Hitler was able to assure himself he'd get no resistance from the French when, in March 1936 as Haile Selassie's forces were choking under Italy's mustard gas attacks, Hitler sent the German army to take over the Rhineland.

Mussolini was pretty shameless in his battering of Ethiopia, and in the widespread bombing of civilians and international aid workers there. Although I have found no reliable record of poison gas being used against international Red Cross units, it was used unscrupulously against Ethiopian troops and civilians. Mustard gas—indeed, all toxic gas—was banned under the Geneva Protocol of 1925, a term of the agreement which both Ethiopia and Italy claimed to uphold; Mussolini's excuse for using it was as retaliation for the brutal torture and mutilation of a captured Italian airman. But it's not clear why Mussolini's air force also felt free to make brazen and relentless attacks on Red Cross field hospitals. Bomb attacks with explosives and incendiaries were carried out on a Swedish unit on December 30, 1935 and on a British unit on March 4, 1936, the event on which I've based the final scenes of this novel. Italians claimed that Ethiopians were using the Red Cross emblem to disguise military units (which is why I imagine they showed no mercy to Ezra's makeshift indigenous field hospital). It's also possible that the Italian commanders really wanted neutral Europeans to leave the country as the native population was being pulverized, since it would be harder for the international press to ignore the witness of educated white men than for them to ignore barefoot Ethiopians.

The Italian use of mustard gas against the Ethiopian forces is pretty well considered to be the tactic that destroyed Haile Selassie's army in 1936. It's amazing how surprised people are when I tell them this. But I didn't know it, either, before I wrote this book.

The village of Tazma Meda, the setting for much of this novel, is itself, alas, a fantasy of progressive modernism for Ethiopia in 1935. The benevolent Sinclairs are very loosely based on Daniel and Christine Sandford, who raised six children on a farm near Addis Ababa between 1920 and 1935, trading coffee and hides and assisting in setting up a "model province" for the Ethiopian government in 1935. But it wasn't until the 1950s that the Ethiopian government began to regulate coffee production; cooperatives were recognized as legal institutions in the 1960s, and coffee cooperatives became the norm only in the 1970s. Ezra, Tazma Meda's forward-thinking educated doctor, is also my own invention. According to the International Red Cross, Ethiopia in 1935 was a country without a single qualified native doctor—doctors in the modern hospital in Addis Ababa were all European. Nevertheless Ethiopia created its own branch of the Red Cross in July 1935, and many trained nurses were Ethiopian, impressing even the most patronizing and prejudiced of Western journalists with their cleanliness and efficiency.

What happened to the Tabot of Zion—also known as the Ark of the Covenant—during the Italian occupation of Ethiopia is something I don't know. It may have been removed from Aksum and hidden, but I have yet to uncover a believable official line verifying this one way or another. My personal view is this: the Ethiopian church would have been crazy not to hide it. The British looting of Magdala in 1868 was shameless: troops hauled the stolen goods out on elephants and mules and then sold off everything in an *auction.* Hoards of Ethiopian church treasures and illuminated manuscripts are still kept in special collections in the British Library and the Victoria & Albert Museum in London, despite repeated requests for their repatriation. And speaking of looting, in 1937 the Italians hauled down the tallest of the ancient obelisks from the Necropolis at Aksum, cut it into three chunks, trucked it overland, and shipped it back to Rome where it stood for over 60 years. I find it pretty inconceivable that they wouldn't also have taken the Ark of the Covenant with them if they had been able to get their hands on it, given that there was no secret about where it was kept; or that the Ethiopians would not have instantly raised a clamoring outcry against its loss. But there is no indication that the sacred Tabot of Zion ever left the country. The story of the Aksum obelisk, incidentally, has a happy ending. In 2005, at a cost of nearly eight million dollars, Italy flew the stolen obelisk back to Aksum and re-erected it there.

How do all the other threads of the story end? The answer is, of course, Ethiopia's story has no real ending. It's like *The Adventures of Black Dove and White Raven,* a series of episodes that continues for years and years with no closure ever anticipated by the reader. After the Italians successfully occupied Ethiopia in May 1936, the local people fought a bloody and terrible guerrilla war against the invaders that lasted five years. Haile Selassie went into exile in Europe; when Italy declared war on Britain in 1940, British troops had the excuse they needed to bring weapons into Ethiopia and drive the Italians out. Haile Selassie returned as emperor in 1941, and with the tables turned another two years of guerrilla warfare raged on, this time with the Italians on the resisting side. When World War II ended, Italians still living in Ethiopia were given a full pardon by Haile Selassie. Some of that aging few still live in Ethiopia today, their descendants speaking Amharic, proud of their mixed heritage.

In 1974, Haile Selassie's aging and failing regime was toppled by a military government known as the Derg (it simply means "council" in Ge'ez, the ancient language of the Ethiopian church), who instituted what was essentially a reign of terror for over a decade. The Derg's rule began a cycle of war, famine, and poverty that has given this beautiful country its current perceived character in Western consciousness; yet the Ethiopian people cling tenaciously to their rich cultural history, optimism, and fierce national pride. The little snapshot of Ethiopian history that this novel gives you is like a captionless picture torn out of a textbook. The scene is fascinating (I hope), but painfully alone and out of context. I hope it inspires the reader to find out more.

This book was hard for me to write. It would never have happened without the unflagging encouragement of my agent, Ginger Clark, and the support of a number of dedicated editors: Stella Paskins, Amy Black, Lisa Yoskowitz, and—the woman who pulled this manuscript together—Kate Egan. Dr. Fikre Tolossa provided careful historical notes, including the culling of information from Amharic sources to which I do not have access. And I could not write a book about modern Ethiopia without thanking Susan and Roger Whitaker, who took me there.

This book's successes I owe to others. Its faults are all my own.

PRAISE FOR

# ROSE UNDER FIRE

2014 Schneider Family Book Award

2014 *Boston Globe–Horn Book*
Award Honor

*New York Times* Notable Children's
Books of 2013

★ "[A] great, page-turning read." —*The Horn Book* (starred review)

★ "At the core of this novel is the resilience of human nature and the power of friendship and hope." —*Kirkus Reviews* (starred review)

★ "[A]nother indelible story about friendship borne out of unimaginable adversity." —*Publishers Weekly* (starred review)

★ "Readers will connect with Rose and be moved by her struggle to go forward, find her wings again, and fly."
—*School Library Journal* (starred review)

★ "At once heartbreaking and hopeful, *Rose Under Fire* will stay with readers long after they have finished the last page."
—*VOYA* (starred review)

"*Rose Under Fire* is bound to soar into the promised land of young adult books read by actual adults—and deservedly so, because Wein's unself-consciously important story is timeless, ageless and triumphant." —*The Los Angeles Times*

"Wein's second World War II adventure novel . . . captures poignantly the fragility of hope and the balm forgiveness offers."
—*The New York Times*

**TURN THE PAGE TO START READING**

Rose Moyer Justice
August 2, 1944
Hamble, Hampshire

# Notes for an Accident Report

I just got back from Celia Forester's funeral. I'm supposed to be writing up an official report for the Tempest she flew into the ground, since she's obviously not going to write it herself and I saw it happen. And also because I feel responsible. I know it wasn't my fault—I really do know that now. But I briefed her. We both had Tempests to deliver, and I'd flown one a couple of times before. Celia hadn't. She took off ten minutes after me. If she'd taken off first, we might both still be alive.

I've never had to do a report like this, and I don't really know where to begin. Maddie gave me this beautiful leather-bound notebook to draft it in; she thinks it helps to have nice paper and knew I wouldn't buy any for myself, since, like everything else, it's so scarce. She says you need to bribe yourself because it's always *blah* writing up accident reports. She had to write a big report herself last January and also be grilled in person by the Accident Committee. She's right about nice paper, of course, and I have filled up a couple of those pretty clothbound diaries that lock, but all I ever put in them are attempts at poetry. Too bad I can't put the accident report into verse.

There were a few other Air Transport Auxiliary pilots at Celia's funeral, but Maddie was the only ATA girl besides me. Felicyta couldn't come; she had a delivery chit this morning. Along with Celia and Felicyta, Maddie and I were the ones who gave out Mrs. Hatch's strawberries to the soldiers lining up to board the landing craft for the D-Day invasion. It made us into friends. Felicyta was very tearful this morning, banging things around angrily. Probably she shouldn't be flying. I know exactly what Daddy would say—three thousand miles away on Justice Field in Pennsylvania—if it were me: "Rosie, go home. You shouldn't fly while your friends are being buried." But the planes have got to be delivered. *There's a war on.*

Boy, am I sick of hearing that.

It never stops. There are planes to deliver every day straight from the factory or just overhauled, painted in fresh camouflage or invasion stripes, ready to go to France. I got thrown in at the deep end when I stepped off the ship from New York three months ago, and before the end of May I was delivering Spitfires, real fighter planes, from Southampton's factories near the Hamble Aerodrome to just about every air base in southern England. I was supposed to get some training, but they just put me through a few flight tests instead. Being the daughter of someone who runs a flight school has paid off in spades—I've been flying since I was twelve, which means I've been flying longer than some of the older pilots, even though I'm only eighteen. The baby on the team.

There was a lull for a week after D-Day, when the invasion started. Actually, I don't think it should be called an "invasion" when really we are trying to get most of Europe back from the Germans, who invaded it in the first place. Our Allied soldiers left for France in the beginning of June, and for one week only military flights got authorized, so there was no flying for us—the Air Transport Auxiliary in Britain are civilian pilots, like the WASPs at home. That was a quiet week, the second week of June. Then the flying bombs started coming in.

Holy smoke, I can't say how much I hate the flying bombs.

V-1 is what the Germans call them. *V* stands for "*Vergeltungswaffe*," retaliation weapon. I worked hard at memorizing the real word for it because I always think it means "vengeance": Vengeance Weapon 1. The only thing these bombs are meant to do is terrify people. Everyone puts on a brave face, though—the English are very good at putting on brave faces, I'll give them that! People try to make the bombs less scary by giving them stupid names: *doodlebugs*—sounds like baby talk. *Buzz bombs*—a phrase for older kids to use. The other ferry pilots call them *pilotless planes*, which should seem simple and technical, but it gives me the creeps. An aircraft flying blind, no cockpit, no windows, no way of landing except to self-destruct? How can you win an air war against a plane that doesn't need a pilot? A plane that turns into a bomb? Our planes, the British and American aircraft I fly every day in the ATA, don't even have radios, much less guns. We don't stand a chance. Celia Forester didn't stand a chance.

At the funeral, the local minister—vicar, they say here—had never even met Celia. He called her "a dedicated pilot."

It doesn't mean *anything*. We're *all* dedicated. But to tell the truth, I don't think any of us would have had anything better to say. Celia was so quiet. She was only just posted to Hamble in May, about the same time I was, and for the same reason—to ferry planes for the invasion. She hardly ever talked to *anybody*. I can't blame her—she had a fiancé who was in Bomb Disposal and was killed at Christmas. It's bad enough being a newcomer without being stuck grieving for your sweetheart. Celia wasn't very happy here.

Am I happy here?

I guess I am. I like what I'm doing. I wanted to come *so*

*badly*—I can't believe they gave me that diploma in December, like Laura Ingalls Wilder leaving school at fifteen so she could be a teacher! And now here I am, in England for the first time, not far from where Daddy was born, and I'm actually helping. I'm *useful*. Even without Uncle Roger being so high up in the Royal Engineers, cutting through the red tape for me, I'd have found a way to get here. And I'm a lot luckier than Celia in other ways, not just because I'm still alive—I'm lucky to have met Nick almost as soon as I got here, and lucky to have had so much flying experience before I started.

I've read over that last paragraph, and it sounds so chirpy and stuck-up and—just so dumb. But the truth is I have to keep reminding myself again and again that I want to do this, because I'm so tired now. None of us ever get enough sleep. Not just because we're working so hard; it's those horrible flying bombs, too.

The tiredness is beginning to show. We're all cracking at the seams, I think. Maddie and I ended up being taken out to lunch by Celia's parents after the funeral because Maddie had still been sitting in our pew, sobbing quietly into her handkerchief after everyone else had left, and I'd been sitting with her and sniffling a bit, too. I am sure the Foresters were touched to find anyone showing so much raw emotion at their daughter's short, bleak funeral, when everyone else there hardly knew her.

But neither one of us had actually been crying for Celia. On the train back to Southampton, Maddie confessed to me, "My best friend was killed in action, in 'enemy action,' like it always says in the obituaries, exactly eight months ago. She didn't get a funeral."

"*My gosh*," I said. I can't really imagine what it must feel like to have your best friend killed by a bomb or gunfire. So I added, "Well, it was brave of you to come along today!"

Maddie said, "I felt like a *rat* eating lunch with the Foresters. So cheap and ugly. Them paying for the meal and me trying to think of *anything* to say about Celia apart from 'She was a nice girl, but she never talked to anybody.'"

"I know. I felt that way, too. Look, we're both rats, Maddie—I was being more selfish than you. I couldn't think about anything all day except having to write the darned accident report. Celia had never been up in a Tempest before, and we only had one set of pilot's notes between us, and she'd refused to take them with her. I should have forced her to take them. And I bet now they won't let any other girls near a Tempest till the accident's been investigated, and if we don't get to fly 'em again it'll be MY FAULT as much as Celia's."

"They'll let us fly 'em," Maddie said mournfully. "Desperate times and all that."

She's probably right. The fighter pilots need all the Tempests they can get. They're the best planes we've got for shooting down flying bombs.

When Maddie and I got back to the aerodrome at Hamble, Felicyta was waiting for us. She was sitting in a corner of the Operations room and had made a little funeral feast. She had a plate of toast cut up into one-inch squares with a bit of margarine and the tiniest blob of strawberry jam on each square—simple but pretty.

"We make do with not much, as usual," Felicyta said, and tried to smile. "Here are teacups. Was it terrible?"

I nodded. Maddie grimaced.

"Celia's mother says we should share the things from her locker," I said. "Mrs. Forester doesn't want any of it back."

Now we all grimaced.

"Someone's got to do it," I said. Maddie began pouring tea, and Felicyta touched me lightly on the shoulder, like she wanted to support me but was a little embarrassed to show it. She gave an odd, tight smile and said, "I will take care of Celia's locker. You must report this accident, Rosie?"

"Yes, I'm writing the accident report. Lucky me."

"These papers are for you." Felicyta patted a cardboard file folder on the table's worn oilcloth. "It is a letter from the mechanic who examined Celia's plane after her crash. He gave it to me when I flew there this morning. You need to read this before you write the report."

"Is it secret?"

I had to ask because so many things are confidential.

"No, it is not secret, but"—Felicyta took a deep breath—"you saw Celia crash. You said you thought the ailerons on her wings did not work. This letter tells why. Celia hit a flying bomb."

Now that I'm sitting here with this notebook, I don't know if I should tell the Accident Committee what the mechanic said, because it is exactly the kind of thing they'll use as an excuse to stop girls from flying Tempests—though I bet any guy would do the same thing, given the chance.

Felicyta wasn't kidding. The mechanic thinks Celia ran into a V-1 flying bomb. No, not "ran into" it—not accidentally. He thinks she did it on purpose. He thinks she tried to tip a flying bomb out of the sky.

Oh—it is crazy.

When Felicyta told me, over the sad little squares of memorial toast, it made me angry. ATA deaths are never that heroic. An ATA pilot is killed *every week* flying faulty planes, flying in bad weather, coming down on cracked-up runways—there was that terrible accident where a landing plane skidded and flipped because of the mud, and by the time people got out to the poor pilot, he'd *drowned*—stuck upside down in a cockpit full of standing water. HORRIBLE. But not heroic. I've never heard of an ATA pilot getting hit by enemy fire. We don't dogfight. Our bomb bays are empty; our gun sights aren't connected to anything. Our deaths don't ever earn us posthumous medals. Drowning in mud, lost at sea, engine failure after takeoff.

So I didn't believe Felicyta at first—she was so convinced by the mechanic's letter, but it felt like she was trying to make Celia's death into a hero's death, when it was just another faulty aircraft.

"Antiaircraft guns on the ground are good for shooting down flying bombs," Felicyta said. "But you know the Royal Air Force Tempest squadron takes down as many flying bombs in the air as the gunners do on the ground, and Celia was in a Tempest—"

"She didn't have any guns," I said. "She wasn't armed." Holy smoke, she didn't even have a radio. She couldn't even tell anyone what was wrong as she was coming in to land.

"You do not need guns," Felicyta insisted passionately, her eyes blazing. "The mechanic says if you fly fast enough, you can ram a pilotless plane with your wingtip."

We leaned our heads in together over the tiny decorated squares of toast, talking in low tones like conspirators.

"I've heard the lads talk about that," Maddie said. "Doodlebug tipping."

"In Polish we call it *taran*—aerial ramming. A Polish pilot rammed a German plane over Warsaw on the first day of the war! The Soviet pilots do it, too—same word in Russian. *Taran*. It is the best way to stop a pilotless plane in the air," Felicyta said. "Before it reaches a target, when it is still over sea or open country, not over London or Southampton. That is what the Royal Air Force does with their Tempests."

"But they're armed!" I insisted.

"You do not need to be armed for *taran*," Felicyta said. "You do not need guns to ram another aircraft."

"She's right," Maddie said. "When our lads come up behind a flying bomb and fire at it, they have to fly into the explosion. Absolutely no fun. But if you tip the bomb with your wing before it's over London, it just dives into a field and there's no mess."

I just couldn't believe Celia would try such a trick, her first time in a Tempest. But, as we all kept saying, we didn't really know her.

"Would you do it, Maddie?" I asked.

She shook her head slowly. It was more of an *I don't know* than a *no*. Maddie's a very careful pilot and probably has more hours than the rest of us put together. She is the only one of us who is a First Officer. But I realized, just then, that I didn't really know her, either.

"Felicyta would do it," Maddie said, avoiding an answer. "Wouldn't you, Fliss? You see a flying bomb in the sky ahead of you, and you're flying a Tempest. Would you make a hundred-and-eighty-degree turn and run the other way? Or try to tip it out of the sky?"

"You know what I would do," Felicyta said, her eyes narrowed. "Don't you believe a woman could make a *taran* as well as a man? You know what I would do, Maddie Brodatt. But I have never met a flying bomb in the air. Have you?"

"Yes," Maddie said quietly.

We stared at her with wide eyes. I am sure my mouth hung open.

"It was back in June," she said. "The week after the flying bombs started. I was delivering a Spitfire and I saw it coming toward me, only a couple hundred feet below me. I thought it was another plane. It looked like another plane. But when I waggled my wings, it just stayed on course, and then it passed below me—terribly close—and I realized it was a doodlebug. They aren't very big. Horrible things, eyeless, just a bomb with wings."

*Pilotless*, I thought. Ugh. "Weren't you scared?"

"Not really—you know how you don't worry about a near miss until later, when you think about it afterward? It was before I'd heard about anybody tipping a doodlebug, and anyway I hadn't a hope of catching it. By the time I'd realized what it was, it was just a speck in the distance, still heading for London. I didn't see it fall."

I haven't seen one fall, either, but I've heard them. You can hear them THIRTY MILES away, rattling along. Southampton doesn't get fired on as relentlessly as London and Kent, but we get the miserable things often enough that the noise terrifies me. Like being in the next field over from a big John Deere corn picker: *clackety clackety clackety*. Then the timer counts down, the engine stops, and for a few seconds you don't hear anything as the bomb falls. And then you hear the explosion.

I hate to admit this, but I am so scared of the flying bombs that if I'd known about them ahead of time I would not have come. Even after Uncle Roger's behind-the-scenes scrambling to get the paperwork done for me.

The mechanic says in his letter that he thinks Celia damaged her wing in a separate incident—separate from the crash, "possibly the result of a deliberate brush with another aircraft." He didn't actually mention flying bombs. But you could tell the idea was in his head.

Now I am upset all over again, remembering the crash. It

took me by surprise, watching—I knew something was wrong, of course, but I never expected her to lose control like that, that close to the ground. It happened so suddenly. I'd been waiting for her so we could come back to Hamble together.

I want to talk to Nick about it. He left a message for me—sweet of him, worrying about me having to go to Celia's funeral. It's after nine now, but it's still light out. They have two hours of daylight saving in the summer here—they call it Double Summer Time. So I'll walk down to the phone box in the village and hope Nick's not away on some mission. And that I don't get told off by his landlady for calling so late.

Horrible war. So much more horrible here than back in the States. Every few weeks someone's mother or brother or another friend is killed. And already I am fed up with the shortages, never any butter and never enough sleep. The combination of working so hard, and the constant fear, and just the general *blahness* of everything—I wasn't prepared for it. But how could I possibly, possibly have been prepared for it? They've been living with it for five years. All the time I've been swimming at the Lake, playing girls' varsity basketball and building a tree house for Karl and Kurt like a good big sister, crop dusting with Daddy and helping Mother make applesauce, Maddie's been delivering fighter planes. When her best friend was killed by a bomb, or whatever it was, eight months ago, I was probably sitting in Mr. Wagner's creative writing class working out rhyme schemes.

It's so strange to be here at last, and so different from what I expected.

I have put my accident report into verse after all. (I think I am trying to trick myself into writing this darned thing.) I wish I'd written this poem earlier. It would have been nice to read it at Celia's service. I will send a copy to her parents.

FOR CELIA FORESTER (by Rose Justice)

The storm will swallow
the brave girl there
who fights destruction
with wings and air—

life and chaos
hover in flight
wingtip to wingtip
until the slight

triumphant moment
when their wings caress
and her crippled Tempest
flies pilotless.

Now that I am an ATA pilot at last, I wish I were a fighter
pilot.

And that was the first thing I said to Nick when I got him on the phone. I did get him at last. He wasn't at home, so I rang the airfield, and they said he was on his way but hadn't got there yet, AND he was "busy" tonight, so he might not be able to call back. I was so desperate I waited in the phone box for three-quarters of an hour till he got in, and we talked for exactly as long as my cigarette tin of pennies held out. In three weeks he will be off to France, and I will not.

"Hello, Rose darling."

"I want to fly Tempests," I said through clenched teeth. "I want to be operational. I want to be in the Royal Air Force, blasting flying bombs to smithereens."

There was a good penny's worth of silence down the wire before Nick answered. Maybe that's where the saying comes from, *penny for your thoughts*. Speak up or the operator will cut you off.

Finally Nick said sympathetically, "What's made you so bloodthirsty?"

"I'm not bloodthirsty. There's no blood in a pilotless plane, is there! I'm a good pilot. I've probably been flying five years longer than half the boys in 150 Wing. I flew with Daddy from coast to coast across America when I was fifteen, and I did *all* the navigation. *You've* never flown a Tempest, or a Mustang, or a Mark Fourteen Spitfire—I've flown them all, dozens of times. They're wasting me just because I'm a girl! They won't even let us fly to France—they're prepping men for supply and taxi to the front lines, guys with hundreds' fewer hours than me, but they're just passing over the women pilots. *It isn't fair.*"

I stopped to breathe. Nick said evenly, "And there's me,

worrying you'd be upset by your friend's funeral. Instead you're after shooting down doodlebugs. What's going on, Rose?"

"How do you topple a doodlebug?" I asked. "The girls say you can do it with your wingtip."

Nick laughed. Then he paused. I didn't say anything, because I knew he was thinking. "You couldn't," he said at last. "Yes, I've heard that, too, but you need to be flying something fast, not a taxi Anson or a Spitfire with only enough fuel to get you to the maintenance airfield. An ATA pilot couldn't topple a V-1 flying bomb."

"Celia did. She tried to, anyway. We think that's why she crashed. How do they do it? Do you just bash it with your wingtip? The Polish pilots have a word for it. *Taran.* Aerial ramming."

Another longish pause. I had stuffed in the entire contents of the cigarette tin right away—after feeding thirty of those gigantic pennies into the telephone, I felt like I'd just thrown away a pirate's treasure hoard. At any rate it added up to more than ten minutes. I didn't want to be cut off.

And, of course, the operator was probably listening in. Nick's job is very secret. I didn't want to get him into trouble.

"No," he said at last. "No, for God's sake, don't try that, Rose. You'll kill yourself. Is that what Celia did? Good God Almighty. The idea is not to touch them at all. The doodlebug's a bloody brilliant bomb, but it's not a brilliant aircraft. It's unstable, and if you get your wingtip just beneath the bomb's wing, half a foot or so away from it, you can upset the airflow around its wing and make it stall. But you have to fly fast enough to keep up with it, and it'll still go off when it hits the ground. Promise me you won't try?"

My turn to be silent. Because I couldn't make that promise. I guess I'll never get the chance, anyway, but if I did—well, I'm a better pilot than Celia was.

"Rose, darling?" Nick had to prompt me. "I'm not a fighter pilot, either. 'They also serve who only stand and wait.'"

Show-off, quoting Milton. He knows I like poetry.

"That's garbage, Nick, and you know it," I said hotly. "You're not standing and waiting. You're dropping off—" I choked back what I was going to say, thinking of the operator listening in. I'm not supposed to know what he's doing, and I *don't* know much about it, but Maddie's boyfriend is in the same squadron—that's how I met Nick—and you figure a little bit out after a while. They've been flying spies and saboteurs and plastic explosive and machine guns in and out of France for the past two years—secret supplies for the D-Day invasion.

"You're on the front line," I insisted.

There was this long, guilty silence at the other end.

"Oh, you *really are* at the Front," I guessed angrily. "What? They're going to transfer you, aren't they, now that the Front's moved back? Or are they getting the Royal Air Force Special Duties squadron to do ferry work so they can weasel out of sending civilian ATA pilots into Europe?"

"They're moving the squadron," Nick gave me cautiously.

I didn't ask where. He wouldn't have told me anyway.

"Far?"

"Yes."

"Oh."

That means out of the United Kingdom. Maybe the Mediterranean.

"Well . . ." Nick hesitated. "We've got three days' leave before we go. It's not much time, but it matches up with your next two days off. We could get married."

I am sorry to say that I laughed at him.

I mean, it is just so stupid. He is sweet and funny and kind and brave, and we talk so easily when we are together, and he is so proud to have a pilot for a girlfriend—"Looks like

Katharine Hepburn and flies like Amelia Earhart" is how he introduced me to his parents (an exaggeration in both cases, but oh, how I burned with joy and embarrassment when he said it!). But we still haven't ever even been on a real date, dancing or to a film or anything like that—it's always lunch in a pub or a quick cup of tea in the coffee shop at the train station just outside Portsmouth, which is halfway for both of us. It is *so hard* to get time together. Apparently, Maddie has supper with her boyfriend, Jamie, at his air base something like once every two months. And the last time Nick and I had the same day off, I had to stand him up because Uncle Roger and Aunt Edie were taking me out. Of course it never occurred to me to stand up Uncle Roger—but I am in debt to Uncle Roger, I mean morally, for pulling the strings that got me here. Nick doesn't get that. I know he was hurt.

And now I hurt him again by laughing at his proposal. I tried to make it up to him and promised we would have a whole day, a real day to remember, all to ourselves before he went away.

It makes me angry. *Why* should it have to be like this, for all of us, all our generation? That the only way for a young couple to be together is to get married? No chance of a honeymoon, no flowers or champagne because the gardens are all full of cabbages and turnips and France is a war zone? No pretty silk dress unless someone manages to steal a parachute for you? No. I know I wouldn't get married suddenly even if it weren't wartime. I'd never do it without Daddy there to walk me down the aisle—with nothing more than a telegram to let him know!

It is the same for every young couple. We are all panicking that one of us will be killed next month, next week, tomorrow. All of us panicking that if we don't do it now, we'll never get a chance. Well, I don't care. I'm not letting the war take over my life.

Maddie laughed, too, when I told her about Nick's proposal.

"I know where he got *that* idea," she said. "Jamie and I are getting married on the twelfth of August. Next week!" She gave another hoot of laughter. "That is Nick all over. He's like a puppy. You said no, didn't you, Rosie? The poor lad! Tell you what—you can give him a good excuse and say you've a previous engagement. Come be my bridesmaid."

"What, *me*? Really?"

I was surprised and very pleased, but what a thoughtless thing to say. Her dead friend wasn't going to do it, was she? And all it did was remind her.

Anyway, of course I will.

I asked her if she knew where Nick and Jamie are going, and she gave me a funny look.

"Careless talk costs lives," she said.

I do know things I shouldn't. I know a lot about what Uncle Roger is doing, because Aunt Edie tells me. She's not supposed to know, either. I am a little uncomfortable about it sometimes, but I think they see it as keeping me Ready for Action—Roger always asks for me when he needs to be taxied anywhere. Felicyta thinks it is very funny that this highly important person wants to be piloted by a lowly Third Officer, and a girl at that! He is building pontoons in France at the moment, as the Allies fight their way inland. The next big push will be to cross the Seine. Then Paris.

It's been a week since Celia's accident. I have submitted my report. I didn't draft it on these pretty, gold-edged pages after all, because I didn't have this notebook with me when I wrote it. The day after her funeral I was stuck at RAF Maidsend for a whole day due to lousy weather, and I couldn't go home, because there was a top-priority Tempest (of course) that I had to ferry away for repair as soon as the visibility was good enough to fly. It felt a bit ironic, and spooky, to spend the day writing about Celia's accident and then take off strapped into a broken Tempest. The plane had a big hole punched in the windshield. It was perfectly flyable, but WOW, was it ever windy! Even with goggles on, my face felt like I had frostbite by the time I landed—absolutely frozen. It's true I was going 225 miles per hour at 3500 feet, but you'd never know it was August. It's been such a cold summer.

You have to fly that high to get across Kent because you have to be higher than the barrage balloons they've got tethered there to try to catch the flying bombs.

I can't get over how beautiful the barrage balloons are. I can't even talk about it to anyone—they all think I am crazy. But when you're in the air, and the sky above you is a sea of gray mist and the land below you is all green, the silver balloons float in between like a school of shining silver whales, bobbing a little in the wind. They are as big as buses, and I and every other pilot have a healthy fear of them because their tethering cables are loaded with explosives to try to snarl up enemy aircraft. But they are just magical from above, great big silver bubbles filling the sky.

Incredible. It is just *incredible* that you can notice something like that when your face is so cold you can't feel it anymore, and you know perfectly well you are surrounded by death, and the only way to stay alive is to endure the howling wind and hold your course. And still the sky is beautiful.